Mark Griffin began his writing career with three successive years of gold medal awards in the Hampshire Writing Festival. In 1996 he moved to Los Angeles, where he turned his attention to acting, script writing and development.

After returning to England, Mark continued in this profession, and in April 2017 was shortlisted in the top five out of 3500 entrants in a national crime thriller writing competition sponsored by Random House Publishing and the *Daily Mail* for his debut, *When Darkness Calls*.

When Darkness Calls was the first novel in the Holly Wakefield series and it was longlisted for the CWA New Blood Dagger Award in 2019. *When Angels Sleep* is the second Holly Wakefield thriller.

Praise for Mark Griffin:

'A thrilling new talent, destined to become a big name in British crime writing' Peter James

'Mightily impressive ... deviously plotted, with a bleak thread of intriguing twists' *Daily Mail*

'Dark, compelling ... one of the best police procedurals I've read for a long time' M. W. Craven

'Meticulously plotted and devious in its execution ... utterly compelling' Lesley Kara

'Wow. I read this in less than a day. As many twists and turns as a rollercoaster! It's the kind of writing which grabs you and won't l

'Deftly  minic Nolan

By Mark Griffin

THE HOLLY WAKEFIELD THRILLERS

When Darkness Calls
When Angels Sleep

When Angels Sleep

Mark Griffin

piatkus

PIATKUS

First published in Great Britain in 2019 by Piatkus
This paperback edition published in 2020 by Piatkus

1 3 5 7 9 10 8 6 4 2

A CIP catalogue record for this book
is available from the British Library.

ISBN 978-0-349-42076-9

Typeset in Baskerville by M Rules
Printed and bound in Great Britain by
Clays Ltd, Elcograf S.p.A.

Papers used by Piatkus are from well-managed forests
and other responsible sources.

Piatkus
An imprint of
Little, Brown Book Group
Carmelite House
50 Victoria Embankment
London EC4Y 0DZ

An Hachette UK Company
www.hachette.co.uk

www.littlebrown.co.uk

To my wonderful sister Melissa,
and her three failed assassination attempts
on my life when we were both children. Her constant
support, love and understanding knows no bounds. To my
amazing niece Natalie, who will one day hold the
torch and guide others.

And to my friend, MJ. May
we all tread lightly on our paths.

One

The man sang to himself on the drive home from work.

He had a lovely voice. Mellifluous, his singing teacher had once told him – a nightingale set free in the dark. When he had sung at school and the local church, he had always closed his eyes and fantasised.

My life is not beautiful, he used to think. *It is not magical. But I can feel the love. Coming closer. Closer every day.*

He had been asked to join the choir when he was thirteen – high praise indeed for a school of two hundred pupils, and when he had been asked to sing a solo in St Mary's church in Chigwell that Christmas Eve, and his mother had watched from the wooden pews amongst the other mums and dads, he had thought for the briefest of moments that he actually was in heaven. There had been no applause or welcome hug after, but the fleeting smile had been enough. That was twenty-three years ago. How he had grown since then.

He turned into his driveway, parked the car and got out. It was February and cold. Blobs of cloudy snow littered the grass and the ground was slippery with wet. A quick wave at the light-sensor so he could see the lock, and then he turned the keys and pushed open the front door. The house was dark. It always was. Black wood panelling, sombre brown floors. A Gothic hallstand with an elephant's foot base. He switched on the hall light. Tiffany stained glass that splashed gummi-bear colours all over the walls. Placed his suitcase on the hallstand and called up the steep stairs.

'Hi, Mum!'

'Is that you?'

'Yes!'

'You're early.'

'I'm going out tonight.'

'What?'

'I'm going out. Remember?'

He went into the kitchen, put the kettle on the stove and made himself a cup of tea. Five minutes later he put two sausages in the frying pan and watched them sizzle like fat fingers until they were brown all over. He boiled some peas, cut the sausages into edible-sized chunks, buttered two slices of wholemeal bread and put everything on a tray with some cutlery.

The stairs were surprisingly noiseless for a house this old, a Victorian throwback that was neither loved nor lost. He hoovered twice a week, but the dust always seemed to settle as if dropped by a sieve, and he couldn't help running his finger over the banister when he got to the top. He took a left on the landing, past two bedrooms, the bathroom, and entered his mother's room. The curtains had already been drawn, and the only light was from a lamp on the bedside table. The sixty-eight-year old woman was perched like a giant crow in the bed. Propped up by pillows, her emaciated arms draped across the duvet and her black lace nightdress was buttoned to

2

the neck. Her head hung forward and was tilted slightly to one side. Her eyes seemed to follow him but her head never moved.

'Where are you going then?'

'I've told you, Mum. It's a works do.'

'Works do?'

He placed the tray of food gently on her lap.

'Come on, eat up before it gets cold.'

His mother stared at the food, then picked up the knife and fork and started to eat. She chewed a piece of sausage loudly. 'What time will you be home? Last time you left me I thought you were dead.'

'I'll probably be late. We're all going to the Cosy Club, it's—'

'You needn't go into detail. I hope I didn't raise one of those boys who always tell you exactly what they're doing when you ask them?'

'No, Mum. Of course not.'

She had spilled peas onto the duvet and they rolled around like baby marbles. The man started to scoop them up but was interrupted by a quick rap on his knuckles with a fork.

'I haven't finished with them. Stop hovering! And where's my tea?'

'I forgot,' he said, and quickly left the room.

Downstairs he re-brewed the kettle and made his mother a cup of tea. He put two Jammie Dodgers on a plate and headed up the stairs again. She was fiddling with the bedside lamp when he entered. The light was flickering like an SOS.

'What are you doing, Mum?'

'Trying to fix the . . . It's always doing this.'

'It's fine. Just . . . hold on.' He put the tea and biscuits on her lap. Went to the other side of the room and pushed her wheelchair to one side. Knelt down by the washbasin and

3

opened a small door that was hidden behind. He went through to the next room, and when he returned a minute later the light had stopped flickering. He closed the door and pushed the wheelchair into place. 'There you go. Nice and quiet. I need to get ready now.'

He had already showered and shaved that morning and opened the bag he had left on his bed. Looked at the clothes inside and added a pair of flat shoes and an iPhone. He shot himself a smile in the mirror but it ended abruptly when he felt suddenly sad. *Stop it*, he said, and he grabbed the St Jude medal around his neck. *Stop it. Stop it.* His eyes went to the ceiling where the painted angel mural was watching and he gave himself a minute.

By the time he went back into his mother's room she was asleep, her gentle snoring like soft waves on a beach. The man wasn't sure whether he should wake her, but—

'I'm off now, Mum.'

'Hmm . . . ' his mother stirred.

He leaned in closer and gave her a kiss on the cheek. Smelled her breath, her old hair. She squinted at him with rheumy eyes and wiped a bit of sausage fat off her chin.

'Where's Stephen?' she whispered.

'Don't wait up for me,' he said, his breath catching in his throat.

He took his mother's tray and went downstairs. Washed everything up, put it all away, and placed a box of Weetabix on the kitchen table ready for breakfast.

'Bye, Mum!' he shouted up the stairs as he made his way into the hall, but he didn't leave yet. He opened the front door then slammed it shut and stood in absolute silence. Listening for a soft footstep or a scrape of furniture. Barely daring to breathe. Five minutes. Ten. Nothing. Then he caught a glimpse of himself in the hall mirror and the sadness returned like a black wave. His head fell forward onto his chest and he cried for a full minute. The sort of crying where he had no idea if he would ever stop and his head hurt and his heart pounded and his face was a mess but he didn't care. And he couldn't see because everything was blurry and nothing looked real and he couldn't feel pain because pain didn't exist any more – there was only the never-ending slog of sadness.

'What am I like ...' he sniffed. And after several minutes he rallied bravely, because deep down he knew exactly what he was like.

He was a lonely man with so much love to give, but nowhere to put it.

Two

'Are you drunk?'

It was a good question.

Someone had banged a nail into Holly Wakefield's head about two hours ago and no matter how much she tried to find it she just kept grabbing tufts of hair. Dirty hair. Smelly hair. Cigarettes and rhubarb gin.

'I think I might be,' she managed.

She pulled herself upright and her eyes flipped open, a newborn shrew seeing the sun. And then there was something she hadn't felt in a long time: the stomach lurch. The room spun and she wondered if she was going to be sick.

'Are you going to be sick?'

Another really good question. Detective Inspector Bishop was on fire today.

'Possibly.'

Hold it in. Hold it in. For God's sake, hold it in.

Who had suggested shots at four thirty in the morning? It had started with gin and tonics at eight last night. A reunion with the girls from Blessed Home, her foster home from when she had been a young girl. Valerie, Sophie Savage, Michelle, Joanne, Rhonda, Zoe. Sixty-two flavours of gin? Who even knew that was possible.

Then they had all decided on something to eat.

Soho – where else?

Balans on Old Compton Street – it had to be.

And after they had been kicked out at 2.00 a.m. they had gone to a members-only club on Shaftesbury Avenue. The Connaught, or something. No – the Century Club, that was it, and they had stayed there until they went on lockdown. Valerie was a member and got them in and then the party had really begun. Sophie had fancied one of the waiters and he had told them one of the funniest jokes about a deer, a skunk and a cuckoo. How did it go? A cuckoo, a skunk and a deer went out for dinner at a restaurant one night and when it came time to pay, the deer didn't have a *buck*, the skunk didn't have a *scent* – and the cuckoo? No, that's not right.

'The cuckoo . . . '

'What?' said Bishop.

'Shush. It was a joke from last night. Trying to remember. It was funny.'

Was it a cuckoo? Maybe it was a blackbird or a partridge? It would come to her. If it didn't she could always ask one of the girls. Ah – the girls. Her girls. All grown up now. All beautiful and smart and strong and lovely. And hard as nails when they needed to be. Good company. Nostalgic until the last round. By four o'clock it had been free drinks, cigars on the terrace and then the singing had—

She was being guided. Gentle hands. One on her shoulder. One on her lower back.

'Where are we going?'

'Toilet.'

'I think I'm okay.'

Stomach lurch number two and then that metallic taste in her throat and she could feel her jaw beginning to lock open as her body was about to—

'Don't watch me, please don't watch me,' she whispered.

The hands lowered her to the floor and she could feel the fluffy bathroom mat under her knees. Her fingers automatically gripped the rim of the bowl and then it all came up.

He held her hair as she vomited.

And kept vomiting.

'Good shot,' he said. And she had no idea if he was being sarcastic.

I wonder if he still fancies me?

And when she finished she found her laugh, because she had remembered the punchline to the joke. It wasn't a cuckoo! It was a duck! The deer didn't have a *buck*, the skunk didn't have a *scent* and the *duck* didn't have the *bill*.

'That's brilliant,' she said as she wiped her mouth with her hand, and all of a sudden everything made sense.

'Better?'

They were sitting in Brickwood Coffee & Bread, an artisan breakfast café in Balham, south-west London. Exposed bricks and wooden planks on the walls and a never-ending supply of healthy food and slow roast coffee. Holly had passed on the food but had taken a kale smoothie. It had tasted like lawnmower leftovers but she had held it down. *Good stomach. Love you.* Now she was nursing a black coffee.

'Do I smell of sick?' she said.

'Coffee and lack of sleep. That's what I'm getting from over here.'

'I'm a classy chick. What can I say?' She smiled and was suddenly conscious that she hadn't even brushed her teeth. Their waitress brought out Bishop's full English breakfast. Holly flinched as if it were part of a horror movie.

'Is that black pudding?'

'Yeah, you want some?'

'I'd rather eat my own feet.'

'What happened to the "hot chocolate and possibly a quiet movie if our mood takes us" evening with the girls?'

'We started with good intentions but then it quickly descended into chaos. It was good food. Good drink. I like my girls.'

'I know you do,' he smiled. 'Did you forget about our breakfast?'

'No.'

Yes.

She had vaguely remembered at six thirty this morning when she had collapsed through the front door and belly-dragged herself into the bedroom.

'I've got something for you,' he said.

'Another coffee?'

'If you want.' He ordered one then handed over a thin paper folder with no labels or words on the front cover. She started to open it but he closed it gently in her hands.

'Not over breakfast,' he said. 'It's the final report from the Sickert case.'

There was a mood breaker if ever there was one. Wilfred and Richard Sickert.

Doctor. Bastard. Patient. Bastard.

It had been nearly four months since she had first got the call from DI William Bishop of the Met Serious Crime squad and been asked to walk into a living room containing the freshly murdered and mutilated bodies of Jonathan and Evelyn Wright. He had been a doctor, she his loving wife. Forty years with each other wiped out by a flathead hammer and a wicked blade.

Angela Swan, the coroner, had concluded at the autopsy that the injuries to Evelyn were consistent with a previous murder; that of a British Airways flight attendant named Rebecca Bradshaw. Rebecca had been killed three weeks previously, left sitting propped up against her bed like a life-sized plastic doll. Wrists slashed, head resting against her chest as if she were asleep. Three murders. Similar MO and suddenly Holly had had a serial killer on her hands.

Before that her life had been quite simple really. Well ... both her parents had been murdered by a serial killer and she had been brought up in a foster home ... but she still considered herself one of the lucky ones. She had stayed in school, worked hard and gone on to major in criminology. Having had first-hand experience of death, she always wanted to know why. Why do you kill, Mr Sociopath? What makes your brain go tick-tick instead of tick-tock? Now she taught behavioural science to students at King's College in London and the rest of her week was spent at the Wetherington Hospital on Cromwell Road in the Royal Borough of Kensington and Chelsea, taking care of mentally challenged patients who had the propensity to kill.

Alongside DI Bishop she had helped track down two of the most brutal and clever killers England had ever seen. Two brothers: Wilfred and Richard Sickert. Born of the same womb, living by the same code. It had taken her to a crofter's cottage by the sea near Hastings – how romantic – and ended with Richard breaking his neck and her stabbing Wilfred in the heart with the broken thigh bone from one of his previous victims. All in all – an eventful two weeks.

The CPS had briefly considered prosecuting her over the deaths of Wilfred and Richard, but the Commissioner and Chief Constable Franks had stepped in and all charges had been dropped. It was the first time in a long time that Holly had felt as though she had help from other people. That she wasn't alone. That she had a family. She looked at Bishop, toying with the file. She wanted so much to read it, but then put it to one side.

'I don't ever want to know where they're buried,' she said.

'I didn't think you would.'

Her next coffee arrived and she downed it in one.

'I'm living life, William,' she said. 'Not staying in the confines of my flat any more. It's quite nice out there. With people.'

'People are nice. Most of them. When's your next doctor's appointment?' he asked.

'A couple of hours.'

'You want me to pick you up? Drive you?'

'Yes please. I might get lost,' she smiled and then his phone went. Holly watched him as he talked. He looked younger than his forty-three years. Maybe he'd had a haircut or maybe he was just sitting in good light. He listened for a while longer then frowned and hung up. Shot a look at Holly then returned to his breakfast. Indecision – fleeting – but it was there.

'I have to go.' He waved a hand to get the bill. 'I'm sorry, Holly.'

'What is it?'

'It's a body. Another case.'

'Can I come? I should come. Hold on, let me get ready—'

'No, stay. Go to your doctor's appointment. Make sure everything is fine.'

'Everything is fine, Bishop. I want to help.'

'I'm sure you do, but not yet.'

'At least tell me what it is—'

'I'll call you later.'

He left enough money on the table and walked away. The waitress returned before the front door had even closed.

'More coffee?'

Holly managed a smile but thought it might have looked a bit wonky.

'Keep it coming.'

Three

Her brother Lee was reading a book when she entered his cell.

He folded over the corner of the page with precision, closed it and placed it face down on the table. Holly sat down opposite. Neutral body-language. Neutral face.

'How are you today, Lee?'

'I'm dandy. How are you? How's the broken leg and mashed head?'

'Still aches.'

'Yeah, your face is killing me.' He attempted a smile but quickly wiped it away. 'Sorry. I get bored with the conversations here. The therapists. You're the only one who gets my humour. Who I can have fun with.'

'When was your last session with Mary?'

'Mary, Mary, quite contrary, how does her garden grow?' He pretended to take a hit on a joint. 'Wretchedly, I would imagine. I saw her two days ago.'

'What did you talk about this time?'

'Gardenias and roses, fairies and hidden treehouses.'

'Seriously?'

'No. We talk about all sorts of things. She's put me on a new type of medication. I'm mixing my pills. She thinks it will help but they're making me tired. Irritable.'

'What has she put you on?'

'Fucking Clozapine.'

'I didn't know. I'm sorry.'

'It's not your fault, Sis.'

'Any other side effects?'

'Cramps. Nothing outrageous. Not like I'm giving birth or anything.'

'What's the book?' she asked.

He turned it over and glanced at the cover.

'*A Beginner's Guide to the Migration Pattern of the Common British Snail.*'

'How is it?'

'*Slow.* A riveting tale of digestion and excretion.' A beat. 'I can smell it on you, by the way.'

'What?' She sniffed her jacket, her hair. 'The alcohol? No, you can't. I had a shower.'

'Good night out?'

'Yes.'

'I had a good night last night as well. I had a Pot Noodle and a wank in my cell.'

'It's not a cell, it's a room.'

'Oh, of course: Hotel Wetherington, I forgot. In which case who do I lodge a complaint with because my waterbed has a puncture and my massage chair keeps breaking down. Oh, and everything smells like mashed potatoes and piss. What would you call this place then?'

'A secure psychiatric facility.'

'Not really selling it to me, Sis. How about a very desirable one-bedroom flat situated in a popular London location, well within walking distance of the communal canteen. The accommodation boasts a single bed, a table and two chairs, a modern fitted music stereo system and benefits from anti-riot plastic windows with stunning views of the surrounding brick walls.'

'Very funny.'

'It includes dodgy electrics, off-road parking for visitors and a small but pleasant garden to the rear that is available for one hour every day, normally just when it's getting dark.'

'Have you finished?'

'Although one of the neighbours does smell a bit funny and sounds like he's fucking a cat whenever he's in the toilets, the property is offered with no onward chain. And the doctors are on call twenty-four hours a day for your convenience.'

'Have you finished now?'

'Yes.'

They sat in silence for a while and she studied him in the low light and felt the familiar flush of guilt. Two years her elder, Lee had actually witnessed their parents being murdered by the serial killer the press dubbed as The Animal, while Holly had come in minutes later and only seen the awful aftermath. Before that day, she had only really started to notice Lee when she was about six years old. He was a noise that annoyed her and kept her up at night, sibling rivalry at an early age that had dissolved when their parents had been taken away. They had clung to each other like limpets for weeks after the murders and as she got older he had kept her company. Held her when she felt down. Kissed her on the cheek when there was no one else and always promised that everything would turn out all right. She wondered if in a way it had.

At thirty-eight Lee's face was sallow and gaunt. Last year the board had talked about his possible parole, and Holly had been asked to come in and interview him about the murder of his male lover – in an effort to garner information that the other therapists seemed unable to extract. She had been successful but parole had been denied and Lee had been in a slump ever since. He probably would be at Wetherington Hospital for the rest of his life, but nevertheless when the candle had been blown out she knew he couldn't help but feel the darkness around him.

'You look as though you've lost weight,' she said.

'I don't think so.'

'I want you to eat up all your food. Even if the eggs are overcooked. Eat it all, okay?'

He nodded absently. Eyes straying away.

'I left my life behind when I was brought inside here.'

'Of course you did.'

'No. I mean literally. In a plastic bag at the reception. I keep thinking about that plastic bag.'

'Why?'

'Wondering if it's still there. In some dark cupboard, collecting dust. Collecting . . . what else would it collect?'

'Nothing probably. But it will be there.'

'Waiting for me?'

'Waiting.'

'That was my life before I was arrested. What was inside. Not much really. Three pounds and fourteen pence. Half a pack of polos. My flat keys, car keys and another key that I found on Latimer Road in east London that I have no idea who it belongs to or which door it will ever open. I think that's sad.'

'Why?'

'Because somebody is missing their key.'

'I'm sure they had a new one cut.'

'But it will never be the same, will it?' he sighed. 'A receipt from M&S – I ate a chicken salad the afternoon I was arrested, and I still had the plastic fork in my pocket. God knows why. It was wrapped in a paper napkin, I think. The physical things that we hold on to. Like emotions, aren't they? We find it hard to let anything go. Three sticks of cinnamon-flavoured chewing gum. A Starbucks loyalty card. A Waterstones loyalty card. A Boots loyalty card. I'm very loyal, aren't I? That's my life in a plastic bag. Lying in a dark drawer somewhere waiting for me to reclaim it. But I know I never will. Does chewing gum ever go off?'

'I don't know.'

'Probably got the shelf life of a nuclear isotope. All the crap they put in it. Killing us softly, but we're so happy in our own oblivion.'

He sat in his chair, hands interlaced comfortably across his stomach.

'I want to go back to reading my shitty book, please. But I appreciate the visit.'

She kissed her fingers and gently pressed them onto his hand. Got up and put her jacket on.

'How's the detective?'

She contemplated, shook her head.

'We're taking it slow.'

'Is it time that I met him, do you think? Introduce him to the rest of the family?'

'No.'

He picked up the book and found his place.

'He knows about me?'

'Not that you're my brother.'

'Interesting. Would he approve? Of course not. Does he know everything about you?'

'No.'

'Secrets are never good in a relationship, Holly. Best to bare your soul and be done with it.'

'Says the man in a padded cell.'

'Says the woman who's lost her way.'

Four

The cold, mechanical whir of an MRI scanner.

Holly lay inside. Pale skinned, her lips slightly parted, eyes closed as if she were asleep. Her light brown hair had been scraped from her forehead so hard it made her face look gaunt. Wearing a white hospital gown she could have been on an autopsy table in a mortuary.

'Holly?'

Her eyes twitched then opened. Deep and dark brown. But the whites were cracked and scarred with tiny red veins. Lost sleep, lost time, lost everything. She stared up at the metal tube as it whirred and hummed around her like a human-sized convection oven.

'How are you feeling?'

'Like a kebab.' Her throat was dry. Scratchy.

'Another couple of minutes.'

Great, she thought. Another one hundred and twenty seconds to think about Bishop, where he was and why she wasn't with him. They'd had a few special evenings over December. Hot chocolate, her evening fix after 6.00 p.m., tucked up on the sofa, conversation and then something on the television. No crime drama though when they switched on Netflix – it was their house rule – and she wondered if they would actually find time for each other this year. Maybe go somewhere for a proper meal. See a show. Cocktails? But not today. Today she was lying in a tube of metal waiting for the specialist to evaluate her recovery after the damage Wilfred had inflicted on her in their final fight.

Living the dream, Holly. Maybe she should buy a cat? Maybe she should get a cat and go and live in the Cotswolds or something. Nice and bland. A distinct lack of sadists and killers hiding in the Cotswolds, she thought. Or maybe not. Maybe they just haven't been caught yet.

'Okay. Holly. We're done,' the voice of God said. 'You can move now.'

She didn't want to move. Today she wanted to stay completely still and do nothing. Today all she wanted was to sleep.

She was sitting in an armchair in the specialist's office.

His name was Dr Breaker. He was in his forties and lean and wore wire-rimmed glasses and had told her when they first met that he liked to paraglide at the weekends. She didn't give a shit.

'Considering the brutality of the assault you suffered, you seem to have recovered remarkably well,' he said. 'The right eye socket is still in a very slight state of dysfunction. Any loss of sight? Zigzag lines at the edge of your vision?'

'No.'

He slipped the colourful scans onto a light board and examined them with the meticulousness of a man who clearly enjoyed his work. 'There's no edema of the brain tissue, which is good news, but we are going to carry on monitoring you for signs of change in your neurological status. The main ingredient for your recovery, however, is rest and quiet. How does that sound?'

Holly put her hands on the arm of the chair and found a loose thread to play with. She was chewing gum slowly as if the act itself required a huge amount of concentration.

'Nice.'

'How's your memory these days?'

'Sometimes I forget why I went into a room, but I think that's normal.'

'It's not.'

'For me it is.'

He nodded slowly, eyes unblinking

'Are you drinking alcohol at all?' he said.

'Haven't had a drop for weeks. Months probably.'

'Good. Best to avoid alcohol at this point in your recovery.'

'Of course.'

He closed her file with a flick of his wrist.

'You're as fit as a fiddle,' he said.

'Thank you, Doc.'

'But we should do more tests.'

She changed out of the gown and into something more befitting a resurrected corpse. A black Cashmere sweater, blue jeans, a pair of low-heeled shoes and a touch of make-up. As she was making her way to her car she was surprised to see DI Bishop waiting outside. She shot him a shadow of a smile.

'Realised you couldn't live without me?'

'Something like that. What did the doctor say?'

'Says I'm fucked up.'

'Christ, I could have told you that.' He took a moment. 'You want to go for a drive?'

She hesitated by her car door. Had to ask:

'Is this the new case?'

He stared at her. Gave nothing away.

'Keep me company.'

Five

Travelling through late afternoon London traffic, the car journey was slow. They went north over Tower Bridge, the Tobacco Dock on their right and Aldgate on their left, dominated by dozens of the high-rise insurance companies and banks. Through Whitechapel, home of the Ripper and lair of the Kray Twins, and then they were out past the London Orbital and heading north. The tower blocks and tenements dissolving to a frosty rural landscape. Tree-covered hills and hazy skies in the distance.

Even though it was cold, Holly had the window down. She liked open spaces now. Having been half buried and fighting for her life in a mud pit with Wilfred one cold November night last year, she didn't much like the feel of being trapped. Closed in. She felt the icy wind fan through her hair and could feel her cheeks going numb. She saw Bishop shiver a few times at the chill but he didn't say anything. Didn't complain.

'How have you been?' she asked. 'I mean your work. I never asked this morning.'

'You know. Same old, same old. Still waiting for that bigger office.'

'How's Sergeant Ambrose?'

'Like a zombie. Can't get enough sleep. But when he's at breaking point he stares at the latest photo of his baby daughter and all is forgiven.'

A pause.

'Christmas was quiet,' he said.

'Same here.'

'Yeah?'

'Yeah.'

Wanstead Park was an easterly area of Epping Forest in the London Borough of Redbridge. Approximately nineteen kilometres running north to south, and about four kilometres east to west it was comprised of woodland, grassland, heaths and gorse with dozens of lakes and ponds of various sizes. They approached from the south via Warren Road, the old gravel beaten down by decades of tyres and millions of feet. A golf course on their left and then they arrived at a series of entrances. Bishop didn't hesitate, took the one that was signposted 'The Glade', a wide muddy path that ran easterly past armies of brown trees and dead ferns. Another left when the road divided, then they hit a dip and the car protested like an old horse at a high jump.

'Sorry,' he said.

A quick pull on the reins and the beast broke through. The buildings up ahead were off the beaten track. Abandoned houses with broken windows and Bishop pulled to a halt in front of an old L-shaped barn. Ivy snaked all over and wild grass grew alongside the steps that led to a wooden front door. Peeling paint. Warped wood. There were two other cars there – one police and one unmarked. In the distance, a constable was rolling out crime-scene tape between trees that looked like bunting at a summer festival.

Holly was suddenly aware of a constant hum in the background but wasn't sure what it was. When she opened the car door, it became obvious. Dogs barking. A cacophony of mongrel noise. She followed Bishop under the bunting to the front door where he rang the bell.

'You expect someone to hear that above the noise?'

'He's expecting us.'

The door opened warily and a man appeared. Shabbily dressed, he stank of wet dog. He had a shock of grey hair, a craggy face. His eyes rested on Bishop.

'Thought you'd be back.'

'Mr Greyson.'

'Come in then. You want a coffee or tea?'

'I'm fine, thank you.'

Holly shook her head.

They followed him inside. A narrow corridor with linoleum floor and a security door at the far end. He opened it up to reveal a room of full of kennels with howling dogs, front paws hanging through bars like furry inmates.

'Been doing rescue for seventeen years now,' Greyson said. 'Lost my funding two years ago but I keep on going through donations. Good people around here. You guys ever want a dog, let me know.'

'We'll keep that in mind,' Bishop said.

They passed through to a kitchen with a workbench, table and chairs. An old black-and-white TV played some obscure vintage film. The room was well kept but there were no real personal touches apart from a few yellowed photos magneted to the fridge.

'You want to repeat what you told me earlier please, Mr Greyson?'

'Not really, but I will if I have to.' He glanced at Holly. 'For your benefit, I think, miss.' He made himself a coffee and kept adding spoonfuls of sugar. Playing for time. Delaying the inevitable.

'Mr Greyson?'

'Yep.' He stopped stirring and looked at Holly with sunken eyes. 'I live here. Have done for twenty-two years. Always up at seven thirty in the morning to take the dogs out for their first walk of the day along Shonks Mill Road. You familiar with that?'

'No,' she said.

'A half-mile away. Got them through the main bracken as usual and then they went crazy. Smelled something. Running, barking. Had three of them on leads but they pulled right away. Never seen anything like it before. Straight through the reeds and up onto the opposite bank. I was calling out to them. Shouting at 'em, but when dogs got the scent they don't listen to nobody. Circling. Howling. I half expected to see a full moon up there it was so wacky. Then I hear a few of them growling, like they're under threat. I pushed my way through and by the time I got there a few of them was wandering around like they were lost, but Ripper – he's my Ridgeback – he was standing on a little grassy mound between some bushes. Teeth bared, fur bristling like he was ready to attack. He calmed down when I came up.' Greyson paused, licked his lips and squared his shoulders somewhat.

'That's when I saw it. The young boy's body.'

*

Dead trees and shadows.

Holly and Bishop walked through both.

There were at least a dozen police up ahead. Tungsten lamps had been erected and cameras clicked and flashed around the scene but there was no other noise. No talking. Just the shush-shush of leather soles on wet leaves as the officers moved among the trees, breath visible in the cold afternoon air.

Bishop put on latex gloves and handed Holly a pair as he led her to a small dark shape lying between two green bushes. He didn't say anything. Didn't need to. Holly moved past him to get a better look.

The dead boy was naked apart from a pair of white underpants.

Lying on his right side, legs tucked into his stomach, hands folded across his chest, his head was resting on a clean white pillow. The boy's face was oval-shaped and very pale, almost chalky, with short dark hair. Eyes open, clear and green, his lips slightly parted as if about to take a breath.

'How many children have been reported missing over the weekend?' she asked.

'One hundred and fifty-seven.'

'This weekend?'

Bishop nodded when she turned to him.

'London averages nearly five hundred missing children a week,' he said. 'Most of them are kids bunking off from care homes. Trying to go home to see Mum and Dad, or they feel safer on the street, but some of them . . . '

Holly nodded absently.

'Can you smell that? Lemons or something.'

'No.'

She wondered if she were imagining it. Looked from the body to the darkening trees.

'No tyre tracks or drag marks,' Bishop said. 'So he would have been carried. He's small, doesn't look too heavy.'

'Afternoon, Bishop, Holly.'

Holly turned and saw Angela Swan walking towards them. An assistant handed her a SOCO suit and she slipped it on with the familiarity of a glove. Holly gave her a smile. She liked Angela. Trusted her.

'Sorry I'm late – matinee panto with the children. Mother Goose will have to find her own golden egg.' She turned to Bishop; 'What do you want first?'

'Cause of death.'

She leaned into the body like a hunter on a corpse. Knelt and put a hand on the child's forehead. Feathery touches around the stomach, torso and head.

'Strangulation.' She pointed to a faint purple welt around the neck. 'But he wasn't killed here. Patches of lividity across the chest, shoulders and front of his thighs. The body was left lying face down for a minimum of six hours before it was moved here and I'd say he's been in the forest less than twelve. Critters haven't got to him yet. So he would have been dumped here in the early hours of this morning.'

'Age?'

Angela opened the boy's mouth. It lowered like a trap door almost immediately, so she had to clamp it before she could shine her torch inside. 'The teeth are all intact with unerupted permanent dentition, consistent with being at least twelve years old. At a guess I'd say between twelve and fourteen.'

She followed the boy's arms, tracing them gently. Moved

on to his hands, clasped across opposing shoulders, forming a cross.

'I think there's something in one of his hands. Holly, can
you ... it's hard to see.'

Bishop handed Holly his torch and she moved closer.
Shone the light as Angela gently prised open the boy's twig-
like fingers and revealed a thin necklace with a silver charm
attached. A tiny figure with ruffled wings.

'What is it?' Bishop said.

A few seconds where Holly seemed almost wistful.
Then she said:

'An angel.'

She took it, examined it and handed it over to Bishop, then
pulled herself to her feet. Her left leg had gone to sleep and
the returning sensation made her wince. She glanced at the
body for a second longer before nodding and striding away.

When Bishop caught up with her, she was on the other side
of the forest. Staring at the treeline. Red sky. Red sunset. He
seemed perturbed, finally spoke:

'You said you were ready for this. Are you?'

She took a sudden breath as she felt the dread washing over
her. Her body going tense. But she knew the answer already.

'Of course.'

She took one last look at the dead trees and cold sky, then
walked slowly towards the car.

Six

When Holly got home that evening, she shucked off her jacket and put a ready meal in the microwave. Poured herself a heavy glass of red and started drinking it before she got to the living room. She lived on the fifth floor of a two bedroom flat in Balham south London. A flat she had renovated herself six years ago and few people were invited across the threshold. It was open plan, minimalist and very tidy. Her own bedroom was east facing, she preferred sunrise to sunset, with floor to ceiling windows that let her guess the weather of the day and ponder the closed curtains of the flats opposite. The answer-machine light was flashing. One message. She pressed play.

The building's supervisor: The couple in number two were having the hallway downstairs redecorated. Simple white to match the rest of the building, but it would obviously involve drop cloths, people on ladders and open paint cans. Could everybody please be especially careful when coming in for the next few weeks? The work was due to start tomorrow. Sorry again for any inconvenience.

The microwave pinged. She emptied the steaming container onto a plate and sat on the sofa. Found herself staring at the Harland Miller painting above the fireplace, 'Death – What's In It For Me?' On the last case she had taken it down and used the wall as an incident board. It had been covered with Sharpie notes and dates, timelines and question marks. Photos of the Sickerts and their victims, all watching her everyday movements with dead eyes. After the case was over, she had scrubbed the wall with bleach. It had been therapeutic. Saying goodbye to the killer in her house and the haunted faces of his victims. Now, the living room wall was pale blue and peaceful again. The painting was once more in place, there was a vase of irises to the left and a card from Bishop still sitting on the other side of the mantelpiece left over from before Christmas. The only one she had kept. *Get well soon, Holly.* Simple. A man of few words on paper but his eyes said so much more.

She opened the file Bishop had given her and scrutinised the photos of the boy in the forest. White skin. Brown leaves. Dead on top of dead.

She imagined him alive again. Pumped his heart rate up from zero to a resting seventy-five. Lungs breathing in and out. Blood pulsing through his veins. Dreams and laughter in his young head. Conversations with his friends at school, kicking stones in the playground during break, tears streaming down his face as someone told a stupid joke. Hands up in class. Questions never answered. Those bright green eyes had seen whoever had done this. Perhaps smiled with him, laughed with him. Mother. Father. A friend of the family? A stranger? Who were you looking at when you died? What did you see in their eyes?

She remembered a case of forensic optography from the nineteenth century – at no other point in time had the Victorian public been so obsessed with murder and death. Contemporaries used to believe you could see the killer's reflection in the dead victim's eyes and the police started to consider optography as a technique to investigate murders. They thought it possible that the eyes retained an image at the last moment of death, the last thing the victims saw. Walter Drew wrote about it being attempted on Mary Jane Kelly, one of the Ripper victims, but the science was soon debunked and turned into nothing more than nineteenth-century hocus pocus.

But what would this boy have seen in his last few moments? He would have seen hate. Anger. Yes. But there was something else there as well. There was love there too. The pillow under his head, the tenderness with which he had been laid down and then there was the necklace in his hand:

You do *look* like an angel. Is that what the killer wanted you to be?

She found the photos of the pendant in the file. The moulding was crisp and she could make out the angel's shallow cheeks, its closed eyes, wings splayed either side, something in its hands. A stick, a flower, a sword?

She put her food to one side and opened her Mac. Googled angels and was hit by nearly half a billion results. Angels of God, Archangels, demi-angels, angels that represented Virtues, Principals, seven days of the week: Michael, Gabriel, Raphael, Raguel, Lucifer, Ariel, Uriel. Seraphim, cherubim, Saint Michael the Archangel, holding a sword aloft, sometimes drawn with a shield. A protector against the wickedness and snares of the devil, a defender in battle. Gabriel, God's messenger found in the books of Luke and Daniel. The fallen angel? Holding a lily in some pictures and she wondered if that was what her angel was holding.

A fallen angel?

She felt her heart pounding when the phone rang. It was Bishop. She watched it for a while, rubbed her eyes before answering.

'Hey,' she said. 'Are you still at the station?'

'Everybody's on late shifts and overtime. We've got three teams out in the forest now, along with a K9 unit walking the grid. They've completed the preliminary sweep but it's a huge area. Hold on a second.' His voice went muffled on the other end, then: 'We've got a station full of worried parents and still have no ID on the boy. The autopsy is tomorrow morning. Nine o'clock,' he said. 'Can you make it?'

'I'll be there.'

'Thank you, Holly.' The silence stretched between them. Bishop cleared his throat. 'The last case, with the Sickerts, I know you almost got killed.'

She suddenly felt out of breath, as if she had run a race. Forced herself to say:

'Yes.'

'I won't let that happen again,' he said. 'I promise I won't let that happen. Okay?'

She nodded but didn't reply.

'You want me to come over?'

It was tempting, but ...

'No, I'm fine. I need to unwind a little, that's all.'

She was silent for a long while and played with her food. When she spoke next it was with careful deliberation:

'Bishop, the scene in the forest may have looked serene, like a page from a storybook even, but underneath this killer is telling us something.'

'What?'

'That he is confused, lost and very angry. And that anger was acted upon and has now become very real. I don't have much to go on yet, but I can start a profile of sorts.'

'Thank you, Holly. As fast as you can.'

The phone went dead and everything was suddenly quiet. The wall above the fireplace badly needed filling in and she could feel the urge to start the inevitable, but there was something she had to do first. She got up, entered her spare room and turned on the lights. She was in her murderabilia room: a mini-museum for her macabre collection of trinkets and trophies from serial killers and their victims. Bishop was the only other person who had ever been inside and she wondered if he knew that. What had he called it? The 'creepy-death-room'. It wasn't a place for the faint of heart, that was for sure.

Annie Chapman's body was discovered at 6.00 a.m. on the morning of 8 September 1888. She was Jack the Ripper's second victim of the canonical five and was wearing a black dress when she had been killed. Holly touched the hem of that dress as she walked past it. Victorian lace. Nothing quite so Lilliputian and delicate.

The knives, the nooses, the belts that had been used to stab, maim and strangle people, all hung from racks, displayed like flags from some forgotten army. A Welsh dresser decorated with auction prizes: Lord William Russell's burr maple snuffbox, the lid mounted with a cabochon in a gold rosette. He had been murdered by his Swiss valet François Courvoisier in Mayfair on 6 May 1840. The snuffbox had been found under his bloody pillow.

A letter from James Berry, an English executioner from 1884–1891, who had contributed to the science of hanging with his drop-method, which was intended to diminish the mental and physical suffering of the prisoner.

John Christie's mahogany chest of drawers from 10 Rillington Place, his Bible laid on top, dog-eared and yellowed, left open at Ephesians 1:7 – 'In him we have redemption through his blood, the forgiveness of sins, in accordance with the riches of God's grace'.

She lingered by an Edwardian kneehole desk. Who had this belonged to? Of course. John Haigh, the acid bath murderer. She pulled open the middle drawer. Heard the object inside before she saw it.

A small brass bell.

There it was. Peeking out of the shadows like a timid creature afraid of the light. Simple and plain but so powerful. This was Wilfred and Richard Sickert's calling card. Their tell-tale sign and token that they left at every murder scene. Their claim to the kill. This was the bell that Richard had used to summon his brother to help to kill her. Bishop had given it to her after the hearing. Thought she might want it. He knew her so well. She lifted it out, gently tapped it and was rewarded by the high-pitched tinny ring. She still had nightmares or visions, once or twice a week when she saw or felt Wilfred's face emerge from the darkness. A knife in one hand, holding her throat with the other, ready to extinguish her life as simply as blowing out a candle. And there were times when she would be watching television or reading and she half expected him to suddenly appear behind the sofa. Whispering in her ear: *Although it will be violent, there is a peace about death which is quite soothing. I promise.*

She returned the bell to the drawer, slammed it shut and went back to the living room. Stood for few seconds by the fireplace, then took down the Harland Miller painting and stuck up the photo of the dead boy's face in its place.

He would watch her now.

Watch her until this was over.

Seven

Holly pushed open the double doors and immediately felt the blast of cold air.

A few more steps and the smell hit her: cold with a heavy hit of decay. Angela and Bishop stood on either side of the autopsy table. Both turned and looked up at her clumsy entrance.

'Traffic, sorry,' Holly said. Bishop gave her a slight nod.

'I won't recap what I've already told DI Bishop,' the coroner said, 'but I'll make sure you get a copy of my findings.'

'Thank you.'

Angela placed the white mask on her face. Spoke into a microphone that hung from the ceiling as she worked.

'Nine twenty-six a.m. DI Bishop and I have been joined by NHS profiler Holly Wakefield as I examine the as yet unidentified boy found in Wanstead Park.'

She pulled down the green sheet, revealing the body of the child. Ribs like green strips under the white stretched skin. Hands resting by his hips, bony elbows on the cold table.

'He measures one hundred and sixty-two centimetres in height, which is average for a boy between twelve and fourteen years of age, and weighs forty-eight kilos, which is below average for a boy of that age range.' She leaned into the body. 'The eyes are open. The irises are green and corneas are cloudy. Petechial haemorrhaging is present in the conjunctival surfaces of the eyes. The pupils measure' – a quick calculation with a pupil gauge – 'nought point four centimetres in diameter. The hair is dark brown and approximately nine centimetres in length at the longest point.'

Angela opened the boy's mouth.

'There is no obstruction of the airway. The mucosa of the epiglottis, glottis, piriform sinuses, trachea and major bronchi are anatomic. He has no tonsils. Surgery would have been at least five years ago. No other injuries are seen and there are no mucosal lesions.' A pause. 'Hold on. There is a small area of inflammation on the right buccal cavity where it comes into contact with the tongue. The surrounding papillae are also inflamed.'

She reached over for a pair of tweezers and lowered them into his mouth. A gentle tug and she withdrew a tiny translucent sliver.

'On first inspection, it would appear to be plastic, but I'll have it analysed.'

She placed it in a Petri dish. Closed the boy's mouth and traced her hands around the neck. Brought the Maglite down to assist. 'The hyoid bone, the thyroid, and the cricoid cartilages are fractured. There is a single ligature mark around the neck, again with evidence of petechial haemorrhaging, which would indicate the boy was strangled while still alive.' She tilted the boy's head to one side. 'The mark is approximately one inch wide, and encircles the neck in an inverted "V" on the posterior side, which meant the killer strangled the boy from the front. Was looking at him. Possibly straddling him. His arms about here' – she gestured close to the boy's neck. Raised her elbows slightly. 'So was lifting him up with some force rather than pushing down.'

'What did he use? A wire, rope?'

'A cord perhaps or fabric of some kind. The lower sections of the wrists show areas of discolouration and bruising where he was restrained. I also found tiny splinters of wood polish and white plastic in one of the scrapings I took from under his nails. The white plastic might be insulating wire. Wherever he was, it looks as though he may have tried to claw his way out.' She turned his hands over. Traced her fingers across the palms and up to the forearms.

'One thing that surprised me was there was no sexual interference.' She stood up slowly, 'and there are no other residual scars, markings or tattoos anywhere on the body. It would also appear that the victim has no broken bones, but I'll X-ray him to be sure. As a summary of his overall health, I wouldn't class him as anorexic but he's incredibly thin. His muscles aren't well formed. Not exactly athletic – let's put it that way. A sedentary life probably spent in front of the computer rather than playing footie in the park. I'd be very surprised if he was a runaway or homeless though. He seems too well looked after. Too loved.'

She moved away from the table and took a sip from a mug that said WORLD'S WORST MUM. Read from a sheet of paper. 'On to the toxicology. Sample of right pleural blood and bile have been submitted for analysis. Still awaiting those. There were no stomach contents. He may have been given a diuretic as well, because his urine was very high in ammonia and an orange-brown colour, consistent with dehydration. Abnormal blood counts and elevated liver enzymes would suggest he hadn't eaten for quite a while. Nil by mouth for at least two days and his fluids were minimal. Barely enough to keep him alive. Toxicology indicates he was given a high dosage of fentanyl.'

'Fentanyl?'

'It's an opiate for pain relief and types of anaesthetic. In this case, it was mixed with a small amount of heroin. It was given before he was strangled. No injection site on this corpse. No patch-mark residuals. My best guess is it was either inhaled or ingested as a pill. On to the poor boy's visage.' She traced the line of his eyelashes with a cotton bud. 'And this is very interesting. Over his body and on his face was a very fine spray consisting of Greek catnip oil, soybean oil and citronella. Any ideas?' It was rhetorical. 'Home-made insect repellent.' A pause. 'Why you would spray a dead body with that, I have no idea.'

'Because the killer didn't want the flies to get to him,' Holly said.

Angela straightened and shot her a look. 'I'm sorry?'

'The killer didn't want the flies to get to him,' she said quietly. She couldn't take her eyes off the boy's face, the shadows around his cheeks, the dry lips. 'Didn't want them crawling over him.'

Angela nodded slightly, went back to the corpse.

'His skin is slightly red and swollen around the eyes and the vermillion border of the lips, so he was allergic to one of the ingredients. It would appear that whoever killed him cleaned him thoroughly before he was brought to the forest, probably to remove trace materials. All of this would have taken time. You have a killer who doesn't like to be rushed. We also have no foreign DNA. The killer wore gloves and was very, very careful.'

She covered the boy up and pulled off her mask.

'As for ID, I've sent DNA samples to the UK database, fingerprints to NAID and had his teeth X-rayed. I'll send them out to the national database of orthodontists this afternoon. But if he cannot be found on our files – and sadly I suspect he won't be – then we are still at a zero re identification.'

'Anything else that jumps out?'

'Apart from the insect spray and the laying of his head on a pillow?' She smiled painfully. 'Nope. Just a run-of-the-mill killer who has a penchant for young boys.'

Eight

Holly and Bishop went up in the lift and walked in silence to the front door.

He held it open and they stepped out into the cold. The branches of the trees were motionless, their leaves long since scattered and decayed. Holly leaned against the railing by the steps. She shook her head with an exaggerated air of patience.

'The smell in the forest. *Citronella*. I knew I recognised it.' She swung around and faced him. 'I had a patient once. Justin Trevago. Over a period of six months he killed three girls. It started off as a burglary – well, that was his defence, only I don't believe it. I'm sure his intention was always to kill. He strangled them. Had sexual intercourse with them when they were dead, and then covered them up with the duvet as if they were asleep. Kissed them on the forehead. Said "Goodnight", then left their rooms. He was very careful. Wore gloves, wore a condom, was waxed everywhere so he wouldn't leave hairs. But it was the kiss that caught him. They got his DNA from the children's foreheads.'

'So why did he do it?'

'Why did he kill?'

'No, why did he put the children under the covers again? Make them look as if they were still asleep, as if nothing had happened.'

'Because part of him hated himself for what he was doing.'

'I didn't think child-killers were like that. Remorse. Guilt.'

'Some are. When he walked out of each house, he convinced himself he hadn't done anything wrong. He could turn at the doorway and stare at the girls – he told me he stared at them – and it was as though they were still sleeping and it had all been in his imagination. It's called symbolic reversal. Whoever killed the boy tucked him up as if he was putting him to bed. He gave him a pillow. Wanted him to be comfortable.'

'Is this Trevago character still around?'

'Got shanked by another inmate in the stomach until he bled to death in the toilets of C Block in HMP Frankland, County Durham. Child rapists don't fare too well behind bars.'

'But this boy wasn't raped. There was no sexual interference.'

'No. Paedophiles prey on children for very specific reasons. Some are simply opportunistic predators, some have physiological and or psychological problems, some are curious, but nearly all are motivated by lust. This killer wasn't.' She paused, staring at the dead trees. The air was cold but she could feel an inner chill that was even colder.

'What about the angel in the boy's hand?' Bishop said. 'A religious killing? The occult?' He sounded unusually tense. 'Christ, what's next? Candles, pentagrams? Ritual sacrifices? There was nothing like that at the scene.'

'Unless we missed it.'

Bishop lit a cigarette.

'I was hoping this would be a one-off,' he said. 'Pissed-off

43

stepdad or uncle. But from what you're saying, I think it's sufficiently fucked-up for me to be worried.' He wiped at his eyes as if the cold air was making them weep. 'I have a hard time with children's bodies. Saw enough of them in Afghanistan. Somehow their faces always looked pretty. No legs, no body, but with their eyes closed … I always thought they would wake up suddenly, stifle a yawn and say something like "What happened? Where am I?" But they never did. Sleeping angels, we used to call them.' He deliberated the lit cigarette. 'We're putting together a list of sex offenders and all recently released paedophiles and predators who target young boys.'

'The killer won't be on that list. He's not a Fred or Rose West. Myra Hindley or Ian Brady. He's not a lust murderer.'

'Then what is he?'

'I don't know yet,' she said distantly. 'But I think a part of him really enjoyed what he did.'

Nine

It was cold in the station car park. A mist had descended. Visibility low.

They had driven separately to Hammersmith police station. A Georgian building off Shepherd's Bush Road near the Hammersmith flyover. The area was home to the Lyric Theatre and rock shows at the Apollo concert hall and busy shops and cafés. Holly managed to squeeze her red MG between two police vans in the station car park and got out right as the heavens opened. She could hear bells ringing from St Augustine's church down the road and wondered if it was a wedding. If it was a happy couple, they couldn't have picked a worse day. By the time she got into the station her hair had been flattened by the rain and was dark almost to the point of being black.

Past the front reception and along the first corridor. Doors left and right, Holly could hear people snatching up phones and the occasional bark of conversation. This was Bishop's home from home and the base where she had worked on the Sickert case. Another door at the end and she saw him walking towards her.

'I'll see you in my office in a minute,' was his only comment.

He disappeared along another corridor, heading towards a frosted door at the end. His head was down and his limp was affecting him badly today, the result of a hit-and-run nearly a decade ago. She watched him until he disappeared, then turned and walked the corridors until she reached his office.

She had forgotten how small it was. The single window behind the desk looked out on to the orange brick wall of his neighbour, there were filing cabinets to the right, and a book-shelf on the far wall. No books though, simply a collection of dog-eared case files. The cabinets looked a little fuller, the desk a little untidier, and there was the ever-present pink orchid on his desk in memory of his fiancée who had been killed in Afghanistan. Holly had never found out her name, but they had talked about her before Christmas and she wondered what she had been like. Wondered how long he would carry the torch.

Bishop entered and threw a file onto his desk

'The incident room will be in S12. We're going to reconvene with the task force after lunch. Shall we eat in here?'

They went to the staff canteen. Holly ordered crab cakes and chips, Bishop an omelette, and now they sat in his office and had their plates balanced precariously on the desk. Bishop took a mouthful of food then started speaking:

'We've had an avalanche of calls since the press reported the story. Over four hundred families, social services and the NCA have all come forward with names and suggestions. So far we've eliminated one hundred and twelve missing boys between the ages of twelve and sixteen through photo ID. We're still working our way through the rest but new cases are being reported every five minutes. Mums and dads

46

are panicking and it's not helped by the fact it's half-term. Children are on holiday with friends, extended family, out of mobile phone range.'

He took a seat behind his desk and flipped open the file.

'We had the preliminary report last night. Let me fill you in on where we are. Wanstead Park has three visitor centres, but we're concentrating on the High Beech Visitor Centre, which is approximately one thousand metres east of where the body was found. The killer could have parked along one of the many side roads there. We've taken casts of tyre tracks and they're being catalogued now. There is no CCTV anywhere in the forest or at the visitor centres.'

'I imagine the killer would have known that.'

'There are, however, thirty-two cameras on the major roads nearby, so we're pulling all the footage of vehicles heading in the direction of the visitors' car park from five o'clock Wednesday evening to six o'clock yesterday morning. Sunrise on Thursday was at seven twenty-four. We've already interviewed some of the regular joggers who arrive between five forty-five and six fifteen every weekday. None of them saw any unusually parked vehicles or new runners. They all take the same route from the visitor centre, which is in the opposite direction to where the body was found. West rather than east, away from the pine trees, as it's less marshy.'

That was interesting. Holly wondered if the killer had noticed that himself. How much of a planner was he?

'We're interviewing dog walkers, ramblers, orienteering groups, and horse riders. There was also a wedding party on the Wednesday night at a local pub called the Robin Hood, which is off Epping New Road.'

'How far is that from the crime scene?'

'A half-mile. The party went on until the early hours of Thursday morning. Over a hundred guests, and some of them would have drifted into the forest. We're working our way through them now.'

'Who takes care of the woods?'

'Run by the Forestry Commission. In this case, the North London department. Why, what are you thinking?'

'He chose the forest for a reason. Which makes me believe he is familiar with the area. He may have lived close by as a kid, may have even worked there at some point. What about Mr Greyson, the dog walker?'

'We've run him through the system and he's clean.'

They sat in silence for a while, both poking at their food. Then Bishop got up and opened a file cabinet, played around with the edges of the folders and finally pulled out a dark blue file. The pink elastic band around its centre snapped when he handed it over.

'Timothy Grent,' he said.

'Who is he?'

'A paedophile.' He waved off her protest. 'I first arrested him eight years ago for procuring underage boys for other paedophiles. Used to hold parties at his flat, but they didn't play pass the parcel, if you get my drift.'

'This killer isn't motivated by lust, Bishop.'

'I know, but Grent has used fentanyl before and that's the drug of choice with our victim. I know it's distant but even if he didn't supply the boy he could have supplied the drug. Four years ago Grent was charged with procuring two thirteen-year-old boys for a paedophile ring. Got three years. The court raised it to four and a half, but he still came out early.'

She opened the file. Took her time examining it.

Timothy Grent. Fifty-five, born in 1963. Glazy-eyed, unkempt, with long curly black hair that hung like frayed rope around his face. Unemployed. From South Wales originally, a small town called Goldcliff, south of Newport. A broken home, abuse from the father; moved to Bristol when he was fifteen, was put in care six months later but ran away and disappeared off the radar until he reappeared in Bristol aged twenty-one. He started working at a local DIY store near what was now called the West End Gay Village, off Park Street, a well-known hang-out where he plied his trade as a rent-boy in the evenings. He was arrested for solicitation dozens of times, and possession with intent to sell twenty-three times over the next four years. Started out dealing cannabis, but a year later he had progressed to opiates. He spent seven years in total at HMP Cardiff, a Category B prison, with various charges including coercion of a minor, inciting sexual grooming, distributing indecent images of children, blackmail and possession of a class B drug (fentanyl). On his release, he moved to London. Within six months he was charged with procuring young boys for clients but the charges were dropped due to lack of evidence. Then he was re-arrested after sexually assaulting a thirteen-year-old boy.

'And he was in prison until twelve weeks ago?'

Bishop nodded. 'What do you think? Is he a killer?'

Holly turned to him and said quietly:

'Not our killer. How would he procure these children?'

'Online grooming or through the rent-boy community.'

'Will he talk to us?'

'I'll bring him in.'

Holly skimmed another page then squinted up at the

strip light in the ceiling. When she looked at Bishop she noticed something resting on the right shoulder of his jacket. She got up, reached a hand over and lifted it off. It was a grey feather.

'Supposed to be lucky,' she said as she laid it on his desk.

'You believe in all that stuff?' he smiled.

'Finding feathers, coins, interpreting cloud shapes? We all believe in something.'

'Are you religious?' he said.

'No. You?'

'Nope. What do you believe in?'

'Good and bad. Right and wrong.'

'What about evil?' he asked.

'Hmm?'

She was staring at the feather again. It was reminding her of the angel.

'Do you believe in evil?'

She shook her head slowly. 'I believe in monsters. I imagine you do too.'

There was a knock at the door and Constable Lipski entered. Holly recognised her from the Sickert case.

'Sir, Mr Eaton is at reception to see you.'

Bishop nodded and got up. 'I'll go and fetch him myself.'

'Who's Mr Eaton?'

'Local parish priest,' Bishop said. 'His son, Elijah, went missing five years ago. Thinks every time there's a body it might be his boy.'

Bishop returned with Mr Eaton within a few minutes and made the introductions. The big man took his raincoat off when he entered Bishop's office and there was a flutter of confetti as he removed his cap. He was large and balding with curly dark hair and his heavy stomach fought against his thick knees as he lowered himself onto the edge of the chair next to Holly.

'I've already been told it's not Elijah,' he pre-empted the conversation.

'No,' said Bishop, 'it's not.'

'Little solace.' He turned to face Holly. 'He would be eighteen now. I don't know these days whether to be happy or sad when it's not my boy.'

'DI Bishop said you work locally. What church are you at?' Holly asked.

'St Augustine's on Fulham Palace Road,' he said. 'Feel free to come in and say hello. We're not as busy as we used to be.' He turned to Bishop. 'Any updates on my son?'

'No.'

'May I, please?'

Bishop passed over the file. 'Nothing has changed since the last time, I'm afraid.'

Mr Eaton opened the pages and his eyes studied each line. He nodded to himself once or twice as if he had remembered some small detail and after a while closed the file and handed it to Bishop. 'Thank you,' he said. 'Was it bad? This one?'

'It always is.'

Mr Eaton stood and put his cap on. 'Thank you for your time, DI Bishop. Miss Wakefield.' He left the office and shut the door. Holly stared after him, deep in thought.

'Was he ever a suspect?' she asked.

'For a while, but he had an airtight alibi on the day of his son's disappearance.' He took another mouthful of food, then crumpled his plate and threw it in the bin.

'How was the omelette?' she asked.
'Overcooked. How are your crab cakes?'
Holly smiled and threw her plate after his.
'More cake than crab.'

Ten

S12 was a large space on the third floor. Open-plan. Several rooms linked like a suite. Holly entered the maelstrom of activity. Most of the officers were in plain clothes, all with an easy air of authority that comes with not having to wear a uniform. At desks, opening up computers, checking printers, filing cabinets with folders of heavy notes. There were a few people she recognised from her last case: Kathy Pembroke, the press officer; Mosely, the sergeant built like a truck; Bethany, victim liaison. But there were many that she didn't. Different departments, different rotas, different shifts. She walked past rows of officers who whispered into head-mics:

'... No, that's okay, you're not wasting our time. What time were you at Wanstead Park?'

'... Thank you, Mrs Prescott. Double "t", yes, I got that. Could you describe your son to me? He's twelve you say? And when did you last see him?'

'... Hold please – I'm going to pass you on to DI Thompson.' A switch of phone lines. 'Sir, I've got a caller on line five. Says she was at the wedding with her boyfriend.

They went into the forest and saw a group of homeless people by a firepit. Didn't see a boy but there was a lot of alcohol . . . '

Someone brushed past her. A quick apology. Quietly urgent as fresh photos from the autopsy were brought in and taped up on the incident board along with a detailed map of the area. A shot of Timothy Grent had already been tacked up to one side under the heading of suspects. She gazed at it, unsure, then turned when she heard Bishop enter and take his place at the other end of the room. A few officers approached and spoke in hushed tones. He replied to each of them in turn and eventually they took their seats. He checked his jacket pocket. It was a habit he had, ensuring the security of his cigarettes. Then he gave Holly a slight nod and turned to face the group.

'This will be our home and our hotel until this case is over. We're missing a few chairs at the moment but that will be sorted by the end of the day. A quick heads-up. I know you know the routines but ... Call-takers, when receiving reports, record, retain and reveal all materials and pass it on to the investigating officer ASAP. Those in the field, remember the axiom: the first chance to obtain material may be the last. Protect and preserve all material collected. We don't want any evidence being contaminated or lost. If any of you are in doubt about the relevance of materials you recover then get advice from the line managers. Non-disclosure agreements signed today, please.

'Last night's grid search of Wanstead Park covered approximately half a mile in each direction from the crime scene, and officers are going out again this afternoon. So far they have recovered the normal detritus – empty beer cans, cigarette butts, shopping trolleys and condoms – but nothing that can be linked to the boy in any way. There are a couple of large ponds further north, which I want to dredge. Critical requests have been logged, but we're still waiting for the go-ahead. Nearly four and a half thousand acres of this park are triple SIs. You all know what that means?'

A few headshakes, a few nods.

'Sites of Special Scientific Interest. Rare birds, wildlife, plants, fungi. We have been advised by the London Forestry Commission to tread carefully, literally, and will be following their protocol. I'll be taking Suspect Management and will be looking at any potentials the investigation throws up. DI Craig Thompson will be heading up Case Management.'

DI Thompson raised a meaty hand in the air so everybody could see him. A bull of a man, uncomfortable in his suit, sweating in the early afternoon.

Bishop carried on: 'Numbers? Alison from the NCA, where are you?'

A sergeant in her forties with striking black hair introduced herself. She was scribbling furiously on a notepad. It looked like shorthand.

'New *mispers* are being reported every hour. For every five we get, three are accounted for within twenty-four hours, but we're playing catch-up all the time.'

'Go through the lists you already have and contact the parents again. Has their child turned up? Utmost priority is to find out this boy's identity. The poison that was used to drug him has been confirmed by the coroner to be fentanyl. Prescription grade, so we know it has been stolen. We need hospital inventories, drug batch numbers and any recent pharmacy robberies. Who's here from Narcs?'

A woman with bright red hair and a spray of freckles raised her hand.

'Sergeant Karla Olshaker, sir.'

'Karla. Put the word out to all your eyes and ears. See if we can get some names as to who is dealing this stuff.' He took a mouthful of water and pointed to the suspect board. 'Timothy Grent. Some of you may have come across him before. A paedophile with a history of dealing fentanyl. He was released from prison three months ago, I want to see if we can get a search warrant for his premises. Possible surveillance as well. Ambrose, can I leave that with you?'

'Sir.'

'Eric, how are the night owls coping on the CCTV?'

Sergeant Eric Brandine blew his nose, sniffing with cold.

'We've got nearly a thousand hours of footage to look through. Tyre tracks we've got VWs, Land Rovers, BMWs, three Citroens and a Volvo so far. We're trying to match them with drivers but it's going to take time. As long as there's coffee and snacks we'll keep going.'

'DI Bishop?' A plain-clothes officer with short cropped hair, wearing a blue suit and tie raised a hand. 'Are we taking this as a domestic murder? Mum, dad, brother?'

'Until we get an ID we can't even begin to lay the corners of this puzzle, but once that is established then all regular routes will be followed as per protocol to eliminate any family members from our enquiries. We are all hoping that this is a one-off, an argument of some sort gone horribly wrong. But because of the unusual nature of the crime scene I have asked Holly Wakefield to come in and consult on this. Some of you worked with her on the Sickert case. Holly?'

She nodded. Took a step forward. Hands clasped tightly in front of her waist.

'I think DI Bishop has covered all we can on the boy so far,' she began. 'So I want to concentrate on the killer, the person who did this.' She brushed some hair out of her face. Her forehead felt cold.

'Although we have no idea of his name or his face, this killer has already given us a huge amount of clues from the crime scene. The killing is foreplay. The choosing of the target, the seduction, it's all the warm-up for what happened in the forest.' She gestured at the photos. 'Look at the staging of the victim. The way he was laid down with his hands across his chest. The angel pendant in his hand.' She turned to face the room: 'Do we know anything about the angel yet?'

DI Thompson gave her a nod. 'The pendant is white metal. Could have been bought from a novelty store or even come out of a Christmas cracker. And the angel could be one of a thousand.'

'But it won't be,' Holly replied. She took a second and sat on the edge of the desk. 'It will be one *specific* angel. In the same way the boy was chosen for one *specific* reason. And the pillow was put there and the boy was dressed in white underpants. This was very important to the killer and we cannot underestimate this. This is his signature.'

'He's a bloody maniac then.' Thompson again.

Holly took a second – cleared her head.

'He's not a maniac,' she said softly.

'I'm sorry?'

'I said he's not a maniac,' louder this time. 'By definition, a maniac exhibits extremely wild or even animalistic behaviour. This was the polar opposite. This killer cared.'

'A caring killer?

Thompson pulled away from his seat and then sat down heavily again. He was frowning.

'Look, I know that may not make any sense to some of you,' Holly said, 'but to him it all makes perfect sense. We need to see through his point of view. Through his eyes. This wasn't someone who suddenly decided to find a random young boy and kill him. He is *not* an opportunist. This was a man who thought about this. Planned this for a very long time.'

She went to the board, picked up a Sharpie and wrote down the pertinent information.

'This was well planned and well executed. He is *not* impulsive. I think in the weeks, possibly months before the kill he would have driven into the forest on numerous occasions. Probably during the day to start with, then again a few times in the really early hours to see what sort of traffic he would encounter. Not simply cars on the roads but people in the forest. Because of this, we know he is mobile. He has a car and doesn't have to rely on public transport. So he would have driven to the forest and parked somewhere along one of the roads leading off from The Glade ...' She took a moment. 'What was the closest vehicle access point to where the body was found?'

'Approximately two hundred metres,' Bishop volunteered.

'So he would have had to carry the body at least that distance. The boy was light, but nevertheless, that's an extra eighty pounds. Through the woods in pitch-darkness.'

'Wouldn't he use a torch?' Karla Olshaker asked.

'He may have, but light and sound travels a long way in the woods at night. He couldn't take that chance, what with homeless individuals living there and the wedding party at the Robin Hood pub. He would have heard them all. The music, the singing. And if he could hear them, they might have been able to hear him. Which makes me believe he is familiar with the area and will have knowledge of the forest. He may have lived close by as a kid, may have even worked there at some point.' She looked at the photos of the dense forest – felt herself get lost for a second.

'We know the boy was murdered *before* being taken into the woods, which means there is a room in a house out there somewhere that has this boy's DNA all over it. I don't care how careful the killer was at cleaning up afterwards, there will be traces of him left behind. So, he strangles the boy, puts him in the boot of the car. Probably wraps him up in something. A rug, a carpet. More likely plastic bags. The longer he travels with that body in the boot, the greater the risk he could go through a red light, get pulled over for something, get caught on a speeding camera. That makes me think he's quite local. Within a ten, maybe twenty-mile radius. If we're really lucky, he'll be right on the doorstep of the forest – but somehow I don't think so. He's smarter than that.'

She went to the map on the wall and drew a circle in black.

'Somewhere here.' Then she turned and ran her eyes over the team. 'Perhaps most importantly – this wasn't a sexual crime. Which means he would have been motivated by something else. As far as his past criminal activities go, this may be his first kill, and it may even be his first act of violence. He may have got close to children before but perhaps the outcome was nothing this tragic. Can we run checks on all cases of abduction of a minor, and attempted abductions with the same variables but that failed for whatever reason. So why did he choose him?'

'He's young. Attractive.' From Lipski.

'Superficially, yes, but it's much more than that. There would have been what we call IVTs, or Ideal Victim Traits in the boy that fulfilled him. Criteria he responded to. His target was a boy in his early teens. Not fully developed, but he would have been smarter and stronger than any eight-year-old. It's a hell of a risk, taking on a teenager, but what that tells us is that the killer has a specific target.' She took a beat and pondered out loud. 'This boy would have been his fantasy and we have to work out why.'

She took a second and re-capped her pen. Her eyes drifted over to the photos on the wall.

'There would have been a tipping point in his own life to make this tragic event suddenly doable. It could either be something drastic, like the loss of a loved one, or something incredibly banal. Robert Lyons stabbed his mother to death because she refused to buy him Avril Lavigne concert tickets. Brenda Spencer – I don't like Mondays – we all know that one. Edward Gutting stabbed his old boss to death when he didn't get the promotion he wanted.'

'So what do we do, look for someone who has a shit relationship and hasn't been promoted?' Thompson said.

'I'm only saying. It's like—'

'Could be any one of us then,' Bishop said. It was an ice-breaker and it was necessary. Gallows humour – the best way to deal with this.

Holly felt herself smiling.

'Look, I can tell you about his personality but I can't tell you who he is. I wish I could. I wish I could wave a magic wand and say he's over there, but I can't. But there are some things that I do know: in appearance this killer will be like you and me. Quiet at times, sometimes lonely, innocuous when he needs to be, but he will also be very well-functioning; after the kill he would have returned to work. The mask once again placed on his face so he becomes your friendly neighbour. The man who takes out your bins for you when you forget and holds the post until you come home from holiday.'

'Do you think he works then? I mean, can he hold down a job?' Karla again.

'Oh, he works,' Holly said. 'He will be very independent as well. That's a good question though.' She turned to the board. Began to write again. 'He won't be a mechanic, work on a production line, or be stacking shelves somewhere. An office job, more than likely. Not a high-level CEO necessarily, but someone who people will recognise as smart and talented. He may not socialise much. He has to be careful – he can't let people get too close. He'll keep them at a distance. The office party, yes, but he won't drink too much in their presence. Can't afford to let the mask slip. "Sorry, I can't stay late, I have to go home." Maybe to his wife.'

'He's married?'

'I believe he will be in a relationship of sorts. He's not a loner. He may be married or have a girlfriend. He will also be very charming. If you ever met him at a bar or a cocktail party, you would probably find him warm and friendly, even likeable. But underneath this mask he will be a master manipulator, and will have a narcissistic and positive self-image bordering on egomania.

'So when you start interviewing people, or when people become suspects, this is when these traits will come out. And this is when you'll go through the list: Is he organised at work? Yes. The kill was well organised. Is he conscientious and methodical? Yes. He left no DNA on the boy's body. Is he physically fit enough to carry a boy's body over two hundred metres from where he parked his car? Yes, he has a gym membership and works out three times a week. Does he live within our twenty-mile radius of Epping Forest? Yes. Is he mobile? He has his own car. Impound it. Look for traces of the forest in the tyre treads and DNA in the boot. Everything I have mentioned will be reflected in his lifestyle and his workplace.' She paused. 'Age is always the hardest thing to predict, but I put him at thirty plus years. Mid-thirties, probably. That's it,' she said. 'I haven't had a chance to write all this up, but I can email everybody tonight with a summary.' Deep in thought. She frowned slightly. 'There is one other thing. I don't think we can discount the fact that the killer may be a woman.'

Bishop looked up at that. Caught her eye.

'I know when we think of women we think of our sisters, mothers, aunties, and most people don't believe we have it in us to do something like this. But we do.'

'Thank you, Holly.' Bishop said and raised his hand to get everyone's attention. 'Are we up to date on everything else?'

The consensus seemed to be yes. He gave a nod to the team and the clamour of the task force resumed.

Bishop had no sooner made his way over to Holly than a junior officer approached. Vickery was his name. He looked a little jumpy as he caught Bishop's eye.

'Sir, we've had another set of parents arrive downstairs at reception.'

'Have they seen a photo of the boy?' Holly asked.

'No. We ask them to bring a photo of their own child with them. That way we can verify it ourselves.'

'Who are they?' Bishop asked, adjusting his tie.

'Alan and Gill Finney. He works for Barnet Council, she's a speech-writer for a local MP.'

'Which one?'

'Ross Winston, sir. He's a Conservative.'

'Go on.'

'Their boy is called Eddie. He's been missing since Wednesday morning.'

Eleven

'Not necessarily missing,' Gill Finney said. 'Eddie may have simply run away.'

They were standing in the corridor. Gill was all arms and nervous exhaustion and her blue power suit looked deflated and creased. Holly had seen her on the local news, a background player against the knights and queens.

'Has he run away before?' Bishop asked.

'Three times last year. The year before too, but we heard about the boy in the forest,' the colour drained from her face, 'and Eddie's not replying to our texts, and other mums and dads are worried so we thought we should come in and talk to you. Someone who can help. We just want to make sure it's not our boy.'

Her husband nodded, out of breath and flustered. Neither of them could take their eyes off Bishop. Gill's lips were still moving but there was no sound.

'Let's go in here, shall we?' Bishop said.

They followed him into a meeting room. He ushered them into the two seats opposite a square table and Holly closed the door and stood at the side of the room.

'So, Eddie runs away quite a bit does he?'

'Yes,' the mother said. 'He takes the train to Scotland. He loves Edinburgh. The last time he went was a month before Christmas, just a long weekend, but he missed two days of school.'

'Does he do that often? Miss school?'

'He gets bullied. The school have tried to clamp down but he's very sensitive. Children seem to pick on him. He's not—'

'—a bad boy,' the father finished. 'But he was dreading going back on Monday.'

'What school does he go to?'

'West Hatch High School.' The mother again. Laying out her son's CV as if this were an interview for a job. 'It's in Chigwell, near Epping Forest.'

Holly felt her pulse quicken. Bishop didn't flinch.

'Have social services talked to you?'

They shared a look.

'They have, and the EWS. We've tried to discipline him, but he doesn't listen to us, does he? Perhaps we've supported him too much? Given him too much opportunity?'

'Did he take a bag with him on Wednesday?'

'He said he was just off to the shops,' the father said, 'but when he didn't come back we looked in his room and his backpack was missing.'

'And how old would Eddie be now?'

'Fourteen. He was born on July twenty-third, 2004.' The scribble of Bishop's pen. 'He was a breech birth,' the mother added quickly. 'Not that that makes any . . . ' She looked over at Holly as if she might have more of an understanding about what that meant.

'Do you have a photo?' Holly asked.

'Yes. Of course.'

Mrs Finney fumbled in her handbag and passed one over. There would be an empty frame lying face down in the house somewhere. The boy was skinny and fair-haired with a slightly crooked smile that made him instantly lovable.

'We brought this one,' she said, and started to cry.

'To make sure it's not him,' added the father. 'We're sure it's not of course. I'm sure he's just run away again but ... ' They both had hold of each other's hands and were circling them together as if trying to tie a knot.

'How old is the photo?' Bishop asked.

'Three months. He hasn't changed much. A little bit taller maybe but ... '

'Can I borrow this for a second?'

Holly saw their eyes fall. Bishop clocked it too but led her out of the room.

'It's not him,' she whispered.

'I know, but I have to be one hundred per cent sure.'

Two minutes to get upstairs to the incident room and load up the autopsy photos on the computer and another two minutes to walk down the stairs through the corridor to the waiting parents. The longest four minutes of Mr and Mrs Finney's lives.

When they re-entered the room, Holly thought the pair might faint. Bishop handed over the photo. 'It's not your boy.'

Gill broke down and her husband started laughing but realised it was inappropriate so stopped almost immediately.

'Thank you. Thank you,' they both said. They seemed to do everything in unison. Nodding their heads, holding each other's hands. Holly wondered if they ate their dinner at home at the same time, raised their glasses together, walked in time together, left foot, right foot, left foot, right.

'Look,' said Bishop. 'It sounds as though he's probably back in Edinburgh, so I can put a call into the local police up there, but I think we should still fill in a missing persons report. That way we have Eddie's information on file, just in case this happens again.'

'Would you like a coffee or tea?' Holly asked.

'None for me,' said Mr Finney.

'Tea would be nice,' said Mrs Finney. 'With some milk.' She still looked terrified, and when Holly passed her the cup her hands were shaking and the tea waterfalled into the saucer. Bishop had taken a form from one of the desk drawers and rested it on its surface.

'This is what's called the Missing Persons Checklist. It's a whole variety of questions that will help us learn more about Eddie. His full name, please.'

'Eddie Brian Finney.'

'Date of birth we have. Birthplace?'

'Thirty-five Dartmouth Park Avenue, Highgate, NW5. It's a flat. Two bedroom.'

'How tall is Eddie?

'Five foot five.'

'Weight?'

The husband pursed his lips, shook his head. 'Don't know. Not much.'

'He never had an appetite,' the mother added. 'I think he'd weigh about six stone. Maybe a little more.'

Bishop nodded, looked at the questionnaire again.

'Any distinguishing marks? Tattoos, scars, birthmarks?'

'No,' the mother said. 'Oh, wait. He had an umbilical hernia operation when he was three. There's a very tiny white scar above his navel.'

'He doesn't smoke, I presume.'

'No. God no.'

'No drugs. Evidence of any drugs of any kind?'

'No,' again. Emphatic. 'I think we'd know,' said Gill.

Holly wondered if they would. Children were experts at hiding things. Experts at keeping secrets from parents.

'When he goes to Edinburgh, do you know who he stays with?'

'We've asked but he never tells us. He seems happy when he comes back. Maybe he's met a girl?'

'You're not the first parent to have to go through this and you won't be the last,' said Bishop. 'I presume he has a mobile phone and you've tried to contact him?'

'Yes. We always say – text or call us back within twenty minutes or we'll get worried.' Gill faltered on the last words. She was holding it together but barely. 'We've told his sister, Samantha, that Eddie's away on holiday again and he'll be home soon.'

'How old is Samantha?'

'Seven.'

Bishop went through to the last item on the sheet.

'Has Eddie ever contemplated suicide?'

'No!' The mother was suddenly out of her seat. Standing like a lioness in front of her empty den. 'He's not that sort of boy! He's made mistakes, we all do, don't we? But he's lovely and nice and kind and charming. And he cooks with me and helps Alan in the garden and we go to car boot sales together and we shop together and we watch TV in the evenings and we eat together and on Sundays he sometimes brings me breakfast in bed with honey on toast and a second cup of tea while I listen to *The Archers*. He's not suicidal. He's not angry. He is simply Eddie. Eddie Finney, and we want him home.'

She sat down, shaking. Bishop took a moment. Let the air settle.

'I'm sorry, Mr and Mrs Finney, but I have to ask these questions. I know some of them are stupid and make no sense to you – but to us they do make sense and they are important. We want to find your boy to make sure he's safe, so what I'm going to do now is pass this information on to the Scottish police. They will be able to look at all the CCTV around Edinburgh and if they see your boy they will contact us immediately so we can let you know where he is.' He had their attention. Red-rimmed eyes and quivering lips. 'And the faster we can find your son.'

They were outside the station and there was a damp airless smell. The threat of rain.

'He's such a lovely boy.' Gill turned to Holly. 'So lovely. I'm sure he'll come back soon.'

'He sounds wonderful,' was all Holly managed. She watched them both walk towards their car. Unbelievably forlorn. Heads bowed, feet scuffing, limp hands touching but not holding.

She felt helpless and sick. There had been handshakes and promises in Bishop's office, in which she took no part, the sense of premonition sweeping over her so strongly that she couldn't even move when Bishop came over to her.

'This is horrible,' she said. He caught up with her and squeezed her arm affectionately.

'They picked up Timothy Grent. He's drunk. Going to sleep it off in a cell. Nine o'clock tomorrow morning okay for you?'

'I'll be here.'

He said goodnight but she wasn't listening. The clouds that had been chasing the moon suddenly covered it in a sullen black mass and Holly felt herself shiver.

Twelve

Timothy Grent was a fucking mess.

He was wearing a stained duffel coat over a thin T-shirt, jeans and boots so scuffed Holly couldn't tell what their original colour was. Three of his fingernails were painted black, the other seven pea-green. His black hair was thin, his face pale, the lines either side of his mouth etched deep. Strain. Tension. Alcohol. It was all there.

'Morning, Timothy,' Bishop said. He and Holly were sitting opposite.

'Morning, DI Bishop.' Grent's voice was liquid-like. He shuffled in his seat. 'Can I have a cigarette?'

'Of course.'

He took a packet out of his jacket and laid it on the table. Flipped open a Zippo lighter with a cartoon blue enamel face painted on one side. Lit the cigarette and took a drag.

'I need a . . .'

Bishop reached under the table into a drawer and pulled out a flimsy foil ashtray. Put it in the middle between them.

'Thank you.'

Grent smoked. Sniffed. Stretched his head from side to side.

'This is Holly Wakefield,' Bishop said. 'She's a psychologist.'

'I know who she is. I read the newspapers. The Sickert case.'

He stared at her through a haze of smoke. A tolerant smile, barely visible. Bishop opened the file in front of him, read it for a few seconds, then:

'I didn't realise you were out.'

'In, out, shake it all about.'

'You're staying at thirty-five Oldfield Road, Stoke Newington. That correct?'

'Yes.'

Holly watched Grent carefully. He was acting indifferent, but it was a pretence.

'And I've already registered with the local plod and the council offices. I don't think they were too happy, although they're too PC to complain. How funny is that?'

Bishop opened a folder and placed a photo of the dead boy on the table. Turned it around so Grent could see it properly.

'Is he one of yours?'

'Never seen him before.'

'Have a good look.'

Grent's eyes went suddenly squirrelly.

'We're all so beautiful when we're young, aren't we?'

'He was found dead in Epping Forest two days ago. You sure you don't know him?'

'Positive. Seriously? What am I doing here? Am I under arrest? I got some kinky in me but I don't kill. I only fuck the little ones. And they're not that little, are they? Thirteen years of age.'

'Very clever I know. Under thirteen and you get fifteen to life, over thirteen and you get what – four years custodial?'

'Something like that. I didn't exactly count the days.'

'We think this boy is about thirteen.'

'Not my kind of thing.'

'Whose kind of thing is it then? Some of the people you mix with don't mind killing, do they?'

Grent stubbed his cigarette out until it was dead. Thin white fingers stained with black. 'I don't know who did it, okay?' He wrinkled his nose and turned away from the photo. 'This is my reality. I have been born with what I would consider a rather unfortunate set of sexual preferences. A desire for a section of the population who are legally, morally and psychologically forbidden to me. How can I put this . . . it will be forever my loss that these children will never be able to fully reciprocate my feelings and desires. But even I, who am detested by so many of the population on this planet, draw the line at murder. So no. I did not kill a boy and take him into Epping Forest.'

Grent reached for his cigarettes again but thought better of it. Clasped his hands together on the tabletop. 'I've never seen that boy before and if someone . . . ' He stopped suddenly, looked at Holly. 'I don't fit the profile, do I?'

'No.'

'So you don't think it was me, do you?'

'No.'

'So why am I here, Bishop?'

'The boy had fentanyl in his system. You sold any fentanyl recently?'

'I'm a changed man. Prison reform and all that bollocks. That's all in the past, and whatever I did in *my past* was purely my responsibility. Nobody else's. I am not responsible for my addiction, but I am responsible for my recovery. And one more thing. I'm not that stupid.'

73

'What do you mean?'

'*Kid-killer*? You know what would happen to me if I went back inside as a kid-killer? It wouldn't exactly be pleasant, would it? No.' He lit the next cigarette. Took a hit. 'I'm never going back.'

Holly tracked the details of his face, her eyes subtly picking him apart.

'This man,' she said. 'I don't think he will have your tendencies. He won't like children the way you do, but there'll be something very different about him.'

Grent leaned away. Wiped a greasy hand over his forehead.

'I bet you're dying to get inside my head,' he said.

She ignored him – and when she started speaking again it was in a low whisper that gradually strengthened.

'This man would have contacted you at a bar, a club, a chatroom maybe. He will be very easy to talk to. The sort of man who will smile in the right places when you tell him a joke. Pat you on the shoulder and make you feel welcome. He would have said he wanted the boy for something else entirely – company, friendship – but he's a pathological liar and would have simply told you whatever you wanted or needed to hear. Deep down, all he will be thinking about is how he can kill this child. Strangle them until they can't breathe. Until their tongues stick out and turn blue and the veins pop in their eyes like tiny stars. He may be a drinker. In which case his alcohol consumption will now increase to cope with the feelings he has inside. The stress he is under. He may reach out to someone. Someone close. Even tell them what he's done. Confide in them. Absurd as it may seem. But he has to be careful. It will be someone who he trusts entirely or someone who he has complete power over and knows they will never tell a soul.'

Grent was staring at her as if she were mad. He shifted away slightly, shot a look at Bishop.

'I don't know him, I swear. Players change all the time,' he said. 'It's like the sand in the desert. Constantly shifting. I don't know.'

'Tell me about you then.'

'What?'

'Tell me about you, Timothy.'

Grent drew on the cigarette. Painted her a smile with brown, twig-like teeth. 'Didn't get the best of starts. Seen a lot of bad things, I guess. But at the end of the day I'm just a . . .'

'A what?'

'A bloke with a bit of fucked-up thrown in.'

'How's your temper?'

'I'm on simmer all the time. Only way I can let off steam is through the drugs and sex. You wanna be my shrink?'

'Who is your shrink?'

'I've been through at least twenty. I discard them like tampons these days. Latest one calls himself Joshua Neate. He's not exactly Harley Street, mind you. Only one sofa but he lets me talk, lets me get things off my chest. Dirty things. And I relieve him of his sexual burdens. A symbiotic relationship, I think they call that.'

'Are you religious, Timothy?'

'What? No.'

'The tattoo on your wrist.'

He held up his hand and looked at it as if seeing it for the first time.

'An angel,' he said.

'You like angels?'

'They've done fuck-all for me over the past forty-odd years. Supposed to protect you, aren't they?'

'What do you need protection from?'

He pulled his sleeve down. Tapped ash into the foil.

'Any more questions and I want a lawyer.'

Bishop was about to say something when there was a knock at the door. It opened and Lipski entered.

'Sir, the Finneys are here again. Said it's urgent.'

'Put them in my office,' Bishop said.

He shook his head and got up, knocked the file off his desk and another photo of the dead boy fell out on the floor. Timothy bent from his chair and picked it up, left dirty smudges on its shiny surface before Bishop returned it to the folder.

'And escort Timothy out, please. You want something to eat before you go?'

'Filet mignon. Medium rare.'

'Give him some rice pudding. Put him in whatever is free. Tell the duty sergeant I've okayed it.'

Lipski led Timothy out and shut the door. Bishop sat down and felt for his cigarettes: still there. Then he turned to Holly: 'Let's see what the Finneys have to say.'

Thirteen

They didn't have to wait long to find out.

Eddie Finney was sitting in Bishop's chair. Blond haired just like his photo, he was slender and pinched. He wore a look between smug and churlish, but at a quick glance from his father he stood up when Holly and Bishop entered.

'This is Eddie,' his mum said. 'We got a text this morning telling us he'd be on the 9.40 train from Scotland and we drove into King's Cross to pick him up.'

She looked washed-out, as if she had been crying again. She would have been a good advert for contraceptives.

'Eddie Finney,' Bishop said. 'You had your parents worried. Had me worried for a while too. Where did you go?'

'Edinburgh.' Churlish was back.

'Edinburgh's a big place. Old Town, Blackford, Dalry. Portobello? You got friends up there?'

'Some.' He looked skittish. He hadn't been expecting a questionnaire. His nails were bitten down to the cuticles. He was fidgeting constantly and his confidence sagged like a waterless flower every time Bishop asked a question.

He was well spoken, though, and polite, and Holly wondered if he had been privately educated in his earlier years. When she'd been younger, she had held a grudge against the privileged. Felt as though she was always working hard against people who didn't have to, so she made up for it by playing harder than they ever could. Made do with the grant money and food packages from her foster mother, but worked after classes either in The Eagle, the local watering hole – *it's Friday night shots – three for five pounds!* – or on Sundays when she had to wear her one good black skirt, white shirt and patent heels for the local car dealership. She hated wearing heels, and thankfully Sundays were slow, but she learned to type fast and managed to stay invisible by focusing on her computer screen and counting the minutes on minimum wage.

Eddie looked suitably contrite. Bishop was wearing him down. He was very good at playing *vaguely annoyed cop*.

When Holly was fourteen, she had run away from Maureen her foster mother. It was the only time she ever had, and it was more of a dare than anything. She had caught the bus out from 'Blessed Home', jumped on the tube at ten at night and got off in zone six, well out of her comfort zone and away from everything she knew. There were people on the streets. Fledgling prostitutes and drunks and alley cats and unlicensed taxi cabs with leery men playing loud music. It had been exciting to begin with, but as the hours lengthened it became lonely, scary and cold. In the early hours she had found herself loitering around the back of a McDonald's. Ravenous, she had dined on half-eaten burgers that had been tossed in the trash, then huddled in a doorway with her knees clasped to her chest. She had slept in five-minute intervals, head jolting up every time she heard a noise. When it was still dark, she realised someone had slipped in next to her. He stank of urine and dirt. A thick beard with long hair and sunken eyes.

'Don't mind me,' he said. He wasn't drunk, just dirty. 'Name's Sandy. Haven't seen you before. You new?' She had nodded. 'Two's better than one for warmth on a night like this. Don't worry, I'm not going to try and fuck you.'

She finally slept and when she did wake the man was gone. She practically ran back to her home, not realising until many years later how lucky she had probably been. Maureen had been waiting for her in the kitchen. The moment Holly flung herself inside, the woman plopped a plate of food onto the table: fried eggs, bacon and beans.

'Glad you could make it.'

Holly snivelled her way through breakfast. She couldn't taste the food for the guilt. When Maureen took the empty plate away, she kissed her on the head. 'Get ready for school.'

'Yes, Mum.' She liked calling her mum even though she wasn't. There was a security about it. A gratitude. But before she left the room:

'You're never going to do that again, are you?' Maureen asked. She was washing up.

'No. I promise.' And she had meant it with all her heart.

'We had the Scottish police looking out for you, Eddie,' Bishop said. 'So trust me, next time you catch the train north-bound, they are going to be picking you up before the stewards can put away the food trolley. You're how old?'

'Fourteen.' It came out as a cough and he blushed.

'You know why your parents were worried, right?'

'Yes, they told me.'

'Told you what?'

'About the boy.'

'As long as you're safe and we know you're okay it's fine, Eddie,' his mother went on and wiped her eyes again. 'Nothing else matters. Just don't do it again, okay?'

'Sorry, Mum. Dad.' Head lowered, but his fists were clenched and Holly could see a knot forming in his shoulders.

'Come on, young man. Out to the car,' Gill said. 'I'll make shepherd's pie for dinner tonight. A special treat.'

Holly wondered if the mother was already making a shopping list in her head. Minced lamb, potatoes, carrots, onions – have we got Worcester sauce? Probably.

Alan's breath whistled between his teeth as he smiled. 'I knew this would be okay. We're so sorry to have wasted your time.'

'You haven't,' said Bishop. 'We're just glad that everything worked out okay.'

The mother led Eddie away with cloudy eyes. A shake of hands from Mr Finney at the door before he turned.

'It was important that we brought him in. Introduced you.'

'You didn't need to do that.'

'No. He's a good lad is Eddie. It was good that he met you.' His face twisted, whether it was anger or relief it was hard to tell. 'See what we've been through.'

Bishop nodded. A faint smile. 'Hopefully next time he goes to Edinburgh he'll let you know first, but if not please give me a call.'

They watched them leave and Bishop sat down.

'See? Sometimes it does turn out for the best.'

There was a silence. The balloon had been popped and all the nervous energy had left the room. Holly leaned back when there was a knock at the door. Lipski again.

'A Mr and Mrs Beasley are in reception now. They brought a photo with them.' She handed it over.

'Oh, shit,' said Holly when she saw it.

It was the boy.

Fourteen

'His name is Noah Beasley,' Bishop said.

'His parents have just identified him at the morgue. Fourteen years old. Son to Aaron and Darya Beasley. Brother to his eleven-year-old sister, Ruby. A regular mum and dad. Mortgage, two cars, credit-card debts and one holiday a year. They went to Spain last summer.'

He dropped a photo on his desk. A holiday snap of Noah with his mum, dad and sister on a beach. Holly picked it up. Sun, sea and smiles. She immediately thought of her brother and the times they had spent at the beach when they were children. The smells reappeared in an instant. Heady and salty with sand in their toes.

'He went to Hopewell Secondary School in Dagenham, well within our twenty-mile radius. According to Mum and Dad, Noah told them he was off to see Granny for a couple of days and was supposed to be home this morning, but he never arrived. Never made it to Granny's house either and Granny said she had no idea he was supposed to be coming over.'

'Both boys lied to their parents about where they were going,' Holly said. 'But Eddie came home.'

'So what does that tell us?'

'That kids lie. That they have secrets and they trust their parents less than they realise.'

'We're still eliminating friends, relatives and work colleagues. We've questioned thirty-seven ex-cons who have charges of abuse or attempted abduction against boys that live within the catchment area,' he said. 'All thirty-seven have alibis.'

'What about Timothy Grent?'

'Surveillance starts tonight. I have to go and talk to Mr and Mrs Beasley.' Bishop was up and putting his jacket on when Holly said:

'I want to see Noah's room.'

'His room?'

She nodded. A tight whisper:

'It's as important to profile the victim as it is the killer. Get a feel for him. Try and understand him a little better.'

'When?'

'As soon as possible.'

'I'll arrange it.' Holly looked relieved and then Bishop turned to her. 'We'll catch up later.'

He left and she sat for a while. Picked up the file and pulled out another photo of Noah. The dreaded once-a-year school photo. Navy blue pullover, white shirt and a blue-and-green striped school tie. A nervous smile, one shade away from agony.

A voice behind the door and a second later it opened. Constable Lipski:

'The final autopsy report.' She handed it over. Was about to leave but said: 'Nice to see you again, Holly.'

'And you. It's Ariane, isn't it?'

'Yes, that's right.'

'How are you finding it here? Being a full-time copper?'

'Love it.' She smiled. 'I'll love it even more when we catch this bastard.'

She left and closed the door as Holly opened the file and started to read: Nothing else unusual but the strip of plastic that had been pulled from Noah's mouth had been analysed and was known by the number five on the resin identification code. A highly recyclable plastic used in bottle caps, toothbrushes and a hundred different utensils.

She pulled out her phone and dialled the coroner. It was picked up on the second ring.

'Holly – how can I help?'

'The piece of plastic in the boy's mouth. Any idea what it might have been?'

'It was sharply curved, cylindrical, so I'm veering towards a straw.'

For a moment Holly doubted her ears: 'As in a drinking straw?'

'Yes. The mucosal damage was caused by it being lodged in the same place for a long period of time. My best guess is that the killer gave him the straw so he could drink.'

Holly paused, her hand suddenly gripping the arm of the chair. 'So he kept him alive?' she said. 'The killer gave him a water supply to keep him alive?'

'It would appear so.'

'Which means he might be away for long periods of time. Work, sleeping somewhere else. Travelling.'

'The Yorkshire Ripper was a truck driver, wasn't he?' Angela said.

'Yes.' Holly rubbed a hand over her eyes. 'Thank you, Angela.' She hung up. Another twist of the screw as she wondered if perhaps the killer had some sort of timeline.

Outside, rain splashed at Holly's feet as she made her way into the street.

Threading her way past cafés and open-fronted shops, she caught the familiar smells of car exhausts, smog and rain. Snatches of music, the smell of hot food. She leaned against a wall and watched a loose knot of people on a corner close by. A woman laughed above the noise of the traffic and she headed in that direction.

A few minutes later she was inside St Augustine's church, two streets away from the station. A shaft of street light came through a massive leaded window in the east-facing wall and to her left a donation box and a table of votive candles beneath carved stone faces.

She sat at a pew, holding the angel pendant in her hands. She'd wrapped the cord around her wrist and now it hung between her fingers. The last time she had been in a church had been at her parents' funeral. It had been busy with death. Black suits, black dresses and black words. She remembered how real it had all felt. She had never—

Someone sat a little down from her. She could feel the weight leaning against the pew in front. Heard his strained breathing. He was staring straight ahead then turned to her, eyes in shadow.

'Miss Wakefield.'

It was Mr Eaton.

'I didn't mean to bother you,' she said. 'I wanted some peace and quiet.' His face was tight with anxiety and she wondered if he thought she was there with news of his son. He didn't ask, simply turned to face the front. 'You have a beautiful church,' she said.

'Thank you. I like to think so.'

'How long have you worked here?'

'Twenty-seven years this month. I still remember my first day but can't seem to remember the decades in between.'

'Your son, Elijah, was thirteen, wasn't he, when he went missing?'

'Yes. I believe he was taken and killed, but I still hold on to the hope. You must. Until his body is found. That ounce of hope . . . ' He cleared his throat. 'I stopped talking about this to other people years ago. I don't know if it does me good any more. I've never understood how someone can take the life of a child. How do they do that?'

'They're very different from us.'

She paused when she saw the expression on his face.

'It doesn't work,' he said. 'God doesn't punish the wicked and reward the righteous. Killers get compensation. Rapists get an opportunity to rape again, thanks to the very laws and judges that are supposed to protect the innocent. The irony is so thick you could choke on it.' She felt Eaton move and he was suddenly standing in front of her. In the church light she could see his eyes were heavy and red with alcohol and his forehead wet with sweat.

'I hope you catch him,' he said before he turned and walked away. Holly's mind went with a rush to her countless unanswered questions, and when she resumed speaking she sounded almost pleading.

'The killer put an angel in the boy's hand.'

His feet rooted to the flagstone floor.

'An angel?'

'Yes. I don't know which one it is.'

He retraced his steps. She offered him the pendant, but he didn't want to touch it. Glanced her way though and took his time.

'Could be one of many. He holds a lily, so Gabriel perhaps. The messenger of the word of God. He appears in people's visions: "Do not be afraid".' A sigh or a groan from the big man, she couldn't tell. Then: 'Which hand was it in?'

Holly had to think. 'The right. His arms were across his chest. So the hand was—'

'By his left shoulder?'

'Yes.'

'Dexter and Sinister. Good on the right and Bad on the left. The angel on a person's right shoulder writes down the person's good deeds, while the angel on the left shoulder records the person's bad deeds.' He closed his eyes. When he opened them they were expressionless, like someone risen from the dead. 'This person knows he's one of the evil ones.'

He passed by her side and lit a votive candle on the table against the wall. Holly followed suit and lit a candle from his flame and thought of her parents with sudden clarity. The stories they would tell her before bed, the smiles come morning, the footsteps on floorboards and the smell of coffee and the sound of the radio. Music and voices that promised never to die and yet they did. And then she thought of Noah Beasley, and by the time her mind had cleared Mr Eaton was gone. But she didn't look for him.

Her eyes lingered on the carved stone faces above the flickering candles as if they somehow stared back.

Fifteen

Bishop went through the motions like a robot.

Third gear. Second gear. Left at Centre Drive, then left onto Broadoaks. Eleven houses either side of a cul-de-sac and the Beasleys' house was the one at the end on the right. Two storeys, thrown up in the fifties with the pebble-dash still intact. A big yard with a double garage and two cars parked on the drive. All the lights were on as if there was a party in full swing. An orange glow behind the curtains. A beacon to guide their son home.

He rang the doorbell, shrill and loud, and wondered if the neighbours could hear it. He had done this dozens of times but every time felt like the first and the pressure in his chest grew and he felt sick. He still got Christmas cards from some of the relatives whose murder cases he had been involved in. A first-class stamp and a reminder that they were inexorably linked for the rest of their lives. Other families he never heard from again and in some ways he was grateful. The pain was just too much. Like little Lizzie Mounter, an aspiring actress who was found face down in the River Thames four years ago.

The case had never been solved and he still thought of the girl's parents. They were divorced now. The father had gone abroad and the mother had simply lost herself.

The wind was picking up and he realised his shirt had come out of his trousers when he had got out of the car. He hurriedly began tucking it in as the door opened and Noah's parents stood there. Aaron and Darya. He was balding and red-skinned, had pushed his sleeves up on his white shirt and although the top button was undone, he was still wearing a red tie. He had one arm around Darya, but it didn't look comfortable. She was small and pale, a little mouse in a human sweater that was way too big for her. There was a quick smear of lipstick across her face as if she had tried to make an effort when the doorbell rang, but it hadn't done her any good. Her lips were pressed so hard together they looked white.

'Sorry to trouble you, Mr and Mrs Beasley,' Bishop said.

Awkward hovering like strangers on a first date.

'You'd better come in,' Darya said. 'I'll put the kettle on.'

The living room was warm. There was a gas fire turned up to the max and every single light in the room was turned on. Spotlessly clean. A sofa with tassels on the hem, a recliner and pouffe, coffee table, and to the left the dining room with a large table and four wooden chairs squeezed underneath.

Darya made a pot of tea and brought it through from the kitchen with a plate of biscuits. Put it down on the coffee table and started to pour. It felt strange – as if they were gathered for a book-club meeting or casual chat over local news. Task completed, she sat on the sofa next to her husband. Aaron gave her a glance then shook his head slowly.

'What happens now?'

There was a momentary pause then Bishop started:

'I know today has been harrowing for you both. And I want to thank you for having the courage to come and identify your boy personally. We've got the whole task force working on this. That's about thirty men and women dedicated to tracking down your son's killer. What we need to do now is try and figure out what Noah was like. Where he went, who his friends were, if he was seeing anyone. Did he have any arguments recently, did he have any enemies. That sort of thing. Any piece of information you have, no matter how small it may seem to you, could take us one step closer to his killer. We've had a preliminary chat with the headmaster from the school and all the teachers say he was a nice lad. One of the reliable ones. But they only see him during the day. You will have seen him every day and all night. You will have more insight than some of his friends.'

Mrs Beasley drew her breath in sharply.

'This half-term he told us he was going to stay at Granny's, didn't he?' And she gave a look to her husband. 'My mother's. We thought he'd gone over there on Monday afternoon.'

'Did he normally go over to Granny's by himself?'

'Sometimes. Have you found his phone?'

'Not yet, but we're doing everything we can to trace it.'

'Because I texted him Tuesday but he never got back to me. I just thought he was having too much of a good time, my mum likes to spoil him. I didn't hear back Wednesday so on Thursday I called my mum.'

'And what did she say?'

Darya's voice was reduced to a mumble and Bishop had to lean in to hear her. 'Mum said she hadn't seen him all week.'

Aaron interrupted. 'He told us he was going there, but Granny knew nothing about it. Where was he going? Why would he lie?'

'We're not sure yet,' Bishop said. 'When was the last time you saw your son, Mr Beasley?'

'Monday morning before I went to work.'

Bishop turned to Darya, encouragingly: 'Mrs Beasley?'

She wiped away tears. 'We had lunch together, sat and watched TV for a bit, then he took his backpack and left.'

'What time was that?'

'About four o'clock. It's a thirty-minute walk to Granny's house.'

'And what was he wearing?'

'His jeans, trainers – Adidas ones with the white stripes. A white T-shirt with a logo—'

'Do you remember the logo?'

'It was a Gap one. And a plain blue hoody and his jacket. One of those jackets with the fluffy hood. It kept his ears warm.'

A pause until Bishop said: 'We need to do a press release now that Noah has been identified. We're going to be guided by you, obviously, but have all the family members been told?'

'They have, yes.'

'Thank you,' Bishop said. He had been making notes and now took a sip of tea. He didn't want to go for a biscuit.

'He was a good lad,' said Aaron. 'Always did his homework, helped me around the garden. He was funny. Had a good sense of humour, you know?'

'Good friends at school?'

'Yes. His best friend was Morris Crenshaw. They're in the same English class, with the same form tutor as well. His parents came round. They were very nice, weren't they?'

'Yes,' Darya said. 'They offered to help. I don't know how they can but – it was nice.'

'Do you know if Noah was seeing someone? Romantically? Did he ever talk about anyone special?'

'Like a girlfriend?' Darya said.

'Yes.'

'No.' She looked a little lost, as if she should have known. 'Not to me. Aaron?'

'No. He was too young for that. Too busy on that bloody computer.'

'Aaron!' Darya almost spat the words and he sagged back on the sofa. 'He played games and things,' she explained. 'I tried to get him away, get him outside. We both did. He didn't much like football. You tried to kick a ball around with him, but he wasn't interested, was he?'

'No. Bought him a rugby ball as well and even tried some cricket but he couldn't get into it, you know. Some kids don't, do they?'

'No, they don't,' Bishop said. 'Where do you work, Mr Beasley?'

'My father's company – Bespoke Signs on Bower Hill. We make aluminium and acrylic signs for local companies, the council. It's a family business. Been going for thirty-two years now.'

'How long have you been there?'

'Since I was sixteen. Left school and went straight to work for Dad.'

'Do you still enjoy it?'

Bishop was veering into small talk and hated himself for it but he wanted them to relax. Although after another sip of tea he realised it may have been for his benefit.

'I like meeting new customers. Every day is different. My brother works with me as well.'

'Do you get on?'

'With Mike?' A brief smile. 'We've always been close as a family. We're going to keep it going when Dad retires. They've been over here all day, haven't they, love – Mike and Sheila – that's his wife.'

Darya nodded. 'They cooked for us. It's hard for them, they loved Noah too. They can't have children, so they really saw him as their son.'

'I think you've already taken statements from them. Checked alibis and stuff,' Aaron said. 'I know you have to do that. Dotting the i's and crossing the t's.'

There was a noise to Bishop's left and he turned. A girl had arrived in the doorway. She had her hair down and it was wet as if she'd just had a bath. She was wearing a blue dressing gown and fluffy white slippers with no heels. She entered and sat down on the sofa, grabbed a cushion and hugged it to her chest.

'Are you Ruby?' Bishop asked.

Her lips were pressed together like her mum's, and when she swallowed her whole head moved with the effort.

'Yes.'

Bishop had seen photos of Noah's room and wondered what Ruby's was like. Small and pink with over-loved teddy bears on the bed. Princess dresses on unicorn hangers.

'She's a swimmer and a runner,' said Aaron. 'Doing triathlon for the school now, aren't you?'

'Are you?' Bishop smiled at her. 'That's good.'

'I like running and cycling. Swimming I'm not that good at, but—'

'You are good,' said her dad. 'Ever so good, love.'

The girl nodded. She was starting to make eye contact.

93

Breaking the wall. And then Bishop's mouth went as dry as a bone when she asked:

'Are you going to catch the person who did this?'

It was as if he were seeing her for the first time, and he was reminded that sometimes he really hated this job. And then she started to cry. A sad image framed by the lamplight as her mother reached over and held the little girl's hand.

Sixteen

The man was finishing his breakfast washing up when the doorbell rang.

A jolt of uncertainty as he placed the bowl and spoon into the drying rack and contemplated. Five seconds. Ten. He checked out of the rear window. If it was the police they would have been knocking on that door as well, and then the front doorbell went again.

The blinds in the wide bay windows in the living room were closed, the thick red curtains pulled tight. He inched one aside and saw who it was.

Her name was Denise Woolcott and she lived at number thirty-seven across the road. Forty-five years old, recently divorced, a sad-sack of a woman who worked as an accountant in Theydon Bois about five minutes from his office. She had started coming over more and more often for a chat during the past few months. An uninvited guest in his driveway.

He opened the door and smiled.

'Hello again. This is a pleasant surprise.' His voice was so controlled. Soft and easy-listening like a chat show host from the radio.

'I made a little something for you.' She frothed at the edges as she held up a circular cake stand with a tea towel half-draped seductively across its contents like a beauty queen flirting with a glimpse of her shoulder. 'It's a Victoria sponge with buttercream icing. Home-made jam from raspberries at the bottom of the garden. We had a big crop this year.'

We?

He knew she lived alone. Perhaps the colloquial *we* that encompassed the whole street. He shook his head in wonder.

'How marvellous,' but made no move to take it, which threw her. He enjoyed watching her squirm. She cleared her throat, scratched her nose, then:

'How's your mother?'

'Had a bit of a funny turn the other day. She doesn't sleep too well, unfortunately.'

'Any news about her hip operation?'

'Not yet. Still waiting for a date. She woke up the other morning and her whole right side was swollen. So painful.'

'I thought it was the left side?'

'Hmm?'

'I thought you said it was her left hip that needed the operation?'

His mouth went dry. A silence until he said:

'No, it's her right hip.'

'Well, maybe I'm confused. It happens quite a bit.' She gave him an embarrassed smile and he stepped outside and pulled the door closed behind him.

'She's sleeping now. Best to keep our voices down.' He

wondered if Denise felt as though she was back at school – being talked to as if she were a particularly slow pupil. 'They want her to lose a bit of weight for the anaesthetic, if you can believe that,' he continued. 'Sixty-eight and she needs to go on a diet.'

'Oh, maybe I shouldn't have baked—'

'She's allowed one treat a day. And today it will be your Victoria sponge.'

He reached over and took hold of his side of the plate. Let his fingers brush against hers. She didn't pull away.

'You have a very lovely way about you,' he said softly. Closed his eyes for a second and shook his head. 'You must have been told that before?' He watched her blush as she raised a hand and ruffled her hair like a teenager seeing her reflection in a shop window.

'I bet you say that to all the women,' she smiled.

'Only the ones that have the time to talk to me. *And* bring my mother Victoria sponge, *and* stand on the doorstep making all the neighbours wonder what's going on over here.'

She laughed again. He took the cake and stepped inside the house.

'Thank you so much. She will love this.'

'It's for you as well.'

'I will love it too.'

She turned as if to leave, but quickly swivelled on her thick ankles.

'Oh, I hope I didn't disturb your mother, but I knocked on the door the other day.'

His whole body went cold. He could feel the hairs on his arms bristling.

'I'm sorry?'

'I had a day off work. I was in the garden pruning and picked some flowers. Roses and larkspur. I wasn't sure if your mother—'

'When was this?'

'Two days ago. I knocked and rang the bell but she obviously didn't hear. I left them on the mat.'

'Yes, thank you. I'm so sorry, Denise, I should have . . . they are in a vase by her bedside. That was very kind of you.'

'And your mother is okay?'

'Mother is fine. I think she wrote a thank-you card, but I'm not sure where I . . .'

Denise smiled. She was warming to her own voice.

'I know you're away quite a bit and you work so hard,' she said, 'but if you ever need me to come over and look after her, I'd love to help. I can give you my number, here—' She handed over a Post-it note. 'That's my number. I don't have any cards, I left them at the office. I know, I should have been a doctor, I have doctor's scrawl. That's a seven at the end. Oh-six-seven.'

He took the note and pondered. 'I really appreciate that. I will call you if there are any problems.' He smiled and retreated past the doorstep. Cocked his head to one side.

'I think I can hear her,' he whispered. 'I'd better go. Call of duty.'

He shut the door and stood for a while thinking. He wondered if she was going to be a problem – something he hadn't taken into account. In the living room he checked through the curtains to see if she was loitering, but the driveway was clear. He returned to the kitchen and threw the cake in the bin. Hiked up the stairs and checked on his mother. Mouth open. Stick-like fingers splayed across the covers.

'Who was that?' she said.

'Denise. One of the neighbours. She says hello, by the way.'

'What did she want?'

'To talk.'

'Look at you – making friends with a fancy woman. Not going to forget about me, are you?'

'Of course not, Mum.'

'Didn't she bake me a cake last time?'

'She did. Not today though. She was out of flour and eggs.'

'More's the pity. I have a very sweet tooth.'

'I know you do.' He spent a moment looking at her and wondered if she needed another bath. It could wait. 'I have to go out this evening. I might be home late.'

He kissed her on the cheek and went into his own room. He didn't lie on the bed though, he chose the floor instead and gazed up at the angel on the ceiling. His mother had painted Gabriel when they had moved house. A hypnotic mix of greens, ochres and yellows. The eyes were jet-black though, with a fluorescent strip for the irises, like tiny stiletto moons. They always watched him while he slept, but when he woke every morning they were gone, as if they had never existed.

'There is an animal inside me,' he said to the angel. 'It's waiting to be called. Waiting for permission and when it comes out, I can't stop it. Some animals can never go backwards. Did you know that? Once they are out of the cage they just keep going until they get cold.'

The angel watched him.

Didn't say anything. Didn't move. But the eyes seemed to follow his thoughts so he turned on to his stomach and tucked his knees into his chest. Wooden floors. Warm and waxy. And as he pressed his ear to them he could hear the faint heartbeat.

The drum of life from below.

Seventeen

Holly's day began with scrambled eggs and avocado on toast.

Phone calls and emails had followed, laundry next and then she had spent the next three hours creating a collage of black and blue felt-pen marks on the wall above the fireplace, all linked with evidence tags and autopsy photos. Listing notes in her head. Poison. Fentanyl. Psychiatric disorders. Symptoms of depression, of psychosis, substance dependence, symptoms of other disorders – antisocial behaviour. Mother or father? Man or a woman. Both? A team? A stranger? No. She crossed that out. The boy would have known his killer. A friend? Parent of a school friend?

She took a step back. A mess of notes. Phrases. Rubbed some out. Cleaned it up.

Her eyes were still fixed on the wall above the fireplace when the phone rang. It was Bishop giving her the okay to visit the Beasleys' house that evening.

She thanked him and left for work almost immediately. Sagged into her car and drove straight to Wetherington. She caught up on paperwork and treated two new day patients and made time for Lee. They walked through the hospital's general ward together: past the canteen, the treatment areas, the chapel and nurses' lockers to what was known as the lounge. A place where patients could converse, play cards, watch TV and generally relieve the boredom of their private rooms. About a dozen patients were already here with their primary carers. Holly said hello to a few as she and her brother passed by.

'I spoke to Mary. It's a short-term cycle on the new meds,' Holly said. 'I know Clozapine has a higher rate of metabolic syndrome, but it's only a three-month cycle, then they're going to switch back to Respiridone.'

'I don't like Respiridone.'

'We'll halve the dosage.'

'Polypharmacy at its best.'

They stopped at the window that looked out over the grounds. Dead leaves, unswept since the winter, blew across the lawn.

'I know this garden so well,' Lee said. 'The grass in the centre with the waterfall at one end. Sixteen beech trees. Twenty-two shrubs. Ten are azaleas: bright pink. Twelve camellias: white, like wet bone in the summer. You can walk around this garden in one minute and twenty-seven seconds,' he said. 'You can walk around it again and go the other way to get a different view. A different perspective, but it's still the same. One minute and twenty-seven seconds and then it's over. You come back to where you started. Life is very short in my garden.'

'Do you take your shoes off?'

'It's too cold.'

'Take them off next time. Feel the grass under your feet. Feel the difference it makes.'

He nodded and sighed.

'I miss the proper walks though, you know? The long walks. The walks that lasted for an hour. Two hours. You would find yourself at some corner café in Covent Garden, sit inside and have a coffee before you decided to walk back. Being a witness as the world goes by. People watching. That's what I miss. Knowing that one day I will be the one who walks past that window and someone will be watching me. The roles will be reversed. Out there you are still part of the world. In here you're not. I want to get out. I want to get out and see things again.'

A pigeon caught their attention as it landed on the lawn. It settled then was chased away by another. Lee leaned an arm against the window.

'At some point last week someone threw a plastic water bottle into the pond by the waterfall. It's still there now, I think, fighting for its life against the constant battering. Just like life. How do you break out of that? How do you get out of the waterfall? Maybe the secret is to not get trapped there in the first place. That's what happens to us, isn't it? Constantly being slapped around. That's how we get our scars.'

'Scars are life,' said Holly. 'I like my scars.'

'I know you do. For you they're a celebration, aren't they? A celebration of survival.'

'It's more than that.'

'What is it then?'

'They're me. Who I am. They are nearly always on the inside, but now they're starting to come out.'

'My my. Look who's all grown-up today. Wearing your big-girl pants.'

'Don't be a dick.' She smiled despite herself. Then said:

'There was a boy killed in Epping Forest earlier this week.'

'I didn't know.'

'I've been thinking about you a lot recently. Mum and Dad. I'm sure I've blocked things out.'

'Hm.'

'Memories. I don't know if they're all true or if I've thought about them so much they've become true. In the summer – did we play hide and seek in our back garden?'

'Always.'

'Where did I used to hide?'

'Behind the fir tree along the path on the left.'

'We had lots of fir trees.'

'You favoured the one by the strawberry bushes,' he said. 'I would always find you there eventually.'

'Yes, you would, wouldn't you? I remember now.'

'How does that memory make you feel?'

'Sad and numb.'

'Comfortably numb is the main ingredient in my life. What would you do without me, Sis?'

He looked around, suddenly aware of music playing from somewhere.

'What is that?' he asked.

'It's the musical therapy dance class. Something we're trying out. There have been good results from other institutions so they thought they should give it a go here.'

'I didn't know they were doing that.'

'Do you want me to book you some classes?'

'Two left feet.'

'Come on. It could be fun. Apparently, it helps us relax. Helps us come to terms with emotions that we can't express verbally. It's very beautiful. I think this is a waltz. "The Skater's Waltz" by Emile Waldteufel.'

'Waldteufel?'

His accent was terrible and she laughed.

'Seriously, say that name again,' she said. 'Just for my benefit.'

'Waldteufel.'

She smiled, then spun around and hit fourth position. 'Five years' ballet, dear brother. The dancing takes place in the conservatory on Sunday afternoon. We could do it together.'

'Ha, now that would be funny. I'm sure I'd embarrass myself. Maybe when I get out of here I'll give dancing a go.'

She faltered. He was never getting out.

'We don't have to wait. I could give you your first lesson?'

He moved away from the window and gestured to her but stopped halfway and then went completely still. There was an odd permanence about it. Then he turned away and bit his lip.

'Lee? Stop it.'

His lip was bleeding now and he kept his teeth pressed into it.

'Lee, stop it now!'

He stopped and spat blood on the window.

Two of the nurses came over. One male, one female.

'Are you all right, Lee? What seems to be the problem?'

'It's fine,' Holly said. 'It will be fine. Deep breaths. Okay?'

'Deep breaths,' echoed the nurses.

Lee closed his eyes and took a deep breath.

Eighteen

The curtains were still drawn.

Holly was perched on one end of the sofa. Darya the other. She looked tired, but probably not just today, it seemed like a profound fatigue.

'I slept in my son's bed last night,' she said. 'He was like me, I think. He was very quiet and peaceful when he was born. We have the funeral to arrange. I need to decide what Noah's going to wear. I don't know yet.' Suddenly stiff and awkward.

'Would you like more tea, Holly?'

'No, thank you.'

'Aaron won't be home until ten. He thought it best to keep working.'

'And where's Ruby?'

'With my sister-in-law. She should be home in an hour or so. She's dreading school tomorrow.'

'Is she going to go?'

'I don't know yet. Mr Rickshaw, the headmaster phoned and said she didn't have to. Said she could take as much time as she needed. They're being very nice at the school. I presume everyone knows by now. It's in all the newspapers. I try not to read them.' She paused, trying to fight off the emotion. 'I can't imagine not being able to speak to him again.'

Holly felt herself nodding, reached out and touched Darya's shoulder. Took in the softness of her cardigan. Felt the emptiness beneath.

'Mrs Beasley, I know DI Bishop talked to you about this, but would it be okay if I go into Noah's room?'

'I don't really understand what for.'

'I want to get a feel for him. To try and help understand what happened.'

'It wasn't his fault.'

'No, of course not.'

Darya shrugged. Sad and teary.

'Was it mine?'

'No.'

The woman nodded uncertainly and Holly got up. Darya did too and Holly wondered if she was going to follow her upstairs but instead she picked up the teapot and proceeded to pour more tea even though the cups were untouched.

Holly left as quietly as she could. She heard the television go on when she was halfway up the stairs and hoped it would provide a distraction. There were four doors at the top of the landing. She should have asked which one it was. She didn't want to go down—

'It's the one on the far left.' Darya was standing at the bottom of the stairs peering up, squinting slightly.

'Thank you.'

Holly followed the directions and opened the door.

First time in the victim's room. First time seeing through Noah's eyes. The walls were sky blue. The ceiling white and the carpet grey with black flecks like the landing. Several posters were tacked up to the wall opposite the bed; a punk rock band and a zany comedian. A chest of drawers and a built-in wardrobe to the right. The bed was from IKEA. Freshly made. The pillow was clean white cotton, like the one in the forest.

The window above the bed looked out on to the front drive. Holly pulled the net curtains aside and stared at the quiet street. She wondered how many neighbours were watching the Beasleys' house right now through their own net curtains. Children safely locked inside, their parents suddenly wanting to spend more time with them. She turned away and opened the wardrobe. The place had been cleared by forensics but she still slipped on a pair of latex gloves. Two black suits that looked brand new and unworn and the normal array of teen-age hoodies, T-shirts and jeans. She shut the doors and sat at his desk. School books and folders stuffed with loose bits of paper and notes, a square of dust where his computer once sat.

What did Noah see when he sat here? An Action Man on the bedside table, along with a lamp and a calendar. No dates marked out. She pulled open the first drawer. School work – maths books, a calculator, history essays on a local cathedral, a half-finished sketch of the steeple in pencil. English books. Literature and creative writing. Notes on *Romeo and Juliet*, comments at the bottom by his English teacher:

A wonderful essay, Noah. You have the ability to delve into people's hearts, to see what is really there and to write about it in an original and respectful way. Romeo and Juliet would be proud! A-

High praise indeed. A folder full of poetry. Love poems, by the looks of them. Tugging at adolescent heartstrings. Some marked with As and Bs, others not.

How many miles. How many feet.
How many hearts with their tremulous beat.
Have failed without valour, have failed without lies
for a moment of love with your beautiful eyes.

She let the words linger then turned to another.

My life is not beautiful. It is not magical.
But I can feel the love. Coming closer.
Closer every day.

Deep and from the heart of a fourteen-year-old. Painfully real. She wondered who it had been written for.

A few magazines in another drawer: *National Geographic Kids* – a photo of a lynx and the caption 'one cool cat', a cooking magazine *ChopChop* with the phrase 'lovin' your oven'. Holly flicked through the pages of recipes: smashed potatoes, roast away your winter blues ...

'He liked to bake.'

The voice startled her and she turned. Darya was leaning against the door frame as if it was the only thing holding her up.

'I'm sorry,' Holly stood. 'It must look strange, me going through your son's things.'

A shrug and then: 'There's a good recipe for butternut squash in one of the magazines. We never actually made it, but we talked about it.'

'What else did you cook?'

'He and Ruby liked desserts. We made a lemon parfait last month. We served it at the dining room table as if we were on *MasterChef*.'

Darya went to the desk and picked up the poems. There was a silence as she read the first.

'"*A moment of love with your beautiful eyes . . .*" that's one of my favourites,' and then the second one: '"*My life is not beautiful . . .*"' She looked suddenly sad. 'I haven't seen this one before,' and she dabbed at her eyes with a tissue.

Holly took it from her and read it again. 'Do you know if he wrote them for anybody?' she said.

'I don't know. He used to write in a diary as well. It will be here somewhere.'

'Did he ever mention someone special? A girlfriend? A boyfriend?'

'That's what the policeman asked us. No . . . ' Then her face formed an expression of terrible puzzlement and she suddenly looked around as if scared of something and started to cry. 'Did they have to cut him up?'

'The coroner. Her name is Angela.'

'Angela?'

'Yes. She would have been like an angel to your son. He wouldn't have felt a thing. She has children of her own and she will have taken care of him like a mother.'

Darya's mouth stretched open in a cry of pain then she walked out. Holly stayed very still waiting for her to come back but she didn't, so she tidied up the desk. Made sure everything was exactly as it had been. She picked up the poems and read them one more time. Sat on the bed then lay down and rested her head on Noah's pillow. There were pale yellow strips of

109

moon and stars on the ceiling – the sort that light up when the lights are turned off.

'What are you doing?'

Darya had returned and was standing by the door. Holly rose abruptly and swung her feet over the edge of the bed. Darya watched her with a certain fascination. 'I've got to decide what he's going to wear. For the funeral.' Her lips trembled and Holly thought she was about to say something else, but instead she removed a small rectangle of card from her jacket and put it on the bed. 'So you don't forget,' she said, and left the room.

Holly felt herself exhale and realised she had been holding her breath. She looked down at the piece of card and picked it up.

It was a photo of her boy.

Nineteen

'How was it?'

'Heartbreaking,' Holly said.

Bishop had picked her up from her flat and now they found themselves walking on Hampstead Heath. They chose a path through to a thin veil of trees. It was busy despite the cold. People walked – wrapped-up shadows in front and behind within the darkness. A dog suddenly broke through a thicket and stared at them, lost interest then scampered away.

'Noah liked to write,' Holly said. 'I found poetry in his room. I wondered if he was writing it for someone.'

'His mother says not and his form tutor at school agrees. Said they can normally spot a classroom romance within minutes.'

'Online then.'

'His parents said he was on his computer a lot. We've eliminated friends, family and relatives. You think he was groomed?' Bishop took a breath that turned into a sigh: 'So before we can go forward I need to go back. How did Noah get himself into that situation?'

'Like any other curious kid. One of my older patients is a

paedophile by the name of Reggie Falder. He was sentenced earlier this year. He contacted his victims on Gumtree initially and it escalated from there. He used to put photos of cute puppies on his profile page to attract the kids.'

'We have Noah's computer.'

'Then you need to look for a young female on his list of social media friends. She'll be slightly older than Noah, not younger. It's a sexual enticement. Someone more experienced. Noah would have thought he was in safe hands. They need to flag anything vaguely sexual in their conversations.'

'What sort of questions would they ask?'

'To begin with? School, homework, TV and friends. Breaking the ice. It's all about friendship and trust,' Holly said. 'Then it would progress to things like: What is your relationship with your mother and father like? Do you have a sister or brother? Are they older or younger? Does your brother or sister ever go into your room?'

'I don't see how that would work.'

'Because, just like you and I, children want someone to talk to. Someone whom they can trust. It's really simple. How did your dad treat you?'

'Seriously?'

'Yes.'

Bishop shrugged, matter-of-fact.

'He bullied me.'

'Same here. My dad used to do the same thing,' Holly said. 'Now, the moment I told you that my father used to bully me – he didn't, by the way – we formed a bond. Your dad bullies you? Same here, Noah. There's the bond between predator and child. Something in common. Two of them together against shitty Dad or shitty world. My dad beats me. So does mine. My mum won't let me watch TV after six. Same here. What a bitch. Friends for life.'

'It's that simple?'

'Frighteningly so. Then comes the final play: Let's meet up, have some fun. Most children will cotton on to what is happening and will tell their parents or end the contact themselves, but the ones that don't ... ' She let the sentence go. The wind was chill with fast flurries that took her by surprise and she wiped at her eyes with her coat sleeve. 'Noah would have had no idea he was being groomed,' she said. 'All he would have thought was that he had found someone to talk to. Someone who understood him. Who loved him.'

'How many children will he have targeted before he found Noah?'

'Possibly dozens.'

'Did Noah have a best friend?'

'Morris Crenshaw.'

'Then we need to talk to him.'

Bishop stopped walking. His brow was furrowed and Holly found herself staring at the path between them. When he finally looked up at her, he said softly:

'We're way behind this guy, aren't we?'

There was nothing she could do but nod. Then she said:

'We should leave, I'm getting cold.'

He didn't answer but they both turned along the path and headed towards his car.

Twenty

Kenneth Rickshaw stood at the front of the Hopewell Secondary School assembly hall at nine o'clock Monday morning.

Noah's headmaster and English teacher, he had a manicured goatee, was immaculately dressed and stood with his arms relaxed in front of his waist. Before him sat the whole school. Four hundred and thirty two pupils ranging from eleven to sixteen years of age and twenty-two teachers lined up on either side.

'Our first day after half-term,' Mr Rickshaw began, 'and we return to Hopewell with a heavy heart. I'm sure you are all aware of the tragic events that have afflicted one of our pupils. Noah Beasley from year ten. I know you will have read the newspapers, their garish headlines, but please try and remember him as he was. Quiet. Gentle. Caring. Noah liked being at school. He was a good pupil and a . . . ' he faltered, '. . . and a fine boy. That's all he was. A boy.'

Holly watched Ken Rickshaw and the pupils from the front of the hall. She couldn't see Ruby and wondered if she was staying at home. Most of the children had their heads dipped low, either as a sign of respect or trying to avoid eye contact, it was hard to tell.

'We are all here for you – the teachers, the staff – as you will be there for us. We have dedicated counsellors being brought in for the next five days, so if and when you need to talk to them, please contact me or any other member of staff and we will make an appointment. Our door is always open. You should all know that. The police are here now and they would like to speak to some of you in the cafeteria after this assembly, and if you have any information that you think may help in any way, please let them know. If you saw anyone suspicious outside the school in the past few weeks, the police are here to take statements and listen. I know it seems pointless now to go to class. To carry on with the day, to go to your lessons after this news – but please do.

'There will be a memorial service next Thursday afternoon at St Thomas's church. School will therefore be closed from lunchtime as we suspect many of you would like to attend. Some of you will be chosen to read something. Something that perhaps will be written by members of his class and his teachers. I know we're not supposed to talk about religion or whether Noah believed in God or angels,' he swallowed hard. 'But whatever religion or beliefs you have, please pray for him tonight. Pray for him and his family.' His hair had flopped over to one side and he pushed it aside with his left hand. Well-manicured. No wedding ring.

'Thank you for your patience and respect. This school will continue as normal and we will not let this sad occasion affect us any more than it already has. Please leave the hall quietly and resume your classes.'

A few of the teachers rose to their feet and held open the

main doors as the pupils began to filter out. Once in the corridors, the chatter started. A background hum. Somehow lonely despite being comprised of a hundred voices.

Ken Rickshaw hung by the door. As the last of the children dispersed he turned to Holly and Bishop and gave a gentle nod of the head. 'Shall we go to my office?'

Rickshaw's office was meticulously clean.

A pot plant either side of the door as they entered. His desk and chair were white and shiny, and there were numerous file cabinets behind. On one wall a print of a bizarre blue-twisted face that could have been a Picasso amidst numerous teaching certificates.

'Take a seat please.' Two comfortable chairs opposite his desk. Holly and Bishop lowered themselves as Mr Rickshaw went over to the percolator and poured himself a coffee. 'Milk and sugar?'

'Thank you,' Bishop said.

'Just milk please,' from Holly.

Rickshaw carried the drinks over then said: 'I speak on behalf of the school, the faculty and all of the other staff when I say we are all at your service. I, myself, have put aside the whole day for you obviously.'

'Thank you, Mr Rickshaw.'

'Ken, please.'

'Ken,' Bishop shifted slightly. 'You were Noah's form tutor?'

'Yes, I was. Every morning when the pupils arrive, they report to their class for attendance and administration. I am responsible for thirty-seven children in all. Have been for the past five years. Noah joined me two years ago. We work on a rotation system so he would have been moved again after the summer holidays.'

'We're trying to build up a picture of Noah,' Bishop continued. 'We spoke to his parents – did you have much contact with them?'

'They were very supportive of Noah and the school. They would both come to parents' evenings, concerts, and of course Ruby has just started with us, but not today. We suggested she stay at home.'

'How did Noah get on with the other pupils?'

'Fine. Good. Not outgoing like some here, but he was well liked.'

'Any bullying? Anything like that?'

'Not that I was aware of.'

'We'd like to talk to one pupil in particular. A Morris Crenshaw.'

'Yes, he was in assembly.'

'Noah's mother told us they were best friends.'

'I think that's safe to say. They'd eat lunch together and spend time with one another during the breaks.'

'And you taught Noah English?' Holly said.

Rickshaw jerked around to look at her. Blinked a few times then found his voice.

'I'm sorry?'

'You taught him English,' she said. 'And he liked to write poetry, didn't he?'

'Yes, he did. He was prolific. In poetry he had really found his voice.'

'There were some poems in his room that weren't in a school exercise book, they were on loose bits of paper. Love poems. Some of them had been marked with a red pen. Comments in the margin. Would it have been you who had marked them?'

'More than likely. He often brought in pieces outside of the curriculum.'

'Do you know who he wrote them for?'

Rickshaw looked up at her with pleading eyes. Holly didn't repeat the question. Let the silence go stale.

'No,' he eventually said and swallowed hard. 'I'm afraid I don't.'

Twenty-one

Morris Crenshaw had one of those spinners between his fingers that he kept going constantly while he talked. He looked as though he had been crying and answered their questions with doe eyes.

'Noah was my best friend, yeah. We're in the same English class as well with Mr Rickshaw so . . .'

They were in the school cafeteria. Mr Rickshaw stayed by Morris's side, casually leaning against the wall. He seemed calmer than he had been in his office. There was another teacher present. The deputy head, Mrs Williams. Safety in numbers, Holly thought.

'When was the last time you saw Noah?' Bishop started.

'On the Friday before we broke up for half-term. We said goodbye at the school gates and that was it.'

'Did you speak to him over the weekend?'

'Saturday, and on Monday as well. He told me he was going over to his Granny on Monday. I guess he wasn't?'

'No. How did he seem when you spoke to him last?'

'Seem?'

'Yes. Nervous? Excited?'

Morris looked confused, turned to Rickshaw as if he didn't understand.

'Answer the question,' Rickshaw said.

'Oh,' Morris said. 'I mean, he seemed normal. He didn't seem nervous and he didn't seem excited.'

'We think he may have met someone online. Did he ever mention anything like that to you?'

He swallowed hard. The spinner picked up pace.

'I don't ... I don't know.'

Rickshaw looked somewhat surprised. 'What do you mean, you don't know?' he said.

'Maybe.'

'Maybe?'

'Best to be honest,' the teacher said softly.

Morris nodded. Shrugged.

'He did mention a girl. I think she was older than Noah.'

Holly leaned forward:

'What makes you think that?' she said.

'The way he acted when he talked about her. Like it was special. I don't know. He said he loved her.'

'Did he ever show you a photo?'

'No. He kept calling her special, that's all.'

'How old do you think she was?'

'Like sixteen maybe.'

'Did you know her name?'

'I asked, but he never told me.'

'Why was that, do you think?'

'He said it was supposed to be a secret.'

A quiet descended. From somewhere a bell rang and Morris turned to Mr Rickshaw.

'Can I go now?'

'Yes, it's fine, Morris. Go to class and then I will see you at the end of the day.'

Morris's chair scraped as he got up. Spinner going at a hundred miles an hour in his sweaty palm as he left the room.

Bishop thanked Mr Rickshaw and Mrs Williams and moved away to take a call.

Rickshaw was raring to go, but Holly asked him:

'Have you always been a teacher, Mr Rickshaw?'

'My calling.' A patient smile. 'I worked at a grammar school before this. King Edward VI in Chelmsford.'

'Why did you move?'

'Change of scenery. I needed a new challenge.'

Holly wasn't sure if she believed him. She was about to ask something else when Bishop returned, pocketing his phone. He pulled her aside:

'Two eyewitnesses have come forward, both claiming to have seen a boy matching Noah's description walking towards the forest on Monday evening.'

Twenty-two

Holly and Bishop arrived at Forest Gate by mid-afternoon.

It was a busy part of London whose main road led towards the easterly entrance to Wanstead Park. Bad drivers and bad congestion, but Bishop managed to find a spot on Sebert Road between two bakery trucks and he led Holly to an office building with half a dozen companies listed on the door.

'Who's first?' she asked.

'His name's John Pickford. He's one of the draughtsmen at Voss Architects. Said he saw Noah from the office windows.'

Bishop pressed a buzzer: 3B. A clicking noise and then a voice:

'Hello?'

'John Pickford?'

'Yes?'

'This is DI Bishop.'

'Ah, yes. Come on up. Third floor.'

John Pickford ushered them inside.

He was five eight or nine, slim, and clean shaven with

receding brown hair. The office was open-plan with rooms around the edges and wide windows that afforded a view of the surrounding buildings and streets outside.

'Good to meet you, Mr Pickford,' Bishop said and shook John's hand. 'And this is Holly Wakefield. She's helping with our enquiries.'

John smiled at her, shook hands.

'Would either of you like a drink?'

'I'm good,' Bishop said. 'Holly?'

'No thank you.'

'So – tell us what you saw, Mr Pickford,' Bishop said.

'Uhh – I was working late on the Monday. One of the junior clerks had messed up with a couple of the calculations on a local council property. Nothing drastic, but I had to stay and fix it.'

'Go on.'

'So I'm at my desk, got up to stretch my legs and looked down at the street, and that's when I saw the boy.'

'You could see him that well from up here?'

'He passed by the street light over there.' He led them over to the south-facing window, pointed down. Holly got her bearings. There was a café to the left, businesses on the right, and in between, the road leading to the main entrance to Wanstead Park.

'What time was this?'

'Six twenty-five? Six thirty? Maybe I'm reading more into it. I couldn't see him that clearly, but he was small, had dark hair and was carrying a backpack, so I thought it had to be the boy.'

'Was he with anyone?'

'No, he was by himself.' He shrugged. 'Again, maybe I'm

reading too much into it. Maybe it wasn't him? Realistically he was in my view for maybe five, ten seconds tops and then he went past the chip shop, and I carried on working. Didn't think anything of it until you started canvassing the area.' He rubbed his eyes. 'Has anyone else come forward? A lot of people at the company are shook up by this, especially the women with children. I hope I've helped but . . . ' He frowned, seemed distracted. 'I didn't see anyone else with him. I wish I had, you know? Sorry.'

'Don't apologise, Mr Pickford. You've been very helpful. Was there anyone else here that night?'

'No, just myself and Dave.'

'Dave?'

John Pickford gave a tight smile. 'Sorry.' He pointed to a wire cage at the corner of the office where something tan and grey shuffled inside. 'Dave the elephant shrew. Damian Voss, the CEO brought him after a trip abroad. He's like the company mascot now. You know you've got a contract when they send their love to *Dave* at the bottom of an email.'

Holly and Bishop thanked him, left the office and shared the space in the lift. Both went for the ground-floor button together, so Holly batted Bishop's arm away and smiled.

'Who's next?'

Hannah Alim had worked at Fish 'N' Chips for the last five years. She was tipping great trays of sliced potatoes into vats of hot oil when they came inside. She already seemed to know they weren't customers before Bishop flashed his warrant card.

'I already told the police everything. Gave them my statement.'

'That's why we're here,' Bishop replied.

Hannah stacked up the empty trays, checked her watch and glanced at them.

'I don't know what else I can tell you.'

'You said the boy went past here at about six-thirty?'

'Well, I think it was him.'

'Think?'

'That's what I said in my statement. I thought it was him, because I remember seeing a little kid carrying a backpack go past the window.'

'From left to right, yes?'

'Um . . .' a second of thought. 'Yes. Left to right. That way.' She motioned with her hands.

'Was he talking on a phone or was anyone with him?'

'No. He was walking fast, but he was definitely by himself.'

'Do you think anybody else in here that night will remember him?'

'I doubt it. The customers are always looking at me, not out the window.'

'Regulars?'

'Maybe one or two, but it's different every night.'

'Do you live locally?' Holly said.

'I'm on Chestnut Avenue. Flat seven B. Turn right up there and you'll find me.'

Bishop took a second and hitched his belt up:

'Any CCTV footage from that night?'

'No. I already told you guys this. A copper came and talked to me.' She reached under the till and pulled out a business card. 'Sergeant Ince.' She held it up as if they didn't believe her. 'Are we done? I've got like a million potatoes to cut up.'

'Sure.'

Hannah scooped up the trays and headed through a door.

They left the shop and stood on the pavement outside. A few cars drove by slowly and there was the constant hum from major roads further away.

'Two witnesses saw Noah go into the forest,' Holly said. 'No one saw him come out. So the killer was waiting there and would have driven him away. Maybe put him on the back seat. Wouldn't have been the front because of all the cameras on the main roads.'

'You think Noah went willingly?'

'Or he was kidnapped then and there. Tied up. Put in the boot. It tells us more about his MO,' Holly said, 'but it's skewed.'

'What do you mean?'

'The killer picked him up in the forest, killed him somewhere else then brought him back to the same place. It's unusual, but it tells us one thing for sure. The forest definitely means something to him.'

Bishop said, 'You ready to go?'

'No.' She gestured to the café she had seen from the window. 'Let's get a drink first.'

They went inside the café and Bishop ordered hot drinks while Holly sat at a table. There were eleven other people inside. Four couples and three by themselves. She wondered if any of these people had been here the night Noah had disappeared. If she walked out now, how many of them would remember her? The man at the window texting on his phone. The couple with their backpacks by their feet, their walking shoes covered in leaves and mud. The woman reading the newspaper, who wasn't really. She'd make the pages flicker but her eyes never strayed far from the other tables and the front door. The woman felt Holly's eyes on her and stared for a few seconds too long. She shifted nervously then put down the newspaper and made her exit. Holly followed her with her eyes until she disappeared from view. On a whim she went over and picked up the newspaper, returning to the table as Bishop arrived with their drinks.

'The woman who just left—'

'Blue trousers, white top and a brown jacket?'

'You noticed her too?'

'Blonde hair up in a bun. Her name is Nina. She's forty-five and has three kids.'

'Seriously?'

'She's one of ours. Well spotted. No end to your talents, is there?'

'How many undercover officers do you have working this case?'

'Only two on this road but we've got another six in the forest. Two joggers, one equestrian and a family of three with a pushchair.' He sipped his drink. Cleared his throat. 'You want me to drop you at home or at the station?'

'Maybe home,' Holly said, although she had no idea what she would do. She had cancelled her classes at King's College until further notice and at her flat she would feel even less useful than she did here. At least when she was outside it felt as though she was doing something.

'What are you doing tonight?' he said casually, but there was tension in his voice. Foreplay had never felt so earnest.

'Nothing.'

'Good,' he said and she caught a glimpse of a smile. 'I'll pick you up at eight.'

Twenty-three

Bishop arrived at eight on the dot.

Mr Punctual. Mr Handsome. Mr Jeans and an old T-shirt. Good job she hadn't opted for the dress and heels. He looked a little grey and she wondered what he had been up to in the hours since she last saw him. He closed the front door and in her living room said:

'You look . . .'

'What?'

'Lovely.'

'Thank you.'

Normally she made no effort at all, so a shimmer of lipstick and eyeliner was, in her books, a huge effort. Maybe her brother was right, maybe she had started wearing her big-girl pants after all.

His eyes were automatically pulled to the details of the home-made incident wall above the mantelpiece. He didn't seem surprised – he had seen the same collection on the last case. The victim photos, black pen lines, question marks and theories.

'So where are we actually going?' she said and for some reason wished she had worn her party frock after all.

He shuffled a bit. Rolled his shoulders.

'Think of it like a date.'

The engine was off and the car was starting to get cold.

They were halfway down Oldfield Road in Stoke Newington, watching Timothy Grent's flat. There was a splash of light behind the curtains on the third floor.

'How often do you do this?' she asked.

He yawned long and loud and shook his head. 'Used to do surveillance all the time in the army. The difference was, over there you couldn't talk. You weren't in a car where it was nice and comfortable, you were holed up in some flea-ridden little desert trench waiting for something to happen. No lights on. No talking. Had to shit into a bag and bury it.'

'You're joking?'

'No. Welcome to my old world.' He paused. 'I won't be doing it in the car. Don't worry.'

She laughed. Then asked:

'Has he been out at all today?'

Bishop picked up a report sheet.

'Left the flat at eleven forty-two a.m. Returned at twelve fifteen carrying a large Sainsbury's bag that appeared to be full of food. Stayed inside and then left again at seven thirty p.m. and walked to the local supermarket. Returned with another bag from Sainsbury's at seven minutes past eight and was also seen carrying a bottle of white wine. Hasn't been out since.'

He put the report down. Looked over at her then along the

street. An awkward moment, then she said: 'Love the place you've chosen for our date.'

'Mood lighting. Service is a bit crap. I haven't seen a single waiter. They do a great packet of crisps apparently.'

'Really?'

'Salt and vinegar or cheese and onion?'

'Salt and vinegar.'

He handed over the packet. She opened it and he opened his.

They both crunched crisps which sounded preternaturally loud in the enclosed space, which made them laugh. A man wearing a cap walked past the car with a dog. Hesitated two vehicles down. Holly noticed Bishop reposition himself slightly so he could see what was going on.

'Do you always do that when someone walks by?' she asked. 'Seeing what they're up to?'

'Force of habit. It's all about body language anyway. Furtive glances from left to right, seeing if they're being watched. Wondering where they can go, where their friends are, who's backing them up tonight. Did you read about the Becky Calthrop case?'

'I followed some of it. Was it the husband?'

'Lover. She was going to retry with the husband. Was carrying his baby. It was all very complicated and ended up with her being stabbed and stuffed into a freezer bag and dumped out Essex-way on a building site.'

'The lover was a contractor, right?'

'Edmond Whistle. Whistle Construction. The company he owned were supposed to be filling the basement of a new building plot with cement but there was an accident on the motorway. The cement truck got held up and one of the supervisors on site spotted the freezer bag with the woman's body in it.'

'How long did he get?'

'Twenty-five. He'll be out in fifteen.' A woman passed on the other side of the street, wrapped up warm with a thick black scarf, jacket, dark skirt and gloves. Holly watched her stop as she checked her phone then carried on walking. 'You think he'll kill again?' Bishop said.

'I doubt it. He will be reintegrated into society and live a somewhat non-productive life.' A pause. 'Unlike his mistress.'

'Misty.'

'That was her name?'

Bishop nodded.

'I like that,' Holly said. 'That's a good name. I wish I was called Misty.'

'Why?'

'Don't know.'

'You're not a Misty. Mist is vague. Transient. Something you're not. Do you want a sandwich?' He reached over and pulled out two meal-deal cartons, angled them to the side so he could read them in the street light.

'Tuna and sweetcorn or Ploughman's?'

'Tuna please.' She ripped open the packet. Hadn't realised how hungry she was. 'Thank you.'

'Glass of wine? I brought a cheeky Pinot Noir.'

'You're joking?'

He was of course.

'Next time,' she said and smiled. Stretched out her arms, pulled her knees up to her chest, her shoes discarded hours ago.

'Do you want kids, Bishop?'

131

'Kids? Eventually, yes. Don't know if I'd be a good dad at the moment. The hours, you know? The workload.'

'You could make time.'

'Maybe. I already have this image in my head of how I'll miss the school concerts, the music lessons, the recitals. Here's Dad – turned up five minutes too late again. Standing at the side of the hall and clapping and giving the kids a nod and a smile as if I'd seen them perform but the reality would be I've only just turned up.' A pause, 'That will probably be on my headstone: "Regrets missing his kids doing things. Worked too hard and didn't understand why." I don't know, Holly. Cases are gathering dust every month because of the cutbacks. Overtime's killing all of us.'

'You could be a house-dad.'

He smiled. 'Early retirement? Wouldn't mind that. Then I would get to hang with the little ones.'

'Plural?'

'Boy and a girl. One of each. Double trouble. What about you?'

'You have it so much easier than us. Our bastard biological clock.'

'Yeah – like you're *ninety*.'

'Shut up.' She felt herself laugh. 'I do want children though,' she said, and tucked her hair behind her ears. 'Part of me thinks I need them.'

She sensed he might ask her something else, but they sat in silence for a while, until Holly looked over because she could hear him tapping his fingers on the steering wheel.

'You'd make a great mum,' he said.

'Thank you. Wouldn't get much sleep. Having said that, I'm not exactly sleeping much now. Four o'clock is the new seven o'clock.'

'Have you ever listened to the shipping forecast?'

'The what?'

'Shipping forecast. It's the weather report on Radio Four.'

'No.'

'It sounds like they're talking in code, but it's very soothing. Like a background noise. Helps me sleep. You should try it when you go to bed.'

Bed.

She could do with her bed right now. Firm mattress, good pillow, light duvet. Bishop . . .

'What?' he said.

'Nothing.'

'Little Miss Secret.'

'No secrets with me.'

'No?'

'No.'

Holly opted for the first shift.

'If anything exciting happens, wake me,' he told her. 'If not, I'll see you at two a.m.'

He closed his eyes and sure enough within seconds his breath had deepened and she could tell he was asleep. She studied his face. Unshaven. Peaceful. They were spending their first night with each other. Not exactly how she had imagined it, but nevertheless it was happening.

She wondered if there was any more food, but the rear seat was empty apart from a woman's magazine. She picked it up and it fell open to the centre pages: *Ten signs that he's into you!* A couple of them had been circled and she wondered where he had picked it up from.

4. He looks you in the eye all the time. Even when

you're not necessarily talking, he'll be trying to make eye contact . . .

She smiled then put it down. Felt suddenly very cold, but at the same time she couldn't think of anywhere else she would rather be.

Holly woke at seven with her head on Bishop's shoulder. There was the whine of a siren in the distance and she wondered if that had woken her. She pushed away slightly, relieved to be awake but sad to be leaving her pillow.

'Morning, bed-head,' Bishop said.

'Morning.' She blinked the sleep from her eyes and realised there was a duvet over her body and legs.

'You were cold,' he said.

'Where did you get it from?'

'The boot. Essential for surveillance during winter.'

'What about you?'

'I kept warm thinking about the coffee we can have when our cover takes over.'

'Did I miss anything?'

'A few mangy dogs. A fox. Oh, and one jogger who was wearing bright pink, which I found vaguely offensive at six o'clock in the morning.'

The siren was getting closer. Bishop turned as a police car zoomed past them. And another. Tyres screeched to a halt. Police units exited their cars.

'What's going on?' asked Holly.

His phone buzzed. He picked it up. Answered:

'Bishop.'

Listened for a few seconds. Frowned and hung up. Was already opening his door and getting out when he said:

'We got a hit on Noah's phone. Someone turned it on and tried to use it.'

'Where?'

'About a hundred metres from Timothy Grent's flat.'

Twenty-four

The arrest had been quick.

Bishop and the team had banged on Timothy Grent's door and the man had opened it with very little protest. He had immediately been cautioned and taken away.

Holly and Bishop arrived at the booking desk as Grent was about to be processed by the desk sergeant. She was in her fifties, sour-looking and tough, but she managed a smile.

'One condom. One lighter and one packet of cigarettes. One wallet. Please check your credit cards and any monies and sign here.'

Timothy counted out the change.

'About three quid.'

'Three pounds it is then.'

The duty sergeant scooped everything into a plastic bag and put it in a tray behind her.

'I'm going to read you your rights. Are you familiar with them, Timothy?'

'Yes, I am.'

'You do not have to say anything. But, it may harm your defence if you do not mention when questioned something which you later rely on in court. Anything you do say may be given in evidence. All clear?'

'Yes.'

'Would you like the duty solicitor notified?'

'That would be nice. A friendly face.'

Grent turned as he noticed Holly and Bishop behind him. There was an air of confidence about him and Holly saw that Bishop had noticed it too and approached him warily. He held up the phone in an evidence bag.

'This is Noah Beasley's phone.'

'Who?'

'The boy who was murdered in the forest.'

'I already told you – I had nothing to do with that.'

'A friend of yours found it at the rear of your property.'

'What friend?'

As he asked the question officers brought in a young woman. Blonde hair in clumps, matted and dirty, ripped jeans.

'Get the fuck off me!' As she tried to pull away from three officers.

'Calm down, love! Calm down,' Vickery kept repeating, but it wasn't any good, she was like a wild cat.

Timothy Grent watched the woman quietly as two officers took him by the elbows and led him away.

'I'll be a while,' Bishop said as he followed Grent and the door closed behind him. Holly turned to the woman who had found the phone. She had calmed somewhat and the desk sergeant said:

'Is she coherent?'

'Barely,' said Vickery, and escorted her to the booking desk.

The duty sergeant began typing the woman's particulars into the computer.

'I've seen you before, love. Come a bit closer to the desk. Ta.' To Vickery: 'Lily-May Brown. Correct?'

'Yes.'

'Time of arrest please, Sergeant Vickery?'

'Seven eighteen a.m.'

'Offence was?'

'Stolen property.'

'It's not stolen,' Lily-May said.

'I want to make it clear you have been arrested on suspicion of handling stolen goods, that's all,' the desk sergeant said.

'I didn't handle it. I picked it up. I keep telling you!'

Vickery stepped closer.

'Empty your pockets, please.'

'Fuck off!'

The duty sergeant glanced at her then pulled away from the computer. 'If you want to behave like that, fine, but until you can be civilised you get to sit in a cell.'

'I want to get out of here.'

'That's not going to happen.'

Lily-May became solemn and shook her head. Set her jaw proudly.

'You can fuck off too then.'

'Put her in number seven,' said the duty sergeant. 'Let her calm down.'

They dragged her away, the kicking and screaming reaching new levels, and when the door clanged shut the silence was a relief.

'Who was that?' Holly asked.

'Lily-May Brown,' the desk sergeant said. 'I first saw her

about ten years ago. In those days she was a screwed-up kid with nowhere to go and no one to look out for her. Screwed-up kid becomes screwed-up adolescent. Becomes a woman. She was first arrested when she was turning tricks around King's Cross. Looks as though she's still on the game.'

She printed and handed over her arrest sheet. Twenty-three pages of solicitation and possession. An accompanying photo of a blonde woman. Fringe, long wavy hair. Sensual, but with an edge to her eyes. Holly felt a stab of pity. The woman today was dishevelled, gaunt-looking. Bordering on emaciated.

'Some of the vice squad used to call her Mary Shelley.'

'Why?'

'She kept falling over when she was drunk. Ended up getting staples in her head like Frankenstein. Used to set the metal detector off every time she came in. Then she got help. Went to a detox centre near Barking and got treatment. That was three or four years ago. I haven't seen her in here since. We'll turn off the lights and let her sleep.'

Holly frowned and sat on the seats by the wall. Read the rest of Lily-May's history. Saw the name of her attending physician in Barking and turned to the duty sergeant:

'Is there any chance I can talk to her?'

'What makes you think you can calm her down?'

Holly pulled out her phone and dialled.

'The Priory, Groveslands House, how can I direct your call?'

'Nick Gross please.'

'Putting you through.'

She was lucky: no answer machine, and she recognised his voice immediately.

'This is Nick.'

It had been many years since they had spoken but Holly was sure he would remember her. They had both spent three months at Broadmoor, looking after Category A prisoners during their final year assessments.

'Nick, it's Holly Wakefield.'

A quick pause and then:

'Holly, how are you?'

'Very well, thank you. It's been a long time I know, but I'm with a patient of yours at Hammersmith police station. A Lily-May Brown – you treated her at Barking detox.'

'Lily? Oh, God yes, is she okay?'

'What's her drug of choice?'

'Whatever she can get her hands on to be honest, but usually meth.'

'Anything I can do to make her more comfortable here?'

Vickery opened cell number seven and he and Holly entered.

'She's calmed down but she's still out of it,' he said as he closed the door. Holly was carrying a blanket and a cup of strong tea. Lily-May looked like a rag doll that had been thrown against the wall. Head slumped on one shoulder, clutching her handbag to her chest as if it were a broken heart. Holly knelt down in front of her.

'Lily-May?' Gently resting her hand on the woman's knee. 'My name is Holly Wakefield. Can you hear me? I spoke to Nick Gross. He says hello. Do you remember Nick?'

A slight nod. The woman stiffened and sat upright.

'Where am I?'

'At the police station.'

'Where?'

'Hammersmith police station.' Holly put the blanket

around her shoulders. 'Got you a cup of tea. Three sugars, the way you like it.'

Lily-May took a sip. 'Thank you.'

'I need to ask you some questions, is that all right, Lily-May?'

'Yes.' Another sip of tea.

'Are you on meth?'

A nod.

'Have you got any other drugs on you?'

She sighed and pulled out her pockets. A baggy containing brown powder.

Holly took it and passed it to Vickery who slipped it into an evidence bag. 'We're going to let you get cleaned up. Sleep it off for a while, okay?'

Lily-May dropped her handbag on the ground. Holly picked it up.

'Have you got any sharps in there?'

'What? No.'

'Lily-May. In your handbag, have you got any sharps in there?'

'Yes. I was going to go to the chemist to get my methadone and swap them over.'

'So they're used ones. In the bag?'

Holly opened it up and saw a few needles. Green sticks. Dirty ones.

'What about your jacket?'

'No. Fuck's sake. Can we get on with this?'

'Take your jacket off.'

'Jesus Christ.' She did and dropped it on the ground.

Holly picked it up, started to feel the hood, the pockets. Nice and gentle.

'How do you know Nick?' Lily-May asked.

'We studied together.'

'You're not a cop?'

'No. I'm a psychologist, a shrink.' Feeling the inside lining, around the zips. 'We've got something else in common as well.'

'Oh yeah.'

'We both went to foster homes.'

'Really?'

'I went to Blessed Home.'

'I don't know it.'

'Mine was in south-east London. St Christopher's Fellowship was yours.'

'How do you know that?'

'It was on your arrest sheet. How did they treat you there?'

Lily-May was about to cry, but she stopped it abruptly, rubbed her eyes angrily until they were red and puffy.

'I don't think they liked me much in the end.'

'You want to tell me about the phone the police officers found in your possession? The phone they took away from you when you were arrested.'

'It's not mine.'

'Who does it belong to, Lily-May?'

'Don't know. I found it.'

'You found it? Where?'

'Will you stop repeating everything I say please.' She rubbed a hand across her eyes. 'Fuck.'

'Where did you find the phone?'

'Round at Grent's place.'

'Timothy Grent?'

'Yes.'

'You know him?'

'I get stuff off him every now and then.'

'Drugs?'

'Yes, Jesus.'

'Is that why you were there this morning, to buy drugs?'

'No.'

'What were you doing there then?'

'Blow job. Forty quid. Did two in one hour. I earn more than you, I bet.'

'Yes, you do. You think you could show me exactly where you found this phone?'

'Maybe. I don't know.'

'Okay – we'll let you sleep it off and take you out there a bit later then, okay?' A pause. 'How long have you known Timothy— Ow! Fuck!' Holly ripped her hand out of the jacket pocket.

'What is it?' Vickery said.

'Just got jabbed,' Holly said. 'You've got sharps in here, Lily-May, that you didn't tell me about.'

'What?'

'In the pocket. Look. It came right through.'

'I thought they was all in my bag.'

Vickery banged on the door. It opened immediately

'Put the jacket down,' he said. 'You need to go and see the nurse.'

Holly got up, somewhat shaken.

'When I get back we're going to have another chat, Lily-May, okay?'

Lily-May rested her head on the wall and closed her eyes. When she opened them they were staring at Holly with a nonchalant defiance.

'Fine. I'll wait up. Put the kettle on.'

'Straight upstairs,' Vickery told her. 'The nurse's name is Jen.'

Holly headed through security and past the booking desk. Up the stairs. Took a left then a right.

'Jen?' she said as a woman appeared from the medical room. She was solid, hair up in a bun above her head. Gloves never off her hands. 'I got a sharp in my finger from one of the girls downstairs. Went through the glove and pierced the skin. No blood but . . . '

She held up her hand. Felt like a fool. There was no pain. Nothing.

'Do you know if she's HIV?'

'Don't know. She's a user though. Said she was off to the clinic to get clean needles.'

'Better get you down to the hospital. Get them to take some bloods and test you. Take some anti-HIV medication.'

Holly nodded. The chances were really slim, but nevertheless, HIV and Hep C could survive in syringes for six to eight weeks. She felt herself shaking, but tried to ignore it as she turned on her heel, exited the station and made her way to her car. She drove fast and left a message with Bishop, telling him what had happened. She would be at the hospital for at least two hours, but maybe she'd have a chance to talk to Lily-May when she got back.

The phone. All the answers could be on that phone.

Twenty-five

Holly had to wait three hours to give a blood sample, after which she had been given a shot, and a nurse had cleaned and gauzed her finger double-tight with a wrap-around plaster. The nurse had left the curtain open when he had left her cubicle and now she watched him talking to another nurse at the centre station. She looked between the two men, studying their expressions. A pantomime out of earshot, unable to tell what was going on. She suddenly felt exhausted. A crick in her neck from the night in the car and that general malaise of no sleep.

She signed a consent form to leave and was exiting the ward when she saw Bishop. He was leaning against a wall, eyes open but looking at nothing, as if he were holding the weight of the world upon his shoulders. He turned as if he somehow sensed her and gave her a thin smile.

'Hey, missy,' he said. 'Too early for a hot chocolate?'

The cafeteria was closed so they both got drinks from the corridor vending machine. Sat on plastic chairs and leaned over a Formica table.

'What's the verdict?'

'A couple of days for the results.'

He counted on his fingers. 'You'll be all clear by the weekend then.'

She smiled despite what she was feeling inside. Changed the subject.

'What did Timothy Grent say?'

'Said he knew nothing about the phone.'

'Do you believe him?'

He shrugged.

'He admitted to knowing Lily-May. Birds of a feather and all that. Hell of a coincidence though, isn't it?'

'Can you charge him?'

'Thompson's putting a case forward to the CPS. See if we pass the evidential test and meet their requirements. I don't think we will somehow, but we can hold him for another eighteen hours, so we live in hope.'

Bishop hesitated and for a second Holly thought he was going to add something, but he simply stared at her blankly, without comprehension.

'There's something else,' she said. 'What is it?'

'Getting a lot of heat on this one,' he said flatly as if he had no choice. 'But I'm trying to deflect it.'

'How?'

'By telling them what they want to hear.'

'And what is that?'

'That we'll catch this bastard by the end of the week.' He smiled and pushed the empty cup to one side. 'They said at the station you knew Lily-May?'

'Knew her primary care physician. We studied together and he told me what she was on. Told me how she liked her tea. She says she found the phone in the bushes. I believe her, she's not involved in this.'

'No.'

Holly took a moment, let the thought drop and sipped her drink again. Bishop's eyes were looking particularly blue today.

'What are you thinking?' he said.

She held up her finger. Tried to smile but felt like crying.

He took hold of her hand, pulled her bandaged finger to his lips and kissed it.

'You'll be fine.'

When she got back to her flat she almost kicked over a can of paint. She'd forgotten about the renovation work. Bill and Ted both said hello, apologised for the inconvenience and refused the offer of a coffee or tea, which Holly was grateful for.

The central heating was on but she still felt cold. She ached all over, felt dazed and sick, and wondered if it was simply lack of sleep or a side effect of the HIV meds. In the bedroom, she slipped on a sweatshirt, and found old recordings of the shipping forecast from the BBC on YouTube.

'And now it's time for the shipping forecast and reports from coastal stations. Here is the general synopsis ... '

She sat cross-legged on the bed, a bottle of prescription pills in front of her. Amitriptyline – they had been prescribed for Lee late last year. They were anti-psychotics but they were also given as a sleep aid. She dry-swallowed two of them and almost unconsciously curled up with a pillow. She thought of Noah, needles and finally found Bishop.

'I'll be fine,' she whispered as she thought of him kissing her hand. She closed her eyes and within minutes everything was beautiful and nothing hurt.

Twenty-six

'How are you feeling?' Holly said.

She had managed to get a few hours' sleep before she found herself back at the station and face to face with Lily-May again. The woman was curled up like a wanton child on the bed in the station cell. She sniffed and wiped her nose on her sleeve. Looked up at Holly with red eyes.

'Starting to feel clean and a little sober. Who knew it could be so good.' She tried to smile. Her teeth were straight but stained.

'You want to come with me,' Holly said, 'show me where you found the phone?'

By late afternoon they were standing with three police officers in the pouring rain at the rear of 35 Oldfield Road, Stoke Newington. Lily-May pointed out the bush where she had found the phone. It was about fifty feet from Timothy Grent's flat.

'And it was definitely these bushes?' Holly said.

Lily-May nodded. Tense and odd, and kept staring at the ground.

'My legs were cold. I remember that.'

The police cordoned off the site and one of them radioed in: 'I need a community police officer to check through the CCTV of this road – the last five days. Who's in?' A pause. 'Cheers.' He turned and nodded a thank you to Holly.

Holly took Lily-May's arm and led her away from the police. They walked through the drizzle, content with the silence while it lasted. Within ten minutes they were at a homeless shelter. They played stepping-stones with outstretched arms and ice-cold feet.

'It's a hard drug area this. Meth, heroin,' Lily-May said. 'Everybody sleeps here. You understand what I'm saying? Close your eyes and everything is free.' She stopped and lit up. Offered one to Holly, who declined.

'Why is this phone so important? Whose is it?'

'A young boy's. He was murdered and left in Epping Forest.'

Lily-May nodded sadly then contemplated her cigarette.

'I ran away from home when I was eleven. I often wonder if my mum knows I'm still alive. I didn't get kicked out. I left because I didn't want her to see me as I was.'

'And how were you?'

'Sleeping with men,' she said slowly, then laughed. It echoed where they were standing and sounded girly. 'I went onto the streets. Stayed there for six months and then managed to get a place. Lost it, got another one. Lost it, got another one. Like a merry-go-round, except not very merry. I haven't seen my mum for years.'

'And your dad?'

'I'm getting to know him better now. They separated when I was three. He took me shopping about a month ago,' Lily-May smiled. 'Bought me a dress. I think one day he wants to see me walk down the aisle.'

'Proud dad alert.'

'Yeah. Funny, isn't it?' She looked away for a moment not saying anything then shrugged. 'You want to buy me a cup of tea?'

They went to a greasy spoon café called Sonny's on Berwick Street, between a vape shop and a place called Underground that sold Rock 'n' Roll footwear.

It was nearly empty at that time and they took a seat near the window and ordered a pot for two. When it arrived, Holly poured.

'Milk?'

'Please. I'm not a heathen,' said Lily-May. She added three sugars and took a sip. 'Thank you.' Lit a cigarette and called out to the man behind the counter. 'Sonny, okay?' Waving the cigarette above her head like a tiny flag. The man nodded. Whatever. She took a drag. Long and toxic. Eyes never leaving Holly.

'What's going to happen to Timothy Grent?'

'I don't know yet. What do you know about him?'

'He's into some weird shit and he's dangerous, but I can't see him killing anyone. People change when they're high though, don't they?'

'How long have you known him?'

'Five, six years. He's good for a fix. Can I?'

'What?'

'The tattoo on your neck.'

Holly lifted her hair, revealed the blue and green butterfly tattoo floating upwards from under her collar to her hairline.

'You like?' Holly said.

Lily-May pulled up her own sleeves. A mix of black, white and polychrome, skulls, names and faces. 'Most of them are stupid. Boyfriend, boyfriend, girlfriend, boyfriend.' She pointed them out dismissively then rolled her sleeves down before taking another drag. She was struggling with something and when she turned to Holly her eyes were wet.

'What hospital do you work at?'

'Wetherington.'

'I've heard of that. Dangerous, isn't it?'

'We have Category A prisoners, but we look after other patients as well. Self-admissions. In that way it's a little like The Priory.'

'I used to fancy my Nick at the Priory,' Lily-May said. 'I think all the patients fancied him. Did you?'

'No. But we were good friends.'

'I can't afford The Priory now.'

She fell silent.

'I can get you into Wetherington for a couple of days,' said Holly.

'Really?'

'Sure.'

'Thank you. People think I'm amoral, immoral, every moral under the sun, but I'm not, am I? I've just made a few shitty choices, that's all.' She tapped her ash. 'What do you do when you're not being a shrink, Holly?'

'I go home and sleep.'

'Ever play drinking games?'

'When I was young.'

'You're still young. You should play Fuzzy-Duck.'

'Fuzzy-Duck, Fives, Chase the Ace. Shot glasses full of memories,' Holly said.

'Kissed my first boy when I was playing Fuzzy-Duck.'

'How old were you?'

'Eight. He was sixteen.' A pause. 'I was on vodka by then. Vodka and glue. Made me float up to the ceiling and never want to come down.'

'But you did.'

'Every time.' She took another sip of tea. There was a sadness in her eyes. Not bitterness. Just a stoic type of sadness. A hard-edged woman who had made her peace.

'I'm sorry,' she said.

'About what?'

'About that poor boy. What was his name?'

'Noah.'

'Noah?' Lily-May took a moment, tracing patterns in the spilled tea on the table with her fingers. 'How old was he?'

'Fourteen.'

'A baby.' She shook her head, eyes in shadow. 'There are some evil people out there.'

'Yes,' Holly said. 'There are.'

Twenty-seven

Noah Beasley was only five foot four and on the CCTV he looked even smaller.

A forlorn figure lugging his backpack over his right shoulder, switching it to his left then over to his right again every hundred feet or so. According to Darya, he had left their house at around four o'clock. There was no CCTV on the local roads but he was picked up on Station Road heading north at four fifteen as if he was heading towards his granny's house. By four forty-seven it had been dark and the cameras had lost him along Hemnall Street, but Eric and his team of night owls had managed to pick him up thirty minutes later, along Kendal Avenue walking south. He had basically done a wide loop of the area, effectively missing out his intended destination. From Kendal Avenue it had been a short walk, crossing between Bower Hill and Station Road, to Epping underground station which was on the Central line, and the TFL cameras had followed him from there. On the train he didn't sit with anyone, nobody approached him or made eye contact with him. He exited at Stratford Station then caught the 425 bus towards Ilford, got off at Stop F and walked the rest of the way towards Forest Gate Station. The latest leg of the journey had taken sixty-two minutes.

Now he walked north on the A114, which led directly to Wanstead Park. Holly paused the screen on the camera shot of the street. Cars parked either side. Businesses, pubs, the café she and Bishop had gone to, half a dozen bars, a gym. The last shot was from a council camera on the top of local offices. And following the road, Noah seemed to shrink into the trees until he vanished into the red darkness.

She stayed at the desk for the next few hours watching and re-watching the tape. Different people traversed the street, left work, entered the café, ran to the train station. Any one of them could have been the killer.

Her shoulders ached from sitting and she suddenly felt hungry. Wandered the catacomb of corridors and offices that seemed as silent as the grave. It was gone 7.00 p.m. and the police station had a skeleton staff fielding calls and working loose ends. A vending machine spat out a chocolate bar. She took a bite and felt herself gravitating towards the large window at the top of the stairs. A misty landscape stared at her. The church spire from St. Augustine's, an empty car park, and halos of yellow halogen.

Bishop was in the incident room when she returned and Holly had never seen him so angry.

Fists clenched, he paced like a caged animal. One cigarette accidentally crushed between his fingers – another on its way. Junior officers kept their ears open but their eyes down.

'There!'

'What?'

'Recognise her?'

Holly was watching CCTV of the person who had dropped the phone behind Grent's flat. After a few seconds she understood.

'That's the woman who walked past our car, with the thick scarf and hat and gloves . . .'

'Right by us.'

Shoulder length blonde hair, flat shoes, black skirt under the heavy black jacket, but her face was obscured by the scarf.

'Is that the best image we have of her?'

'There's only the one camera on that street corner and that's it.'

The CCTV followed the woman as she walked around the rear of Grent's street. Holly recognised the garages, the wheelie bins and the scraggly bushes. The woman became fuzzy the further she went away from the lens, but it was clear enough to see her arm shoot out and something drop from her hand as she passed.

'Start looking at rap sheets for women in their thirties or forties who have ever abducted or tried to abduct a boy,' Bishop said and sat on a desk.

'I can't see her carrying Noah's body two hundred metres on her shoulder through the forest.'

'Working with someone then? A boyfriend? Husband?'

Two killers working as a team? She was getting déjà vu about the Sickert brothers when an officer in plain clothes rushed in, breathing heavily.

'Sir? We've had a breakthrough on Noah's phone.'

They followed him through to a separate office, Bishop making the introductions as they went:

'Holly, this is Simon Hachette, he's a data analyst with our

IT division.' They shook hands as Hachette hovered at his desk, Noah's laptop and phone in front of him. He took his glasses off for a second and wiped them on his shirt.

'The motherboard on Noah's computer has been compromised, which basically means the laptop has been wiped clean by a virus that was sent from an unknown IP address. The same process was applied to the phone and it should have been wiped clean. No SIM card, no memory – no good, right? Wrong. Most people think things are deleted when you destroy your phone or SIM card but it's not, we managed to pick up all of Noah's text messages from the iCloud on the day he went missing. Everything the killer thought was deleted – it's still there. Specifically the directions he sent Noah for the pick-up point.'

'Jesus Christ,' said Bishop.

Hachette nodded. Took a breath.

'Are you familiar with the dark web, Holly?'

'A little.'

'We found a dummy link on Noah's phone that looked like a Facebook account but it wasn't, it was a link to the dark web. Now, you need special tools and log-ins to access these websites and it's kept hidden for a very specific reason – the darkest corners of this area of the web are used to engage in human trafficking and exchanging child pornography. A blog, a chat room, a forum – it can all be generated on the dark net, and when people are asked to join, they will have no idea it's not a public site. That's the case with this hoax Facebook site.'

He held up the phone and turned it on.

'See? And the profile of the person who set up this fake account is here.' He pulled up an image on the tiny screen and Holly found herself staring at a photo of a teenage girl.

Fifteen, sixteen. Mediterranean probably. Dark skinned with dark eyes and a cute smile. She was standing by herself on a beach, leaning over a café wall.

'So behind this photo is our killer?' said Holly.

'Yes,' said Hachette. 'And she calls herself Grace.'

'Grace,' Holly said under her breath. 'Can we access the killer's phone through this? A back door or something?'

'Not exactly,' Hachette said. 'It's a GSM mobile with SMS encryption, so he's covered his tracks, but he did make a mistake, albeit inadvertently. On the day Noah went missing, the iCloud added four new telephone numbers to Noah's contact list. Each contact number was given directions to another meeting place in Wanstead Park.'

'Other boys he was targeting?'

'It would appear that way.' He laid a topographical map on the table and Holly grabbed a pen and drew a cross at each of the coordinates as he read them out. Linked together they looked like a tight constellation.

'Did any of the other boys respond?' Holly asked.

'Only one and that was five weeks ago, but we have the coordinates of where they were supposed to meet.'

'Show us,' said Bishop, and Hachette pointed to the map.

It was late and this had been the longest day but they couldn't stop now.

'So if the boy did go and the killer is following the MO,' Holly said, 'there should be another body there.'

Twenty-eight

A flashlight played over grass and dense undergrowth revealing a wide brick wall.

The flint facing had fallen out leaving the core of the wall exposed to the elements. Ivy had taken over, sucked the moisture from the mortar, left it crumbling and covered with weeds.

'This way I think,' Holly said.

Bishop had parked on the narrow road and they had made their way through the thick brush and now entered an area of knee-high weeds and toppled bricks. Navigating over bumps in the earth, eyes finding the remains of a Victorian folly. The roof had collapsed, the lead was stripped away, the pale stone beaten to the ground. A sheet of hardboard covered up one of the windows at the front.

They picked their way through the open entrance, shattered glass crunched underfoot and it was strewn with debris and animal faeces. The walls had been sprayed with graffiti and vandalised and the air was damp and stale. A pair of crows erupted to their right, cawing loudly and flying overhead. Circling until they landed in the branches of a dead tree.

Holly took in the desolation, head bent against the drizzle that fell through the open roof. High above the back wall one window was still unbroken and on either side was a pair of stone gargoyles carved as winged angels with pointed tongues.

'There's nothing here,' Bishop said.

'No.'

'Maybe the boy backed out. Maybe he's sitting at home with Mum and Dad watching shit TV and eating a home-cooked meal.'

'Maybe. I don't like the gargoyles though. The angels. It makes me feel as though we're missing something.'

She shone her torch towards the remains of the roof. 'What do you think?'

He nodded, bent his knees and linked his hands together. Holly put a foot on his wrists and he levered her up until she could clamber onto the old frame. Fingers slipping on wet slate and splintered wood. A cold premonitory dread swept over her as she aimed her torch across the wooden slats, the rain a silver mist. Something shuffled quickly to her right, disappearing behind an old chimney stack.

'Bishop, can you lift me higher?'

A grunt and a noise from below as he repositioned his feet and she felt herself rise gently. She spun her torch – nothing but old bricks and broken planks. Movement to her right again and the thing – a pigeon? – suddenly appeared from behind the chimney and aimed towards her, glistening hideously. It was a black rat with red eyes and a thick tail that flapped from side to side like a heavy whip.

'Shit!' She put the torch in her left hand, felt across the roof with her right until she found a lump of brick. She aimed and threw in one fluid motion. It bounced over the rat but the noise made it stop. It didn't retreat though. It hunkered down and feasted its eyes on her.

'What is it?' Bishop said.

'A rat.'

'Anything else?'

'Nothing,' she said, so Bishop lowered her to the ground. She wiped her hands on her thighs, walked a few paces and sank to her knees. Slipped on latex gloves and started examining a pile of sodden rags. An old jacket, a pair of trousers, a pair of men's shoes: once polished and bright, now faded by time. Bishop came over and gave the items a cursory glance.

'Can I ask you something?' he said.

'Sure.'

'You never really talk about your brother.'

She felt herself shiver and wondered if it was just the cold.

'No. Our relationship is . . . fractured to say the least.'

'I'm sorry. Do you still see each other?'

'When we can.'

She stood up.

'What about you?' she asked him. 'You're an only child, aren't you?'

'Yes, although I wish I'd had a sister or brother. Someone to play with and spend time with. There were the kids on the street. Two brothers opposite. We'd play kick-a-brick in the winter, tennis in the summer.'

'Kick-a-brick?'

'We used to draw out goals with chalk on the road and kick a block of wood around because we couldn't afford a football.'

'And the tennis?'

'Street tennis with sticks from the footpath and an old

tennis ball we nicked from the dog at number seventy. We got pretty good.'

'At stealing tennis balls?'

'At tennis,' he smiled then shone his light to their right. 'Someone's lit a fire over there,' he said. A circle of burnt logs and carbonised beer cans. Bishop poked at them with his foot, picked up a stick and ran it through. Another beer can emerged from the ashes.

She walked past him, eyes lost in the twisting ivy and fallen bricks. There was a hollow in the wall behind. A bird had nested there last summer and had left an abandoned egg. Speckled dull blue, a thrush probably. She was about to call Bishop over when she slowly raised her head and pulled aside the curtain of ivy. More graffiti behind, but these were words she immediately recognised:

My life is not beautiful. It is not magical.
  But I can feel the love. Coming closer.
  Closer every day.

She felt herself go cold.

'Bishop! This is one of the poems from Noah's room. The one his mother didn't recognise.'

She felt him move silently to her side.

'Which means maybe he didn't write it,' he said.

She nodded and looked at him but he wasn't interested in the wall any more, wasn't reading the words. He was looking down, amongst the dead leaves, the ashes, the bracken and the old bricks. Something had broken through the ground. Like a flower searching for the sun.

It was a small twisted hand.

Twenty-nine

It was eerily quiet.

The road had been closed in both directions and Holly could see a fuzzy blur of blue flashing roof lights against the sky. There were four other cars and an ambulance parked bumper to bumper along the narrow road. Progress of the police had been hindered by the clusters of trees and bushes and there was talk of cutting some of them down, but the forensics crew had already gone ahead and set up lights and a tent. Angela Swan had prepped her team on the road. Given them a brief talk on the scene's forensic strategy and a reminder to make sure everything was stored in accordance with national and force protocols. Then they had all dispersed, their white suits shuffling like gloomy marshmallows through the long grass towards the body.

Holly followed them and found Bishop with the photographer.

Flash-flash

The glare of the bulb was making her see stars. She was silent for a long while.

'You okay?' Bishop asked her.

She waved off his question then said to the photographer: 'Get close-ups of every letter of the poem. Even where the paint ran.'

Angela's team had scraped the earth from the shallow grave and the remains of the boy lay inside. A sodden mess of old flesh and pale bone. The remains of white underpants, a semi-skeletal head resting on a rotten pillow. Angela looked up and took off her mask as they approached. Got up from her knees. Sweating despite the chill.

'So . . . our killer comes here with the body, digs the rather shallow grave and proceeds to bury him. The pillow and white underpants look similar, although I will need to compare them to the others in the lab.'

'Was he drugged?'

'Cards tricks I can do, DI Bishop, but a magician I am not. Toxicology will take at least twenty-four hours to confirm whether he was drugged or not. Fentanyl being the most obvious opioid. As for similarity in MO it will have to wait until I can get him back to my office. I need him out of situ ASAP before any more damage is done. The elements have taken their toll and the foxes and badgers have got to him. There are no larvae or bluebottles present, which would indicate they have already departed. This leads me to believe he has lain here recumbent for at least four weeks.'

'Age?'

'Not fully developed but he's very similar to the other victim. I'd put his age at fourteen again, possibly younger.'

'What about his right hand?' Holly asked. 'Is there anything inside?'

'Melissa, can you flash me, please?'

A marshmallow suit waved a torch in Angela's direction and the pathologist pulled a pair of tweezers from her kit.

'Holly?'

Holly knelt down and kept the boy's clenched fist steady. It felt glassy and slick as Angela pushed the tweezers inside and within a few seconds removed a silver pendant.

She passed it to Holly, who stood up and examined it. Another angel although in her mind there had never been any doubt. She held it up for Bishop to see. He blanched and turned to Angela.

'Anything else?' he said.

'I suggest a closed casket for this one.'

They left the forensics team and walked to a nest of trees and stood stock still. Watching the black skies overhead and listening to the howling wind, waiting for it to catch up with them again. Holly stared stoically ahead, lips set tight.

'The angel in his hand is Gabriel. An archangel who delivers his messages to people in dreams, acts as their guardian.'

Bishop turned slightly as he spoke, but she noticed he avoided her eyes.

'Christ, he's already got an insanity plea organised.'

'And I think I was wrong about him,' she said.

'What do you mean?'

'He doesn't care. This boy. The way he was half-buried. Dumped. It makes me think it was a rehearsal for Noah,' Holly said. 'I think this was his first kill. This was the one he didn't want to be found. That's why he attempted to bury the body. He strangled him but something wasn't right. The body didn't look how he wanted it to look. He couldn't present him how he wanted him to be seen. A picture, a painting, whatever image he has in his mind. His MO is developing. Shifting . . .'

'Two bodies – two angels,' said Bishop. 'We've got a lot of forensic possibilities here. We have to be patient.'

'We can't be patient, Bishop. There will be another one.'

'We don't know that yet.'

'There will be.'

Thirty

Back at her flat there was a staleness in the air and Holly opened the windows and straightened the pillows. She brushed her teeth, showered, then brushed her teeth again.

Angela had called and confirmed the same MO as Noah. Partial lividity in what was left of the distal portions of the limbs which meant he was lying still for a couple of days after he had been killed. Evidence of petechial haemorrhaging around both wrists and ankles, which would indicate restraints or handcuffs and strangulation occurred from the front, consistent again. No trace fibres, of course. They had no ID on the second body yet, but it would only be a matter of time. Another mother and father somewhere out there were going to have their lives ripped apart. Weeks of worry and phone calls and late nights and no sleep.

Outside her bedroom windows the London skyline seemed subdued and cowed by the relentless rain. She pulled the curtains shut and picked up the photo of Noah that Darya had given her and held it in both hands, gripping it like a bunch of flowers.

'Why would he kill you?' she whispered. 'You're lonely, aren't you, Mister Killer? Lonely. Inadequate. Lied to? Persecuted.' She tried to visualise him. 'Definitely persecuted. So how are you going to fix that? What can you do to get your power back? That wonderful feeling of fullness. Of love. Do you love? Can you? Possibly. Perhaps yourself. You'll be narcissistic, judging by the way Noah's body was cared for after he was dead. That's not normal for a killer. You're a dichotomy. Angry, aggressive, but there's another side to you as well. The fantasy of having a real connection with him? A real relationship? But when Noah would have come face to face with you, Noah would have resisted, and the fantasy would have collapsed. All he would have had in front of him was a frightened little boy. He had had no choice but to kill

'Once you had made that decision then there was no going back. Hours spent on Twitter, Facebook, Gumtree, Snapchat. You name it, you went on there.' Holly had seen it so many times before.

'Who are you chatting to on your computer, Sarah?'

'A friend, Mum.'

'On Facebook?'

'Yes, Mum.'

'Are you sure they're who they say they are?'

'Jesus, Mum. Give me a break!'

And little Sarah leaves for a date and is found the next morning face down in a river.

Choosing your victim at night after work? Couldn't chance doing it at the office. And you do work, don't you? Maybe not totally fulfilling, but it keeps you going. Keeps the wolf from the door and allows you the freedom to do what you really want to do, which is what? Fantasise. So you scroll through social media. Narrow it down from dozens and dozens of children. And then all of a sudden there he is. He matches everything you want. He's perfect for you. Little unsuspecting boy.

Her brow furrowed and she found herself staring at the floor. When she looked up again she took a deep breath and held it. Counted the seconds. Let it out. Close your eyes, Holly. Take a trip. With a final breath she stepped into the killer's shoes.

I make contact with you through Facebook. Nice and easy, zero protection and I can be anyone I want to be. I send out a few feelers. I'm new on here and need some friends. Any takers? A few respond. How wonderful! I weed out the ones I don't want. The ones that aren't quite right. Too old, too smart, not the right look. And the look is important. I cancel over a dozen friend requests or block them, but here's one. He replied to me. Now I have his attention and he has mine. He's polite, cordial, but funny as well. He looks so beautiful in his profile – as do I. For my profile I use a photo of the young European girl with olive skin, dark hair and dark eyes. I screenshot it from an online Eurocamp holiday website. It's perfect. I call myself Grace and I can almost hear her soft accent as I type. I know he likes girls because of what he posts but he's so shy. Maybe I can help him. How perfect that I can be his guide.

At first he takes his time getting back to me, but after a week we're messaging nearly every day and if he's late I ask have I upset him? Is he angry with me? Apply the guilt with a light feather. He'll respond faster if I'm needy. *Of course I'm not angry with you, Grace,* he replies. *Had to do my homework first.* We text about homework and I help him with his. Forming a bond. And then we move on to other subjects such as activities at school and his parents. He doesn't get on too well with his dad and I reciprocate. Same here. My dad used to beat me but then my mum and I managed to get away from the house. It was so daring. A midnight escape in a hire car. My mum is so smart and brilliant. But let's change subjects – let's talk about fun stuff.

I tell him I did something goofy the other day and show him a screenshot of me in a dress with my bra showing. He says I look beautiful and sends a kiss. I say I feel embarrassed now, but he says not to worry and then the next day he sends me a photo of himself without his top on. I stare at the screen for minutes that seem like hours. *Wow*, I put. *Wow*. He lets me into a secret – he's been looking for someone like me all his life. The other girls at his school are full of themselves and dull, apart from his sister, he says. I get anxious at this, I didn't realise he had a sister. How old is she? Eleven and her name is Ruby. Eleven and a girl. She'll be smart and savvy. A red flag. I tell him that he must never let her know that we communicate. We're special friends – the two of us. His sister must never know. It has to be our secret, okay?

I don't understand. My sister and I are really close. We share everything.

Noah, please. I really like you but . . .

I go off-grid for an hour then re-surface. I tell him that years ago, before my mother and I escaped from my abusive father, I told my sister a secret and she betrayed me. I haven't seen her since. He feels sorry for me and says that Ruby would never do that. I tell him I trust him but please don't tell her about us, okay? I'm tempted to end it now. This is dangerous. I've invested too much time and he's perfect but—

Don't worry, I won't tell her, he says.

I say thank you so much and then don't return his messages for two days and he leaves me a dozen more. Now he's worried that he's upset me. I say no. I've been thinking about things. *What things?* Things that . . . well, I find this really hard but – okay I have to put it out there. My mum said I should always be honest with my feelings. *Okay, he says. What?* Then I do it. I tell him I think I love him. I'm worried, what work I have put into this could well be undone, but within one minute I needn't have. He sends me a cute message saying *I think I love you too.* And he sends me the sweetest poem. Young and awkward but so full of love.

'How many miles. How many feet. How many hearts with their tremulous beat . . .'

That's so beautiful, Noah. Thank you!

I send emoticons of beating hearts and flowers. Rainbows and dancing girls. I've been doing this for over three months, it's been gradual but I'm learning as I go. I've already lost three other boys. Their accounts were all closed down and I worried for a while that maybe their parents or the police had been notified about me, but I hear nothing after a month so I know I'm safe. Now it's time to play the ace. I'm really doing this, aren't I?

My fantasy is becoming real.

I send Noah a few more photos of me – taken from another website that I have access to – they're blurry but it's enough for him to believe they're me. Things are going well and then I hit Noah with the bombshell. I tell him I have to stop communicating with him. Why? he asks. I can feel the sudden uncertainty of his fragile life. I have to go because my father has found out where we live again and is trying to squirm his

170

way back into our lives. He beats me and he said he will take my computer away from me. I'm so sorry, Noah. I'll never see you again. I'm so sorry. Lots of crying face emoticons come my way. *Please don't go we have such a great connection. We love each other* – and then the most beautiful clanger – *I've never felt like this before, he says.* Me too, I lie. He is distraught – I can feel it in his messages. It's so sad. *Where are you going?* he asks. Overseas I say. Probably Spain, where my mum is from, that's why I've got brown eyes. *Lovely brown eyes,* he says. Thank you. Hold on, I've had an idea, Noah. Perhaps we could meet? OMG OMG! Noah – what do you think?

Okay! One day after school? Come and meet me?

No, I can't do that. We'll have to be careful because of my dad. Nobody else must know. You mustn't tell anyone, Noah. Promise? He promises again and I feel so in control. He is totally mine now.

So we agree to meet. It has to be on my terms though because of my dad but he's okay with that. He's already told me about his granny's house so I tell him he should tell his mum and dad he's going to stay with Granny for a few days over half-term, but instead you can come and stay with me and Mum for a SLEEPOVER! – and then you can go to Gran's and nobody will ever know. *Okay – that sounds like a good idea.* It does, doesn't it, I say. Where shall we meet though?

Holly opened her eyes. He can't go to the forest as he is, so he has to get someone else to drive to the forest. Pretending to be Grace's mother. Noah feels safe with women. He loves his mum and she loves him. So he enlists the help of this woman on the CCTV. She's medium height and blonde. A wife or a girlfriend? Someone who will be complicit and who you can have complete control over. But who? A sister? A mother?

Girlfriend? – it has to be. So this woman will drive and perhaps the man is on the back seat of the car or in the forest already waiting. Noah stands no chance against two adults. Holly closed her eyes again.

It's okay, Noah, I say, I can get my mum to pick you up – she's like my best friend.

Really?

Yes. She's so gorgeous as well, and she's so funny. I pause. Let the silence speak. I've told her about you, Noah.

You have?

Yes. I showed her your photos as well. She thinks you're amazing. *Really?* Yep. She thinks you're very handsome. This would be like our first proper date. I laugh and say, I've got nothing to wear. He laughs and says:

Don't worry. No matter what you wear, you'll look beautiful.

Ahhh, you're so sweet, Noah. Thank you, my love. I can feel him blushing. Okay, I'll text you the directions on the Monday after you break up from school. We can meet up that night. Is that okay?

Okay.

Follow the directions and I'll see you soon. Mum and I are super excited! Love you!

Love you too, Grace.

I press enter on the keyboard. A breath. I've done it now and I have to go through everything again in my head. No mistakes.

So I suggest a route into the forest. *The forest?* I love it there, Noah. It's so romantic! Bus from home. The underground, then change to the overground and get off at Forest Gate, then the short walk into Wanstead Park where there is no CCTV.

Monday arrives and I'm nervous at work. Try to keep my

cool, try to be as normal as possible. Stop trying to be extra funny and extra nice because people will pick up on it. You must stay as you are. After lunch I text him directions. Keep him satiated with promises of dreamy fun. He texts me to say he's on his way.

My heart is in my mouth. What am I doing? I'm texting my partner too. She's as calm as I am. I tell her to keep to the speed limits. Don't get a ticket now. She promises she won't. Pulling into the entrance of Wanstead Park. Travelling down the curving roads. She texts me every minute. Tells me her hands are sweating. She's past The Glade and on to the side road. She turns off the ignition and waits. And then she lets me know she sees him walking along the forest road behind her. Noah. There he is, carrying his rucksack over his shoulder like it weighs a ton, face set in grim determination. Off on an adventure, aren't you, Noah? She's watching him in the rear-view mirror coming closer. There are no cars here this time of night. I chose this spot well. She follows my instructions, turns the engine on so he can see the rear lights and knows it's her. Noah starts to run. Stops and takes a breather. Checks his phone. Coming closer now. This is the last chance to stop this, she tells me, but I tell her no, because the animal inside doesn't want to go away. She understands and plays the role perfectly, winds down the window. 'Noah?'

He turns. Startled bright green eyes.

'Hello, Noah, I'm Grace's mother.' A delicious smile. Disappointment on his face like a flat balloon.

She's not here?

No – she's got a half-term assignment to finish tonight. You are both very smart, you know that, Noah? Tentative. She can't grab him, there's no one here but if he runs there's no way she can catch him in the forest. She has to get him into the car. Get in, Noah. He's still hesitant.

Where are you from? he asks. Where am I from? Madrid. In Spain. He nods as if she has passed the test. Still hovering though, he looks in the rear seat as if Grace might be there. Get in, you little shit! He looks about him once more as if weighing the odds and then he leans in to the open window and smiles. A little cheeky. *Grace said you were beautiful.* Her heart melts.

Come on. Get in. We're having beans on toast for tea.

He opens the rear door and sits inside the car. She drives him home. A little light chat. She asks him questions that she already knows the answers to. He laughs like a bell. He keeps looking at the trees as we drive by. *Is it much further?* No. Nearly there.

My phone suddenly beeps. Noah is texting me. Letting me know he's on his way. My heart is in my throat and twenty minutes later I hear the purr of the car as it pulls into the driveway. The tall bushes cover everything and there's no one on the street. She gets out, helps Noah with his bag – God this is heavy I hear her say – what have you got in here? She laughs. He laughs with her. I can hear them both from the living room. I mustn't come out until the front door is closed and then I hear it open. Hear the patter of his little feet on the wooden floors.

'*Grace, it's me, Noah. I'm here,*' he says.

The silence that follows and I feel . . . what do I feel? Anger. Sorrow. Perhaps nothing. I feel nothing. Just that I must now complete this journey. I walk into the hallway. Noah still lingers at the bottom of the stairs, excitement plastered all over his little face, sticky hands touching the banister.

He turns and stares at me. A heady mix of eagerness and confusion.

Who are you? Where's Grace?

I close the front door. Click the lock. Noah drops his backpack, the stark panic is gone, but there is fear now – blind, nameless fear, like that of an animal run to the ground. And then I tell him the truth.

'It's just you and me, little one. Just you and me.'

Holly reared up from the bed with a deep wrenching breath. The noise out of her mouth from some dark place within, more animal than human. She looked at the crumpled photo of Noah still gripped in her hands and realised there were tears rolling down her cheeks.

Thirty-one

Holly couldn't sleep.

She couldn't get the image of Noah out of her head and at 1.30 a.m. was sitting upright in bed debating whether to turn the television on or lie down again and count dead bodies until she fell asleep.

She did neither. She stretched and got up as if it was morning and put the kettle on and made herself a coffee. Noah's face was still watching her from above the fireplace in the living room and seemed more beautiful in the witching hours. She wondered how soon the other boy would be identified and accompany Noah on the wall.

She was almost half-dressed before she realised what she was about to do. Checked outside and saw the rain was staying away but she knew it would be hideously cold. Jogging bottoms, T-shirt, sweatshirt, hoody, jacket and scarf. She found her car keys and headed for the door.

Exited the lift on the ground floor, the smell of turps hitting her as she manoeuvred around the drop cloth and tins of paint. Outside, a fast walk to her car. Beep-beep with the alarm and she clambered inside. Whacked the air conditioner on, maxed it to the red and let the air blow over the windscreen and bounce off her hair. Cold as ice, but after a minute it was a sauna and the windscreen was clean and toasty. She pulled out and started the drive. No traffic for the first five minutes and it was as if she were driving through the metropolis after a zombie apocalypse.

It only took her fifty-five minutes to get to the forest. She followed the route that Bishop had taken, past Greyson's dog shelter, and there it was – The Glade – the signpost looking eerily hand-drawn in her headlights. Following the path until she felt rather than knew she had arrived.

She parked and turned the engine off. Opened the door, got out and flipped on her torch. Dark trees, deeper shadows. Tiny whirring noises. Moths' wings against a night light.

She stepped off the road and into the forest. Slowly now, careful not to make too much noise, although she didn't know why. More than once she caught sight of a trembling branch in the beam of her torch as a tiny four-footed local found her presence unwelcome. After ten minutes – there it was: the police tape. A bright yellow game of cat's cradle.

Ducking underneath. Flashes of silver birch, elm and trunks of corrugated oak and then, after another few minutes, an oval zigzag of tiny red flags where the body had lain.

What exactly was she looking for? Greyson the dog-walker had said it was the strangest thing. Yes, she wouldn't disagree with that – a child crunched up on his side with a pillow under his head and an angel pendant clutched in his hand. There was no way Greyson would have seen the pendant but that was what Holly kept coming back to, and the second body was found beneath stone angels at the folly. Come on, throw me a bone. Give me a sign. A killer with a God complex? The voices told me to do it? She started to search the surrounding trees. Examining the trunks, looking under fallen branches and hollowed logs. A cross, pentagrams carved into the wood of the thick trees. Another angel hanging from a branch. Anything other than what was here. Just an empty space where Noah had been and endless trees that disappeared when her torch passed them by.

After half an hour of searching she had come up with nothing and she was getting cold. Maybe she was wrong about the torch? Maybe he had used one. A pause. No. he wouldn't have. Too much of a risk and this killer wasn't into risks. In which case – how dark would it have been that night without a torch? Only one way to find out. She turned off her own.

The instant blindness was paralysing. Something flittered past her face, surprised her. A bat? Zigzagging as moths and insects buzzed close by. She felt like a canary in a coal mine. Vulnerable and out of her natural habitat. She found a Mars Bar in her jacket pocket, sat on her haunches with her back against a tree and devoured it. Her eyes were becoming accustomed as she continued to stare at the dark that would only fade when the sun began to rise. It was beginning to look beautiful. So beautiful that it might be something from a dream.

Another minute passed and then she heard it. The snap of a twig. Startlingly loud, and she knew immediately it was human. No soft-padded badger or nimble fox. A curious local wanting to come out and scare themselves shitless by standing where the body had been found? A journalist? Or the killer? She stayed very still. Nothing was cold any more and her heart was beating faster. She forced herself to breathe slowly. Waited. Another snap, not as loud as the first, but closer and directly behind.

Five seconds of silence.

Snap.

Less than ten feet away. If it was the killer, she had surprise on her side. She was hidden behind the trunk of the tree. There was no way he could see her. What to do? Wait until he passes and then jump him? No. Stupid idea, although she was already bunching her fists. Shush-shush on the leaves and she felt him drift past on her left. She could barely make out his silhouette. He was large and bulky, dressed all in black, a hood covering his head.

The figure made it to the little red flags and it was there that he crouched. She was directly behind him as he turned his head slowly from side to side, craned his neck up to one of the trees, walked forward and touched the bark. Rubbed it slightly. Holly swallowed hard. Hadn't realised she had been holding her breath. Then as if hearing her swallow, he shifted and turned around to face her. His body immediately stiffened, then crouched as if ready to fight. He seemed to be staring directly at her. But there was no way he could see her. Neither of them moved. What the hell was he doing?

It's him, thought Holly. I know it's him.

Fuck it.

She turned on her torch and shone it in his eyes.

Thirty-two

When the light hit him, the figure shouted and reared away.

He stumbled backwards through the undergrowth, fell to his knees, picked himself up and started to run. Strobe-like flashes in her torch light – black trousers, trainers, and a black hoody under a thick black jacket. He twisted and turned, fell again and it was then that Holly caught up with him and landed on his back.

About one month ago she had started MMA training. After fighting Wilfred Sickert to the death, she still felt unprepared for another encounter. Her instructor, Anthony Kleeman, an Australian stick-fighter, had told her in her first lesson: 'In a fight you never have enough time. You're in a pub drinking and things kick off. You put your glass down to punch some-one. That someone has already smashed their glass in your face. That's how fast things are in real life.'

Hands fighting for a grip on his jacket that felt like slippery canvas under her fingers. Her torch was knocked from her hands and went out, and in the darkness he seemed bigger and stronger. He rolled away and suddenly all advantage was lost.

But instead of attacking her, he picked himself up and started to run again. She lashed out with her left hand, grabbed his ankle, felt the trousers shift and then for a split second felt his flesh, warm and clammy. He pulled his leg free, kicked out at her, his foot catching her on the temple. Her head felt numb and she went deaf. And then he was up and away like a gazelle.

She dragged herself after him, her hunter's instinct in full play. The wet earth spitting upwards against her tired feet with every step. She could hear him moving fast, hear branches snapping as he ploughed ahead. Massive trees, a slow-moving river on the left. A gorse bush like shards of glass. She fought against it, fell over, picked herself up and fought her way free. How the hell could he move so fast? Her left shin was starting to ache. She had to be careful – it was only just healing and she didn't want to break it again.

I'm fucked, she thought. I couldn't beat a five-year-old in an egg-and-spoon race. The ground was now marshy and wet underfoot, but then she heard the sound of footsteps sprinting on hard ground. Maddeningly fast, like castanets. He must have made it to the road. She was still struggling to get her bearings when she heard the sound of a car ignition turning over. A gentle purr that slowly dissolved and flattened out into a distant buzz.

She pushed through the disappearing treeline until she felt tarmac under her feet. Finally caught her breath – leaned against a tree that was slimy and dank with moss and wiped a hand across her face. She felt in her pocket for her phone but it wasn't there. Must have dropped out during the fight. She checked the other pocket. The jangle of car keys. Thank Christ for that. Slowly she recovered and began to follow the path through the forest. She might have lost him and taken a kick to the head, but she held her left hand high above her head as she walked.

She had touched him.

She had his DNA all over her.

It took ten minutes to find her phone and another ten to get back to her car.

Once there she rummaged in the boot, found a plastic shopping bag, placed it over her left hand and tightened it to her wrist with a hair band from the glove box. She then drove on to the main road and exited the forest. She needed to get forensics to take samples from her left hand and fingernails as soon as possible. She was twenty minutes from the police station but decided to go somewhere closer.

Bishop opened his front door wearing blue track pants and a white waffle sweatshirt; his face was colourless in the shadows.

'Jesus Christ,' he said. 'What the hell have you been doing?'

She smiled somewhat pathetically and held up her plastic-bag hand as if it were a balloon without a string.

He sat her down in the living room and she filled him in on what had happened.

He only interrupted once to ask if she wanted another drink – he had made them a hot chocolate when she had first come into the kitchen. Then he had cleaned the cut above her left eye and put a plaster on it. Brought out a bag of frozen peas, wrapped it in a damp tea towel and rested it on her bare shin.

'Thank you,' she said, feeling the cold burn all too quickly.

'If it was the killer, why would he go back? Relive the fantasy?'

'I don't think so.' She leaned up against the sofa, eyes closed, fighting a headache. 'He was touching the trees.'

'Touching them?'

'I couldn't see very well. And when I shone my torch at him he shouted and turned away – that was when I chased him. He could run fast. I don't know how he did it. The only reason I managed to catch up with him was because he tripped. And then when he got away the second time I didn't stand a chance.'

'Did you get a look at him at all?'

'He was wearing a hoody, maybe a balaclava. I thought it was a gas mask to start with. I think he wears glasses. There was a reflection from the torch light.'

'Jesus Christ, Holly.'

'I know, I'm an idiot. But if it was him, he was there for a very specific reason. He either left something behind and was looking for it, or he wanted to add something else to the crime scene. Something to confuse us.'

The packet of peas had melted on her leg and she rose stiffly to her feet. Bishop took them from her but stayed his ground.

'Why didn't you tell me where you were going? What the hell were you thinking?'

'It was a spur-of-the-moment thing.'

'You could have been killed.' Voice no higher than a whisper. 'I told you I'd take care of you.'

'I don't need anyone to take care of me.' She shrugged, not really caring to analyse herself too deeply. 'I don't—'

'I'm not saying that, Holly. I'm saying *I* wouldn't have gone out there alone. I always have back-up. Always, and you should start to think like that too.'

She felt her cheeks flush. Staring at him.

'Fine. Next time I want to go out to a forest, I'll call you up at one o'clock in the morning.'

'Do it. I'll be here.'

'All right, I will.'

'I look forward to it.'

'So do I,' she said. She held her breath. Their faces were inches apart now. His head shifted slightly. Angled closer to her and the colour had returned to his face. She had forgotten how handsome he was. Square jaw, clear eyes, soft lips. She felt herself moving forwards ... lips parting—

A knock at the door.

Startled them both. He shrugged backwards, more involuntarily than anything.

'Anton,' he said.

'Who the hell is Anton?'

'Forensics.'

And whatever had happened between them had now passed.

Anton refused a drink. Removed the plastic bag from Holly's hand and swabbed and cleaned her fingers and took samples from under her nails.

'How long for results?' Bishop asked.

'Twenty-four to seventy-two hours.' Then Anton asked Holly to remove her sweater and bagged it before he left. Bishop gave her one of his sweatshirts and made more hot chocolate. She found herself on his sofa, a cushion under her head. He was in the kitchen tidying up and she could hear the occasional clink of glasses or cutlery. It was a nicely decorated living room, a few old paintings at either end and the only photo was on the far wall. A black-and-white shot of a blonde woman.

'That's Sarah,' he said.

He had entered without her noticing.

'She looks very beautiful.'

'She was.'

'Who told you when she was killed?' Holly said.

Bishop wasn't melancholic when he spoke, just stayed very matter-of-fact:

'The company padre – Cassidy Little was his name. He came into the mess. We were all awake anyway. News of an IED spreads fast through the ranks. A lot of the time it was goats or dogs, sometimes kids from nomad tribes. No, this time he came in and said: "Bishop, got some shit news for you. You want counselling?" I thought it was a joke. We'd always joke with each other over there. Anything to break up the monotony and the heat. "Nah, I'm good thanks, Sarge, lay it on with a shovel." And he did. "Sarah, your fiancée, is dead. She's the one that got caught by the IED." There's certain things you don't joke about.'

'What did you do?'

'I think I sat very still for about five minutes. Maybe more. Everybody left me alone. Don't know. Can't remember what went through my head, but I'm sure it wasn't rainbows and buttercups.'

She checked her watch, then said: 'I should go home.'

'Let me drive you.'

'No, it's fine. I need—'

'I'll follow you then. To be on the safe side.'

She agreed and she watched his car in her rear-view mirror for the next thirty minutes until she pulled over at her block. He offered to walk her up, but she declined. Waved goodbye and immediately showered when she got inside her flat. Hot and soapy, washing out the leaves and twigs in her hair. It made her head sting when the soap hit the graze above her eye and she pulled the plaster off.

Her head hurt like hell so she took some pills with the leftovers of a bottle of red wine and was walking to the bedroom when she realised she had put on Bishop's sweatshirt again. She didn't want to wash it. As she lay on the bed her eyes closed and she drifted off to sleep with the scent of Bishop filling her dreams.

Thirty-three

It was a grey cloudy afternoon, but the sun was higher and the morning mist had already evaporated.

A phone call from the hospital – a simple message to say she was all clear and no HIV or Hep C antibodies had been detected. She thanked them and hung up. Took a second, inwardly both excited and relieved. She had eaten lunch and was playing with the idea of opening another bottle of wine. For some reason her body was gravitating towards a drink. What would Dr Breaker say? She pulled out two bottles from the rack in the kitchen – a Malbec and a Château Musar. She opted for the Malbec.

There was still no face, no name, but she was getting a feel for him. She was starting to understand how much this meant to him and how careful he had been. This killer is not irrational. He knows that if he ever gets caught for this he will lose everything and will be going away for life. Thirty, forty, fifty years in a twelve-by-twelve cell and it wouldn't be HMP Berwyn. Oh, no. At Berwyn, the governor allows you to walk and talk with the other inmates, a bit of gym of a morning, a light breakfast, then an afternoon on your own laptop, TV and phone in your en suite room. Always wanted to be an actor? We've got drama classes for you three times a week. And what can you do on a rainy Wednesday afternoon when even the all-weather football pitches can't entice? I know, go and sit in the assembly rooms or the cafeteria, order a decaf cappuccino with chocolate sprinkles, and listen to people from the outside world come in and give talks about making the best of yourself and how you can change the world for a nicer place once you have left Her Majesty's Pleasure.

Oh no, it wouldn't be Berwyn for you.

It would be Belmarsh, Full Sutton or Woodhill. The type of prison where you would shiver at night as you heard the echoing howls from the lucky ones who had bargained for their spice, and you would look forward to spending time in solitary to avoid being raped in the showers every week. You would never survive your term. No way. News would spread about your crime and the other inmates would stare at you with blood-red eyes and salivating mouths. Timothy Grent was right: kid-killers don't fare too well behind bars. They are the most detested of them all, and for obvious reasons. It would be like shoving an antelope with a busted leg into the eyeline of a cackle of hyenas. Counting the moments until you would walk into their path and give them the opportunity to bite you, claw you, suffocate or kill you.

That's why this man was being especially clever.

He had everything to gain but everything to lose.

She poured herself a glass. Swirled it and took a sniff. Heady and rich. Followed her feet into the living room where she let her body recline on the sofa.

He would have planned for everything, but he couldn't

have planned for her. There's no way he could have known she would visit the crime scene. So he had waited for the body to be cleared and the police presence to have reduced, which meant he had probably visited the forest since the kill. He will be one of the joggers, a birdwatcher, a walker, waving at the police, asking what's going on. 'We're packing up tomorrow, sir. You can enjoy the forest again,' and that's when he had returned.

If he had approached from the south, he would have seen her car, which meant he must have approached from the north. So there was another clue. He's more likely from that side of the woods, from that side of London. Which narrows down where he lives. More or less halves the houses where both boys will have taken their last breaths. North London towns: Harlow, Bishop's Stortford, Theydon Bois, Chelmsford to the east. Dozens and dozens of them, but we're getting closer.

But now he knows someone is on to him. He knows I wasn't a cop, otherwise I would have shouted: Police! Stop! I didn't work for the Forestry Commission, but he doesn't know that. Let's turn that thought on its head. When I saw him I thought he could have been the press, a local wanting a quick fix or the killer. Perhaps he thought the same about me? Minus the killer bit, obviously. Perhaps he thought I was a reporter trying to get a scoop?

When I startled him he recovered so well. Like Bishop said, he didn't panic, but now he would definitely be in fear. I don't care how much self-control he has. Fight or flight has no friends. He had played it safe but this would have jolted him. Sweaty palms at midnight. How would he cope with this new pressure? More drinking? Paranoia every time he gets in the car. Even worse when he gets home after work. Driving slowly, looking for the cars by the kerb that shouldn't be there. The police cars. They're on to you. Should have had a better plan. How long before the calm takes over again? A day? A week? He had taken Noah over a week ago, so perhaps he had relaxed his grip when he came back to the forest? By then he thought he had got away with it. Wow, I actually did it. No one came knocking at the door. No flashing lights outside and gravelly voiced cops asking questions. But then I showed up and now you are sitting at home. Sitting at home shitting yourself, going over everything in your mind.

Another mouthful of wine.

The angel pendant. The pillow. She tried to get a better picture in her head although she already knew what was coming. Another boy would go missing soon, and this time the killer would be even more careful. In one sense, she had forced his hand.

She had been so close. She had touched him, for God's sake.

And as she finished her wine and got ready for the day, she wondered if the killer was thinking of her.

He was.

Thirty-four

The man sat at the kitchen table.

He had slept badly, woken at nine, slept again and now sat with his lunch uneaten in front of him. He had lined up the knife and fork so they were perpendicular to the salt and pepper. He had re-folded his napkin until it was the perfect triangle but he could still not eat. He was constantly reliving the early hours of the morning in his head.

He had called work and apologised for his absence. Had told them he had a horrible cold, might even be the flu, and was stuck in bed. They totally understood – there was something going round at the moment. Take the day off, another if you need to – we can cover until you feel better. He thanked them with a sniffle and a fake cough, hung up and poured himself a fresh glass of wine. A Château Musar.

When he had returned home from the forest this morning, he had immediately wanted to get into the safety of his bedroom and shower, but good sense had prevailed, and he had stood on the rear porch of his house for twenty minutes before going inside. Using his phone torch he had painstakingly removed every leaf, twig and scrap of forest from his clothing. He had then stripped naked and bundled his clothes into a black bin liner from the shed. He would burn it in the garden later today. Only then had he deemed it safe to go inside. Any residual leaves left from his trip would be blown from the porch during the night to mix with the leaves in his own garden and make them nearly impossible to separate and therefore identify. He was being fastidious. Had to be. He knew that one scrap of Wanstead Park on his body would link him to the forest and from there it would be a downhill journey.

Who was she?

Her hair had been pulled into a ponytail. He remembered that. She had been wearing a scarf and he hadn't seen her face, but he had kicked her in the head. I wonder if I left a mark? A cut. Blood. Did my trainers leave an imprint on her skin? Tread marks. Should I get rid of them? Do it at night. Too early to start a fire outside now. Don't want the neighbours getting suspicious. Never do anything to warrant interest.

He would have to buy the newspapers today. Listen to the radio and watch the television. *Appeals for the mysterious figure nearly caught at the crime scene.* Yesterday he had returned to the forest, one of the many joggers in old track bottoms and sweat tops, so he knew the police had left the scene. He had worn headphones but hadn't turned them on. It avoided conversation but also let him hear when people thought he was deaf. The police had left but she – whoever she was – had come by night. Had she been the police? If so, why hadn't she called out? No. She was something else.

He felt cold, but the wine was warming him. Then he went on autopilot and made himself a sandwich. Brown bread – the local store was selling home-made and it was worth the extra sixty pence – butter first, then a slice of local ham and squares of strong Wiltshire cheddar with pickle and salad. He sat and devoured it with a certain bovine complacency. Afterwards he washed everything up, put the kettle on and made himself and Mother a pot of tea.

Had the woman worked out why he was there?

Up the stairs we go. Taking the tray with the tea and two chocolate biscuits. He knocked once on the door. Didn't wait for the reply before entering. Put the tray on the dressing table, and closed the right-hand curtain. His mother liked both curtains fully closed otherwise the sun got in her eyes in the mornings when she began to read. He laid the tray on his mother's lap. She sniffed once and cleared her throat. Picked up the spoon and gave it a cursory clean with the sleeve of her dressing gown.

He watched from the side. The ritual was the same as it had been for a decade now. Very occasionally, his mother would nod and smile, and he would feel that he had done something right for once. Now, however, his mother wanted to talk.

'What were you doing coming home in the early hours? I heard you on the back porch but you didn't come in. You stayed out there for a very long time.'

The question caught him off guard but he managed to lie convincingly enough.

'Oh, I was thinking.'

'Thinking?'

'Yes. I came home from another works do and had a few things to work out in my head. Boring things, Mother. Things that you don't need to bother yourself with. I didn't want to come inside, turn all the lights on. You know what I'm like. Banging around, causing a disturbance. I thought you'd be sleeping.'

'Clumsy is as clumsy does,' his mother said and looked at him with dead eyes. She didn't seem convinced and slurped a mouthful of tea. 'If you want time to think you should come inside to do it, otherwise you'll catch your death. Better to have you upstairs near me. I don't sleep well at the best of times so you probably wouldn't have disturbed me.'

'Next time then.'

'Next time, next time. Maybe there won't be a next time ... '

Another slurp and his mother poked at a bit of biscuit that had become caught in her teeth. 'How's work been?'

'Oh, you know. Same old same old.'

'I don't know why you bother. Seems like a miserable existence to me.'

He checked his watch.

'Keeping you, am I?'

'It's was a hard night, that's all. I might not go in today. The bosses say I can have a day off.'

'A day off? Look at you – goody-two-shoes! Well I never.'

'I still need to get ready for tomorrow. The next few days are going to be very busy.' He smiled at her. 'I'll be up in a minute for the tray.'

He went downstairs and finished off the glass of wine, was tempted to pour another but his instincts stopped him. No mistakes. Last night had been his first. Then he suddenly remembered Denise, his neighbour. She had been curious. Asking questions. *No.* There was no way it had been her, although perhaps he couldn't take the chance?

Curiosity blanched to anger. Then anger moved to its old friend hatred. Stop it, he said. She could never identify him. The goggles would have shielded his face and he was all in black. He had been very careful but now he had to think. He was supposed to go to the forest again soon but she had put a spanner in the works. Was it safe to return? Not with the extra police – they would be out in force now. He would have to delay, which would mean his MO would change, which might affect future MOs. Domino effects. This was a dilemma.

He filled up a water bottle and put in a fresh straw. Took a sip himself. Nice and cold.

Another twinge.

Oh Jesus ... she touched my leg, I think. Did she? He started to sweat again. Goosebumps on his arm. A vague memory, but it had all happened so fast. He remembered the flash of light blinding him as she scored a direct hit on his eyes with her torch. It was like a million suns exploding in his head. He must have shouted. There was no way she could identify his voice. He had been lucky. No, not lucky. He had kept his cool. He had practised what he had preached and it had paid off. But had she touched him? He checked both his ankles. There were no scratches, no bruises. He had shaved his entire body again earlier in the week and was grateful he had.

Even if she had got DNA from his skin, his sweat, it would have been lost on her hands as she floundered in the forest behind him, lost as she tried to find her way back to wherever she had come from, and lost when she had showered as soon as she got home. But, had she worked out why he was there?

The only way he could stop thinking about her was if he kept himself busy. A distraction. He needed something to do so went into the hall, unlocked his briefcase and pulled out an envelope. He had had the idea earlier last week but had only acted on it yesterday at lunch break. He decided to tell Mother. The ever-responsive audience.

'What do you think?' he said as he entered her room again. She was mopping her chin with a tissue.

'What?'

'What do you think?' He opened the envelope and fanned out a series of travel brochures. 'You always said you wanted to get away. Go on an adventure. We could go together.'

'I hate cruises.'

'How do you know? You've never even been on one.'

'I'm not a people person. Never have been. Not like you.' A rare compliment and he felt his cheeks flush. 'I couldn't think of a worse thing to do. Being cooped up on a boat with two thousand people that I don't like and don't want to talk to.'

'A ship.'

'What?'

'Nothing. You might like some of them.'

'I won't. I'd rather relive my twenty-four hours of labour again. Rather face the surgeon's knife with no anaesthetic while having that C-section as well.' Her eyes were black as coal. 'Giving birth to you again would be more fun than going on a cruise.'

The story never changed, no matter how hard he tried.

'Sometimes I wish …' It was barely a whisper but his mother heard it. She heard everything these days. Sometimes he believed his mother could even hear his own thoughts.

'Wish what?' She was staring at the ceiling. Opened her hands and the brochures slipped to the floor.

'Nothing,' he said. 'Sometimes I just wish.'

His mother laughed. It crackled through the room like dry twigs catching fire.

'Nearest is dearest. Blow a kiss. Make a wish! Remember that? You want me to blow you a kiss?' His mother twisted her head around and took a breath. 'Come closer, child. Come closer.'

Thirty-five

Bishop got to the station early afternoon.

A quick hello as the shifts changed and he was in his office with a coffee and a handful of biscuits from the communal tin. He often wondered who bought the biscuits, as he never did, but whoever it was had good taste. Three chocolate Hobnobs, four custard creams and a Penguin. He sat quietly in his office as he made his way through them, dropping the occasional crumb, flicking it onto the floor. The case was at a standstill. Half the task force had shifted their focus to the mystery woman on the CCTV but it was like searching for a ghost. He answered a few emails and when he had finished he was starting to feel sick, but wasn't sure if it was the sugar or the thought of what he was about to do.

The cabinet on the far left of his office held case files that he had closed over the past ten years, but at the back was his personal collection of photos. There were three of Sarah, his ex-fiancée, a few of her family, whose names were becoming misty, one of his own parents, a photo of a dusty Seawolf HAL-3 helicopter that had been adapted for war, and lastly the four-by-six colour photo of a group of six men from his old regiment, all dressed in desert gear and staring warily at him. Two had been killed on duty a month after the photo had been taken and two had committed suicide when they had returned to the UK. That left two others. One he had no contact number for – he could probably find him but that would take time – and the other was a sergeant he had last seen three years ago. Bishop had no idea what he had been doing since then, but a few phone calls confirmed he was still in London. He was a difficult man and had problems with drugs and alcohol after returning, but he could be trusted and that was what mattered.

He lowered the photo as two officers approached his door, wondering if they were going to come in, but they passed by. Don't do it, Bishop, but deep down he didn't think he had a choice. He picked up the phone and dialled the number.

It was answered on the second ring.

'Hello?'

The voice was whisky. Burnt cigars and RPGs. The sounds of gunfire and bullets smacking into running flesh.

'Max, it's Bill Bishop.'

There was a silence followed by a dusty breath.

'Bill? Long time, Bill. Hey, how you doing?'

'Good. Keeping straight. Yourself?'

'Not good today, Bill. Not good at all.'

'I'm sorry to hear that, Max. We should meet up. Let's have lunch for old times' sake.'

'You buying?'

'Yep.' Bishop slowly raised his head and squeezed his eyes shut. 'I need a favour.'

There was a long pause and he wasn't sure if Max had heard him, but he had.

'What sort of favour?'

'For old times' sake. Will you be able to help me out?'

'I'll be at the Lyric in forty-five.'

The receiver went dead.

The Lyric pub was off Great Windmill Street in Soho.

A Victorian happy-hunting ground with open fires and draught beers. Crowded, sweaty, full of lunchtime noise. Bishop pushed his way to the bar and ordered two pints of snakebite. Carried them over to a corner table and sat opposite the man. They shook hands. Max was in his forties, had long hair and a beard. He had kept fit, looked big and strong, sleeves pushed up, black tattoos underneath, eyes constantly roving towards both exits – old habits die hard. They chinked glasses. Max spoke first:

'How's civilian life working out for you?'

'It's warming up,' Bishop said. 'Where are you sleeping these days?'

'Lost my accommodation six months ago because I broke the rules, but I'm making it work.' A mouthful of drink and half the pint disappeared. 'What sort of favour are you looking for? Surveillance, interception. What?'

'Close protection.'

Bishop pulled an envelope from his jacket pocket, passed it over. Inside was some money and a photo of Holly with her information on the back. Max glanced at it with no expression. Put it away.

'I can think of a couple of guys that would be suitable. They're all top class. Security specialists. Ex-regiment the lot of them. I've weeded out the dross over the years.'

'I don't want any guys. I want you.'

A pause.

'Is this official?'

'No.'

'What's the urgency?'

'Immediate effect,' Bishop said.

Max nodded. Finished the rest of his pint and walked.

Bishop watched the door close behind. Thinking of bad things, bad places and a whole lot of pain.

He took a mouthful of snakebite but didn't enjoy it. Was contemplating another when the phone call made him jump. It was Ambrose.

'A message has come in from Wanstead Park Forestry Commission about one of their cameras, sir.'

'I didn't think there was any CCTV there.'

'There isn't. These arc hides set up to capture rare birds and wildlife, but they caught sight of something that you and Holly might want to look at.'

Thirty-six

'Marsh sandpipers are waders who breed from easternmost Europe to Central Asia. Very distinguished with a fine bill and long yellow legs. Incredibly rare over here.'

Holly and Bishop were sitting in a room that was part of the Forestry Commission's buildings in Epping Forest. A shelf of computers and monitors to one side. A desk to their right, behind which were charts and catalogues for identifying rare species. They were listening to Marcus Edmonds, mid-fifties with tiny half-moon glasses.

'The wader was first spotted two weeks ago by one of our regular twitchers, Brad Duesbury. He didn't have time to capture an image, but we promised to set up a camera as soon as possible. What with the poor boy being found we waited until the police had cleared the scene and then hid the camera in the vicinity hoping the sandpiper might return. As their name implies, they like marshes or wetlands and we have an abundance in Epping. We set up hides and cameras all over forests, part of the WWF, and my remit is Wanstead Park.'

'I'm guessing we're not here to see the image of the bird?' Holly said.

'Quite.'

Marcus turned on a television that had been linked to his computer and pressed play. 'Height-wise, the camera is attached to the base of a tree, about two feet off the ground. They're well disguised so as not to disturb any of the wildlife.' A time code appeared at the top right of the screen: 3.19 a.m. 'Here we go.'

'What day was this?' she asked.

Bishop nodded at the screen.

'Watch.'

The screen was pitch-black but Holly didn't take her eyes off it. And then it suddenly lit up. Bright white and phosphorous. Tree trunks and leaves, branches dipping into frame. A badger walked ponderously from left to right. Sniffed at nothing in particular then stopped and stared at the camera.

'Can it see the light?'

'No, it's infra-red. It can't see a thing.' The badger looked once behind it and waddled off into the bushes. After ten seconds the screen went dark again.

'How many of these hides are throughout the forest?'

'Twenty-seven. We place them all across the grounds and change their locations every season. Not that the wildlife ever finds them, but some creatures will always tread the same path and every different set-up reveals something new to us. I've been doing this sort of thing for over twenty years now. Started as a ranger and then—'

The screen lit up again. A whitewash of vegetation.

'This is it,' he said.

Holly waited and waited.

'I don't see anything.'

'The camera is very sensitive. It senses movement around it and will react even if an animal isn't in frame.' He leaned forward and turned up the sound. 'Listen.'

A gentle shush-shush. Stopping. Shush-shush again.

'What is that?'

'The undergrowth being disturbed. It's precisely three-twenty-two a.m.'

Holly felt herself leaning forward, watching the screen as if waiting for the end of a magic trick. The rustling noise was getting louder and louder. But it wasn't simply a noise now, it seemed to have become consistent. Slow but regular. Footsteps? Then from the right-hand corner of the frame a leaf flew into view. Twisted over in the middle of the screen, landed and settled. Silence. The rustling noises stopped. Total stillness. Holly held her breath. Five seconds. Ten. And then she couldn't believe her eyes.

She saw a figure walk into frame, crouch down against a tree and start eating a Mars Bar. Oh, Jesus.

'Hungry?' Bishop asked.

She felt herself smile.

'I had a Twix in the other pocket.'

'Good job you didn't eat that as well,' he said, 'otherwise you might have scared away the wildlife.'

He gave Marcus a nod and the video was fast-forwarded. Holly felt privately relieved she had pocketed the wrapper and not let it drop to the ground. Then she felt her stomach tighten and the adrenalin started to course when Marcus said:

'Three-twenty-five a.m. Here we go.'

There was a loud *snap* and she felt herself flinch as she

saw the figure wearing black, as clear as day, moving swiftly towards the tree she was resting up against.

'Jesus Christ. He was right behind me.'

'Yep,' said Bishop. 'Which is why he didn't see you. The tree blocked you out.'

Don't ever do that again, Holly. Don't ever go into the forest in the dead of night to a crime scene by yourself. What the hell had she been thinking?

The figure paused within touching distance and then moved past her towards where the red flags were. Marcus stopped the tape as the figure was about to pass out of frame, and the infra-red outlined his head and his face. There was no way of getting an ID, because Holly had been right. It looked as though he was wearing a gas mask over his face – small glasses with a thick rubber surround.

'What is that?' she said.

'That's why he could move so well in the dark,' Bishop told her. 'He was wearing night-vision goggles.'

Thirty-seven

It was early evening when Holly crouched down by the camera in Wanstead Park and peered along its line of sight.

Vague shadows of trees either side as she shifted on the wet leaves, elbows balanced on her knees. 'So I was here and he walks in from my left side and leans against the trunk. Then he went to the flags where the body was. Over there. Crouched down and looked up at the trees.' Re-playing it in her head. Her torch flickered over the forest floor. 'He went over to that tree there and touched it.'

'What height?'

'Five, maybe six feet off the ground.'

Bishop followed her directions and shone the torch on the tree.

'You see anything?' she asked.

He took his time, then: 'Nothing.' Walked across to her. 'Try these.' He handed her a pair of night-vision goggles. They resembled mini-binoculars held together by rubber bands that formed a cradle-like swimming cap. She put the torch in her mouth as she tried to fit it over her head. Struggling, like trying to wear a four-fingered glove.

'Hold on.' He adjusted the straps on her head. They felt way too tight and the rubber was pressing into the cut above her eye. 'How does it feel?'

'Like my head is about to explode.'

'You won't be able to see much at the moment.'

Pitch-black through the goggles. She could hear her breath as if she were underwater.

'How easy are these to get hold of?'

'These are mine.'

'You think he could be ex-army?'

He didn't answer but she could tell he had been thinking about it.

'I'm going to turn them on. Never look directly at my torch, okay?'

'Okay.'

He flicked a switch on the side of her head. There was a tiny electronic whir and she suddenly saw another world. Green on green. The trees, the leaves, the sky. Everything was a different shade like the cameras from the hide. A million gnats danced in front of her and Bishop was a green blob with shiny teeth and white eyes. He raised his torch and directed it at the tree. The sudden brilliance made her squint and turn away quickly.

'This is what he saw, Holly. Walk through his shoes.'

She did, took a step forward, still in awe of this new landscape. Got to the flags where Noah had lain. Pointed to an oak in front of her.

'That's the tree. There.'

'Do what he did.'

She followed his instructions. Leaned towards the tree and mimicked the man. Wondered where to put her hand. Saw nothing but twisted trunk. Felt nothing but rough bark.

'I don't see anything.'

'It was definitely this tree?'

'Yes. I'm positive. Then he heard me – I don't know how – and turned around.' She turned herself and Bishop was where she had been by the tree opposite

'You want me to eat some chocolate, set the scene?'

'Very funny.'

'And then you ran at him?'

'No, I turned on my torch first, shone it in his eyes and then he fell and shouted and then got up and started moving.'

'Right. So you followed quickly?'

'Yes.'

'Start moving then. Be him. I'll be you.'

Holly floundered for a few seconds as if she had fallen, then started to move. It was like running in daylight. She could hear Bishop behind, breath loud against the quiet.

'Where did you tackle him?'

She looked around and kept going for a few feet. 'About here. We struggled on the ground. I lost my phone and torch and this was when I grabbed his leg. And then he kicked out at me and he was off. I was blind compared to him.' She turned. 'Can you see me, Bishop?'

'Barely. I think there's more moon tonight than the other night but if I were to turn my torch off I wouldn't be able to see a damn thing.'

They both stayed silent for a while.

'But what was he here for?' she said. 'Maybe there was something on that tree and he took it away.'

'Maybe.'

'But,' she said, 'he knew exactly where to run as well. It wasn't as if he got lost or anything. He kept going and I could hear it when he made it to the road, but I still couldn't see him. There was no way I could have caught him. Then I heard his car and he was gone.'

'Can you see the road from here?'

'No.'

'You'd scared him, made physical contact with him, but he didn't panic. He didn't get disorientated and run anywhere. He recovered and kept going on the same course. To his car. Somehow he knew how to get there.' She could see Bishop's breath, a cloud of green smoke.

'There was a bush,' she remembered. 'With thorns – I ran into it. I'm not sure how far it is.'

'Let's go.'

Walking the rest of the way in silence until she saw the mass of green ahead.

'This is it.'

Bishop stopped next to her. Voice low: 'Look away,' as he shone his torch at the bush. Even with her head averted, her eyes started to ache. After a minute he turned his torch off and she spun round suddenly.

'Hold on. What was that?'

'What?'

'I see something on one of the trees over there,' she said. 'To your left. Something's shining.'

'Lead me to it.'

She felt his hand on her shoulder, gentle but firm, and as she walked towards another oak, his footsteps fell in time with hers and she thought about the Finneys. Left foot, right foot.

Left foot. Right. There. Above her head on the trunk was a tiny strip of bright white.

'Can you see it?'

'No.'

'It's fluorescent,' she said. 'An adhesive fabric or masking tape about four inches long.' She pulled off the head-gear and passed it over. She was suddenly aware that her head and hair was wet with sweat. He placed the device on his head, she heard the tiny whir and saw the shadow of his arm lift to the tree.

'I'll be damned,' he said. 'It's a marker of some kind.'

She took them back and held them up to her eyes. Ten steps forward. Ten more and there it was on a tree up ahead – a second fluorescent strip. 'Bishop! I've found another one.' And twenty feet beyond that – a third. And then a fourth and finally she reached the road.

'That clever bastard. That's why he was here. For whatever reason he didn't have time to remove these markers when he placed the body there. That's how he went through the forest in complete darkness.'

'My God. He's a planner,' she said quietly. 'Like Hansel and Gretel. He left breadcrumbs in the forest.'

They were getting closer.

But to what, she had no idea.

Thirty-eight

The man had been surprised at how familiar it had felt when he had first gone into the attic to see if it was suitable for his purpose. He had found so many things from his past. Memories shrouded in bubblewrap and hidden in boxes. Faded photographs, old spelling books, scribbles of crayon on paper. The hurt was still there, but there was also a certain comfort to the cruelty.

The space was dark but he knew it like the back of his hand. He had spent hours playing here as a child. Hide and seek, catch me if you can. Holding his breath behind the chimney stack, trying not to cough on the soot, sweaty fingers playing with crumbly bricks.

He shook two drops of tea-tree oil into a handkerchief and placed it across his mouth as he climbed the narrow stairs. Turned on the light at the top – a single bulb that always seemed to be swaying – and tiptoed his way through the stacks of furniture and other-worldly odds and ends.

The smell was becoming more intense, something he had adapted to, and by the time he arrived at the other end of the attic the handkerchief was pressed firmly against his face. He should have cleaned the space after he had removed the last boy, but there was something comforting about the smell. The boy had curled himself into the side of the rafters, like an animal under a hedge seeking shelter from the rain. His hands tied behind him, his little white legs bent up at ninety degrees. His skin had been so cold and he had expected to see a leak in the roof, a trail of rainwater dripping like sand through an hourglass. Nothing. Secure and as it should have been. The restraints had worked well but the boy's pulse had been slow and this time he had put electrolytes in the water bottle which had made the water go orange. He set it down with the straw. Preparation is the key. He thought he heard a noise behind him. A whimper. But it was just the empty attic. And then the doorbell rang.

'Thank you so much for coming at such short notice, Denise.'

The man opened the door and the neighbour from number thirty-seven was ushered inside. She had obviously made an effort: a heady perfume and a slash of pink lipstick.

'Oh,' she said as she saw the elephant-foot umbrella stand. 'Is that real?'

'Very,' he smiled. 'Mother was a bit of a hoarder. Went all over England and kept buying odd pieces from charity shops and auctions. I think it's African rather than Indian. Not sure if there's any way to check, to be honest.' He took her coat and hung it up, headed towards the kitchen, then turned quickly and retraced his steps. Met her eyes with an odd blend of innocence and apprehension.

'I'm so sorry, Denise, but I brought you here under false pretences.'

'You did?'

'Yes. Mother is fine. She doesn't need help and I'm not going out. I wanted . . . ' a short sigh, 'some company. It's been a rough few weeks and . . . '

She looked suitably taken aback but then suddenly smiled. 'That's okay.'

'Really?'

'Yes, of course. You don't need to – well – I'm here now and I'm all yours. So shall we have a drink then?'

'I can do better than that. I did cook. I hope you're hungry?'

There were three plates set on the dark mahogany table in the dining room. Burgundy painted walls, white coving and a French crystal chandelier. Pristine red napkins, ivory placemats and silver cutlery.

'How lovely. Will your mother be joining us?'

'No, she prefers to eat alone, but I will prepare a plate for her here and take it up. She loved your Victoria sponge, by the way. I caught her trying to come downstairs and help herself to an extra slice the other day.'

'Oh, how funny. Did you give her one?'

'I certainly did. Rich and creamy, and she enjoyed every second of it.'

He smiled and she laughed.

'Please, take a seat,' he said, and he picked up Mother's plate. 'The food's almost ready. Red or white wine to accompany?'

'Red, please.'

He disappeared into the kitchen, knowing full well she would be sitting there staring around the room like a child looking up at the stars. He poured her wine first and took it through, then prepared his mother's plate, apologised profusely as he traipsed past her and up the stairs, and then came down about two minutes later and ladled out the thick stew.

'It smells lovely,' she said.

'Thank you,' he said, taking his place opposite. They toasted each other in silence.

The crunch of the peppercorn and the tap of cutlery scraping across the plates like heavy nails. He poured more wine and wondered if she would have liked some music in the background.

'I do love the elephant stand in hallway,' she said. 'Probably not very PC of me to say it, what with them being almost extinct and everything. But I think it looks nice. It's different, isn't it?'

'Yes, these are all Mother's things.'

'And your father?'

'He was away most of the time. He left when we were rather young.'

'We?'

'Mother and I. Do you have brothers or sisters, Denise?'

'No, no family to speak of. No cousins or uncles, and both my parents have passed away.'

'That's right, you did mention that. How tragic.'

'Yes, it was.' She sipped some more wine. The glass was half empty again – she was like a funnel. 'I don't know,' she brushed her hair from her eyes. 'I find myself quite solitary the older I get. I have a few friends at work but I don't socialise much. I think I'm at a point in my life where I don't know what I'm doing. I feel a bit lost.'

'I think that happens to all of us sometimes.'

'It does, doesn't it? So tell me more about you,' she said.

'What would you like to know?'

'I know you're single.' She smiled. 'Have you ever been married?'

'No, I find it hard to manage the time. I like ... moments to myself. And of course there's Mother.'

'You're very dedicated. You really are.'

'Yes, I am, aren't I? And yourself?'

'What?

'Were you married to your partner?'

'Yes, I think I mentioned I was married for seven years but it wasn't particularly pleasant.'

'I'm sorry.'

'He was quite controlling.'

'Did he hurt you?'

'Sometimes. I mean he wasn't all that physical. It was more mental cruelty, to be honest.'

'He belittled you. Made you feel unworthy. Like a fool.'

'Yes, he did.'

'And where is he now, this Hades of a man?'

'I think he still lives at the same address, but we don't have contact any more.'

He wrinkled his nose and there was that sad and empty feeling again.

'I was seeing someone until very recently but we went our separate ways,' he said.

'I'm sorry.'

'Thank you. Perhaps some things in life naturally have to come to an end? That's the way the world works. The bizarre tapestry.'

She nodded and smiled.

'I do like your moustache, by the way,' she said. 'People think they're old fashioned but I don't think so. It's very distinguished. Makes you look like a captain in the army or something.'

Captain was one of the lowest ranks but he thanked her anyway before she asked:

'You haven't told me what meat this is yet.'

'I want you to guess,' and a smile flittered across his face.

'Is it chicken?'

'No.'

The man watched her put another forkful into her mouth. She ate very daintily, like a little mouse.

'It's not venison, is it?'

'No, it's not venison. Closer though. A wild animal who shares the hedgerows.'

'Oh, no,' and she looked horrified. 'Not badger?'

'Badger?' he laughed. 'Nobody eats badger! Can you even eat a badger? How would you even do that?'

'It's very tender. From something small, I would imagine.'

'Very good.'

'Shares the hedgerows ... There's no way you would serve me rat.'

'I wouldn't serve rat to my worst enemy.'

'And who is your worst enemy?'

He thought briefly as he placed another delicate morsel into his mouth.

'Time.'

'Time? That's very philosophical.'

Her colour was changing. Her cheeks were becoming flushed and there was a hint of blue around her lips.

'Did you ever watch *Watership Down* when you were a young girl?' he said.

Her eyes went like saucers.

'No!'

'Yes!' he smiled.

'Rabbit?'

'Rabbit!'

'How wonderful! It has a very distinctive flavour, doesn't it?'

'It does, although that may be the fentanyl.'

'Fentanyl? What is that – a herb?'

'No, it's a drug.'

Her mouth twisted to one side and stayed there, and when she eventually found her voice, it came as a bewildered stutter.

'What sort of drug?'

'How are you feeling?'

'I don't know. I think I'm ... '

'It's fast acting. You still have another ten seconds then you'll start to feel slightly odd.'

'Why? What's going on?'

She tried to stand up, but as she did, it looked as if she were on the deck of a ship in high seas. She shifted to one side, and then to the other with nothing to take hold of. The table must have been slippery as she suddenly fell and banged her elbow. He wondered if she had broken her arm as she went down. She pulled off his wig as they struggled on the floor and it ended up like a dead beast on the carpet, but he didn't care.

'I don't understand,' she said, as he knelt above her and put the cord around her neck.

'Neither do I,' he whispered.

Thirty-nine

Twenty officers and over thirty members of the public turned up to help.

The search party was split into two groups and started along a north-easterly route. Two sets of single horizontal lines, arm's length apart. Most were wearing waterproofs as rain had been forecast and there was already a slight sheen to the leaves underfoot. Slow steps in the morning cold. Dry sticks poking into wet bushes.

Holly joined one of the groups and fell in between a couple of locals. From time to time she would see a hand go up from one of the uniforms or civilians in the line. An officer would pull out a bag and place whatever he or she had seen inside. Seal it up. Pass it on to an investigating officer. Carrying on slowly forwards. Not missing a thing. Eyes on the ground. Necks starting to ache after hours and hours of repetitive movement.

They had discovered three separate routes from the crime scene with the strips of fluorescent material. One from The Glade to where Noah had been left, an alternative exit from the forest which he had used after his confrontation with Holly, and the third one which they were now all following that headed directly south through bumpy marshland.

Holly wondered if the killer was among them, returning to the kill zone to relive the thrill. She couldn't stop staring at everybody, trying to catch their eyes, see something that would give them away, but she knew he was too clever for that. He would be nondescript, blending in with everyone else, but a wolf amongst the lambs.

After three and a half hours they had followed the route all the way through from the beginning to its conclusion, stopping at a series of white flags that had been planted by a dip in the ground. That was where the final strip had been discovered. It seemed a funny place to end. The road was at least four hundred metres away through thick forest.

After the first run, over seventy evidence bags had been collected with the eagle-eyed officers doing the best they could in the drizzling light. Everything was bagged up and tagged and ready to be taken to the forensic laboratory. Put in folders, itemised and time coded.

A local business in a white van had turned up and was serving hot drinks and hot food for lunch. It was welcome. People were hungry and it was cold. Holly added herself to the line and for the first time this morning saw Bishop as he was about to address the volunteers.

'I know for a lot of you this is your local woods,' he said. 'You come here all the time, so you are looking at the forest with different eyes than ours. There is a chance, however slim, that you may help catch the killer, so thank you so much. Food and hot drinks have been provided, so please help yourselves. We'll carry on the search going the other way in about forty-five minutes.'

She saw him shake hands with a few who came over to talk to him, then he met up with her and they both ordered burgers with all the trimmings and a hot coffee to go. Fatty food had never tasted so good. They had started to move through the forest away from the group when Bishop's radio crackled. He grabbed it.

'Bishop.'

'We've found something, sir. You need to see this.'

'Location?'

'About fifty feet south of the white flags.'

Holly shot him a look and the two pushed through the dead trees, nearly falling over themselves as they crossed a marsh and eventually saw an officer waving them in. One of the constables was already cordoning off the area with police tape.

'What did you find?'

'Sergeant Ince has the details.'

Bishop led Holly another thirty feet until she saw a wooden shack with the remains of a corrugated roof. No more than six feet square, it was old and dilapidated, the bleached wood collapsing, old bricks scattered close by. Two constables stood guard as Sergeant Ince appeared from within the hut.

'Couldn't see it from any of the roads or paths, the ground dips lower. It's almost like we're in a valley here,' he said.

He led them inside the shack and shone his torch on an old barrel that had recently been used as a firepit. He pointed inside with a stick. Holly's body stiffened when she saw the burnt remains of a child's clothing. Blue jeans, white T-shirt, a blue hoody.

'Give me the stick,' Bishop said.

Ince handed it over and Bishop lowered it into the barrel and hoisted up the T-shirt on its point. It used to be white and had a Gap logo on the front. Holly noticed the remains of a few cotton threads where a name tag had been ripped out.

Bishop poked around a bit more. Pulled a glove on, reached down and lifted an object slowly from the barrel and into the light. It was a notebook or diary. Green, leather bound, perhaps six inches high, four inches wide. Badly burnt.

Bishop pointed to the corrugated ceiling. 'Did you check up there?'

'Not yet, sir.'

'Check. Double check. Get a ladder and send someone up.'

'Yes, sir.'

Bishop handed over the notebook to Holly and she flicked a page. There was writing inside, but it was illegible.

The fire had done its work.

Forty

It was the lunch hour, but in the incident room nobody seemed to be eating.

Officers floated quietly, moving from desk to desk, computer to phone. Some of them seemed nervous, some perplexed, all in a constant state of anxiety. Most of them had children themselves and this was affecting them so much.

Holly was mesmerised by the map of the forest on the crime board. Black lines zigzagged from the dirt road to the place where Noah had been found and where the clothes had been burned. Sixty-seven trees had been marked with the fluorescent strips, entrances and exits for the killer.

There was still no news of the mystery woman who had dumped the phone, the female accomplice, and anyone could buy night-vision goggles on eBay for less than a hundred pounds. Darya had tentatively identified the Gap T-shirt as having been the same style that her son had worn, it was now being tested for his DNA and the notebook had been sent to a specialist forensics lab in Millbank.

A phone rang two desks down. There was nobody there to

answer it and both Holly and Karla went for it but Holly got there first.

'Incident room.' A beat. 'Hello? Incident room.'

The phone went dead.

'Who was it?' Karla asked.

'Nobody there,' Holly said, and hung up as Bishop entered. Somehow Holly knew not to talk and the silence was infectious.

'Everybody, please.' He held up a file. 'A social worker from Loughton council has identified the second boy's body at the morgue. His name is Matthew Cotton. He was thirteen years old.'

They made their way to his office. They seemed to gravitate there – the seclusion from the rest of the task force working well for them both. She studied the photos as Bishop handed them over. The boy looked a little like Noah. Slim, attractive. Almost waif-like.

'Are these modelling shots?'

'His mum wanted to get him in the business. Thought he could make some money. Contacted a local photographer who then passed him on to another photographer. Both photographers came back clean,' Bishop said. 'No previous arrests, convictions or anything untoward. Matthew Cotton was originally from Woodford in Essex. It's well within the twenty-mile radius.'

'Parents?'

'Separated. His dad left when he was five, his mum's given up on him. Won't take the social worker's calls any more.'

'When did he actually go missing?'

He passed over another file – the final autopsy report from Angela. 'Five weeks ago, Angela concludes he was in the forest

223

for about a month. Which means the killer took him, kept him alive for a few days then killed him and dumped him in Wanstead.'

There was a silence and then she said:

'Where was he last seen?'

'Less than a mile from Epping, at a pub in Chigwell called The King's Arms.'

'A pub? He was thirteen.'

'Liked mixing with the older crowd.'

'Alcohol, drugs?'

'He and his school mates used to sip a crafty vodka before class. Experimented with drugs, mainly marijuana and cocaine.' He handed the last sheet of paper. 'And this is where it gets interesting. He's got a low-level rap sheet. Petty theft, possession. Then he upped his game and got arrested four times last year by the Camden Police for solicitation.'

'He was a rent boy?'

Bishop nodded.

'You want to have another chat with Timothy Grent?'

Forty-one

Timothy Grent was dripping with sweat.

He sat opposite Holly and Bishop, rolling a cigarette with shaking hands, packing it tight, licking the strip. He finally lit it and shook his head slowly, pale face flushed red.

'Fuck's sake,' he said.

Bishop leaned forward slightly, claiming the space. 'We should get you your own room, Timothy. Can't stay away, can you?' A breath. 'Let me tell you how this is going to happen. We have another dead boy, and this one has been identified as Matthew Cotton.' He laid down an eight-by-ten shot. 'You want to see the autopsy photos?'

'No.'

Bishop pulled them out anyway and spread them on the table between them. Flesh-ragged bones that used to be arms and legs stretched out on a bright white sheet.

'He was a rent boy. Your patch.'

Grent shuffled and looked away.

'I need my pills.'

'Which ones?'

225

'The beta-blockers. That's why I'm shaking, look.' He raised a hand.

'You're not shaking because you know who Matthew Cotton is, and very soon we will be able to link him to you?'

'I took four this morning, but I need some more.'

'That's a lot of beta-blockers,' Holly said.

'I suffer from anxiety. What more can I say?'

'You can tell us if you knew Matthew Cotton.'

Grent stared at her then pulled away. He looked like an angry bird today. Beady eyes, black hair pulled into a pony-tail, stick-like limbs.

'I'm not going back.' Barely a whisper. 'I can't.'

'Go back where?'

He became solemn, set his jaw. Took a hit on the cigarette and tapped the ash. When he finally spoke the words came out of his mouth like a great lump of spit. Hung in the air then dropped.

'The man contacted me through the noticeboard,' he croaked.

'What noticeboard?' Bishop said, leaning in.

'A pub in east London. It's called The King's Arms. It's a good place. The people have no idea of what goes on, has been going on there. I use it as a meeting ground.'

'A meeting ground?'

'To set up clients with young men.'

'Matthew Cotton was thirteen. Legally he was still a minor at that age.'

'I didn't know he was thirteen. He told me he was seventeen.'

'And now he's dead. Talk me through it.'

He was silent for a while before he went on.

'I have boys come to me. Sometimes I go searching. I find whatever strays cross my path and then I put a notice on the board at the pub with my number. Someone sees the notice, calls me direct.'

'Who contacted you about Matthew?'

'I didn't know his name, he never—Christ, you think we use our real names? I never saw him. I passed on his details to Matthew. It was Matthew who made contact from there and decided what to do. I was the go-between, that was all.'

'Did you sell Matthew fentanyl?'

'Yes. He liked getting high when he had sex. Apparently the man wanted some as well, so Matthew bought some for him. It was part of the deal.'

'And you had never come across this man before?'

'I don't think so, no.'

'Where do you get your fentanyl from?'

'I can't . . .'

'It's prescription grade, so we're already narrowing down the field.'

'Jesus, you don't understand . . .'

'Two boys are dead, Timothy. Both were drugged with fentanyl.'

'I know but I didn't—'

'Did you put this man in contact with Noah Beasley as well?' Bishop put Noah's photo on the table. 'They're both similar age, look a little like each other. How many children did this man want?'

'I didn't know about the other boy—'

'How many, Timothy? How many more parents are we going to have that horrible conversation with? How many more mums and dads are going to see their son wrapped up in a white sheet on a metal table in some cold room—'

'Jesus . . .'

'—Two bodies so far, but we think there'll be others. And if there are, the CPS will rate this as one of the worst episodes of child abduction and murder they have ever seen.'

'Ahh . . . shit.'

'—One of the worst. So now we have to follow procedure here as fast as possible. The press are already nicknaming this killer "The Grim Sleeper"—'

'The what?'

'You heard me.'

'The press are calling him that? And two boys – this is a fucking mess. How the hell . . .'

He sat up and suddenly clenched his head as if in the middle of a migraine. Holly watched him coldly. Dispassionately. Gradually, he pushed out of the pain and dragged on the cigarette. Some of the spark had left his eyes and when he looked at the ground he said in a small voice:

'My therapist.'

'Joshua Neate?'

'Yes. He has . . . clients. And he also sells to one dealer.'

'Who, Timothy?'

'Jesus Christ – he'll kill me.'

'Who?'

Grent chewed the inside of his cheek, eyes screwed shut.

'His name is Mash. I don't know if that's his real name. I think he's Greek or Cypriot. I know he sells to other men of my persuasion. He's not the most pleasant of characters. I think you both understand what that means?'

Bishop wrote something down. Timothy turned his eyes to

228

Holly. White with pin-pricks of black. He was still staring at her when Bishop said:

'How much did the man pay you to contact Matthew?'

'Two hundred pounds. He left it at the pub in an envelope.'

'Have you got any of it left?'

'The cash? No – of course not. And I don't have a number for him either – it always came up as caller ID blocked. You've got my phone. You can check.'

Bishop paused for a while. Glanced down at his notes.

'So you never had any actual contact with this man, physical or otherwise?'

'Never. I don't know what he looks like. I spoke to him on the phone a few times, that's all.'

Bishop pulled a CCTV photo from the file.

'Do you recognise this woman?'

He looked at it curiously.

'I don't know, I don't think so – why?'

'That's the woman who dropped the boy's phone behind your house.'

Grent studied the photo with new eyes. Took his time. Again:

'It could be anybody. Somebody trying to set me up? I would never— You think I would kill a boy and then chuck his phone out my window?'

'What about Lily-May?'

'What about her?'

'She says you deal fentanyl to her all the time.'

Grent laughed, and for a split second he looked like a friendly uncle who could bounce nephews and nieces on his knee. But then the smile faded and the light disappeared.

'She's a crackhead. She's full of shit.'

He pulled his eyes away from Holly and Bishop. 'I can't go back,' he told the linoleum floor. He stared at the dirt and scuff marks between his boots as if the conversation was now officially over.

And in a way it was.

Forty-two

Constant rain and gutters half-choked by winter's leaves.

Lily-May sucked the last vestiges of life from her cigarette, dropped the stub on the ground and entered her building. It was a bleak place with very little comfort. A tenement flat that should have been pulled down after the Grenfell fire, but somehow the council never found the finances. She climbed the flight of rickety stairs to the second floor. A few people milled on the landing, but she pushed past them and knocked on the door. It was opened by Natasha, early thirties with flaming red hair. Tired and drawn, another working girl. She took one look at Lily-May and said:

'You're like a drowned dog. Come in, come in.'

Lily-May could smell Indian food and wondered if there was any left for her. The place was squalid and dank, the wallpaper bloomed. She kicked off her boots and sat cross-legged on the sofa, a few baggies of pills in front of her, prescription bottles without labels.

'You going out tonight?' she said.

Natasha was in the kitchen. Stirring a pan on the stove. 'In that? No point, luv. Where you been?'

'Runnin' around.'

Lily-May lit up, fingers stiff with cold. Her cheeks went hollow as she took a long pull and tapped the ash into an empty mug. 'I thought we took it down?' she said, staring at the far wall. There was a plastic Christmas tree on a stand with an angel on top and a few strands of tinsel.

'Eh?'

'The Christmas tree.'

Natasha came back in. 'Shall I lock up?'

'Nah, only came home to change then I'm off again.'

'Where to?'

'Casper wants to see me.'

'Casper? What the fuck? You're not going back with him, are you?'

'God, no.' More decisive. 'No. He said he wanted a chat.'

A silence as stale as the cigarettes.

'I'll make you a cup o' tea before you go then,' Natasha said.

She went into the kitchen and Lily-May's eyes strayed once more to the Christmas tree and she smiled, remembering the pre-holiday excitement of flushed faces and drunken laughter. She'd always had a soft spot for Christmas.

An hour later and Lily-May sat at the same corner table in Sonny's where she had taken Holly.

Sonny had given her a cup of tea, but she was nervous and wanted something stronger. She had known Casper since he'd given her her first Quaaludes behind the bike shed. She had been eleven, he'd been sixteen. She'd downed one, was about to take a second, but he had stopped her, and just as

232

well – she had puked up in history class five minutes later and then passed out for the rest of the afternoon. When she turned fourteen they had started dating and he had become her pimp – daisy chains and laughs on the grass between blow jobs on sticky sofas and damp carpets. The first time he hit her was when they had had a particularly bad argument about how much money she was bringing in. She was always tired and sore and some nights she didn't want to play the game. He'd found the old ginger jar under her bed where she'd been stashing loose notes, and a half-bottle of vodka and some Doom Bar later and no amount of loving could calm him down. She didn't even realise he had hit her until she woke up with a bloody nose, sprawled on the floor in the kitchen. She wiped the blood off her face and went out to work that night, but a precedent had been set. It seemed inevitable that history would repeat itself, and it had. Casper had controlled her for over six years, but then after one final beating, where he had almost killed her, he had let her go out on her own. She had no idea why he wanted to see her now, but she knew deep down that he would always be violent. A rotten man who—

The bell over the door rang and she saw him enter. Casper Faulks: scruffy and balding with a pasty smile and half-closed eyes. She hadn't seen him for a few years and he looked closer than ever to death. Take your pick: battling heart, perforated liver or an OD. He gave her a peck on the cheek that smelled like patchouli. It made her feel sick.

'Do you want a tea?' she said.

'Fuck no. I'll have a sip of yours though.' He reached over and slurped from her cup. Dumped the teabag onto a napkin and rubbed the weariness from his eyes.

'Fuck me, what a day.'

'So what do you want, Casper? I've got things to do.'

'The only thing you have to do right now is listen to me. What the fuck are you doing helping the police?'

'What?'

'Don't play dumb. Timothy Grent got word to me. He's banged up because of this dead kid and you're the one who put him there.'

'No I didn't. All I did was pick up a phone behind his flat. I didn't put it there. Then the cops arrested me.'

'I'm going to spell it out for you, little lover. Timothy Grent is my go-between. He has access to a very legit contact who supplies me with some top-quality merchandise. I lose Timothy Grent, I lose my quality merchandise. I lose my quality merchandise, I lose my share of the market – and you know what happens then, don't you? I lose my money. Therefore, I cannot afford to lose Mr Grent to Her Majesty's Prison Service – so I want you to retract your statement and say you found the phone somewhere else.'

He stared at her hard and she shot him her best smile. Sipped her tea and spilled it, her hands were shaking so much.

'I can't do that. I've already shown them where I got it.'

'Who?'

'The police and Holly.'

'Who the hell is Holly?'

'Holly Wakefield. She's a shrink.'

'A shrink? So you showed her where you got the phone? Why?'

'A kid is dead, Casper!'

'Cry me a fucking river, Bono. I don't give two shits about some kid. But I do care about Timothy Grent.'

'Don't talk like that, it's not like—'

'You tell this shrink anything else?'

'Like what?'

'About Timothy Grent?' He leaned closer. Thick arms pressed on the table. 'About me?'

'No.'

She started suddenly as she saw someone outside the café. There were people loitering, but she couldn't see the details.

'God, you're dumb, Lily-May. She's not a fucking shrink. She's a cop.'

'No she's not.'

'Yes she is. She's playing you.'

'I didn't do anything wrong. Christ, I didn't know you were involved in all this!'

He reached over and took her right hand. Interlocked his fingers with hers. Twisted them slightly. Enough to make her gasp. 'I can make all this go away, Lily-May.'

'What do you mean?'

'Retract your statement. Tell the police you lied.'

'I can't, they'll lock me up.'

'I'll get you out, then you can come back to me. I'll take care of you. Be like old times.'

'I'm not that nostalgic, Casper.'

Hunched over, breathing hard.

'You're either with me or you're not.' She could hear him grinding his teeth. 'As a sign of good faith, you can give me a blow job.'

'Fuck off.'

'I'm serious. Blow job under the table.' He turned to Sonny. The man leaned on one elbow across the counter, leafing idly through a local magazine. 'Sonny? Five minutes, yeah?'

Sonny looked up, nodded and left. Whatever. Just the two of them now.

'And you promise I'll be all right, Casper?'

'Pinky-promise.' He gave her a thin smile.

'Fine,' Lily-May said. 'Pull your pants down. I'll be back in a minute.'

She got up and headed for the bathroom. Casper glanced out the front of the café again, but now there was no one there. He undid his belt and tugged his jeans to his knees. Started playing with himself. Every few seconds his eyes darted towards the toilet, but Lily-May didn't appear. Paranoid now, he pulled his pants up, waddled over to the bathroom door and pushed it wide. His face went red and he almost had the coronary he was scheduled when he saw all the stalls were empty. No sign of Lily-May and the rear window was open.

When he sat at the table again he was calm. He was always very calm when he had important things to do. He dialled a number. When it was answered he said:

'Get Saulius and Mash. Find Lily-May.' A pause. 'And someone called Holly Wakefield.'

Forty-three

Friday morning and the phone rang and woke Holly.

It was Bishop. She was so tired she still had her eyes closed when she started talking:

'Hey.'

'Were you sleeping?'

'I was about to get up.' It was a lie but she thought he might appreciate it.

'The notebook we found in the hut with the burnt clothing. It was Noah's diary. The forensics lab deciphered some of what was left of the writing, and the mother has confirmed it was her son's. Get some more sleep. I'll text you the address and meet you there at two.'

She hung up and lay on the sofa. Within a minute she was asleep again. Her alarm woke her two hours later.

Holly had never heard of the London Forensic Laboratory. It was on the north bank of the Thames, adjacent to Lambeth Bridge. Originally used as offices by DuPont, it had served as the headquarters of the forensics lab since 1998.

Bishop was waiting for her in front of the art deco-style façade, the result of a 1930s facelift. They showed their IDs at the door and were buzzed through and ushered into a reception where one of the forensic analysts was waiting for them. Introducing himself as Jericho Brown, he was in his thirties, not a hair out of place and the sort of person who wouldn't be seen dead without a tie.

All three of them passed through a series of security doors and into a lift. The metal grille closed with a crash and they descended into the main building. The lab itself consisted of a series of connecting corridors with frosted-glass doors. Each door led to a different field of research but Brown led them to his own lab at the rear of the building.

The room was crammed with computers and technicians, all of whom ignored the newcomers, concentrating on the screens and equipment in front of them. At the far end of the room was what looked like an industrial photocopier, and when they stopped beside it, Holly saw the separated pages of the remains of Noah's diary lying flat on a glass table underneath its sensors. A laser moved slowly across the surface, humming gently.

'This is an infra-red scanner,' Brown explained. 'We use it to see the things people don't want us to see.'

He introduced them to another technician who was loading a flash drive into the scanner.

'I'll let Michael talk you through the finer points of what we've done.'

Michael Pearson was the exact opposite of Brown – younger, fitter, with tousled blond hair, and Holly would have expected to see him wearing board shorts rather than a lab coat.

'This was an interesting one you guys gave us. There

wasn't much to work with but we're hoping we've shed some light.'

Pearson nodded eagerly. 'Most documents are made from paper which is primarily cellulose, composed of atoms of carbon, hydrogen and oxygen. Now, when you burn paper it becomes blackened and curls up, that's because the fibres that make up the paper have different expansion rates. We had to use chloral hydrate first to soften the paper so we could get rid of the curls, lay it out flat and start to read what was left of it. Whoever wrote on these pieces of paper used a ballpoint pen, and most ballpoints contain a small amount of metal in the ink and of course metals can survive a fire.'

'How does this scanner work exactly?' asked Holly.

'The scanner takes a photo of the paper, enhances the metal in the ink and makes it more visible. We were lucky here, this paper was good quality, probably an expensive brand. The fire that was lit didn't burn for long, but enough for the person to think they had destroyed what was necessary. The range of incident angle is the interesting factor here.'

'What is that?'

Brown had been loading up images on his desktop. 'You know when you have a coin and you hold it up to the light and then you change the angle so the light reflects better and you can read the date more clearly? That's what the incident angle is. We found with this charred white paper and this black ballpoint pen, the optimum incident angle was sixty-two degrees. This method works on any written document, whether it's been burned, buried for a hundred years or chemically cleaned; it's called infra-red reflected photography. Jericho?'

Jericho pointed to his screen where Holly could see an extreme close-up of a fragment of the paper under a microscope. Streaks of silver against dull grey. 'So we have here what we believe is the remains of an eighty-page diary, with a faux green leather and gold covering, the lower rear section of which burned through which would normally be where you would find the retailer's stamp and possibly the manufacturer's name. Now, because of the randomness of fire and its ignition pattern, we estimate about ninety to ninety-five per cent of the paper was destroyed; but we still found some interesting things in the first part of the diary. January through to early February.'

Brown leaned over the computer and moved the mouse. Images of the salvaged pages appeared in order. Grey tattered sheets with lighter smudges. 'Watch what happens when we create a sharper angle of incident on the first page of paper in the book. We found six words on page one. Here – see?'

'I can't make them out,' Holly said.

'But we increase the incident angle.' He turned a dial. 'Fifteen, twenty-five, thirty-five, forty-five. It's getting clearer, because the light is being reflected more significantly off the metal from the ballpoint pen. There you go. Sixty-two degrees. Now we can read what was before unreadable.'

Holly read the six words. Chest suddenly tight.

'This diary belongs to Noah Beasley.' She turned to Bishop. 'This is it.'

'It would appear that Noah was a bit of a poet. Nothing remains of the first three pages. Notice how he always starts writing something on the odd page numbers, never the even ones – and here we get to see the remains of one of his poems on page eleven.'

If I were
Run away

There
end my life with you

'End my life with you?' Bishop said.

'That's what we thought at first. Maybe a suicide pact or something like that?'

'If it was, only one of them stuck to the deal.'

'Maybe '*Spend* my life with you?' Holly said. 'Rather than *end* my life with you? The "e" isn't capitalised, is it.'

'Nothing on the reverse of this one. Page thirteen is even more damaged. And we were only able to salvage six words: *love, me, belief, flight, white* and *angels.*'

'Angels,' Holly said.

'Some significance?'

'Possibly.'

'Page fifteen is in the same sort of condition, and we simply have the words *love is.* Then there is nothing for a page. Now, remember Noah would never write on the reverse of his poetry but this last one here is the odd one out.'

He highlighted the page on screen. Smoke-stained and with a few holes, they could see the indent of the pen coming through from the other side. 'We're at ninety per cent recovery on this one. Some letters no longer exist but we have tried to guess what was written, based on the previous pages and the wider context of the contents.' Brown adjusted the incident angle and the words suddenly sprang to life.

*My life is not **be**autiful.*
  It is not magical.
  *But I can feel the lo**ve**.*
  *Com**ing** closer. Closer every day.*

'And here's the sting in the tail,' carried on Pearson. 'Whoever wrote this last poem – it wasn't Noah.'

Holly leaned forward.

'Are you positive?'

'Handwriting analysis confirmed it. Note the loopy "s" and the theatrical "e". Five years ago we would have missed another clue, but thankfully we now have the technology to see through different colour spectrums. The final character wasn't written in black ink. It was written in red.' He adjusted the screen and switched to infra-blue.

Holly couldn't believe her eyes.

'It's a B plus,' she whispered.

'Right,' said Pearson, smiling. 'Like a grade at school.'

She looked at Bishop.

'The English teacher.'

Forty-four

Ken Rickshaw sat nervously behind his desk.

He had a folder in front of him that he kept playing with. Closing and opening it as if it were more important. As if he had somewhere else to go.

Holly placed the poem in front of him.

'Do you recognise this?'

He glanced at the sheet of paper quickly. Looked up at her with pleading eyes then down to the poem. He read it very slowly, his mouth moving with every word.

'My life is not beautiful. It is not magical. But I can feel the love. Coming closer. Closer every day.'

He took a breath: 'I don't know. It doesn't look familiar.'

'This poem was in Noah's diary. The diary had been burned in an attempt to destroy it, along with his clothes. A T-shirt, his trousers.'

'Dear God.'

'Can you see what we found written next to it?'

'No.'

'Look closely.'

A pause.

'A *B plus*,' Rickshaw said. He shook his head. Eyes on Holly but his mind was elsewhere.

'Have you seen this poem before?' she said.

'No.'

'But you marked it?'

'No. God, no.'

'Who put the B plus there then?'

'I don't know! Christ, not me!'

The door suddenly opened and a boy in school uniform walked in.

'Mr Rickshaw?'

Blissfully unaware of what he was walking into. No one answered. When he dragged his eyes away from the carpet he saw two strangers and Mr Rickshaw's red face screwed up like an angry fist.

'Knock, Harris! How many bloody times?!'

'Sorry, sir.'

'Outside now! I'll see you after I have finished. Go on!'

More shocked than sullen, the pupil backed up and exited. Closed the door. Holly wondered if he was outside listening, shell-shaped ear pressed up against the thin wood of the door when Bishop asked:

'Did you ever see this diary?'

'No. And I've never seen that poem. Never.' He went over to one of the cabinets. Opened a drawer and fanned through a selection of files until he found the one he wanted. A thick grey one with Noah's name written at the top.

'It's all here. His coursework. Everything. That poem will not be in here. You'll find . . . hold on.' He laid the folder on his desk. Stopped at the section entitled *poetry*. Couldn't find it for a second. 'The one you showed me the other day that began – "how many miles, how many feet", here it is.' He pulled out a sheet of paper and handed it over to Holly. 'See? That same one I've marked it *B plus* in red pen. But I never saw his diary and I swear to God and I've never seen that poem.'

'Where were you on the night Noah went missing?' Bishop said.

Rickshaw sat again and put a hand up to the bridge of his nose.

'I worked from home all day until about six. I had some marking to do. Literature – Thomas Hardy and *Tess of the d'Urbervilles*.' He was very quick to answer. 'I had to get petrol so I went to the M&S garage on the Bolton road. It's twenty-four hours. I filled up and bought some wine and a packet of crisps. I have the receipt somewhere, I'm sure.'

'Red or white?'

'I'm sorry?'

'The wine.'

'Red. Why?'

'I'm curious,' Bishop said. He was looking around the office as Rickshaw was talking but Holly knew he was all ears.

'When I got home I started marking exam tests. For about an hour. Then I watched some television afterwards. Made myself some pasta and had a glass of the wine. It was a Riesling, I believe.'

'What was on television?'

'Christ, I can't remember. Um . . . you have to let me think, okay? I need time. I don't like this.'

'Neither do we.'

'An old episode of *Morse*? I'll have to check. Then I went out. Yes. I did. I met a friend.'

245

Holly glanced at Bishop. She cleared her throat to get Rickshaw's attention, then asked:

'Do you write poetry, Mr Rickshaw?'

'Me? I've dabbled, but nothing—'

'We're going to need a sample of your handwriting.'

Sudden realisation.

'What? You think I wrote that?' A shake of the head. 'Take whatever you want. I wouldn't— Christ. Take everything.'

'What friend?' Bishop caught him off guard.

'I'm sorry?'

'On the night Noah disappeared. You said you spent the night with a friend.'

'I didn't say I spent the night. I . . . we had a drink.'

'We'll need to talk to this friend.'

Mr Rickshaw took his pen out and wrote down a name and number. Swallowed hard as if to force down some overwhelming emotion.

'He's an accountant. Works in town, near Bloomsbury.'

'Thank you for your time,' Bishop said as they saw themselves out.

After they had left, Mr Rickshaw sat very still and tried to compose himself. That idiot boy was probably still standing outside his door, but he would have to wait. He wondered how much of the conversation he had heard. Harris was his name. Scott Harris. He was a little shit. Fifteen years old and he still picked his nose and put it under the tables. Very delicately, Mr Rickshaw took his handkerchief from his pocket, removed his glasses and wiped the tears from his eyes.

*

At the station things were moving fast.

Timothy Grent's shrink, Joshua Neate, had been arrested but was refusing to talk. The police had obtained a search warrant and found a stockpile of expired inventory fentanyl in his office and garage, as well as a large quantity of ketamine and MDMA. The case had been handed over to Narcs and Karla Olshaker had been sequestered off the murder squad to her own department to build a case against both the psychiatrist and his patient. Joshua Neate would post bail, but Timothy Grent would not. He was still locked away in a cell down below asking for filet mignon but getting rice pudding instead.

The DNA on the T-shirt found in the firepit had been confirmed to have come from Noah Beasley. There were no other traces of DNA apparent. Holly wondered why the DNA results from her left hand were taking so long and she called Anton in forensics. There was an anomaly that they were looking into and it needed specialist help. She had no idea what that meant but left him to it.

'Holly?' It was Sergeant Ambrose. 'Your teacher, Mr Rickshaw, his alibi has been confirmed.' He took a breath and slouched for a few seconds with his eyes closed. 'One of those days today,' he said. 'A lot of answers, but none of them any good.'

She half-smiled as she watched him return to his desk. Things were winding down and she felt like a spare cog. Lily-May was supposed to check into the Wetherington tonight and Holly wanted to go home and shower before she visited. She felt as though she might actually be starting to smell like the incident room.

Forty-five

Holly was lucky and managed to park at the end of her street.

She bought herself another microwave meal at the local supermarket, promising that next week she would start cooking fresh food again. As she got to her block of flats she thought she could see someone waiting in the shadows by the porch. She approached warily, eyes slitted against the wind, but the figure melted into the street and shambled west towards Wandsworth without giving her so much as a second glance.

There was only one of the decorators at work in the lobby and she couldn't work out whether it was Bill or Ted. As it happened it was neither.

'Charlie,' he introduced himself. 'The management want this wrapped up by next week so I'm on the late shifts,' he smiled.

'Do you want a drink? Tea or coffee?'

She shouldn't have offered. But—

'Actually, a tea would be nice, love. Wouldn't mind stretching my legs for a bit as well.'

Great.

'Come up then, I'm on the fifth floor.'

He put down his paintbrush and they got into the lift. As the doors were closing, a hand pushed between them, making them open automatically. A man stepped inside, attractive but weary. Holly recognised him as one of the neighbours on the same floor.

'Peter?'

He had moved in late last year and Holly had seen him at an Italian restaurant when she and Bishop had gone out for a meal during the Sickert case. In fact, that night she had compared him to Ted Bundy: attractive, charming, but in this instance probably not a sociopath.

'Holly, nice to see you again. I haven't seen you around much recently.'

'Work keeping me busy.'

'Same here.'

She suspected he worked in the city, financial trader or something, and tonight he looked ready to drop. He turned to the painter:

'How much longer, do you think?'

'Should be done in another couple of days.'

'Thank you.'

The lift doors opened. They all got out and Holly said goodbye to Peter. Charlie waited by the door as she made him a cup of builder's tea.

'Shall I put the mug outside when I'm done?'

'No, it's fine,' Holly said. 'Leave it downstairs and I'll pick it up in the morning.'

He thanked her and left.

Holly shut the door and kicked off her shoes. The central heating was on but she felt cold. She made herself a hot chocolate, shoved the ready-meal into the microwave and collapsed on the sofa as she saw the answer machine was flashing. Jackie from Wetherington: *Lily-May never made it to her appointment. There's an empty bed. What to do?*

Holly cursed. The microwave pinged, but her plastic-wrap meal would have to wait. She put her jacket on again and went outside.

She arrived at Lily-May's block of flats within forty minutes.

The buzzer hadn't worked, but after a few minutes a young girl went into the building and Holly followed her through the lobby. Climbed the stairs and stopped at the door. She was about to knock when she realised it was already open. Pushed it tentatively.

'Lily-May?'

Through to the living room. The place had been turned over and trashed, but there was no sign of Lily-May. The sagging sofa, tinsel and an old Christmas tree lying on the floor. The TV was on, but it was mute, jerky reflections against the glass coffee table in the middle of the room.

'Hello?'

Kitchen, bathroom. Then she saw a smear of blood on one wall. She traced it to the first bedroom and realised the blood was on the handle as well. She pushed open the door.

A body in baby-blue pyjamas lay on the floor. Arms locked across her chest, fingers backwards as if broken. Long red hair. Not Lily-May. Her flatmate? Friend? Holly fell to her knees and checked for a pulse. The woman was non-responsive and cold.

A noise from behind. She turned and exited, followed her feet to a second room. Pushed open the door and saw

250

Lily-May lying on the bed. There was a terrible amount of blood – a sticky wetness on the sheets. Holly went to her, put her arms around her waist and lifted her slowly. Sounds came out of Lily-May's mouth. Groans. Words. Snatches of her life.

Holly tried to move her. Leaden-limbed, as if in the middle of a nightmare, and they rolled together in a heap on the floor.

'Come on. Come on. I've got you,' Holly said.

Lily-May was mumbling. Repeating soft words over and over again, and she leaned to one side and was sick. Barely breathing as Holly pulled her closer. And then Lily-May grabbed Holly's arm so violently she almost dropped her. Eye to eye, and this time she did hear:

'Get . . . out,' Lily-May pleaded. 'He's followed you—'

Holly shifted about-face and looked up. A man was standing above her. She hadn't heard him come in. A hint of recognition.

'I know you.'

'You just made me a cup of tea,' Charlie said.

He smiled and then something flashed in his hand.

Forty-six

Holly sat bolt upright and took a huge breath.

Her head was crackling with static, her eyes going in and out of focus. Red with dirt and pain. Wiping her mouth with the back of her hand. Checking the saliva as if looking for blood.

Everything had happened so fast she could barely recollect. The man – the painter – Charlie had moved towards her. A shadow had come from behind him and she had been pushed backwards. Felt a sharp blow on her head. Blackness for a while, seconds perhaps, and then she had heard a gurgling noise. Breath being stifled. And now she was sitting up. Her elbows were sore, her left arm hurting. The man called Charlie was lying next to her. Dead. An old kitchen knife sticking out of his chest. Another man was kneeling by his side, rifling through his pockets. He turned to look at her.

'Are you hurt? Did he get you?'

'What?'

'There's blood all over you. Are you cut? Did he cut you?'

'No. I don't know.' Frantically checking her body. Hands rolling over limbs and face. Stomach and chest. Lily-May's blood. Not her own.

'He said his name was Charlie,' Holly said. 'I met him at my flat. He was painting the hallway—'

'His real name was Saulius Yosovov. He was supposed to be killing you there.'

'Why didn't he?'

'A witness got into the lift with you. Your neighbour, Peter Asquith.'

'Peter?'

'You got lucky. Saulius had to wait for another opportunity and followed you here. So did I.'

The man was already moving the body closer to the side of the wall. Stripping the pockets and pulling off labels. He put a baggy of white in the dead man's hand. Wrapped stiff fingers around it and turned to her.

'You need to call the police. You're safe now.'

'Am I?'

'Yes. Call them and let them know what you found. Do it now. This man was stabbed as a drugs deal was going down. You didn't see who did it.'

'Who are you?'

A half smile but the eyes were still on work mode. 'My name is Max. I'm a friend of Bishop's.' And now there was a bite to his voice. 'One girl is dead, the other might live. Seriously. Call the police now.'

Twenty minutes later and Lily-May was wheeled out on a stretcher, Holly by her side, holding her hand. The paramedics had wrapped her in a thermal blanket and wiped her down, cleaned up her face. It was then that Holly had seen the full extent of her injuries. She had broken teeth, split lips and it looked like half her head had been sliced open.

'Is she going to be okay?'

'Too early to say,' one of the paramedics offered. 'Christ, what a mess.'

Holly watched them lift Lily-May into the ambulance, shut the doors and drive away. Sergeant Ambrose approached and whispered something to her. The response was a long silence.

'Holly?'

She turned and stared at him as if he were a stranger. Ambrose. She had barely seen him at all on this case. He somehow looked different tonight. She headed away from the tenement block, past the flashing lights and milling crowd.

'Holly? We need a statement.' One last attempt and he reached out and grabbed her arm. She turned, her brow furrowed as if she didn't quite understand. Suddenly pulled away and shook her head.

'Where's Bishop?'

'Over there.'

He pointed and she followed his hand. Bishop was standing by his car talking to someone on the street. He sensed her, looked right at her. Their eyes met and she felt as though he was about to come over and say something, but instead he nodded ever so slightly. She felt her feet moving towards him and life suddenly seemed to be going too fast. An officer walked in front of her, and another, and by the time they had cleared her line of sight, Bishop had gone.

Forty-seven

Gill Finney stared at her son's empty bedroom.

He had left the house that morning. No argument. Just a simple shrug and it was time to leave again. A wanderer. A traveller, and a part of her envied him. She wanted to leave sometimes, but this was it. This was life. A canteen of opportunities, but she felt as though she had chosen the sausage, baked beans and mash rather than the beef wellington and fondant potatoes.

Alan was in the living room reading the evening newspaper. Alan always sat in his armchair. Safe and secure like a nut in a shell. A flicker of a page to signify he knew she was hovering at the door but he didn't lower it. She went into the kitchen and made herself a cheese and tomato sandwich. Heavy on the butter, thick on the cheese and thin on the tomatoes with a sprinkling of salt. She wasn't hungry, but ate quickly and mopped up the breadcrumbs with a wet finger.

'He promised he'd call when he got there,' she said as she sat on the sofa. The newspaper didn't flinch, stayed covering his face, but he spoke:

'You mother him.'

'I'm his mother. What else am I supposed to do?'

'Are you going to phone the police?'

The business section shuffled and bowed.

'Gill? Will you phone the police?'

'I don't know. I get frightened.'

'About what will happen to him?'

'About what's happening to us.'

The paper bowed further. Was folded neatly and placed on the side table.

'One day we're close, the next we're poles apart,' she said. 'Our behaviour to one another is dictated by our son's actions.'

'Yes. I wouldn't disagree with that.'

'Then what do we do? We only seem bonded in an emergency. I feel like Mrs Brown on the *Titanic*. Panic and mayhem everywhere around and I am the one who girds my loins and shepherds everyone to safety. Whilst you . . .'

'Go on.'

'You're still playing "Nearer my God to Thee" in the lounge. Quite content at your own immortal requiem, as everything you hold dear sinks around you.' He blinked slowly like a lizard. 'You do still hold things dear, don't you? Don't you, Alan?'

His face soured. He looked away from her and stared at the tips of his toes. His slippers were old. The felt had run through but he refused to let her buy him a new pair. He wore them with beleaguered pride, somehow comfortable in their inevitable decay.

'Alan. Please say something.' A beat. 'Anything.'

But he didn't and he couldn't and he suddenly started to cry. Great sobs that wracked his body and he heaved himself forward, head in hands, body shaking as if incredibly cold and she went to him. And held him. And comforted and soothed him, and he apologised and she said don't. And told her he had let her down, let Eddie down and he had been a shit father and a bad husband and he couldn't cope and he wanted everything to just go away, but he knew that it wouldn't and after the tears had dried and the shaking had stopped they were somehow both standing back in the kitchen. And somehow he laughed and so did she and everything was all right again.

'Would you like a cup of tea?' he said.

'That would be nice.'

They held each other's hands and stood in interminable silence waiting for the kettle to boil.

Eddie texted his mother later that night.

He was in Edinburgh again. *I think I've met an angel,* he said. *Could you pick me up from Kings Cross Station tomorrow morning? My train gets in at 10.41. Sorry. Thank you. x*

Forty-eight

Some days you wake up changed.

Holly rubbed one side of her head with a fumbling hand. She had slept, woken, and slept again until her alarm had pulled her out of bed and she had opened the bedroom curtains. For once the morning sun was shining and she had to hold up her hand to shield her eyes.

She had no idea what state the living room was in. She had conjured up an image of her driving home from Lily-May's flat last night, covered in blood. There would be red impressions left by her feet in the plush carpet. A zigzagging path like crocodile tracks as she had dropped her clothes and made her way to the bedroom. But it wasn't like that. The living room was neat and tidy as it always was and she remembered she had somehow had the energy to shower and then slump onto the bed of cold pillows. Listened to hushed tones from the radio as the light had faded and her head had rolled down to her chest.

She made coffee and then a phone call to Cromwell Hospital. Lily-May was still in critical condition with a perforated lung, but they would keep Holly up to date. Bishop had left two messages, checking up on her, making sure she was okay, and she wondered if she had dreamed seeing him at the scene last night. She ran a hand through her hair and saw there were still traces of dried blood. Another wash was needed and stepping into the shower she was suddenly nine years old again and washing red paint from her hair after she and her mother had spent the morning playing with a box of new acrylics and an old canvas from the garage. After time, brushes had been discarded in favour of fingers and they had both ended up painting their faces. Vibrant smiles and butterfly eyes. Now the rainbow-blood dribbled down her shins and across her feet until it frothed and finally washed itself away.

And as she followed herself to the bathroom mirror and tried to find a patch of skin that wasn't bruised, she wondered if this was her new normal.

White shirt, black trousers and jacket, and her hair tied in a neat French braid. She may have felt beaten, but she didn't want to look it. Her pulse was racing again when she got to the station and knocked on Bishop's door.

'Come in!'

He was at his desk and stood up as she entered.

'How are you feeling?' he said.

'Lucky.'

She felt very small and strangely vulnerable, as though something inside her had been broken. There was a nervous tension, but he quickly crossed to her side and touched her on the shoulder.

'We don't have time to talk,' he whispered. 'Things are

moving fast.' There was something in his eyes. Something dangerous that she picked up on.

'Bishop—' She felt clumsy. Lost for words.

Then Vickery entered after a knock.

'Got the address, sir. Ready when you are.'

Bishop nodded, watched Vickery go, then looked around as if he had lost something and finally picked up his car keys. She wanted to get him alone, have a minute with him, but he was already putting his jacket on. He exited the office and she followed. He turned his head sharply to the left, looked along the corridor and gave an apologetic wave to Vickery, who was waiting by the door.

'Where are you going?' she asked him.

'We got the forensics results from your late-night trip into the forest. No sweat or human DNA, but they found a tiny animal hair.'

'An animal? What are we dealing with?' Holly said.

She saw his mouth twitch slightly, but it could have passed as a smile.

'Dave the elephant shrew.'

Bishop had wanted to talk to her, but the station walls had eyes and ears and he couldn't take the chance. Max had called him last night. The job had been more complicated than he had thought but he had taken care of business. Bishop had thanked him, but felt a general sense of unease.

He had read the police report and the killer had been a contract killer, a certain Saulius Yosovov, unknown to him, but known to Karla and the Met drug squad. Saulius had worked closely with several high-level organised crime bosses, including a certain Casper Faulks. Arrests were already being planned.

260

He wanted Holly to go home and rest but she had flat-out refused and he tried to stop thinking about her as he drove with Vickery towards the City of Westminster. It was a haven of chic restaurants and old-school pubs and they double-parked a street down from the Saatchi Gallery. Bishop exited the car and when the back-up vehicle arrived he was already at the front door of the large house and pressing the doorbell which recited a toneless rendition of the *Magic Flute* Overture.

The door opened and a woman stood there.

Goth style, black eyes. Silk dressing gown with koi carp decoration tugged in tight at her waist. Bishop flashed his warrant card. She raised her eyebrows and was about to speak but Bishop raised a finger to his lips for quiet and then whispered:

'Is Damian Voss in?'

She nodded, not particularly bothered, and moved to one side.

The kitchen was large and open-plan. Shiny white cupboards and shiny black floors. Past a central island that led to the living room and there sat Damian. On the sofa, a bowl of cereal in one hand, spoon in the other. He was watching the football. Red and white shirts on one side. Blue and white on the other. Man United and Chelsea, Bishop remembered. Early league game.

'If it was the bloody Jehovahs again I hope you told them to piss off.' Damian spoke but didn't turn. Then he saw everybody's reflections in the TV screen and his bald head spun around.

'What the fuck is this?'

'Damian Voss of Voss Architects?'

'Yes.' He tried to get up. Splashed milk on his T-shirt and ended up with soggy bran flakes on his crotch. He was wearing a matching silk dressing gown. He might have been naked underneath.

'I need to ask you some questions.'

'Now?'

Yes, now. Fuckwit.

'Who are these people, Sylvia?'

'They're the police.'

Bishop was aware that Sylvia was now standing amongst them and he got the sense that she was enjoying this. She was on their side. Staring at Damian as if he were pondlife.

'Why did you—'

'Can you look at me please, Damian?' Bishop said.

Damian was about to have another mouthful of cereal but thought better of it. He looked at Bishop.

'Where were you late on Wednesday last week?'

Doubt crossed his face. 'Fuck. I don't know.'

Damian attempted a charming smile but it went south. 'I think we had a Thai. The Blue Moon or something. Isn't that right, Sylvia?'

'I can't remember.'

'Sylvia?'

The woman shrugged and wandered off.

'I've got the receipt somewhere. I'm sure I have. Then we came home and went to bed.'

'You didn't go out again?'

'No.' Starting to get flustered. 'Why are you all here? This is my house.' Sudden indignation. Like the starter's gun going off when the runners are already halfway down the track. 'Don't you need a warrant?'

'Sylvia let us in.'

'Right. She did, did she?'

262

Damian took a mouthful of cereal. He was trying to compose himself.

'We need to talk to you about Dave.'

'Dave who?'

'Dave the elephant shrew.'

'The what?'

'The elephant shrew at your office. Your mascot.'

A pause. Almost a laugh.

'Are you serious?'

'Very, Damian.'

'Why? Is he dead? I mean … Jesus … we only gave him a bit of speed to see what would happen to him. I wanted to see how fast he could run on that wheel. That's all.'

'Dave's not dead. He's very much alive and in custody.'

'Custody?'

'Safekeeping.'

'Okay. Well – that's nice. So, what about him?'

'Who has access to him and your office?'

'You mean the staff?'

Bishop nodded.

'Everybody. People come and go all the time. Clients as well.' A pause. 'What's so special about Dave?' He sounded almost jealous.

'We need to interview all of your employees immediately.'

Damian nodded but he looked confused.

'I don't understand.'

Forty-nine

The man sat in his favourite armchair and had a cup of tea by his side.

He was still very angry with himself. He had strayed from the path but what was done was done and he couldn't bring Denise back, couldn't unbury her. It had been necessary and although it had been wrong it had felt so good. Deep breaths, time with Mother, and he had treated himself to a biscuit, but now he brushed the crumbs off his lap and contemplated.

The second body had been found and it had thrown his timing off. There were too many police in the forest again for another visit. Too many warning bells so he had to be patient. He couldn't alter the mission but he could adapt.

He picked up the phone and dialled the number from memory. By the fourth ring the calm had caught up with him again and he was ready to hang up when the answer machine kicked in with the mother's voice, soft and lilting like a Welsh chorister:

'Hello, this is the Finney residence. We're not able to come to the phone right now, but please—'

'Hello?' A different voice cut off the answer machine. 'Who's calling?' Inquisitive and fresh. A young girl's voice. It wasn't who the man wanted to talk to, but he could almost see the little hands holding the phone. The big phone that Mummy and Daddy normally use, but now I'm using it and I'm going to behave like them. 'How can I help you?'

'Is that the lady of the house?'

'No.' A pause. Very grown-up. 'This is her daughter.'

The man closed his eyes. Tried to picture the face on the other end.

'Her daughter? Oh, how lovely. Is your mother there?'

'No.'

He thought for the briefest of moments and then the words just bobbled out of his mouth.

'Maybe you can help me?'

'I can try.'

'Well, let's get to know each other first, shall we? How old are you?'

'I'm seven.'

'You're seven?' The man smiled. 'You sound so much older than that. Like a young woman. You're really just seven years old?'

'Yes.'

'What are you wearing?'

'A dress.'

'Is it blue?'

'How did you know?'

'I like blue. Blue is my favourite colour.'

'Blue is my favourite colour too.'

'Are you wearing your hair in a ponytail, Samantha?'

'Not today. Sometimes I do.' A beat. 'How do you know my name?'

'You have really nice long hair, don't you. Is it blonde?'

'Yes.'

'Just like the sun. Do you pluck your eyebrows?'

'No!' The little girl giggled at that. 'My mum does, but I'm too young.'

'You're never too young, Samantha. Ask your mummy if you can borrow her tweezers and you should give it a go.'

'Doesn't it hurt?'

'A little to start off with, but it's worth it. You get used to it. And then your eyebrows look amazing. Like little sleeping caterpillars that arch their backs whenever you smile.'

Samantha giggled.

The man giggled as well.

'That's funny. It's almost like we're friends already,' he said.

'Who are you?'

'Hm?'

'What's your name?'

'I'm a friend of your mother's.'

The man got up and went into the kitchen. He had been stewing some apples but had left the heat on too high. Now there was an acrid smell and as he placed the phone between his shoulder and his ear, he stirred the burnt stickiness off the bottom of the pan.

'Do you have any brothers, Samantha?'

'I have one brother.'

'What's his name?'

'Eddie.'

'And where is Eddie?' he asked.

266

'On holiday in Scotland again.'

'Really? Does he like Scotland?'

'Yes. I've never been.'

'Nor have I. Very cold in February. I hope Eddie took a coat.'

The girl's voice suddenly changed. It was heavy. Uncertain.

'I don't know. Mum and Dad were arguing about him. I heard them last night. He keeps missing school.'

The man nipped a mouthful of the apple from the edge of the spoon. It was oh-so-hot and oh-so-delicious.

'When's he coming back?'

'They're picking him up from the station now.'

'That's nice. And they left you all alone?'

'No. My neighbour, Mrs Jenson is here with me.'

The smile became strained. The hand holding the phone tense.

'Is she next to you listening to this phone call?'

'No. She's in the living room watching TV.'

'Can you see her from where you are?'

He heard her moving. Imagined her craning her little white neck around the sofa so she could look for Mrs Jenson. Squinting her bright little eyes.

'She's watching a show.'

He paused. 'I should go now, Samantha. I have to go back to the attic.'

'We have an attic.'

'I know you do. It's been lovely talking to you. Say hello to your mother from me.'

'I will do. Maybe ... '

'What?'

'I was thinking. Maybe you could come over and say hello to Eddie when he gets back.'

The man pondered for a second. Shook his head.

'No. Eddie's never coming back.'

A silence.

'What do you mean?'

'He's fucking dead, you little cunt. And you'll never see him again.'

Fifty

When Holly returned to the incident room another long briefing was ending and DI Thompson was giving out assignments to the officers who weren't otherwise occupied. He turned and smiled at her, but it was an effort.

Lipski and Ambrose were both staring at the map on the incident wall showing the route the killer had taken through the forest and Holly wondered if they were all missing something. Vickery put a cup of tea down on the table for her. She picked it up but couldn't face it yet.

The phone call came two minutes later.

DI Thompson was the one who answered it and his face went ashen. When he hung up, he sought her out, and as she watched him speak she couldn't ever imagine him doing anything other than this job.

'We've just had Mrs Finney contact the station.'

'Finney?'

'Gill. Her kid is called Eddie, the one who keeps bunking off to Scotland.'

'I remember.'

'He went AWOL again yesterday morning, texted her last night to say he'd be back at 10.41 today. They went to pick him up from King's Cross station, but Eddie never showed up and while they were out, a man called them at home and spoke to their daughter. The answer machine picked up the conversation by accident. You need to hear it.'

By the time Holly got to the IT room, voice experts were already trying to verify it.

Was it the real killer, or was it a fake? Almost impossible to tell, as the information given by the caller hadn't mentioned any of the previous victims and gave no hint of the real where-abouts of Eddie. There was no ransom demand – not that Holly had expected one – but there was something quietly chilling about the control with which the man had spoken.

The recording had then been broken down into three sections. The ambient noise had been removed to listen to inflections in the man's voice, homing in on his speech patterns, his characteristics and biometrics. These acoustic clues would help them determine his anatomy, i.e. size and shape of the throat and mouth, and what are termed learned behavioural patterns, detectable in his pitch and speaking style. The results were that he appeared to be well educated – college or possibly university level – and he possessed incredible self-control.

Next, the voice had been deleted and the background noise had been amplified in the hope of picking up any distinctive sounds such as trains, ambulance or police sirens, ship horns, church bells, local radio stations, television programmes, and anything else that might give a clue as to the location of the caller. There were none.

Finally they focused on what he had said. What clues had been given out in the short two-minute-and-fifteen-second conversation?

Everyone on the task force had listened to the recording numerous times. Transcripts of the conversation had been printed and emailed, and now Holly was in one corner of the incident room with a pair of headphones on, listening to the tape again and again.

Holly recalled the Yorkshire Ripper case; in 1978 a hoax tape had been sent to Chief Constable George Oldfield, the investigating officer. The voice on the tape had a Wearside accent and the police had re-directed their search to the Castletown area of Sunderland. Forty thousand men were investigated. A complete waste of time, and in the meantime the Ripper killed three more women. The hoaxer, John Samuel Humble, eventually confessed twenty-two years later. Now that she had listened to the recording several times she had no doubts.

She saw that Bishop had entered the room. He was watching her from the doorway, deep in thought. She took off her headphones and leaned against the nearest desk.

'I think it's real,' she said. Choosing her words carefully: 'But he made a mistake here. There's no way he knew he was being recorded on the answer machine.'

'So why did he call?'

'He was either reaching out to the mother or wants a connection,' a beat, 'or he was being vindictive. There are other clues here as well – he told us he has an attic. I bet that's where Eddie is.'

'Christ, it could be anywhere.'

'But it's not anywhere. It's within twenty miles of both

victims. And yes, I know there are thousands of houses out there that could easily fit that description, but this house or flat – three boys have been taken there without alerting any neighbours. So it would need to be off the beaten track. More likely to be detached, rather than a semi or terrace. Thin walls are no good if you have a kidnapped child. Probably a covered driveway or a garage as well.'

'Maybe we're wrong and he's keeping Eddie in an old warehouse or something.'

'He wouldn't risk leaving the boy out of his sight. Someone could stumble upon him, he could escape from his restraints. No, I think the killer needs him to be close. Needs to be able to watch him, I think that's part of his psychology. It all comes down to his need to control.' A pause. 'I believe Eddie is being kept at the killer's house. Which tells us that he either lives alone, or lives with someone who he can dominate without them asking awkward questions.' A beat. 'Where are the Finneys now?'

'At home. They confirmed Eddie left Friday morning and then sent a text message to them Friday night asking to get picked up at the train station this morning. I spoke to the Scottish police. They've checked all CCTV of trains from Friday evening arriving at Edinburgh Waverley, Park and Gateway. No sign of Eddie. Same with the trains coming back this morning.'

She watched Bishop's face as she thought to herself, putting something together.

'He was abducted before he ever got on the train.' She was silent for a while before she went on. 'Which means it was the killer who texted Gill and Alan last night.'

She hesitated for a second, and felt compelled to say

something, but before she could, Hachette shouted from the other side of the room:

'Sir! Eddie Finney's phone has been turned off but we've retrieved some of his text messages via the iCloud. He was sent directions to a meeting place in the forest just like the other boys. There's a canine unit en route now.'

It was fifty feet behind an old bus depot about a mile and a half into Epping Forest and eight hundred metres from where Matthew Cotton had been found. The dogs were already there when they arrived. Rambling through everything like curious children let out of their playpen for the first time. Paws black from the mud, noses wet from the rain, trained to bark when they found that familiar smell, but the air remained still and silent. Bishop came over to Holly and the two stood next to each other for a time in silence. Then he shook his head, perplexed.

'He's not here.'

'No.'

'Why would he change his MO?'

'He wouldn't,' Holly said. 'It was working.' And she looked slightly on edge now. 'Which makes me think Eddie Finney may still be alive.'

Fifty-one

Holly parked in the Finneys' driveway.

Birch trees either side, but the surface was pitted and the shrubs in the heavy stone pots were leafless. It was a three-storey Georgian mansion with sash windows that had been turned into flats and the house had been freshly re-painted. There was money here and she was sure Eddie had never wanted for anything. Holly had been the girl with the hand-me-downs from her foster mother. Charity shop jeans and dresses – but her weapon had been hard work. There was a certain feel to wealth, a certain scent, and Holly was well aware she didn't possess it. There had been jibes from class-mates at school which was why she had rebelled. Piercings and tattoos. But dead is dead. We all turn to ash in the end no matter what we start with, and as she rang the bell her thoughts went to Gill and Alan.

White-faced. Hollow-cheeked. Sitting by the phone, making sure it's charged. Checking the home phone. The wire – has it been unplugged? Is the phone off the hook? No, love, everything's fine. But it's not fine, is it, Gill would say, and then they would stare into the silence. The horrible silence. And seconds would seem like hours, a slow drag between endless cups of coffee and closing your eyes for a minute of sleep but you can't, just in case the phone rings. Just in case there's a knock at the door.

Gill opened the door and Holly followed her into her living room. It was painted white, but full of colour, a casual arrangement of paintings, family photos and heirloom collectables. Gill gestured Holly into a comfortable chair and then lowered herself onto a sofa, paused, remembered something, got up, went to the kitchen and returned with an old coffee mug to use as an ashtray. Holly wondered where their daughter, Samantha, was. Tucked safely away somewhere she hoped.

'There's a chance that Eddie may not be dead,' Holly said.

Gill held the tears, but Holly could sense the sick empty feeling as she began to talk.

'Don't say things like that.' She was looking directly at Holly as if she was being particularly crass and cruel. 'Why say that?'

'The killer has a method. An MO. He has killed two boys so far. He sends them instructions via social media to meet him, and on both occasions – with Matthew Cotton and Noah Beasley – he has then taken their bodies to the exact same place where he picked them up. We have the coordinates for where we think Eddie met him.'

'Where? Where was it?'

'Near an old bus stop in Epping Forest off Thurwell Road. The police sent out twenty men and K9 units—'

'Dogs? They're called cadaver dogs, aren't they?'

'Yes, they are. And they didn't find him. If he had been there they would have found him.'

275

'Maybe you got the directions wrong? Maybe he's really close to where you looked but you missed him in the under-growth. Behind a big tree. You could have missed him.'

'We wouldn't have missed him. That's why we want you to go on television. Make an appeal.'

'I don't understand.'

'Appeal to the killer. If Eddie is still alive it's important that we let him see you.'

Gill picked up her coffee mug and took a sip. It was too hot and it burned her mouth, but she didn't say anything. Put the mug down and kept staring at it. Her voice was low when she spoke:

'Why would he call me?'

'To connect to you. To talk.'

'Why?' She answered her own question. 'To gloat? It's about power, isn't it?' She shrugged and held her shoulders up by her ears for a long time as if she had an itch that she couldn't scratch. 'It must be hard for you as well. You know things we don't. More than we ever will about this. That's not easy, carrying that sort of truth inside you.'

No, it's not, Holly wanted to tell her. It eats me up. Every minute. Every second.

'The other dead boys,' Gill said distantly. 'Do their parents know about their sons?'

'Yes.'

'Do they get help? I mean counselling, when this sort of thing happens?'

'The police have bereavement counsellors on call,' Holly said.

'On call?'

'Twenty-four hours a day. Part of the service.'

'Right,' Gill whispered. 'Part of the service.'

She lit a cigarette. Her mouth set angrily.

'I keep asking myself: if I could change one thing about my life what would it be? Perhaps if I hadn't given birth to Eddie, then I wouldn't be in this situation, would I? No – I can't say that because that's selfish. I would have taken him away from the rest of the world and they wouldn't have had a chance to meet him, to see him and to grow to love him. It's not as if I didn't want him. So what would I change? Watching him more closely. Being more attentive. Not judging him. How could I have stopped this?'

'You couldn't have.'

'No?' She paused to look up. Straining her eyes. 'I could have lived somewhere else. If I had lived in France in some quaint village, this would never have happened, would it? If I had divorced my husband, that's a possibility.'

'Is it?'

'You know whenever I'm in bed he puts his head on his pillow, closes his eyes and sleeps. How does he do that? I can't. He always sleeps so soundly. Like a baby. He's had a few rough nights perhaps, but nothing like me. I saw myself in the mirror this morning in the bathroom. I'd been sick again. There was a mad woman staring back at me. Who the hell was that angry, *angry* woman staring at me? The woman with the sad eyes, the sad face. The worried hair. What has become of me? Why am I like this? I'm punishing myself, I know. Slowly killing me. Taking revenge on motherhood in the worst possible way.'

'You need to stop now.'

'Says the woman with no children.' Gill closed her eyes briefly, smoked for a few seconds. 'Do you want to be a mother?'

'Yes.'

'Will you be, I wonder? What would you be doing in my position?'

'Probably the same thing.'

'I'm going to make myself sick again, I think.' She had turned pale.

'Please don't.'

Gill ignored her. Got up and went to the bathroom. She didn't bother closing the door. Holly took a cigarette out of the packet and laid it by Gill's cup of tea.

The toilet flushed. Gill returned, wiping her mouth, and picked up the cigarette.

'Thank you.'

She lit it and inhaled. Began to play with the collar of her shirt.

'Sometimes it's so easy to think that I've gone crazy. I haven't, have I?'

'No.'

'When you look around. See what's going on. Do you ever think like that?'

'That I'm crazy?'

'Yes.'

'Sometimes.'

'There is a dark side to this world that I'd never seen before. Now I have. Men who kill – and you look inside them, don't you?'

'Yes.'

'My God, you must live a soulless life.' Her voice sounded suddenly loud. 'Sorry, that was rude. I'm angry. My husband is asleep and you're here. You're my punching bag.'

'That's okay.'

'I feel as though I should stand up and tell the world.'

'Tell the world what?'

'The truth. That none of this is real. The people walking and the people shopping. Ordering their frappuccinos and their one-shot decaf soya lattes and their lemon poppy-seed muffins. None of it is real.'

'It's real.'

'But it's not what's really happening, is it? Behind the curtain.'

A pause before Holly answered. 'No, it's not.'

Gill smiled. It was the first time Holly had seen it. It was curious, but it was cynical too.

'I have prepared something for the press conference, although it is the one speech I never thought I would have to write.' Gill tipped her cigarette into the old mug. 'What a horrible host I've been.' A pause. 'Since Eddie has been gone, my imagination has been going crazy and I can't stop it. You see, there are two sides to this coin. There's one side where I think he's still alive and he's out there and he's running around and I think of him shopping and eating at Pret or going to the library and looking at his phone and thinking "Hey – I'm going to text you, Mum. I'll text you today. Ah – you know what? I'll text you in a minute." Why does my mind do that when I know where he is? Some sort of coping mechanism?'

'Yes.'

'And then there's the other side, the flip side, which I don't like: I think of him lying down. Face down in the mud with leaves under his head and twigs in his hair. And he's cold and needs a blanket. Lying there with his . . . I don't know. I have to stop myself because I don't want to see him like that. I want to return to the first image when he's sitting down and having a coffee and he's smiling, about to call me. And that's how I get through my days.' She contemplated Holly through a spiral of smoke. 'But I don't know about tomorrow.'

Holly got up. 'We should go. They'll be waiting for us.'

Gill stood. She seemed unsteady on her feet but managed to right herself. They stared at each for a long while. Knowing each other, but strangers at the same time. Gill reached out to Holly's hands and circled them in her own. Her grip was strong, her fingers cold.

'I don't care.' Gill spoke slowly. 'I don't care if you find a fingernail or one piece of his hair. One damn piece. I don't care. I want you to find out where he is. Find out where that beast put him. I want a piece of my boy brought home, so I have something to bury and I can put him to rest.'

Holly looked at her and added gently:

'I will find him, Mrs Finney.'

'You're not supposed to say that, are you, Holly?'

'No.'

'Then don't lie to me.'

Fifty-two

'Eddie, we need you to come home now. We miss you. Your mum, your dad, your sister. Your friends miss you at school. They wrote you a lovely letter. They did it all together in assembly. I'll read it out to you.'

She fumbled for her glasses and rested them on the bridge of her nose. She blinked a few times as she focused on the piece of paper in her hands.

'Dearest Eddie. Where are you? Our friend, Eddie. You have walked away but have not come back. We need you here for sports day. We need you here for the art exhibition this summer. We need you here for the playground games and for the maths lessons. So we can copy your homework! Please come back. We're keeping your chair empty for you. We love you.'

Gill folded the letter and put it away.

'We know you are with someone at the moment, Eddie, and we are now asking that someone to let you come home to us. Please, let him come home, so he can be with us again. You may have made a home for him. But it won't be his home.

281

It will be a foreign home that he doesn't recognise. That he may not feel comfortable in. And you may not know that. You may think he's happy there. You may think he's comfortable. But deep down he won't be. And he may even have told you he is happy to be polite because he's such a lovely boy. But deep down he won't be comfortable. He won't be happy, and he'll want to come home. Come home to his own bed. To my cooking, to his dad's bad jokes, and to his sister. But we know he's going to come home. We know you're going to do the right thing. We know you're going to let Eddie go. Let him come home to us. And we won't press charges. We won't. We don't know why you took him. And that's not relevant to us. But you do have him. Somewhere in London. We know that and we want him home. I can't say this or stress this enough. But we love him. Perhaps you feel as though you love him too. Perhaps you feel as though you have a bond with Eddie. But my bond is stronger. Because I am his mother. And no matter what you do, that bond will never be broken. I gave birth to him. He'll always be mine. Always be the one that I think of. And the one that I know I will find and will be able to hold again. And carry on loving him like I have done ever since the day he was born.'

She stopped and glared at the camera. There was a hush. An anticipation of what would come next, but—

'That's all I have to say,' she said.

Holly watched Gill leave amidst the flash of cameras and barking questions. Stared after her, until Bishop found her and gave her a nod:

'Briefing in one minute.'

Bishop had positioned himself in front of the incident board when he said:

'Everybody? A second, please.'

All heads spun around.

'We don't know if the appeal will work. If the killer will perhaps try to contact the family again or if he will respond to their pleas and release their boy – the latter being highly unlikely. But what it may do is give him pause for thought, make him think about what he is doing and perhaps delay the next kill. Eddie went missing yesterday afternoon. We know that, for whatever reason, the killer kept Noah Beasley alive for one day and gave him water, so let's hope he is doing the same for Eddie. If he is not – then he will probably already be dead, but we have to go with the assumption that he is still alive.' He pulled down the photo of Eddie from the incident board and held it up, showing it to the room, missing no one, and Holly thought he seemed to pull everyone's thoughts together.

'Edward Brian Finney.' A double beat. 'Eddie to his friends. Therefore I think we should all refer to him as Eddie from now on. That's what his mates call him at school. And as from now we are also his mates. His best friends. The buddies he hangs out with.' Holly saw Ambrose wipe his eyes. 'So we'll call him Eddie. This is him. Look at him. Connect to him. Get a copy of his photo and stick it on your computer. That way, he is with you every second from now on. Fourteen years old. Blue eyes. A skinny little kid really. Frail and fragile. Not like any of you. He wouldn't be able to defend himself when someone attacked him. Didn't know how to fight. But you all do. You fight.'

Holly felt a lump in her throat.

'And now you fight for Eddie.'

Fifty-three

Even though it was a Saturday, all of the employees at Voss Architects had rallied themselves to help the police.

Half of the staff had driven to the police station and the rest had given DNA samples at the office. Clients who had come to visit in the past three months had been contacted, as well as catering staff for an office lunch from the previous month, and the three cleaners who worked rotating night shifts.

Because the office was now a location of interest, everybody had been asked to stay away from the premises until further notice and it was empty apart from Lydia Smith, Damian Voss's joint investment partner, and a half-dozen forensic officers. Holly had spoken to Lydia after she had given a buccal swab and now she sat in the leather chair in her office and carried on as if nothing was happening. Holly could hear her laugh every now and then as she fielded phone calls from clients. She wondered if Lydia was telling them what was happening or if she was keeping quiet and carrying on as normal, pretending that the police hum in the background was her regular weekend employees. There was an empty cage to her left; Dave the elephant shrew had been whisked away by Anton and his team with the promise of fresh earthworms and a millipede.

Holly looked around at the unfamiliar room, went to the window that John Pickford had seen Noah from, and stared at the grey landscape outside. The click-click of cameras made her turn and she began walking the length of the office, stopping at everyone's desks along the way. Untidy, neat, neat, untidy. Different personalities, different lives, different rules. An unwashed coffee mug, crumbs on one desk from a snack that would probably still be there in a month. Neat desk again. Another untidy one and she wondered if the cleaners were left instructions never to touch anyone's personal workspace. She stopped at one without touching anything for a few minutes. It was the neatest desk in the office. Everything had its place. The computer dead centre, stapler to the right. Three pencils laid out in a row. Four pens behind. All perpendicular to each other. An empty *In and Out* tray. A coaster with a photo of a young teeage boy on it. It looked hand-made, from one of those make-your-own pottery shops that had sprung up in the past ten years. She put on latex gloves and turned it over – a simple layer of cork underneath – then put it exactly where she had found it.

She lowered herself into the chair and wondered who sat here during the day. A good view of the whole place, and directly in front of her was a montage of cut-outs from newspapers and magazines, pinned to a square of cork.

Man searches for dog but finds a wife!
    Buy one bottle of bleach and get—
    4. He looks you in the eye all the time

She read that last one again. Why was that familiar?

4. He looks you in the eye all the time.

She walked over, unpinned it and pulled it down. Started to read. Then it came back to her – the magazine she had found in Bishop's car – *Ten signs that he's into you!* It was the same article. *Even when you're not necessarily talking, he'll be trying to make eye contact.* Why had Bishop had it? Holly tried to remember what else had been in the magazine but couldn't. She was about to pin it when she turned it over and saw the photo of Noah on the reverse:

Boy's body found in forest. Epping Forest is no stranger to dead bodies but local residents are saying this is the most mysterious case they have ever seen. Turn to page five for more details!

She replaced the cut-out on the cork board and read the next one along:

Raising money for the new sports centre roof

On a whim she removed it and turned it over. A shot of Darya and Aaron holding a photo of their son, and below it the headline:

Missing boy identified as Noah Beasley

She replaced it, deep in thought. The next one was an advert for bleach:

2 for 1 special on Vim

She removed it and held it as if it were either incredibly hot or unbearably cold. Turned it over. It was a photograph of the crime-scene tent from another newspaper. She couldn't tell which one but it didn't matter. She took a step and stared at the board. There must be forty or fifty cuttings.

'Mrs Smith?'

Lydia had come off the phone and was over at the window watching the forensics team with a quiet detachment, but she heard Holly and approached.

'Yes?'

'This collection of newspaper articles. What is it?'

Lydia looked at the press cuttings as if seeing them for the first time.

'It's the company ideas board of local events that we can use for pitches. One of John Pickford's creations.'

'Sorry, whose?'

'John Pickford's.'

Holly paused.

'John Pickford did all this?'

'Yes.'

'How long has John been here?'

'Just over a month.'

'And when did his ideas board start?'

'A couple of weeks ago. It didn't make sense to me, but Damian let him play.'

Frowning slightly, Holly chose another scrap of newspaper at random and took it down.

Man searches for dog ... turned it over. Another photo of Darya and Aaron with Ruby clutched between them, and the headline:

She put it exactly as it had been and asked one of the forensics officers to take photographs of the whole board. When he was done, she pulled off all the clippings and laid them on the closest table. Forty-seven articles from newspapers across England. Thirty-nine of them had photos or headlines about the case on the reverse.

'Which one is John's desk?' Holly said.

'That one over there. The one you were sitting at a few moments ago.'

Holly went and sat in John Pickford's chair. The neatest desk in the office and the board was right in front of her.

She held up the coaster of the boy.

'Does John have a son?'

'I don't know.'

Lydia was watching her with a mix of disgust and astonishment. 'What does this mean?'

'Where does John live?'

A pause. Recollecting.

'Out by Theydon Bois, I think. Not too far from here.'

'I need a sample of his handwriting. Can you supply that to me?'

'Of course.' The slow burn was building. 'What's going on?'

Holly turned away, grabbed her phone and dialled Bishop. He answered on the first ring.

'Holly.'

'Is John Pickford with you?'

'I think he's downstairs giving his statement. Why?'

A long pause.

288

'Holly?'

She had to slow herself down. Had to think. She kept the excitement close to her, nothing must show. And then she said very quietly:

'It's him.'

Fifty-four

'Shit!'

Bishop took the stairs down three at a time.

No one coming the other way, thank God, or he would have bowled them over. He landed on the ground floor with a thump, his right knee twinged but he kept going, smashed past the double doors, out to the booking desk and through to the interview rooms where all of the Voss employees had been questioned. Vickery was exiting an office and Bishop grabbed him and the folder of papers he was carrying.

'Is John Pickford still here?'

'He left about fifteen minutes ago.'

'I need his information, now.'

Vickery handed over the folder like the British 4x400 relay team on a bad day and all the papers cascaded to the floor. They both went down on hands and knees, knuckles scraping, eyes trying to focus on the handwriting and ticked boxes. There were only thirty-four employees, it shouldn't have been—

'Got it,' Vickery said and passed it over.

Bishop scanned it. Full name: John Andrew Pickford; Age: thirty-six; Address: 4 Station Approach, Theydon Bois, CM16; Car make and model: Ford Mondeo; Registration number: FTH Y78Y; Next of kin: blank; Work contact details: Voss Architects; Emergency contact: Eileen Palmerston—

'Sir?' Vickery was standing with his mouth open. 'What's going on?'

'Don't know yet.'

Bishop retraced his steps to the stairs and pressed the lift button. The light flashed but stayed on the fourth floor. Seemingly for ever.

'Shit!'

He started the climb, trying to read the form at the same time, cursed as he tripped, picked himself up and cursed some more because he didn't exercise as much as he used to, and he probably still smoked too much – three floors up and he was still ruminating when he went through the side doors. This time there were officers milling about but they swept themselves to one side as he bellowed something indecipherable and then managed a gruff *thank you* forty feet later. By the time he got to the incident room he was sweating.

'Listen up!'

Heads swivelled.

'Drop everything! John Pickford – one of the Voss employees. He drives a Ford Mondeo, registration number FTH Y78Y. I want immediate ANPR and CCTV of when he left the station today. He lives at number four Station Approach in Theydon Bois, so plot a route-tracker from here to there and find him.'

A chorus of: 'Yes, sirs' as heads swivelled to screens.

'I also want a recent photo from this morning, when he

came into the station. Grab something from the internal CCTV and stick it up on the incident board under "Suspects". I want a record of his online activity – Facebook, Instagram, Twitter – all the usual haunts.'

Five minutes. Ten. Bishop dropped his eyes to the floor to hide his impatience. If it was John Pickford and he had been at the station—

Lipski shouted: 'Sir! ANPR picked him up on camera ten miles away, heading north on the Finchley Road towards the A406.' A murmur of voices as the whole room seemed to come to life.

'How many active units do we have in the vicinity?' Bishop said as he came around to her screen.

'Only one. Foxtrot Two, sir. Three quarters of a mile away in Seven Kings.'

'Get them over there and have them follow him home.'

'What's going on, Bishop?'

A conspiratorial whisper from Thompson.

'John Pickford,' Bishop said.

'One of the eyewitnesses?'

Bishop stayed mute. Holly had said it was him. She had explained about the 'ideas board' at the office. It was staring us right in the face, she had said. Staring all of the other employees in the face as well. He was basically telling everybody at Voss that he was the killer but he knew none of them would ever cotton on to what he was doing. He was showing everybody that he was in control, yet at the same time keeping it a secret. Bishop hadn't asked for anything more, he had taken her word for it, hung up the phone and completed a mini assault course through the station in record time, and now he was up here, pulse still topping a hundred.

'He's joined the M11. Heading north.' Jump-cutting from camera to camera. 'Going to be passing Chigwell in about two minutes.'

'How close are Foxtrot Two?'

'Two hundred feet behind him. He's coming up to the exit on Rectory Lane.'

'Tell them to close in. I don't want to lose him.'

'Foxtrot Two. Close the gap. Beware there are lights at the exit.'

Bishop realised his hands were sweating.

'Hold on, sir,' Lipski said in disbelief. 'He's driven past the exit.'

'Where the hell is he going?' Thompson leaned in. 'You think he saw the tail?'

'Christ, I don't see how,' Bishop said. But he could see how. If Pickford was smart and a planner, like Holly had said, he would be so careful, extra careful. If it was him. Maybe it wasn't? Perhaps John Pickford was simply doing his civic duty and the 'ideas board' was a silly coincidence and he had nothing to do with this and Holly was wrong. The trouble was, he didn't think she was.

'He'll be coming up to junction twenty-seven in two minutes.'

'Can he get to his flat from there?'

'Yes, sir. He'll go first left onto the M25, two miles east and left on Theydon Road. It's a weird way of driving home though.'

Lipski's eyes were white and wide and never left the screen, and Bishop wondered if she had ever tracked a high-speed situation before.

'He's at junction twenty-seven now, sir. Stopped at the lights. Foxtrot Two are three cars behind.' She spoke into her head-mic: 'Be advised, Foxtrot Two, target will be taking the next left at the roundabout on to the M25, then first exit on to Theydon Road.'

A silence in the room as all of the squad watched John Pickford's stationary car. Ten seconds passed. The lights changed. The car moved forward and suddenly indicated right and switched lanes.

'Shit,' said Bishop.

'Foxtrot Two have lost him,' Lipski confirmed. 'They've had to exit.'

'Tell them to proceed to his residence and wait for him.'

Lipski gave the order as the cameras switched and followed Pickford around the roundabout. He stopped at a second set of lights and indicated left.

'Looks like he's going west on the M25 now. Southbound will take him through Stapleford Tawney, the next junction will be number twenty-eight. North leads to Brentwood, south to Gallows Corner and Romford. There's also Hornchurch and Upminster off the A124.'

'He's making a run for it?' Thompson said.

'Christ,' Bishop swore. 'There is no way he's—'

Suddenly the car signal switched to the right again as the lights changed. He moved over two lanes and exited east-bound on the M25, taking the main road towards Theydon Bois.

'Looks like he's back on track, sir. Twenty-nine minutes until he gets home. Foxtrot Two will be in position in seventeen.'

'Let me know when they get there.'

Fifty-five

'When John Pickford came in he gave his fingerprints and a buccal swab, same as everyone else.'

Holly was rushing with Vickery towards the incident room.

'Did he seem worried? Nervous?'

'No, very chilled. He even cracked a few jokes. He was quite funny.'

'Is there any previous with him?'

'He's as clean as a whistle, but we've got four other employees from Voss's with minor infractions. Two for speeding, one for assault – but it was thrown out of court—'

'What type of assault?'

'Nightclub argument with a bouncer – the bouncer came out on top. And the last one is for drugs possession, a bit of cocaine, three years ago. Damian Voss, the boss.'

'Nothing else?'

A shake of the head as Vickery pushed open the doors and they entered the bustle of the incident room. Bishop waved her over and they found seats on one of the desks by the monitors.

'What did you want to show me?' she said.

Bishop took a moment, wiped his face with his hands and gestured to the CCTV:

'It might be nothing – but when Pickford was heading home he totally ignored the exit towards Loughton, which would be five minutes from his place, and carried on up the M11. Gets to the roundabout, indicated left for the M25 but changed his mind at the last second. Here' – he started the replay – 'Theydon Bois is to the left and see, he signals that way, but then he signals right, crosses two lanes and gets to the next set of lights. Hesitates and does the same thing. Indicates to get off, but when the lights change he completes the roundabout and carries on with his original route home.'

Holly nodded. She had seen enough.

'So in those fifteen, twenty seconds at the lights he was deciding what to do,' she said quietly. 'I've left the police station after giving my DNA samples. I'm nervous. Do I go left and head home? Home is safe.' She stood up and walked over to the map. 'Or do I go right and head over here somewhere . . . where though? A place where he's keeping Eddie? We need to check on all properties under the name of Pickford. Companies as well.'

Bishop got up and stood next to her, both mesmerised by the map.

'He lives in Theydon Bois,' he said. 'And rents a single room in a two-bedroom split-level maisonette flat. I've asked for a floorplan, to be on the safe side, but—'

'He won't be keeping Eddie there.'

'No. We've got two teams watching the property and he hasn't moved since he got home at eleven o'clock. His flatmate is called Julien Framer, an interior designer who works in Streatham. He's not there at the moment but we've already put a call in to him.'

'Any social media at all from John?'

'Nothing. No digital trace whatsoever.'

'That's interesting.' She was about to—

Bishop's phone rang.

'Yeah?'

He seemed to age in front of her eyes before he hung up and sat down on the closest desk. 'No CCTV of any Mondeo either entering or leaving the forest that night on any of the roads.'

'Maybe he's got a second car?' Thompson said.

'What the hell was he thinking?' Holly said aloud. 'In those fifteen seconds he wanted to go somewhere. But where? Can I see Pickford's statement?'

He handed it over. She scanned through it and stopped on the second page.

'No next of kin.' Turned to the third. 'Eileen Palmerston, his emergency contact. His fiancée. Do we know who she is?' Her eyeline lifted to the CCTV of the blonde woman who dropped Noah's phone and she wondered if it was her. Walking into the forest. Driving a different car?

'Her contact details list her as working at a company called Bainbridge and Co,' Bishop said. 'They're architects as well. We have her home address. An estate called Waterloo Gardens in Romford.'

'Romford?' Holly put a hand up to the map. 'That's on the A12 off from the M25. He could have been going to see her.'

'I'll drive,' Bishop said.

Fifty-six

A seventies block of cement and glass in Romford, Essex.

Bishop parked the car, they got out and he pulled open the main doors and headed up the stairs. Fourth floor and they entered a long corridor where every other light was broken. There were a few potted plants outside number fifty-seven, but the door needed a coat of paint. Bishop rang the bell. No answer.

'We have her number.'

He pulled out his mobile and punched it in. Behind them a woman entered the landing carrying two shopping bags. A woman with short blonde hair. Black bomber jacket, jeans and trainers.

The phone started to ring. Echoing in the enclosed space. Holly watched the woman walk closer, suddenly lower one of her bags and pull a mobile from her purse.

'Hello?' she said.

'Hello,' Bishop said.

All three clocked what was happening at the same time. The woman glanced over at them, eyes wide. She froze for a second and then her mouth fell open and she suddenly dropped both bags, turned and ran.

'Eileen!' Bishop shouted.

No good – she slammed open the landing door and was out of sight in a matter of seconds. Holly gave chase, dodging past fallen groceries, pushing open the door, Bishop close behind. Following the figure down the stairs, arms and legs flailing until a door banged open somewhere and thirty seconds later Holly went through the same door and was outside. Slick and wet, because in the past few minutes it had started raining. The woman was straight ahead. Shooting looks behind her, a scarf flapping over her shoulder like a manic tongue.

'I'll go right,' Bishop shouted. Holly felt him peel off as the council houses flashed by in a grey drizzle. The woman skidded to a halt at the end of the road and took the right onto a footpath. Holly was gaining ground until the concrete jungle turned into a fence of ivy on either side with a dark curving tunnel up ahead.

Inside the tunnel, everything suddenly became quiet. Her footsteps stopped. Just darkness. And then a scuffle and Holly heard a familiar voice:

'Holly?'

'Bishop? Shit – I'm sorry, I lost her.'

'Don't worry,' and she could hear him smiling in the darkness. 'I got her.'

'Why did you run?'

'I didn't know who you were. I thought . . . I owe money to some people. Figured you might have come to repossess my things. I'm sorry.'

They were at her flat, carrying her salvaged groceries and hovering on the doorstep until Bishop broke the ice.

'Can we come in? Maybe easier to talk inside?'

She opened the door and led them through the corridor and into the kitchen. She put the kettle on and leaned against the kitchen counter. The place was used, needed a wipe-down. Today's breakfast bowls in the sink along with fallen coffee cups.

'We'd like to talk to you about John Pickford,' Bishop said.

Eileen prickled and her lips became thin.

'That's a name I never want to hear again.'

'You were engaged to him?'

She shook her head. 'No. John and I were never engaged. We dated for a few months when I first joined Bainbridge and Co, but it didn't work out and he left and went to work over at Voss Architects. Why are you interested in him?'

'Routine questions for an ongoing enquiry. Tell us what you know about him.'

She wasn't totally convinced, but answered anyway: 'I moved to town about six months ago. Needed a new start. Bainbridge and Co were hiring and they were like a Godsend to me. John was one of the draughtsmen – we bumped into each other in the canteen, started to chat. He seemed nice. Laughed at the right times. We decided to meet up for a drink one night after work at a bar on Neasden Lane. It was quiet. Tapas and wine – intimate. We ordered food, started talking. Casual but by the end of the evening he had his hands everywhere. I told him to stop and he did. Felt embarrassed by it, I think, and the next day he sent me a massive bouquet of flowers. Total overkill. Fifty roses or something. I felt a little awkward at the office after that, but he was persistent and so we went out again.'

'What was he like this time?'

'A perfect gentleman. He dropped me off at home by ten and we started dating.'

'During that period did he ever get violent with you?'

'Violent? No. He was always very gentle. I couldn't imagine him hurting anyone.'

'What went wrong?' Holly asked.

'It started to get a bit weird. He seemed so intense. And then I discovered he had lied about a few things. Stupid things. I saw him driving past my house once and I called him and he said it couldn't have been him because he was at home watching TV, but I saw him, I know I did. And then after that I started getting a red rose every day at work.'

'From him?'

'Well, I said thank you to start off with, but then after a week I asked him to stop. It was too much.'

'And what did he say?'

'He said it wasn't him sending me the roses. I thought he was joking, but he kept denying it and said I obviously had another admirer. So one day I followed him at lunch and sure enough he was at the florist around the corner, ordering another rose for me. I confronted him and he laughed and said he didn't want me to know. But he had been so adamant that it wasn't him. Had lied so convincingly that it made me pause for a second. I've been out with possessive men before and it's not a good fit. So I called it off, there and then. I broke up with him.'

'How long ago was this?'

'Six weeks ago.'

'How did he take it?'

The kettle boiled. She grabbed a mug from the cupboard, but didn't put it down.

'Not well is the understatement of the century. He was angry. Then upset. He came over to my house wanting to talk about it. I let him in because I felt guilty, but after three hours he wouldn't leave. I called my neighbour over and she managed to get him out. After that I refused to answer his calls, and tried to avoid him. At work he would just stare at me and other times ignore me. And then he started spreading rumours, saying that I had cheated on him. I hadn't, God no. But he was so manipulative, and some of the staff believed him, you know? I've never been in a situation like that. It was horrible. I lost my confidence, I thought I was going to lose my job, so after a month I went to my boss, Mr Chambers, one of the CEOs and told him what was happening. He heard my story, backed me and two days later the board asked John Pickford to leave.'

'How well do you know Voss Architects?'

'I know their reputation. They're good. After he was there for about a week he left me a message at home. He was like – "*Hey – thought you'd like to know I've settled in okay over here – they're treating me really well. Hope all's good. Be great to see you again.*" As if everything that had happened between us didn't exist. As if we were best friends or something. It was creepy. He even came to the office once – one of the staff saw him lurking outside. Told her we had made plans to meet up for coffee—'

'Had you?'

'No! God, no! That's the thing: he lies.' A pause and Holly noticed Eileen had been inching forward throughout the story and was now upright in front of them. 'I alerted security and told the receptionist not to let him in. She's blocked all of his calls since then.'

'Has he called much?'

Eileen led them through to the living room. A half-hidden sofa under clothes and old pillows, plates on the coffee table with knives and forks.

She pulled a file from the bookshelf. Opened it and read from the first page:

'John Pickford has called my office twenty-seven times since he was asked to leave Bainbridge and Co. The times and dates are all noted.' She handed over the sheet to Bishop.

'Did you ever see him again?'

'I saw him once – about a month ago. At the coffee shop around the corner from work.'

'Was he with anyone?'

'He was sitting at the same table as a woman, but I didn't know if they were together.'

'Could it have been this woman?'

Bishop showed her the CCTV image.

'It's possible. I don't know. Maybe … I mean … I don't know, sorry. The moment I saw him in that café I walked backwards and went in the opposite direction to the train station.'

Eileen checked her watch. Gathered her jacket and picked up her car keys.

'Sorry, I have to go now and pick up my son from school.'

'Your son?' Holly asked.

'Yes.'

Heading to the door. Passing photos on the hallstand that Holly hadn't seen when they first came in. It was the same boy on the coaster by John's desk.

'How old is he?'

Eileen suddenly sounded dry and strained.

'Twelve years old. His name is Harper.'

'How did John get on with your boy?' Holly asked.

'He treated him as if he was his dad. Harper is autistic, his own father died when he was three and it's hard for him to form relationships, but John was very patient with him and they took to each other almost immediately. He and John used to do homework together. Writing, maths, art. Harper drew some pictures of John. I can show you, if you like.'

'Please.'

She went to a bureau in the living room and pulled open the bottom drawer. Handed over a couple of sketches in pencil and wax crayons.

'Can we keep these, please?' Holly said.

'I'll need them back. Harper will know they're missing.'

'Did you ever go to John's flat?' Bishop said.

'Once. I met his flatmate. I can't remember his name. We didn't stay long. I never got to meet his mother.'

'His mother?' Holly breathed out slowly.

'Yes. She lives near him, I think.'

'What makes you say that?'

'Because once I was cooking a meal for us and I needed some cream, I called him up and asked if he could bring some over. He said he could come right away, because he was at his mum's. He was at my house within ten minutes.'

'But you never met her?'

'No. John had arranged for us to meet on a couple of occasions, but then he told us she was either sick or had a ladies' lunch or something and he cancelled it on her behalf.' She checked her watch. 'I do have to go.'

'One more thing,' Holly said. 'When was the last time you spoke to John?'

'He called me a week ago on my home phone, to make sure Harper and I were okay.'

'What do you mean?' Holly said.

'After the murder of the boy in the forest. Noah, I think his name was. Poor thing. His mother must be . . . ' A beat. 'John called me up and asked me if I'd read about it. I said yes, I had obviously, it was front-page news. He told me not to worry. He said he'd always protect Harper. I said – that's kind, I know you will – but we're not together any more so . . . He wanted to make sure that I knew that Harper would never get hurt.'

'Have you seen him since then? Since that phone call?'

'No. Look – what's this about?' She took a breath. 'I hope he's not caused any trouble, has he?'

'Thanks for your time,' Bishop said.

They went outside and she locked the door. Bustled off in a hurry and Holly and Bishop followed at a slow pace, still watching her as they talked.

They got down to the street in time to watch Eileen's car disappear.

'You think he'd try and hurt her son?' Bishop said.

'No. I think he cares for him too much. Loves him. I think that's what this is all about.' Squinting at the cloudy sky. It was as if her mind was coming out of a deep sleep.

'Hell hath no fury like a sociopath scorned.'

Fifty-seven

Holly pulled out a road map of London from the glove box of Bishop's car which she unfolded onto her legs. Bishop turned on the interior light as she tried to get her bearings.

'How certain are you that it's John Pickford?' Bishop asked her.

'Ninety-nine per cent.'

'Not one hundred?'

'I'm never one hundred per cent sure on anything. There are too many variables.'

'Why draw attention to himself by being an eyewitness?'

'A lot of killers ingratiate themselves with the police.' Holly turned to him. 'It gives their ego a massive boost. Here I am among you and yet you still have no idea who I am. Edmund Kemper used to drink with the cops at the Jury Room Bar in Santa Cruz California after he had murdered ten people. But in this case, I think Pickford needed to know what was happening in the investigation. How we were progressing. For whatever reason he was getting spooked. Do you have a pen?' He passed her a felt-tip. 'Eileen told us that she thinks

his mother lives within ten minutes of her flat. So that is . . .'
She drew a circle on the map. 'Within this area. This morning
on the M25 he came to the roundabout. He ended up going
left towards his flat but if he had taken the right he could have
come to Eileen's house – and then where? Somewhere within
ten minutes.'

'Dagenham.'

'Too far, I think,' Holly said. 'Rush Green, Hornchurch,
Upminster? It makes sense that the other property is in that
direction, so east of where he lives with Julien and within ten
minutes of where Eileen lives.' She drew a circle around each
of the towns. Rush Green, Hornchurch, Upminster. They
were narrowing it down. Closer and closer. 'If John Pickford
has another house somewhere around here, and if Eddie is
still alive—'

'If?'

'I hate that word so much,' she whispered and stared at
the map. 'Eddie will be tied up, restrained and unable to free
himself. But,' she paused, 'if John Pickford is sticking to his
MO he will have given Eddie some water. It will be limited, it
may have already run out, but if not, it will be there.'

'Why not just kill him?'

'Because he has to put the body in the forest. But there are
too many police there ever since Matthew was found. There's
no way he'd be able to get away with it without being seen and
he knows that. He can't take the chance.'

She folded up the map but left it on her knees.

'How long can you survive without water?'

'You want to talk variables?'

She shot him a look, didn't rise to it.

'An adult – up to three days – but a child will be less, and

307

under these conditions – the stress – maybe a day, day and a half if he's lucky,' he said.

She shook her head. Neither of them liked the odds.

'Why the hell is he doing this, Holly?'

'I think a part of him is trying to punish Eileen.'

'So he wanted a relationship with her—'

'Not her, no. Her boy. That was his fantasy – I don't know why yet. Eileen took that relationship away and effectively destroyed it. It made him lose control and now he wants that control back.'

'By killing other children?'

'He won't kill her or Harper. But he can put the fear of God into her. You heard how she talked, I'm sure every mother in London is double-locking their doors at night – and that's all down to him. He wants Eileen to fear for her child's safety. We have to bring him in,' she said.

'The CPS won't touch him with what we've got.'

'He's the only one who knows where Eddie is.'

'Then what do we do?'

She glanced at him. He was looking out of the window and had one hand resting on his chin.

'You're right, if we arrest him now he'll clam up and shut down. We need to make him relax, appeal to his vanity, his ego. We need to get him on our side so we can make him talk.'

'How?'

'Bring him in as if he's helping us with our enquiries – he's a key witness, after all – but also bring another two employees from Voss Architects to the station.'

'To question them?'

'Yes, and we have to make sure John sees them. He sees

them, he'll think he's safe and that we're fishing, that we don't have anything.'

'We don't have anything, Holly.'

'Not yet, no.'

'And what do we do with these other two employees?'

'After John has seen them, put them in one of the conference rooms and assure them that they have nothing to worry about.'

She felt unsure and unready, but thought it might be the last thing John Pickford would suspect.

'All right,' Bishop said. He sounded flat, almost resigned. 'I'll make the call, and what do you want to do in the meantime?'

'I want to get a look inside his flat.'

Fifty-eight

When John Pickford was asked if he could be of further assistance to the police enquiries he left the Station Approach premises with a nod and an assured walk.

His flatmate, Julien Framer, had been given the minimal amount of information by the two forensic officers left on site and when Holly arrived he had blanched, checked IDs, fidgeted and followed her as she moved from room to room. The flat was simply decorated: magnolia paint, with a few cheap prints on the walls and second-hand furniture. He had offered everyone tea or coffee but there had been no takers.

'How long have you lived here, Julien?' Holly said.

'Five years. I tried to sell in October but I didn't have any offers and then I stopped because of Christmas so I'll probably put it back on the market in spring.'

'Why are you selling?'

'Time for a change.' A pause. 'John has been here for two years, he always pays the rent on time. What's he been helping you with? I mean – he's been good as a tenant. Friendly. He likes his own space, but takes the recycling out when he needs to, does his share of the washing up.'

She opened a utility cupboard and found an ironing board, a towel rack, folded laundry.

'Does John drink?'

'A little. Not much.'

'Socialise?'

'No. He ... I had a party here at Christmas but he wasn't around much. He spent a few nights away, I think with his girlfriend.'

'Eileen Palmerston.'

'That's right. I met her once. She seemed nice.'

'Did John ever mention his mother?'

'No.'

'Any other female partners or family members?' A shake of the head. 'You're sure?'

'I don't think so. I mean he's not the most talkative of people, you know? He'll come home from work. Eat watching the TV or sometimes in his room.'

'Was he here last night?'

'I've already told the officers, I was away so I have no idea. John said he was here. To be honest, I barely see him. I'm away nearly every Thursday through Saturday with my partner in Lewisham, so John basically has the flat to himself on those days.'

'But when the police called you and you came back home, John was here?'

'Yes, he was in his room.'

'Did he mention he had been to the police station this morning?'

'He said he was helping you with a case.'

'Did he say which one?'

'No.' A pause. 'Is he helping you?'

She moved towards an open door.

'Is this John's room?'

'Yes.'

First time through his eyes and it was as she had expected. Neat and tidy. Taking in every detail. Suits in a row in the cupboard with polished shoes underneath. Folded clothes. Two black-and-white prints of London houses on one wall. They were asymmetrical to each other, which surprised her. She felt as though there should have been another one in the middle and when she ran her hand over the wall she felt a hole where a nail had been.

'Julien?' He was in the doorway. 'What was here?'

He squinted, uncertain. Then:

'It was another black-and-white photograph.'

'Of what?'

'It was like the other two. A photo of a residential street.'

'Was it removed recently?'

'John came in Wednesday afternoon after work. He went into his bedroom and left carrying a box with the painting.'

'Was there anything else in the box?'

'I don't know.'

One bookshelf with three rows of neat books. Travel destinations, chess strategy, a few autobiographies. She picked up one and flicked through it. A celebrity she had never heard of, photos she didn't recognise. Replaced it on the shelf. This wasn't him. This wasn't John Pickford. This was the side that he let other people see. But the real John – the real John Pickford – was somewhere else. With his mother? She was looking at the surface of the iceberg but she needed to see what was underneath.

Fifty-nine

All three men shrugged and half-smiled as they passed each other at the booking desk.

'Hello, Damian,' John Pickford smiled. 'Get you as well, did they?'

'Unbelievable, right?' Damian Voss said and laughed, but he looked ill. Mitch Robinson from the accounts department coughed constantly. They were all led through security and into separate interview rooms and, once there, Damian and Mitch were both immediately removed and taken upstairs where they were thanked and told they were free to go whenever they liked. Mitch left immediately, but Damian wanted to stay and so Lipski made him a cup of tea.

Holly was in the observation room, staring through the one-way glass. John Pickford was wearing a well-cut suit: charcoal grey with a white shirt. He had no tie, but his shoes were incredibly shiny. Sitting casually, his legs crossed with one knee raised, he brushed at the threads of his trousers as if shooing away specks of dust. Perhaps it was the room, the shadows cast by the light or her own imagination, but

John Pickford looked different today. More alive. Thompson joined her and the two watched him in silence, took a second then said:

'You really think it's him?'

'I do.' A beat. 'Do you have children, Craig?'

'Two.'

'Can you tell when they're lying?'

'Of course.'

'We have to work out when John Pickford is lying. What his tells are. He may have sociopathic tendencies, but his central nervous system will work the same way as ours. Stress caused by lying will make his eyes start to dry so his blink rate will increase and he'll get thirsty. He's drinking coffee, right?'

'Yes.'

'Next time he asks for one, make it really strong. And if he asks for decaf, don't give it to him.'

'Seriously?'

'Tell him it's decaf but give him the strong stuff. Can you get me one as well, please.'

'Coffee?'

'Yes.'

'You look as if you need sleep, Holly.'

'So do you.'

He couldn't argue with that. The door in the interview room opened and she watched Bishop and PC Karen Switch enter and take their seats. Smiling introductions and firm handshakes. Holly leaned into the table microphone in front of her.

'Can you hear me, Bishop?'

A quick nod from inside the room.

'I'm ready,' she said.

*

'You understand you're not under arrest, Mr Pickford?'

'Yes, I do.'

'But you were brought here because we'd like to talk to you about a few things.' Bishop held a folder that he set down on the table. He turned the recording device on.

'This is DI Bishop of the Serious Crimes Squad and—'

'PC Karen Switch,' Karen said.

'We are talking with John Pickford of number four Station Approach, who has come here voluntarily to help us with our enquiries.'

John shifted gently in his seat.

'I'd like to start with Noah Beasley, if I could please, Mr Pickford.'

'That's the boy from the newspapers? The one I saw from my window.'

'That's correct. I presume you've seen his photo. Know what he looks like?'

'Only from the newspapers.'

'His body was found in Wanstead Park on the morning of Thursday the fifteenth of February. He had been drugged and strangled and then his body had been left in the forest. We traced him from his home on CCTV. The last image we have of him was recorded on Monday the twelfth of February at 6.26 p.m. He was heading towards Wanstead Park on the road where your offices are located.'

'Yes, that's right. That must have been when I saw him.'

Bishop took a moment then:

'Did you have any involvement in the death of Noah Beasley?'

'Excuse me?'

'Did you administer any drugs or noxious substances to

Noah with the intention of causing him any harm? Fentanyl in particular.'

'No. Definitely not. I don't understand. What's going on?'

'We have to ask. We're asking everybody.'

'Is that why Damian and Mitch are here? They're getting the same treatment?'

'Yes, they are. It's routine. We're trying to be systematic and eliminate everybody at the workplace from our enquiries.'

'Of course, I understand and I'll do anything to help.' A pause. 'No, of course I had nothing to do with his death. Carry on, DI Bishop.'

'Thank you. Have you ever taken drugs?'

'I have taken a few drugs.' An embarrassed shrug. 'Yes.'

'Could you be more specific? Which drugs?'

'Cocaine. Marijuana.'

'Where did you purchase these drugs?'

'The street.'

'A dealer?'

'Yes.'

'One in particular?'

'Depends who and what was available.'

'From this man?'

Bishop laid down a photo.

'I don't know who that is. It's not as if I look at their faces when I buy the drugs.'

'So you don't recognise him?'

'No.'

'His name is Timothy Grent.'

'I'm sorry, no, I don't know him.'

Bishop placed a photo of Noah on the table. Then another, and another. Three autopsy photos.

'This is Noah Beasley. And you don't recognise him? You haven't seen him before?'

'No. I mean, when I saw him from the window he was walking away from me carrying a backpack, wasn't he?'

'Yes, he was—'

'And his photo has been in the newspapers, so I do recognise him. That's how I would know who he is. No other way.'

Bishop placed a photo of Matthew Cotton on the table.

'How about this boy? Have you seen him before?'

'No.' He straightened suddenly. 'My God, he's not dead as well, is he?'

'Yes, he is.'

'That's so sad.'

'Have you ever been into the forest, John?'

'I don't think so.'

Bishop paused.

'You've never been there?' he said. 'You live in Theydon Bois, and yet you've never been into the forest?'

'Do you mean Epping Forest?'

'Yes. Wanstead Park specifically.'

'Oh, yes, I have been there. I thought you -- you didn't say which forest so I couldn't answer properly. Do you understand?'

'Yes. Sorry, John. So you have been to Wanstead Park?'

'Yes. I have.'

'When was the last time you were there?'

'Last year sometime. I honestly can't remember. I took my girlfriend at the time. We went for a walk. Had a picnic.'

'What was the weather like?'

'Quite sunny, I think.'

'You didn't need umbrellas?'

'No.'

'So it was more than likely in the summer or the spring last year, rather than the winter.'

'Oh, yes. I see why you were asking now. Yes. More likely the summer then.'

'So seven, eight months ago.' Bishop wrote something down. 'What was her name?'

'Her name? I don't understand why you want to know about a relationship from last year.'

'Just routine.'

'Her name was Mary Radcliffe. We were both at Bainbridge and Co.'

'Mary? I used to go out with a girl called Mary once.' Bishop smiled and checked the file. 'And now for something completely different.'

John suddenly laughed.

'Sorry,' he said. 'I couldn't stop myself, that was funny. It's what Monty Python said between sketches on their TV show. "And now for something completely different!" John Cleese would dress up in a pink bikini or pretend he was being roasted on a spit and say it. Do you . . . ' He looked at Karen. 'You're probably too young for that, but you might remember, DI Bishop?'

'I do remember actually,' Bishop said and he laughed. 'Tommy Cooper was my favourite.'

'He was a genius,' said John. 'Heart attack on stage. Everybody thought it was part of the act. Quite sad really, when you think about it. Sorry, I'm digressing, let's go back to the questions.' He took a sip of water.

'And now for something completely different,' Bishop repeated with another smile and John laughed again. 'Do you remember Holly Wakefield? We both came to see you at the office.'

'Of course, yes. She seemed very nice.'

Bishop nodded.

'She's a psychologist. She helps us with our cases from time to time.'

'I didn't know that,' said John.

'On Wednesday she took a trip into Wanstead Park and at three twenty-five a.m. encountered a man in the forest at the spot where Noah Beasley's body was found. She thought it curious that someone should be there and a scuffle ensued. The man fled, but not before Holly touched the man's ankle. You obviously know about DNA, John?'

He said nothing. His face became strained.

'The DNA from the man's sweat was inconclusive, but one thing our specialists managed to salvage from her left hand was a rather unusual hair. A hair from an elephant shrew.'

'An elephant shrew?'

'Like Dave, the mascot at your office. That was probably the first elephant shrew I've ever seen. Are they rare? Do you know anyone else who has one?'

'No, I don't.'

'Being that they are quite rare, it was very strange that the DNA from the one hair that Holly provided for us matches the DNA from Dave at your office. It's a billion to one that the hair is from a different elephant shrew.'

'Yes, I understand why you've invited us here now. Of course. Damian bought the elephant shrew. It's his. He feeds it, bathes it, talks to it. Um . . . I'm sure he can provide more answers than I can. I guess it's possible that if Damian left the office and bumped into someone in the street, then the DNA could have been transferred, couldn't it?'

'It's possible, yes.'

'So perhaps it wasn't someone from the office.'

'That is possible, John.'

Bishop opened the folder and pulled out a photo. He took his time looking at it then turned it over and laid it flat on the table.

'This is a photo of your ideas board and the clippings from your office. They're all taken from local and national newspapers. Do you have a morbid curiosity with the abduction of children, John?'

'No.'

'Did you cut out all these clippings? Did you choose them?'

'It's a joint effort by the office staff. We all contribute.'

'Not according to Lydia, the senior partner at your work. She says this is all your handiwork.'

'Well, Lydia is wrong.' He examined the photo more closely. 'Sarah Green from marketing put one up last week. I think that one there, about the recyclable bins changing from blue to green.' Pointing to another. 'Geoff Star in marketing cut that one out about a local archaeological dig in Oak Hill Farm. Ask him if you don't believe me. He's a history geek. It's collaborative. They're just newspaper clippings, they don't really mean anything.'

'No, you're right, they don't. Not by themselves. But you know why I'm asking, don't you? On one side is an innocuous story about some local event, or an advert or discount coupon for the shops, but on the other side we have a series of photos or headlines all concerning the missing or dead boys. That's odd, isn't it?'

'I don't think so.'

'You don't think so?'

'The missing boys made the headlines in every newspaper.

If I bought a paper now and cut out an advert or some crazy story that I think I might use in a pitch, the chances are that there will be a piece about one of the boys on the other side. I don't understand why you're asking me these questions. For God's sake, I wouldn't harm anyone. I'm not—'

'Where were you yesterday evening?'

'Why?'

'That was when Eddie Finney went missing.'

'I don't know who Eddie Finney is.'

'This is Eddie.'

Bishop placed a photo of Eddie on the table.

'Do you recognise him?'

'I don't, no. I was probably at my flat. I rent with a friend called Julien Framer.'

Bishop checked his folder and nodded slightly.

'Yes, we've already talked to him. He was away yesterday evening so can't verify you were there.'

John was suddenly very still. He glanced around the room as if weighing something up.

'Do you want to tell us about what happened at Bainbridge and Co?' Bishop said.

'You've been there as well?'

'We have.'

'You're working very fast. Very efficiently.'

'The statement we received concerned your relationship with Eileen Palmerston. You listed her as your emergency contact. You were in a relationship with her up until six weeks ago.'

'She was my fiancée.'

'According to her, you were never engaged. Did you buy her a ring?'

'I was saving up. We had talked about it. We went to a jeweller's in St Albans and had a look at some. She likes diamonds. Emerald cut. Christ, ask at the jeweller's if you don't believe me, there's even a brochure at my flat. We . . . ' he trailed off.

'What?'

'It doesn't matter. What else did Eileen say?'

'She said that after she split up with you, you started hassling her. That was the reason you left Bainbridge and Co, wasn't it? You were asked to leave.'

'Hassling her? Is that what she said? Oh, wow.' He chuckled but it dried out a little too fast. 'What a stunt. Wow. Congratulations, DI Bishop. Okay – so I had a relationship with a woman at my old workplace. Maybe I shouldn't have. You know what? Tie me up. Arrest me. Shove me in the deepest dungeon for my crimes. Here you go.'

He held out his hands. Pleading.

'Seriously. Arrest me for having a fiancée and loving her and trying to treat her like the woman she is. Trying to treat her with respect that she deserves when she's too drunk to do it herself. Oh, what, you didn't know that? Didn't know she's a drinker? Have you been inside her flat? The whole place stinks of alcohol. I was the person who was helping her do the steps. You know? AA? She goes to the local church near her. They have meetings every Tuesday and Thursday. Seven o'clock start. Go ask them if you don't believe me.'

He went to check his watch, paused and took a breath.

'She fell off the wagon every bloody week and I was there for her.' He said it slowly, as if it was the hardest thing to do. 'To try and rekindle the life which she deserves. And now here I am. Accused of . . . of I don't know. Killing children? Jesus Christ.' His tone sharpened. 'No, I will not sit here and listen to these accusations any more. I have tried to help you, I have tried to assist and answer your questions, but you have managed to bully me and bring my character into question.' His lips flared. His cheeks burned red. 'How dare you! How fucking dare you!'

Absolute silence.

'Um ... ' Bishop looked a little lost. The slightest of hesitation in his eyes. 'We need to have a think about you've told us, John,' he said. 'Digest this new information and start making enquiries.'

'Yes, you should.' To Karen: 'I'm sorry I raised my voice and swore. I shouldn't have done that in front of a woman, but I'm sorry.'

'That's okay,' Karen said.

'I'd like to leave now, please.'

'Leave?'

'Yes, please. I should go and talk to Damian and Mitch. See how they're getting on. If they are being treated like this then – well – you're going to have a massive lawsuit on your hands. Damian is a powerful person with a lot of contacts and a good friend. He's still here, I presume?'

'I don't know,' said Bishop. 'They'll be in different rooms. I can't interrupt—'

'Well let me out so I can talk to them. I'm sorry, but I feel a bit ... '

'A bit what?' said Bishop.

'Bullied.' A beat. 'I'd like to go now.'

Bishop paused, said delicately:

'I don't think you can leave yet, John.'

'What do you mean?'

'I still have some more questions for you.'

'Are you arresting me?'

'No, but we'd like to talk to you some more. Is that okay?'

'I was under the impression I was helping you?'

'You are, Mr Pickford. Very much.'

Bishop nodded at Karen to do the necessary:

'This is PC Karen Switch. We are terminating this interview at 5.45 p.m.'

Holly watched John being led from the interview room by Lipski. The second the door shut, Karen started to shake her head and Holly could see she was visibly shaken. Bishop stood up and rubbed the ache in his knee. Stared at the one-way, knowing full well she could see him through the glass. She heard his voice, suddenly tinny and far away.

'We need to see if any of this corroborates.' He took a breath. 'Holly?'

'I'm here,' she said.

'What do you think?'

She sat back in the chair and felt the tension building in her body. She barely recognised her own voice when she spoke. Flat. Impersonal.

'Don't buy it, Bishop. Don't buy anything he says.'

Sixty

'He is planting the seeds of doubt,' said Holly.

They were all in the incident room. 'There's just enough truth mixed in with the lies to make them believable. He is manipulative. Controlling. And he's fucking clever.'

She started pacing.

'He's telling us things that are plausible but unverifiable. Eileen and AA? They don't call it Alcoholics Anonymous for nothing. Was it random bad luck that the clippings from the newspapers found at his place of work had stories of the murders on the reverse? Will the CPS believe that? A jury? Reasonable doubt. I can't stress enough how much of a planner he is. Trust me, he wasn't surprised when you hit him with the "ideas board", Bishop. He already had an escape route ready and it worked.'

'I thought he'd react more when we brought up your name in the forest.'

'Externally he won't. Internally, he's trying to resolve the situation. But the fact that he knows about DNA transfer means he is more aware and up-to-date on police procedure than I thought.'

'What do we do?'

'We need to keep up the pressure. We're in his head now. We're getting to him. Break him down. Ease off, then break him again. Constantly take him to the edge.'

There was a disturbance behind her. Four officers were bringing in cardboard boxes and emptying their contents onto trestle tables.

'Evidence bags from Pickford's flat,' Bishop told her.

There were over fifty items in all, and she poked through them until she found something that caught her eye. A photograph of a young boy, maybe ten or twelve. Skinny and attractive, wearing knee-length shorts, a school shirt and tie, probably in the summer as the flowers behind him were in full bloom. She turned the photo over. Blank on the reverse. She put it down. Picked it up again. Played with it between her fingers.

'Where was this found?'

'In his sock drawer.'

She tried to remember photos of herself when she had been that age. One of her holding a mackerel after sea fishing with her father, another holding a tennis racket that was way too big for her. If a stranger looked at them, would they recognise her now?

'Do we know who this is?'

Nobody did.

Thompson approached with a file in his hand and an update:

'Mary Radcliffe from Bainbridge and Co isn't our mystery woman. She emigrated to Portugal six months ago. Passport control confirm she hasn't been back since. There are no matches on any other homes listed under the name Pickford within a fifty-mile radius. John Andrew Pickford does not own any companies, corporations or charitable businesses. No sign of his Mondeo on any of the CCTV near Epping Forest, which makes it more likely that he has access to another vehicle somewhere.' He flipped over a page. 'John Pickford's computer from work and the one we confiscated at the flat on Station Approach have been accessed by IT and there are no nefarious links to the dark web or dummy accounts of any kind.'

Holly had to look away, felt the words being forced out of her as if she didn't really want to say them.

'Is there any good news?'

'Yes. Voice analysis has confirmed that the message left on the Finneys' answer machine is John Pickford—'

'A defence lawyer will rip it to shreds,' interrupted Bishop. 'He admitted to nothing and it could simply be construed as a horrible prank.'

'The call was also made on an untraceable GSM mobile phone with SMS encryption, probably the same one that was used to send messages to his victims, but we'll never know,' Thompson added. 'He's smart, but we do have something: a ninety per cent match on the handwriting analysis from the burnt diary. Comparisons to the sample provided by Voss Architects and the sample from the forensic boys over at Millbank.'

'Will it be enough to charge him?' Holly said.

'I've sent everything off to the CPS. We have to wait for the phone call. It's Saturday night, we could be a long time.'

'We don't have time,' Holly said. 'A day or a day and a half without water, right, Bishop?'

'Yes.'

'If Eddie hasn't had any water since yesterday evening

when he was taken we're already at twenty hours.' A shake of her head as the realisation sank in. 'If we're lucky, Eddie has got about four, maybe six hours left.' She went over to the whiteboard on the wall and wrote *4 hours* in thick black pen.

No one spoke. Holly could almost feel their thoughts racing and the silence began to grate. She felt as though all eyes were on her and ended up leaning against the far wall. She had led them down this path. She knew she was right but—

'*Ask Geoff if you don't believe me,*' she said it under her breath, but Bishop heard her.

'What are you thinking?'

'The history geek, Geoff Star from his office. *Ask him if you don't believe me.* He said it on three separate occasions when you interviewed him. "Ask Geoff. Ask at AA if you don't believe me . . . Ask at the jeweller's – if you don't believe me".'

'What does it mean?'

'He's taking our attention there. *If you don't believe me,*' she said again. 'He's becoming a paragon of truth. It's to prove a point. That he is always telling the truth.'

'Why would he want to do that?'

'So that when he tells us a lie, we won't be as sure. He's testing us. At some point when he says – "if you don't believe me", I think he'll be lying.'

She turned and stared at the team. Their faces were colourless and lined with fatigue and she pulled her gaze away to the ceiling.

Four hours.

'We really need to push for the location of his mother's house,' Bishop said.

'We could always ask him?' From Thompson.

'He won't tell us,' Holly said. 'He's a sociopath. You can't appeal to his morality. We've got to be smarter than that.' The simple statement ended the conversation. 'I need to get in there,' she said to Bishop. 'I want to talk to him.'

Chief Constable Franks entered the room and made his way over to her. In his sixties, he was tall and slim but his brow was creased, his head down.

'You honestly think there is a possibility Eddie Finney is still alive?'

'I do.'

'And you believe you can find out where he is?'

'Yes.' She hoped she looked and sounded convincing.

Franks chewed on her words for a few seconds then gave her a nod.

'What do you need?'

'Change the room. Put him in the smallest one you have and put the table up against the wall – I don't want anything between us, there should be no barriers, nothing for him to hide behind. Change his chair as well – make it plastic, uncomfortable – and turn the heat up. Not too obvious but . . . And there will have to be an officer in there with me?'

'Of senior rank, yes. DI Bishop will accompany you.'

A tight smile between them. Holly turned to go but hung back. 'One last thing. He's a narcissist. And that's dangerous because it means he thinks he's smarter than us.'

'Is he?'

'We'll have to find out.'

'Good luck, Holly.'

She heard a voice as she walked past the kitchen. Stopped and looked inside. Bethany. Making herself a coffee.

'Thank you.'

Through the main office. Then into the incident room. The hum of conversation died as all heads turned. Everyone at their desks, on the phones, knee-deep in paperwork, they all stopped whatever they were doing and stared. Bloodshot eyes and bloodshot souls. Some of them looked as if they hadn't slept in a fortnight, pale faces, scruffy hair. Stinking of cigarettes. The stale smell of never leaving the office. Uniform and plain clothes, it made no difference, they all cleared a way to let her pass as if the whole team was one living, breathing being. Thompson straightened his tie, gave her a nod. Karla had her fingers crossed. Didn't care if anybody saw it.

A phone rang but Ambrose ignored it. And then it began:

'Go get him, Holly,' he said.

'Do it,' from Henderson. The man-monster who knew no fear.

'Bring that bastard down,' Kathy the press officer.

Shouts of encouragement from the others. Wishing her well. She stopped at the other side of the room and turned.

'Find Eddie,' a lone voice said.

She felt the hairs stand up on her arms. It had sounded like his mother. It wasn't. Couldn't have been. But for some reason she took it as if it was.

'I will,' she whispered.

And then she left the room.

Outside cell number five, Lipski and Vickery were waiting for her.

'Has he asked for anything else?'

'A decaf,' said Lipski. 'We gave him a double espresso.'

'I'll have the same,' said Holly.

Lipski headed towards the kitchen. Vickery had been standing at ease but snapped his feet together when he handed over the file folder.

'It's all there. Just as you asked.'

'Thank you.' Everything was ready.

So, she told herself, was she.

She squared her shoulders and took a deep breath. Nodded once at Vickery who then unlocked and opened the door. Holly stepped through and heard the interview door clunk shut behind her. The slow grating of the key.

Bishop turned and looked at her when she entered but Holly ignored him and simply focused on the other man. She took her seat opposite. Didn't say anything for a while, then lifted her head and smiled.

'Hello, John. Do you remember me?'

'Of course. You came to the office last week.'

'That's right. We also met in the forest in the early hours of Wednesday morning.' She straightened and folded her arms: 'You should have killed me when you had the chance.'

Sixty-one

'Excuse me?'

John Pickford paused, searching for the words, then: 'I have no idea what you're talking about.'

'Really?'

'No, of course not. What are you saying? How can you sit there and tell me I should have killed you? I don't ... Is this some weird sort of joke?'

'No, no, no. You were in the forest the other night.'

'What other night? We've ... hold on, hold on. Slow down. DI Bishop, Karen and I have already had this conversation. You weren't here so – he asked me about this already and I told him it wasn't me. I don't lie. I'm not one of those – yes, I have been to Wanstead Park, last summer – and I was there with an ex. We had a picnic. Her name was Mary. Christ, call her up if you don't believe me.'

If you don't believe me.

'Well, do you want her number?' he said.

Holly looked into his eyes. So many layers within.

'No, it's fine,' she said and shook her head. 'I'm sorry, John, okay? I'm sorry. My mistake.'

'That was a very strange thing you said – talking about murder.'

'Yes. I know. It's been one of those days. Do you ever get those days when everything clambers on top of you and nothing makes sense? I think today is one of those days. Not just for me but for everybody in the police force here.'

She sipped her cup of coffee and watched his eyes. Flickering ever so slightly. From cold to warm and back to cold again. Then he switched as if nothing had happened. A smile. A gentle laugh that floated across the room. He shook his head and stretched his arms into the air above his head. Two old friends having an easy and inconsequential discussion about nothing in particular.

'Well, I told DI Bishop and Karen that I would love to help. How can I start helping?'

Holly looked down at her notes. Circled a few things. Underlined others. There was no eye contact but she didn't want it at the moment. When she judged the time was right, she stopped on a page and looked up again.

'Tell me about Eileen's son, Harper.'

'He's a lovely child. Heavily autistic. Did Eileen mention that?'

'Yes, she did.'

'So you have talked to her?'

'We have.'

'She probably hid all the bottles before you got there. She's not an idiot. They're under the sink, by the way. Between the bleach and the Windex – if you ever happen to go there again.'

Holly took a second and skimmed to another page. She

could feel John's eyes trying to read what was inside, but she didn't speak for a while.

'You have a photo of him on your desk – a coaster. You were obviously close.'

'If Eileen was away or went out in the evenings, I'd sit with him, make his food. We'd watch television together. We liked those quiz shows, the ones in the early evening, the ones on the higher channels.'

'What did you talk about?'

'What do you normally talk about to a twelve-year-old autistic boy? Autism is ... you have to think outside the box, have to be very patient, but it's worth it. We talked about everything that interested him from *Sesame Street* to model train sets. We talked about books. About the garden. He liked the garden. We'd walk to the end of it and look at the bees. There's are lots of flowers there in big bunches, they're purple, with an orange middle. I can't remember what they're called. Like daisies but—'

'Asters,' said Bishop.

'Yes, you're right. I think that's it.'

'I used to have them at my old house,' he smiled.

'Right. They attracted a lot of honey bees. Legs thick with pollen. Yes, he liked watching the bees. We'd put out a plate of honey for them and some water. Make sure they were well looked after.'

'It sounds idyllic,' Holly said. 'How long were you and Eileen together?' She checked the file. 'Two to three months. But it was quite intense?'

'I guess so.'

'I mean, you were talking about getting engaged. So I think that's fair to say that qualifies as rather intense for only knowing each other for eight weeks or so. How angry were you?'

He looked up quickly.

'I'm sorry?'

'How angry were you when Eileen split up with you?'

'A little. I mean it's sad when things come to an end.'

'Describe how that felt. The anger.'

Shaking his head, a look to Bishop and then:

'We've all been there, haven't we? It's difficult to measure though, isn't it? How do you measure a kilo of anger or a pound of hurt? Ten ounces of love? You can't, can you? My hurt *hurts* more than yours. It's not . . . I love more deeply than *you*. I *care* more than you do. How can you measure that? You can't. There's no spectrometer for measuring, love, hate or hurt.'

'No.'

'It's how we react to things. Isn't it?'

'Yes it is. It's how we react to things.' Holly took a breath. 'Did you ever pick up Eddie from school?'

A hesitation, then his face creased into a frown and he answered her as if talking to a particularly stupid child:

'Eddie?'

'Sorry.' A pause. 'Harper.'

'Yes,' John said. 'I did pick up Harper from school. I used to take the route over on Lanceford Lane. Three hundred metres along past the lollipop lady and he was always waiting outside the gates with one of the teachers. Holding their hand. Then he would wave goodbye and get into the car. Put his seat belt on and then put both hands on his knees. It was a routine he had. "Ready to go? Off we go." And then I would drive and he would hold a pretend steering wheel and drive next to me. He used to love that.'

'Eileen said you used to help with his homework as well.'

'He's very good at English. I corrected only when I needed to. He has a wonderful imagination. And his maths is good if he remembers to show his working out. Art as well. He's very talented.'

'Yes, Harper drew this picture of you.'

Holly pulled a drawing of John from the folder and held it up. John turned his head away quickly.

'I don't want to look at that.'

Holly could feel the tension coming off him and she wasn't sure whether he wanted to rip it to shreds or hug it to his heart.

'Why was it so important that you had a relationship with him?'

'I wanted to help.'

'Help?'

'He's autistic. He needs . . .'

'Needs what?'

Holly looked away when she asked the question, started writing on the notepad, made sure John couldn't see the words. She looked up when John didn't answer. His mouth was moving and she leaned forward, listening intently. Amid the breathing, the ticking of the clock, she could hear the low murmur of his voice. Soft, almost delicate.

'Could you repeat that please, John?'

'*Needs me.*' So faint it was barely a whisper, and when he half-smiled it seemed to take every ounce of his effort. 'I'm being sentimental, that's all. I'm sure she'll find someone else and so will Harper.'

'But while you were with Eileen you saw yourself as his stepfather?'

'I was more than happy to give up my time to take care

of him, but it didn't work out. Eileen wanted something different.'

'What did she want?'

'Not me.'

'But what did she want?'

He lifted his head up slightly. Chin at an angle.

'Not me.'

Sixty-two

'Where were you born, John?

'Chigwell.'

'Chigwell? That's a beautiful part of the country.' Holly smiled. 'Do you remember where?'

'Vicarage Lane.'

'And you went to the local school?'

'Chigwell School, off the High Road.'

'Was it peaceful there, growing up? I mean, are you country born and bred?' Another smile. 'Log fires, home-made bread, vegetables in the garden?'

'Yes, to all of the above.' He smiled as well. 'All the children used to hunt rabbits during the summer in the wheat fields, running around with big sticks. Sometimes we got lucky.'

'DI Bishop, do you have that map from the car?'

'Sure.'

Bishop pulled it out of a folder and opened it up. Handed it to Holly, who got up and laid it out on the table by the wall. She searched for a while until she found Chigwell and circled it, made sure John could see what she was doing.

'Whereabouts was your school, John?'

She pointed and he had to get up and see for himself. He couldn't stop his eyes from looking at the three other towns that had already been circled – Rush Green, Hornchurch and Upminster; it was human nature and Holly knew that. A vulnerable point of truth between them. *I know your mother is here somewhere. Now you know that I know.*

'The school was around there,' he said and sat down again quickly and reached for his coffee. An instant distraction to take his mind off what he had just seen.

'If there's anything you want to talk to a lawyer about, please let me know,' Bishop said.

'No, I'm fine.' But he wasn't; he was sweating.

Holly left the map open so they could all see it. John now angled his body slightly away from the table so he wouldn't have to look at it. He was moving his hands more. Getting anxious. Holly wondered which one of the three locations he was worried about.

'Geographically you are connected to both of the dead boys, would you agree?' Holly said.

'What do you mean?'

'Both boys were found in Wanstead Park, the entrance of which is within half a mile of your place of work.'

'Yes.'

'Do you often socialise in Forest Gate? Go to the bars, the gym there?'

'I have a gym membership, yes, but as for socialising, unless there is some sort of function at the office I normally go straight home after work.'

'When you talk about going home, where are you referring to?'

'The room I rent off Julien.'

'Right,' Holly said. 'That's number four Station Approach. Julien says you're a good flatmate, by the way. Always pay your rent on time, take out the rubbish.'

'I do my bit. We both do.'

'When you were in the relationship with Eileen, did you ever stay over at her flat?'

Holly asked the question quietly, kept her eyes fixed on the file in front of her, staring at the words on the page, but neither reading nor taking them in.

'Some nights. And others I stayed at Julien's.'

She nodded and finally looked up. He stared at her for a few seconds then gave a half-hearted wave of his hand.

'What?'

'Do you ever stay at your mother's house?'

'My mother?'

'Eileen mentioned she lived close by, within ten minutes. I mean, is she okay? Does she know you're here?' A pause. 'Would you like us to send someone around to the house?'

'It seems bizarre to me that you are so concerned about my mother.'

'You haven't called her, that's all. She may be getting worried.'

'Nearest is dearest,' he whispered.

'Sorry, what did you say?'

'*Nearest is dearest.* That's what she used to say when I would sit on her bed. *Blow a kiss. Make a wish . . .*'

'You're still very close to her then?' He kept silent. 'You're still very close to your mother?'

'No. No, you misunderstand. My mother is no longer with us.'

'She's not?'

'Cancer. Pancreatic, it was very fast. When she got the diagnosis she went downhill.'

'I'm so sorry.'

'She couldn't cope and took an overdose in 2005. She was only fifty-two. I wasn't with her at the time and didn't find out until I came home for the weekend.'

'That must have been such a shock. You must miss her terribly.'

'She may be gone, but I still see her every day.'

'What do you mean?'

There was no expression on his face, but his eyes were half closed as if he knew something she didn't.

'It's a figure of speech,' he said and shook off the nostalgia. 'I was an only child, of course. The apple of her eye. Mother didn't want any more children.'

'Didn't want or couldn't have?'

'Couldn't. I was a troubling birth, apparently. Caused some damage down there. Sorry, I don't want to talk about this. It makes me feel funny. I love my mum ... ' He started playing with the cuticles on his nails. 'Look – you've upset me.'

'Would you like a tissue?'

'Thank you.'

Holly passed one over and John dabbed at his eyes gently. He sniffed and blew his nose.

'I always get emotional when I think about her.'

'Do you need a moment?'

'No, it's fine. We had a simple burial.'

'We?'

'I'm sorry?'

'You said *we* had a simple burial.'

'We. *Mother* and I. She's in Isleworth Cemetery.' He smiled, but it didn't make it to his eyes. 'Go and check if you don't believe me.'

If you don't believe me.

Holly smiled. 'I don't think we'll bother.' She gave the signal by tapping her fingers twice on the desk.

In her ear she heard Thompson say: 'I'm leaving now.' She imagined him running out of the observation room, along the corridors. Down the stairs and out of the building. Getting into his car.

God speed, Thompson.

Sixty-three

'You're a draughtsman at Voss Architects, aren't you, John?'

'Yes. I trained at Farnborough College, attained my diploma, then got a job at Cillian Graphics in Slough when I was twenty. Stayed there for seven years until I was head-hunted to Bainbridge and Co.' A shake of the head. 'We've already discussed how that ended.'

'So you draw all day, I would imagine?'

'Yes, pretty much.'

'Do you write as well?'

'Write? What do you mean? Proposals, contracts?'

'Poetry. Creative writing.'

John shook his head. Didn't reply.

'I can't write,' Holly said. 'I'm probably the least creative person in this station.'

'I doubt that,' John said and he frowned.

'I want to show you something.' She reached into the folder, showed it to Bishop first, then contemplated the photo for a while before finally revealing it. The graffiti on the ruin walls.

My life is not beautiful. It is not magical.
But I can feel the love. Coming closer.
Closer every day.

'These words were written on a wall that Matthew Cotton's body was found underneath. Do you recognise this poem, John?'

Silence.

'Did you feel the love when you killed Matthew? Or was it fleeting? A few seconds of absolute bliss and then nothing again. Back to that feeling empty.'

'I don't know that poem. I've never seen it before.'

He wiped his lips with his hand. One of his cuticles had started to bleed.

'That's interesting,' Holly said, 'because the police found this same poem in Noah's diary, which had been burned, along with some of his clothes. Our experts compared the poem to a letter from Voss Architects that you had written and handwriting analysis confirms with a very high probability that you wrote that poem in Noah's diary. Can you explain that to me?'

'No.'

'You can't explain that?'

'No.' He took a second. Gestured miserably with one hand. 'Have you told Eileen that I am here?'

'No.'

'I don't . . . I'd like her not to . . .'

'Not to what? If you want discretion, you have to give me honesty, John. You understand that, right?' Holly had to be so careful. Like a surgeon with an unpredictable patient. 'One of the things that we kept out of the press,' she said, 'was that both victims, Matthew and Noah, had a tiny angel pendant clasped in their hands. Why put an angel in Noah's right hand? He was already dead. You killed him then brought him to the forest. But the angel? Is it Gabriel? "Do not be afraid." To protect him on his journey wherever he was going? To protect you?' A beat. 'Or was it for our benefit? Giving us a clue as to what you are.'

'You have no idea what I am.'

'I think I do, John.'

She paused. Let the words sink in and deaden the air. Then she showed him a photo of the pendant.

'I thought you were going to give me honesty, John.' Holly watched him. Five seconds. Ten. Then said: 'Matthew was the first, wasn't he?'

'This is a joke. DI Bishop – are you going to let her continue with this line of questioning?'

'You don't have to answer,' Holly said, 'but I think you should hear what I have to say. I think you panicked with Matthew. I think everything was good until it came to that moment when you saw his dead body in front of you, which is why you tried to bury him. It wasn't right, was it? It didn't match your fantasy.

'By the time you got to Noah, you were more prepared and you planned it better. You took his body to the forest in the early hours of Thursday morning. And this time it's different. He is everything you thought he would be. Noah was presented perfectly to us. The white underpants, the pillow under his head. The angel.' She quietly turned a page as if she were reading a bedtime story. 'He looked beautiful, by the way. You never got a chance to see him in daylight, but Noah looked quite beautiful. The citronella was a nice touch. Kept him safe. Safe and sound until we found him and could take care of him. Wrap him up and keep him warm for his parents.'

John stared at nothing in particular but Holly could see his mind was filled with deep, dark thoughts that wouldn't stop spinning. She didn't stop, kept on:

'The police have impounded your car. They're going to see if there are any traces left behind.'

'Traces?'

'Of Wanstead Park. Of Matthew. Noah or Eddie. If there are . . .' she knew he wasn't listening any more. He was thinking of himself, of the consequences, of the mess he was in.

'Are you a parent, John?'

'No.'

'You have no children of your own?'

A pause and he scratched his nose.

'No.'

'If we were to do an investigation into your background, is there anything you can think of that may be misinterpreted or anything in your history that somebody might say John Pickford did this?'

'No. Of course not.'

'You've had no problems with young boys in the past?'

'Problems?'

'Your lifestyle – you haven't got close to any boys before?'

'No, of course not. I'm not a paedophile. I read about the murders but there was never any mention of sexual interference, was there?'

'No, there wasn't.'

'Right – then you should be careful about what you say. This killer is not sexually interested in young boys.'

'You're right, this killer isn't a paedophile.'

'No, he's not. And as for my lifestyle – I think you can safely assume that for me one day is very much like the other. I get up, I go to work, I come home. My life is rather dull.'

'What's that?'

'My life is rather dull.'

Holly got up and placed a photo of each of the boys onto the desk.

Noah, Matthew and Eddie.

Then she opened the file and took out the black-and-white photograph of the young boy wearing a school uniform and placed it next to them.

'Who is this, John?'

He picked up the photo, eyes riveted. Holly knew he was trying to think five steps ahead of her so she was trying to think six.

'I'm struggling to work out who this is,' she said. 'It's not you. You told me you don't have any children and you said earlier you didn't have a brother. So why would you have a photo of a young boy hidden in a drawer at your flat?'

He was staring at the photograph as if he were a thousand miles away.

'I know your mind is racing, John, but as soon as we get that bit of evidence that we need, it's over. You have to show your hand now. All these children that you say you don't know – look at their faces. I have a photo of Noah on my living room wall at home and I look at him every night.'

He folded his arms – retreated.

'Essentially the photo of this unknown boy – that's what the police are looking at now. You're a very intelligent person so you can see how something like this could set off alarm bells. Two boys are dead, one is still missing and you have a photograph of an unknown boy hidden at your home. You have to be honest with me, John, because this is getting out of control really fast. You know there is only one option. Who is he?'

'Stephen,' he said. His eyes were bloodshot. The tiredness creeping in. 'His name was Stephen.'

'And who was Stephen?'

'He was my brother.'

She felt Bishop stiffen next to her. In the incident room, the search for the brother would already be underway.

'And what happened to Stephen?' Holly said.

'He went missing.'

'Where, John? Where did he go missing?'

He looked up at her as if to mark the moment.

'In Wanstead Park.'

'Wanstead Park?'

'Mother loved him so much.'

'Of course she did. Did they ever find him?'

'No.'

'And where is Stephen now?'

'My brother?'

'Yes. Where is your brother now, John?'

'Being watched by the angel.'

John shook his head – a gesture of exhaustion and futility. He seemed stunned, as if nothing made sense. Holly reached out her hands and touched his.

'Well done, John. That's really good.'

Sixty-four

Holly was watching John Pickford on the live camera feed from his cell.

He was lying on his back, his left hand behind his head, his right hand resting across his stomach. Fingers drumming – no particular rhythm, a random tap-tap-tap. He had unbuttoned his shirt and a small silver medallion floated close to his neck. Every now and then he would finger it with his left hand. She could see he was sweating and wondered how warm the room was. Clammy. Lifeless air. Turn the heat up more, she thought. Make the bastard sweat.

She felt Bishop move to her side. He dropped a cigarette into his palm and put it in his mouth. Didn't light it but played with it as if he had. She suddenly realised how much she missed his smile.

'The Finneys are downstairs,' he said.

'They know we have someone?'

'They know we're talking to someone of interest.'

She wanted to smile at the cliché but it would have been too painful.

'What did the CPS say?'

'We can't charge him. Not without a body. His Mondeo has been professionally cleaned. There are no traces left behind so we can't put the car in the forest. No mud, no leaves, no nothing.'

'There must be a second car.'

'That we can't trace.' He handed over a police report. 'And then there is this. Stephen Alistair Pickford's police report. He went missing in the spring of 1999.'

Holly turned to the first pages. Old type settings and hand-written notes at the sides.

Stephen Pickford was reported missing by his brother John Pickford at 2.28 p.m. on Sunday, 1 March 1999. He arrived at Epping police station in rather a state saying he could not find his brother. The boys had attended a church service at St Mary's church in Chigwell that morning to commemorate the founding of their school – both were wearing their school uniforms. They had then returned home with their mother to 137 Stony Path Road at approximately 10.30 in the morning and then started the walk into Epping Forest at approximately 11.15.

She looked up quickly:

'The mother's house?'

'Which was destroyed the same year for redevelopment. His mother's name was Grace Florence Pickford—'

'Grace . . . '

'Yes. We have no evidence of any other properties under that name and we have no idea where they relocated to.'

'But they relocated somewhere. And nothing under Stephen Pickford? Then there must be someone else.'

'The mystery woman?'

'A relative, a friend of the family, someone we don't know about yet. What did the mother do for a living?'

'On a voting form from 1977 she lists herself as a housewife.'

Holly tried to hide her dispirit. Carried on reading.

The two brothers had walked to the forest many times before. They started playing 'cops and robbers' and then moved on to 'hide and seek'. Stephen went to hide and John counted up to one hundred. He spent the next two hours searching for his brother. Numerous witnesses (appendix 7) say they saw John calling out his brother's name and rushing from one part of the forest to the next. Other witnesses (appendix 8) say they saw him eating a packed lunch by the River Lea from between 1.00 and 1.30 that afternoon. John's initial statement was taken by DI Tracy Rhones, and by 4 o'clock two officers accompanied the minor back to the forest and continued the search. At 6 o'clock it was getting dark so they walked the boy home where they were met by the boy's mother – Grace Pickford.

The boys' mother was distraught when she heard the news and could not be consoled. A statement was taken from her and a search party was sent out that night. At 10 in the evening it was called off because of the bad weather and resumed the next morning at 10.00 a.m.

Two dog units were used but after a week of searching there was still no sign of the missing boy. No more clues were ever forthcoming and it was presumed he had met his fate either by a tragic accident or at the hands of an opportunistic killer.

Holly closed the folder and sighed as Bishop sat next to her.

'You think that because John lost his brother he was looking for some kind of substitute? Someone he could care for?'

'No, I think it's darker than that,' Holly said. The story was coming together. But it was loose, there were holes and she couldn't quite fill them yet. Out of the corner of her eye she saw Vickery get up from his desk and walk to the whiteboard. The officer checked his watch, wiped off the number *4* and wrote *3 hours*. She glanced at her own watch. Had time gone that fast?

Bishop's phone rang. He scooped it up, answered and listened. Held the phone loosely but Holly saw his hand go white and his body tense.

'No Grace Pickford was ever buried at Isleworth Cemetery,' he whispered.

'There is no death certificate or anything?'

He shook his head. Staring at her but talking into the phone. Disconnected a few seconds later and rubbed his eyes. 'Which means she's still alive,' he finished.

'Christ,' Holly said. 'If she was fifty-two in 2005 she'll be what? Sixty-five now. Could be suffering from dementia. An accomplice but an unwilling one?'

'The woman who dropped the phone?'

'It's possible. We have to find out where that house is.' She stood up and stepped away from the desk, nodding as if still connecting the dots. They were so close. They just needed a little luck on their side. A little guidance.

'The necklace John's wearing around his neck,' she said. 'Does anybody know what it is?'

'It's a Saint Jude,' Vickery said.

'Saint Jude?'

'Yes.'

'Who is Saint Jude?'

'The patron saint of lost and desperate causes.'

She felt herself shiver. She rubbed her arms but it didn't get rid of the goosebumps, so she put her jacket on.

Bishop met her outside.

She held out her hand and he gave her a cigarette. Lit it for her and pressed it between her lips. She took a deep breath. It was like breathing fire – and memories were being lit up like a flare. She hadn't smoked in twenty years. Why did she need it now? Why was she going back? Because I have to, she thought. The past tells us everything. It makes us who we are. What are John Pickford's scars?

She took a long pull on the cigarette. Stared at it, as if it were somehow speaking to her. It was reminding her of when she was young. A teenager. Stockings under ripped jeans, peroxide hair and piercings. Pass the fags. Play the game. I'm in love. I'm out of love. Doubt and the never-ending search for the *lack*. The *lack* of what she had. The lack that everybody has. No matter how much money, how much fame, how much of everything we still always lack something. She stared at the wet ground. It was dirty, grey and black. Like the carpet in Noah's room. An empty crisp packet suddenly started fighting with the wind by her feet. Quavers or something. Twisting and flicking like it was being stung by a bee. She hadn't had Quavers for years. Then suddenly she was hungry although she didn't have time to eat.

She felt Bishop's hand on her shoulder.

'You okay?'

'What?' A pause. 'Yeah, fine.'

'I've been talking to you for a couple of minutes.'

'You have? Sorry.'

'Don't be.' He backed off. Squinted in the dark light. 'Do you need anything?'

'More time, Bishop. I need more time.'

Tap-tap-tap with his thumb.

John Pickford was still lying in his cell when the partition opened in the gun-metal door and in popped his hot food on a plastic tray. Some sort of chicken casserole with green beans and mashed potatoes.

'Twenty minutes,' said the voice. He took the tray and sat down on his bed and poked at the food with the plastic fork. He tried to make a face out of the mash, but it didn't want to play. After two bites he put the food down and lay in his grey cot with his grey thoughts. Closed his eyes and began to wish.

He was running through the fields.

Hands tipping the tops of the corn as he fluttered up the side of the path. His brother was ahead of him, his school blazer and tie blowing out behind him like a cape. Somehow faster, always more sure-footed. He never managed to catch Stephen, but he always felt happy knowing he was there again. John could feel the wind in his hair. The sun on his face. He closed his eyes as he ran. He had done this once before and had tripped over a flint. Bruised his knee and cut his hands. But he didn't care now. It felt so good to run with his eyes closed. When he was blind. There was something unimaginably freeing about it. Dangerous but it made him smile. And if you didn't think you would fall, you never would. If you kept picking your legs up you'd always end up going in the right direction.

'John.'

His mother was calling him, but he didn't want to talk, he wanted to carry on running. The forest was right in front of him. There was so much freedom here. He could run for ever.

'John.'

He opened his eyes and the little boy in the school uniform and the field was lost for ever.

'John Pickford.'

He didn't recognise the woman. She was wearing a police uniform and had a harsh face.

'They're ready for you again.'

Sixty-five

'I've finished reading the police report on your brother.'

Holly entered the room and sat. John took a breath and pushed his coffee away. Half to himself he replied:

'DI Tracy Rhones – the investigating officer. I still send her a Christmas card every year.'

'Do you blame yourself for Stephen's death?'

'They never found his body. I like to think he's still alive.'

'I think he's dead. The same as Noah and Matthew. I can only see what you want to show me, John. Do you want to tell me what's going on?'

'Not really.'

'Can we talk about Eddie Finney now?' she said.

His shoulders went forward and his neck swivelled around at the mention of the boy's name. He gave a rare smile.

'I'm sorry, but I don't know who that is.'

'Where does she live, John?'

'Who?'

'Your mother. We've had an officer do an inventory of Isleworth Cemetery. She was never buried there. In fact we have no death certificate anywhere for a woman named Grace Florence Pickford who died in 2005. Which means either you lied to us about the year of her death or there is a high probability that she is still alive. Wouldn't you agree?'

He was looking down – avoiding eye contact.

'The thing is, John, and there is no easy way to say it. I think you killed these boys and the next hour or so are going to be the most important of your life,' Holly said. 'You understand that? You have to decide how you want to be remembered.'

He looked up.

'How I want to be remembered?'

What did she see in his eyes? Regret? Doubt? Something else perhaps. Not rapture, that was too strong a word, but relief perhaps. Relief that something was coming to an end.

'As a hero?' she said. 'As the man who saved a young boy's life, or the man who had the opportunity to tell us where Eddie was but decided against it. Child-killers don't make good friends in prison. You'll be mixing with a lot of angry fathers in there. And you will be hated beyond anything you have ever seen.'

Nothing.

'Why not let us know where Eddie is? Why the reluctance to help? There's something else, isn't there, John? Something you think is worse than what we've seen. What is it? Nothing you say will shock me. I've heard everything.'

'You think so?'

A flicker in his eyes made Holly take a second. Regroup.

'Where did you move in 1999? Tell me where your mother's house is and we can end this. We can go and get him now. If he's alive, fantastic. You'll be the saviour. That's how people will remember you. Not as the animal who killed three boys. They will remember that when John Pickford came into the police station, he talked to them. He told them where Eddie was and they managed to get him. They pulled him out of that place and saved his life. That's you, John. You will be responsible for saving his life. That's what the headlines will read. We've got hundreds of officers ready to do this. Volunteers on the street. Thousands of people will join the search, and they will find him eventually.'

He licked his lips. Dry and salty.

Holly said: 'I can understand how it would have felt when Eileen split up with you. The loss of power. Of control.'

'You have no idea . . . '

'A kilo of hurt. A ton of pain? You do measure it, don't you? You tried to reach out to Eddie's mother, John. You called her, wanting to talk about her boy, didn't you? Think of his mother, how much she loves him. Tell me where he is.'

He pulled himself upright. Sweat trickled down his face and he blinked to clear his eyes.

'What do you think of me?' he said.

'Where is Eddie?'

'Do you think I'm crazy?'

'Where is Eddie?'

Silence.

'You always put the bodies in the forest. Their final resting place – like your brother. That's where they belong, but Eddie's not there.' She held up a photo of the old bus stop. 'See? And the police are very good at finding bodies. If he was truly dead, I think you would be rejoicing. You would show us to his body, roll out the red carpet for us. But you weren't there to do it because you were in here with us. And you want him to die, don't you? But you'll never get to bury him in the forest.' A pause. 'Do you think it will fix you? Because it won't.'

'Oh, you know, do you?'

'I have spent nearly all my life looking into the eyes of people like you. Murderers, rapists, paedophiles. They all say the same thing. And what they are looking for – what *you* are so desperate to find – you never will. That's the sad truth of all this. You're looking for something that isn't there. We know you gave the boys water. We found a piece of a plastic straw in Noah's mouth. That's how they kept themselves alive, isn't it? Tied up on the floor, but with enough water to keep them alive while you were at work or staying with Julien. In a bowl or a bottle. Sipping it every five minutes, trying to stay conscious. How much longer has he got? How much water did you leave him?'

She stared at him, more angry than anything else. Moved her chair closer. Rested her hands on her knees.

'Did Eddie say *Don't kill me*? Did he beg? Can he feel the love? Coming closer and closer. The love of his mother. He'll fight for the love of his mother. He'll be lying there now on the attic floor. Lying there and saying. "I will survive this. I will survive so I can see my mother again. My father. My sister." And every second that you are not there he's going to get stronger. Because he expected to die. But now you're not there, he's thinking to himself – He hasn't come back. Something's happened. I might actually get out of this. I might survive. And our survival instinct is so strong when it kicks in. We think we're mice, don't we, but we're not. We're savage beasts who will bite and scratch and kill in order to survive. And I bet that's what Eddie's doing right now!'

'Enough,' he said.

She took a moment. Made sure she really had his attention.

'You're never leaving here, John, you know that, right? And after tonight – after tonight – you don't get to take any more of our children.'

'Don't look at me like that, Holly.'

'Like what?'

'As if you're judging me.'

'I'm not judging you,' she said. 'I have a brother too. I don't get to see him much. Think about him all the time though. Every day. How different life has turned out. Picking at the scab, re-watching the film, hoping for a different ending. Tell us where Eddie is.' She fell silent for a while, knowing John was trying to think. 'What are we going to do? Is he in another part of the forest or is he at your mother's house? Rush Green, Hornchurch, or Upminster? It's one of those, I know it is. Can I make one phone call and get him, or do we have to go somewhere? What are you struggling with here, John? Is there anything you want from me?'

A silence that stretched. John was suddenly very calm. Detached almost:

'Fucking hell, I'm so tired.' he whispered. 'So tired.' His hand went up to his face. The red-bitten cuticles – flecks of blood against his cheek. 'Let me take you to Eddie, then.'

Holly felt her stomach fall to the floor.

'Is he alive?'

Nothing.

'Are we going to find him alive when we get there?'

He was stunningly matter-of-fact:

'You take the A112 from the M25 and head north towards the forest for four miles. Sewardstone Road turns into the Crooked Mile. Take a left at the signs for Waltham Abbey, the

360

Gatehouse and the bridge. It's a narrow lane. Stoney Bridge is about three hundred metres ahead. You can park there. He'll be in the river below.'

John closed his eyes and put his hands on the table. He was done. He wasn't going to say anything else. Holly looked up at the one-way mirror. Inside the observation room, she knew Chief Constable Franks was watching. She heard him clear his throat before he spoke into the mic. He only said one word:

'Go.'

Sixty-six

'How long to get there?' Holly asked as she and Bishop ran towards his parked car. John Pickford was being placed in the rear by Vickery who then took his own seat next to him.

'Forty-five minutes, max. We've got local police en route. It's a high tide because of the rains – quite a fast-flowing river underneath – but there are three divers getting suited up as we speak. By the time we get there, they'll be ready.'

Bishop barked out orders to three other vehicles and then the convoy skidded away into the night.

Outside, the trees flashed by in the darkness. John's face was impassive and Holly wondered what he was thinking. She wanted to talk to Bishop but couldn't because John would hear, so she said nothing. After thirty minutes there was a sign for Waltham Abbey up ahead.

'Why the river, John?' Bishop said.

'I thought he might like the ducks.'

Police cars up ahead. Halos on the street lights with pelting rain. A policeman waved them down, gestured to pull into the right. Bishop did as asked, parked and turned off the engine. Holly glanced in the rear-view mirror. John's eyes were slitted, his lips pursed. He sensed rather than saw her watching him.

'Go straight down,' he said. 'You'll find him.'

A sergeant handed them an umbrella as they exited the car and walked past police who were still taping off the area. Spotlights had been erected at each corner of the grass and Holly squinted every time her gaze flashed past them. Waltham Abbey was to their left. Eleventh-century stone, mortar and memories. They were led to a little tent where it was cold and crowded. Three video monitors had been set up and a dive-captain watched the screens with headphones on.

'We're using sonar as well as cameras,' he explained. 'Bodies relay different signals, but the water is fast flowing and we haven't found anything yet. We've done one sweep east to west, about to start north to south. It's deeper than we thought though.' A radio crackled. 'They're going in again now.'

Each camera had a different screen and they watched the replay as it came through. Murky depths. Floating detritus. Moss. Stones and old bricks. A few minutes later they got the call:

'They've found something.'

'Shit,' said Bishop.

Holly felt her heart flutter. Two of the cameras showed the dark water but the third was aimed at a black tarpaulin, fuzzy with moss. There was a rope around its centre and bricks weighing it down.

'They're going to cut the ropes, bring it up.'

They saw a diver enter the frame and slowly saw at a rope. It took two minutes, but then the signal was given and each diver took a side of the tarp and slowly escorted it upwards. One of its edges flapped open in the current and Holly got a glimpse of a pale bleached face in the helmet lights. She turned away quickly, and felt her legs walking out of the tent into the night. They had been so close, but it had been too much to ask. She felt Bishop put a hand on one of her shoulders. It felt good. It was what she needed right now. Human touch. They stood in silence for a few seconds then Bishop said:

'I have to tell the parents.'

'I'll do it with you. Gill, she . . . ' And Holly thought of her promise. Thought of the poor woman making herself sick all the time.

'The mother always thinks it's her fault. There is no such thing as closure, there never is.' He put his arm around her shoulder. Drew her in close.

'We'll do this together,' he said.

They turned and walked slowly away from the bridge. The air was suddenly colder and the spotlights suddenly brighter.

Silence behind them, then a voice from the bridge:

'Sir.' And again, but louder this time. 'Sir!'

They turned.

'Sir, now, sir!'

Jesus Christ, thought Holly. There was no way Eddie was alive, no way they could have brought him back. She had seen the moon face, the round open eyes. What the hell were they shouting about? Bishop caught her thoughts but there was a spark in his eyes. Hope? He started to pick up the pace and she followed suit. Feet slipping on the wet road, rain stinging her face.

They skidded to a halt at the bridge and looked over. Holly dug her toes in so she wouldn't fall. All three divers were clumped together on the shore in the dark, their wet-suits looking like shiny seals. One of them pulled his goggles off and ripped out his breathing apparatus.

'Fucking hell,' they heard him say.

'What is it?' asked Bishop.

'It's a blow-up doll. It's a bloody blow-up doll!'

Held down with rope and bricks: wrapped in the black tarpaulin was a shiny white inflatable doll. Naked apart from a pair of white underpants. Holly felt the anger rise in her throat and she turned and looked towards the car.

John Pickford was leaning up against the passenger door. Somehow he had managed to convince Vickery to let him out. He stood watching them, arms folded. Then he gave them a wave and started to laugh.

Sixty-seven

Holly didn't think she had ever felt so exhausted.

Another coffee but it was making her sick. She freshened herself up in the bathroom and walked through reception. Swiped her pass-key. The corridors towards the rear of the building seemed cold and long. Never-ending shiny floors and fluorescent ceilings. She was exhausted. Drained. And the most sickening thing was, she had no idea what to do next.

A left, then a right and then she saw Vickery coming towards her. He was putting his jacket on, car keys jangling in one hand.

'Where are you going?' she said.

'It's two in the morning, Holly.'

He gave her a quick nod and opened the incident room door for her. She sat at the nearest desk. The few souls that were still there seemed to have been put on mute but someone, somewhere was using a stapler – the monotonous clip-clop and the shuffle of paper.

The countdown clock on the whiteboard had been wiped clean and someone had put a zero. That was it – game over. She wanted to rub it off when Thompson came to her.

'Why the hell would he send us out there?'

'To waste time. It may have been a practice run months ago. He wants Eddie dead, but he knows he'll never get to bury him in the forest now. He doesn't bury him. No-one else will.'

'Bastard. It's never complete without the body. We'll always keep looking.'

'I know. I'm not giving up either,' she said.

She couldn't tell if it was pity on his face or disbelief – either way he nodded and walked away. Sat at his own desk and stared at his computer screen. She picked up the files on John Pickford again. Now that he had successfully wasted their time, he had asked for a lawyer and was refusing to speak, so she started systematically going through everything they had on him. The files and folders, the photographs and statements. Looking through every piece of paper. The crime scenes, the autopsy reports, the angel pendant, the witness statements. Then moving onto the photos of Julien and the flat they shared.

The clues are here. The clues are here . . .

She banged her fist on the desk. The coffee cup jumped and a dark circle of brown flooded across the paperwork. She lifted up the paper page by page. Drip-drip with the coffee. Looking underneath. Most of it was okay, wasn't damaged. Eddie Finney, where are you? If you're still alive. Where are you? She was halfway to the coffee machine when she suddenly had the idea, turned and snatched up the wet photos of John's bedroom like her life depended on it.

Bishop approached quietly from behind. Holly saw his reflection in the window and pulled herself upright. He hovered by her shoulder. Sensed something in her.

'What? What do you see?'

'It's what I don't see. That's what interests me. There was another framed picture on the wall in John's bedroom. He took it away earlier this week.'

'What was it of?'

'According to Julien it was ... Jesus Christ – "I see her every day" ...'

She picked up the phone and dialled. It was answered by Julien on the fourth ring.

'Hello?' he slurred.

'Julien, it's Holly Wakefield. The picture that John removed. Do you remember when he put it up?'

'What picture?'

Wake up, Julien! Wake up!

'The one in his bedroom that's missing. How long has it been hanging there?'

Muffled noise on the other end.

'Since he moved in.'

'Really?'

'Yes, it was one of the first things he put up two years ago.'

'Thank you.'

Was about to put the phone down when—

'One last question, Julien. When you tried to sell your flat, who was it listed with?'

The rain was getting heavier.

She thought the man might be angry when he finally turned up. After all it was nearly three o'clock in the morning, but he wasn't. He was wide awake and even managed a smile as he lowered his umbrella and unlocked the front door to Soloman Estate Agents. Only when they were both inside did he speak.

'I'm David Soloman, this is my company. I received instructions from DI Bishop at the Met Police to help in any way I can.'

He flipped a series of switches and overhead strip lights popped on as he walked ahead of her to his office at the rear of the building. Desks and dead computers sat either side, posters of houses and flats for sale and for rent.

He unlocked the door and stepped inside. A gentle hum as he turned on his PC and sat behind his desk.

'You want to see the photographs of Julien Framer's property. Number four Station Approach, correct?'

'That's right.'

He brought it up on screen. 'The flat was listed here last October. On at three-fifty-seven. No offers, but we had a few show-arounds. One second. Here you go.'

He stood up and invited her to his seat. Holly sat and started to scroll through the photos of Julien's flat. The kitchen, living room, dining room, outside patio. Julien's bedroom. Kept scrolling. John's bedroom. Here we go. Photos of the bed, the bathroom and there it was – a single shot of the far wall with the three hanging photographs. The two either side were as she had seen them, and Julien had been right, the middle one was another black-framed photo of a single house in its centre.

'Those photographs on the wall in John's bedroom. The two either side I'm not concerned with, but the one in the middle with the detached house. Can you zoom in on that? Enlarge it? I want to see if we can tell where that house is.'

'Sure. Hold on.' He edited it and enlarged it. 'I'll print it out for you.' A few seconds of fumbling for the mouse and the printer started whirring: a detached Victorian house, white-walled with black windows. A covered drive that was hidden by hanging vines and ivy. Two storeys and a third-storey attic.

'Any idea where this house could be?'

'Not off the top of my head,' David said. 'There's a number on the brick by the front wall. Number forty-two, and there's a street sign on the right-hand edge of the frame. First letter only. Looks like a K. There'll be hundreds of streets or avenues in London beginning with a letter K.'

'It won't be anywhere in London. It will be close to . . . ' she pulled out Eileen Palmerston's address, 'Waterloo Gardens in Romford.'

'How close?'

'Within a ten-minute drive. Four or five miles. Do a five-mile radius.'

David's fingers twitched over the computer. 'There are only two streets, Katherine Street and Krepton Street and one terrace, that's Kildarre Terrace, within that vicinity with a house number forty-two. It's in Upminster.'

A beat.

'Can I take this photo with me?'

Sixty-eight

Holly drove as fast as she could.

Lipski had already checked out one of the streets, which had been cleared, and was on her way to the other. Now GPS pushed Holly around a corner to the right. A set of red lights and she went right through. A camera flashed her registration plate – dutifully logged her details and would no doubt be issuing her a fine.

A left and a right and into a cul-de-sac. This was it. Kildarre Terrace. Semi-detached houses, a few single ones with large lawns. She counted the numbers: thirty-six, thirty-eight, forty, forty-two. Here it was at the end. A Victorian detached with a long driveway with hedges either side. A car parked in front of the garage. A pale blue mini. Ten years old but it looked immaculate. Holly's car swerved into the driveway and sent a scattering of gravel as the brakes were applied. She felt suddenly very calm and still. Either Eddie was alive or he was dead.

She ran up to the front door. It was locked and she rang the doorbell then shouted through the letter box.

'Mrs Pickford?'

Grabbed her phone and dialled Bishop:

'Bishop, I'm here. Number forty-two Kildarre Terrace.'

'Lipski has cleared the other property. She's on her way to you. Five minutes.'

She hung up, moved around the side of the house, pushed open a wrought-iron gate and stepped into the rear garden. Let her torch guide her past old trees with motionless branches. She ran to the tree-line and peered through the windows of an old shed. A lawnmower toppled to one side and a hedge cutter hanging from a nail in the wall. A rockery closer to the house with an abundance of purple and white daisies. The earth looked freshly dug in one section and she wondered if Eddie was buried there, but he wouldn't be. John would stick to his MO. She pondered for a second, reached down and grabbed a big flint from the loose mud. Stepped up to the back window.

Five minutes is too long.

She threw the rock.

The old glass smashed and clattered. Holly took her jacket off, laid it over the sill and climbed through. Cut her hand but barely noticed it as she fell to the other side. She was in a kitchen. The table was set for breakfast: one bowl, one spoon, one coffee cup and a box of Weetabix. Everything else was clean and tidy and put away. She opened the old-fashioned larder. Painted wooden shelves with neat pots and cereals.

Into the corridor and the toilet downstairs on the left behind a mahogany door. A rosette of lavender hung from the door handle.

A burgundy painted dining room to her right, the front door straight ahead, an oval mirror on the left wall and opposite, an elephant foot umbrella stand and a rack with two pairs of men's shoes and a pair of jogging trainers. She turned them over. Faint traces of mud on the soles and she wondered if it was from Wanstead Park. She realised she was dripping blood from her wrist and took off her scarf and wrapped it hard around the cut. She entered the living room and turned the light on. Old brown furniture from another century. An iron fireplace with sea-green tiles either side. It looked cold, ashes neatly gathered in the hearth. Lots of books on shelves and a grandmother clock ticking like a metronome.

She returned to the hallway. Climbed the stairs.

'Grace Pickford?'

The first door on the right had a white and black tiled floor, a sink, toilet and a bath with an opaque shower curtain suspended from the ceiling. A shadow behind it. Human-shaped. Standing. Holly reached forward, arm trembling and slowly pulled away the curtain. A woman stared back at her. Ghastly pale, plastic eyes and no arms. A mannequin on a wooden stand.

Her phone rang. Made her jump. It was Bishop.

'Yes?'

'Two minutes and Lipski will be there,' he said.

She was in the corridor again. Moving.

'I'm already inside.'

'You are?'

Eyes intense. Deciding which door to open next.

Nearest is dearest.

Slowly pushing past the carpet. Flicking the light on. A bed at the far end, wrought iron with fairy lights entwined, a full-length mirror, a large walk-in wardrobe and chest of drawers.

'I'm in a bedroom.'

'John's room?'

'Possibly.'

Again the furniture was dark wood and old and there was

a staleness about everything. A deadness – a snapshot from an old postcard. Holly opened the wardrobe. It was larger than she had first thought. Men's clothes: neatly arranged on hangers. Suits, shirts and ties, sweaters and polo shirts.

'Hold on, there's another door,' she said.

That opened into a small dressing room. She flicked on the light. A chair and a theatrical mirror with a dozen bulbs in an oval setting. And straight ahead, clothes hanging against the far wall. A woman's black skirt, scarf, heavy black jacket and gloves. She blinked and looked again. Her eyes moving swiftly from the jacket to the skirt and then to the floor. A pair of flat shoes. Crossing to the mirror. A blonde wig on a stand. Maybelline, Kiehl and Pantone. Cosmetics everywhere. A lipstick kiss on the mirror.

'I think I've found her.'

'Who?'

'The woman from the CCTV. It's was him, Bishop. There never was any accomplice. He was trying to throw us off the scent.'

She pulled open a drawer to reveal another wig   this one black, along with a black moustache . . .

'So where the hell is Eddie?' Bishop said.

'There's one more room.'

In the corridor. The last door on the right.

'Lipski is going to be there any second. Wait for her.'

'No time, Bishop.'

'Holly! Be careful of the mother.'

'Christ, she's in her sixties.'

'I don't care. Be careful!'

She pushed open the last door. Noiseless oiled hinges and she had a sudden jolt of fear.

The room was dark, the curtains drawn and the smell hit her immediately. Made her gag. Stifling, heavy perfume, masking a dead smell underneath. The smell of rot.

She straightened from behind the door. Fingers trembling, flicked on the light switch and took one step inside.

Sixty-nine

A creature lay across the bed.

A creature wearing a black lace nightdress. Human? Dead and mummified. The body christened with a dull waxy sheen and then that smell again. The smell was too much. Holly gagged but held it in even as her stomach tightened. The woman had been propped up on soft white pillows. Hands draped across her lap, yellow fingers clutching at an empty cereal bowl. The eyes had rotted away years ago. The mouth was wide open and Holly stared into the silent scream. Only two teeth remained and there was a tube of some sort in there. Looked like plastic. Holly gritted her teeth as she fought to keep from losing it entirely. She didn't want to touch anything. It was too disgusting.

She forced herself away and into the en-suite bathroom. Pulled aside the shower curtain. Empty. Hadn't been used in decades. A layer of dust and rust. Stains. Checked inside the cistern. Came out and looked under the bed.

Did she miss something? Must have. There must be a way up to the attic. No stairs. Nothing.

'Eddie!'

Silence.

The bedside light suddenly came on.

'Eddie?'

Flickering like a moth catcher. Highlighting the grotesque figure on the bed like some bizarre fairground attraction. Roll up, roll up, the freaks are in town and have I got a show for you! The flickering stopped. Then quiet. No sounds and she could hear her own breathing.

A fuse out or maybe it wasn't plugged in properly. She went to find the plug. Couldn't see it. Followed the white wire from the lamp. White wire? Traces of white insulating plastic under Noah's nails? It went into the base of the wall by the skirting board. She moved an old wheelchair and a stand-alone washbasin to one side. Couldn't see the plug. Felt around but the wire disappeared straight into the wall. She pushed and pushed, ran her hands up and down, the wallpaper rough on her palms. A keyhole and a catch at waist height, a simple hook and eye that lifted easily but she needed the key. A fumble on the windowsill but she found nothing. She kicked at the door. Felt her left shin almost give way. Changed feet. Kicked hard and the thing splintered at the hinges on the second hit. Cracked the wood in two and Holly pulled it apart and saw the staircase behind.

A massive crash and thump from downstairs. Glass breaking and then Lipski's voice:

'Police!'

'Up here! Top bedroom!' Holly shouted as she grabbed her torch and turned it on. Pushed through the narrow opening. Dusty stairs with no handrail. Follow the wire, Holly. Follow the wire. Up the stairs. At the top she teetered on the edge and took a moment. The smell was overpowering. Faeces and blood and death and pain. The smell of panic. Of uric acid in tensed muscles. She played the torch around. Dusty antique furniture, drop cloths, piles of magazines.

Follow the goddamn wire! A thin white snake that seemed to slither away in her flashlight. She shoved a stack of chairs to one side. The wooden arms and legs scattered on the floor like an old skeleton.

Around the corner past the chimney stack, under a heavy plastic drop cloth. Another mannequin appeared in front of her. Bald and dusty with baby-doll make-up that looked so wrong. She pushed past a drape of coloured beads – another room behind – Christ, how big was this place?

There! Red stains on the floor! Blood or was it brick dust? Orange and wet. She rubbed a finger across it. Couldn't tell. Kept thinking of the mummified corpse in the room below. Deep brown waxy skin. Empty eye sockets.

'Eddie?'

A grandfather clock that never chimed, more chairs, piles of magazines. And she had a horrible thought that the wire would lead to a window or simply out of the attic and behind the bricks to the outside world. An empty race. She pulled aside another drop cloth and coughed on the dust. Put a hand over her mouth as she saw something move in the corner of the room and she thought quickly of the rat with the red eyes on the roof of the folly. She spun the torch. It wasn't a rat and it was still there. A piece of cloth or something. Pink and dirty. That suddenly twitched. It was a . . . had to be . . . it was a foot? Or it looked like one. Something that made her think it was human. Not the shape because it was bent backwards, but the form. The delicate form of life in a shell of skin.

Delicate life. Young life.

Eddie Finney?

She ran over, brushing through cobwebs. And there he was.

'Eddie!'

She dropped to the floor and turned the boy over. A grey face. The ghost of the photo she knew so well. Hands and feet bound, naked. She instantly saw his mother's lips and his father's nose. A straw in his mouth, brown with old spit, an empty water bottle. She cleared it away. Checked his breathing. Nothing.

'Eddie!'

His hands were freezing and limp. His pulse – one faint beat. She linked her fingers and formed a fist. Punched it downwards and started CPR. One-two-three-four – felt a rib crack. Ribs can be fixed. Get him breathing first. Get that heart pumping. Get him to safety and you can always fix the ribs after. Crack. Another one went. Maybe the same one. Had to be careful. Didn't want to push so hard the piece of bone went through a lung. One-two-three-four—

'I need help up here!'

Pause.

Deep breath.

Blowing in his mouth.

Dry lips.

Like kissing toast.

Another breath then compressions again.

One-two-three-four—

A voice from behind: 'I'm coming!'

A paramedic manoeuvring towards her past the old furniture like Bambi on ice. De-fib case in his right hand. Thank God for that. Her arms were getting tired.

'He's non-responsive,' Holly said. 'Severely dehydrated.' She felt herself fall away as the paramedic eased in, checked the boy's carotid artery then he ripped open the box and snapped on the de-fib battery. A tight buzzing noise.

'Stay clear.'

He lifted the paddles then pushed them onto the boy's sunken chest. Smash. Like a puppet being jerked out of a coffin. Stiff and gangly. Arms flailing then sinking down to earth.

Somehow she heard her phone. Answered it.

'Holly?' Bishop's voice in her ear.

'Yes.'

'Did you find him? Is he all right?' A beat. 'Holly?'

Watching the boy.

Buzzzzz.

Eddie's head shot forward and rolled to one side. His eyes gaped open as if he was looking at the ground, searching for something.

'I found him.'

'Is he still alive?'

'Don't know yet.'

She wiped her eyes and got up.

Buzzzzz.

Upping the current. Black marks on the boy's sunken chest, the outlines of the paddles. She could smell the burning skin.

'Holly?'

'I don't bloody know!'

If she had got there ten seconds earlier she might have saved him? Ten minutes? An hour? John Pickford the child-killer. Twisted John with his mind as warped as . . . as what, Holly? Mind as warped as what? Why is it always like this? Why is everything I do linked to life and death? I should stop this. I should stop the pain. The isolation. This feeling inside that rips out my guts.

BZZZZZZ

The paramedic checked Eddie's carotid again. Gave her a quick nod: 'Manual compressions again please.'

She lowered herself over the boy and clasped her hands. Got to work. Chest heaving, covered in dirt and blood, she was sure she looked like the devil herself. One-two-three-four—

'Come on, Eddie,' she whispered between her teeth. 'I made a promise to your mum.'

One-two-three-four—

'Breathe, Eddie, breathe!' Holly shouted. 'Come on!' She leaned down. Breathed into his mouth, stroked his cheek.

More voices behind. Two more paramedics arriving. Working around each other in perfect sync. One of them attaching a blood-pressure cuff, the other lining up a saline drip.

'We'll take it from here, Holly.'

He knew her name. She wasn't sure how and then she pulled herself away and let them get on with their job. Her body didn't feel like her own. She felt as though she was falling and there was nothing else, so she sank to her knees. Stalled, an arm's length away. It was ghoulish to watch. Somehow even worse to hear. She saw one of the paramedics move away and close his eyes, felt another lean over to her as if to say something—

And then a sigh.

And it wasn't from her. And it wasn't the paramedics.

One of Eddie's eyes opened. Closed. Opened again. The lid fluttering like a tiny bird's wing. Desperately trying to fly, desperately trying to connect with the living.

'We got him!' one of the paramedics said. Into his

walkie-talkie: 'We need help up here! Transport down and a second saline drip.'

'His blood pressure's too low – he's going to flatline again.'

Erratic heart rate, palpitations.

'Where's that goddamn IV?'

Holly crawled over and gently eased some water on to the boy's lips. He coughed and spat. Blood, mucus and phlegm. Took some more and managed a gulp.

'Not too much, he'll be sick.'

'Let him have what he needs,' she said.

A fourth paramedic arrived and another IV was ripped into his arm, saline bag held up high. The drip-drip of life. Eddie kept his eyes open. He was staring at Holly and she somehow saw the horror within. Then he rested his head as the colour started to return to his cheeks. A soft pink glow. The most beautiful candle in the darkened room.

She moved away, past the drop cloths. Leaned against the chimney; brick dust and cobwebs dusting her face. Took her phone, pressed it firmly in her hand. Staring at nothing but empty space.

'We got him, Bishop.' She had no idea how frail her voice sounded. 'We got him.'

Seventy

'Not a happy camper,' Angela said flatly as she stared at the mummified corpse.

'The mother,' Holly said.

'DNA will confirm.' Nothing seemed to shock Angela and this was no exception. She simply raised an eyebrow as she pulled away the sheets. 'Could have been dead ten years. Fifteen. Hard to tell in this instance, but the sheets look fresh. Whoever keeps her here cleans the bed and the ... Are you getting this, Bishop?'

One of her marshmallow assistants was filming the process.

'Yes,' his voice loud and clear from the speakerphone.

'There was a plastic tube inserted in the mother's vagina. Traces of spermatozoa. He was having sex with the corpse.'

'For how long?'

'Years. There was one in her throat as well.' A beat. 'I think it will make an interesting case study, but I wouldn't recommend it for bedtime reading. Would you like me to complete the formalities, Bishop?'

'Please.'

'I, Angela Swan, Chief Coroner for the county of Middlesex and London District, and as defined by section 1(2) of the Coroners and Justice Act 2009 will be opening an inquest immediately as I believe there is reasonable suspicion that the deceased has died a violent or unnatural death. Therefore, in the interests of the police activities I can confirm to DI Bishop, that there is indeed a dead body in the room at forty-two Kildarre Terrace and the circumstances appear somewhat suspicious.' She turned to Holly and smiled. 'You'll have my report in a couple of days. She is all yours, Bishop. Your investigation may begin.'

Holly went outside, to the other world, where none of this existed, but outside the sounds of the street seemed to sharpen, the police radios, the idling of the ambulances. There must have been twenty police cars along the road and a crowd was beginning to gather.

'Is it him?'

'Is it the boy?'

Questions coming from all directions, faces pressed against an invisible window, neighbours and onlookers that stood in a shuffling arc by the police line. A member of the press suddenly broke through and was shoved back roughly by the elbows. A fearsome protest and then his camera flashed in the officers' eyes and he smiled. The casualness of one not involved.

A surge of noise from the crowd and Holly turned. Eddie Finney was being led by the paramedics down the gravel driveway on a stretcher, oxygen mask over his mouth, fresh drip in his arm. A cheer from the crowd. People were clapping. It was then that Holly spotted Gill and Alan Finney.

They were being led by Bishop between vehicles: Alan looked utterly confused and Gill was hunched over like a woman twice her age. When she saw her boy she started crying – a terrifying noise – like an animal braying. Moving quickly, brushing past officers who were still trying to get inside the house – clamping herself to her son, stroking his half-hidden face, his blond tousled hair. Gentle hands persuaded her to move to one side as Eddie was hoisted into the ambulance and Gill and Alan were guided after him. As Gill sat by Eddie's side she caught sight of Holly. The two women's eyes met and Gill became very still and stared at Holly with an odd mixture of bewilderment and savagery. In some strange way Holly felt ashamed, as if she had done something wrong, and then the ambulance doors closed and the vehicle drove away.

Holly turned too quickly and felt suddenly dizzy. Dizzy and surprisingly empty as she walked into the house. Up the stairs and into John Pickford's bedroom. The lights were off but she left them as they were. She wanted darkness now because with the darkness came the quiet that she hoped would fill her head. There was a Victorian nursing chair in one corner. Green suede, the back of which was pressed pale where once a mother's head had rested and a baby had been fed. She sat and took a breath. Didn't know why she did what she did next, but over the next few weeks she would wonder if she had been guided.

For as she rested in the nursing chair, she saw a pair of fluorescent eyes staring at her from above. Strips of silver, and she was reminded of the trees in the forest. She got up and turned the lights on and saw the painted angel on the ceiling. Gabriel. Looking down at her, neither smiling nor frowning. No judgements. Wide eyes somehow seeing all and knowing everything.

Her breathing slowed and she blinked away the tears as suddenly everything became clear.

'Where is your brother now, John?'

'Being watched by the angel.'

She went down on all fours, rubbed her hands across the wooden floors. Dusty and waxy. Warm despite the cold.

Within five minutes, two of the forensics team had started to wrench up the floorboards. The whole world splintered with massive cracks as wood and nails flew in all directions. A torch was shone down into the crawl space. Holly didn't smile because she had seen what she needed to. A dusty mix of plastic bags, mouse droppings and a young boy's skeleton wearing a pair of white underpants.

Seventy-one

Timothy Grent rested his head in his hands, keeping his face covered.

He was wearing headphones and listening intently. Bishop was playing him the voice recording that John Pickford had left for the Finneys. He turned it off after a time.

'Well?' he said.

'It's him,' Grent said. 'I never saw him, but I'd recognise that voice anywhere.' He gave Bishop a subdued look. 'But I told you already, I never had any direct contact with him. I didn't know what was going to happen to Matthew Cotton.' His voice was a little slurred. He lit another cigarette from his old one. Eyes haunted, turned his attention from Bishop to Thompson, but Thompson merely shrugged.

'I can give you evidence against Casper as well as my therapist. That will help, won't it?'

'It's not going to be enough. I think you know that,' Bishop said. 'Would you like us to call your lawyer?'

Shivering like a newborn.

'Yes.'

'Come on. Get up. We need to move you to a different station.'

Grent breathed out slowly. Shrugged, almost ashamed.

'I'm not going back.'

'Yes you are, Timothy.'

When Timothy Grent left the cell it was Bishop who led the group towards the main door.

Grent had been told he would be transferred to a holding wing where he would stay until his trial started, which would be in approximately sixty-seven days. The other station was twelve point two miles away and he had no intention of going there. When they got outside he stood very still and stared at the car park and open gate that led to the main high street. He bent down and took his shoes off.

'Do you mind? I'm getting a blister.'

They didn't mind. He handed them over to Bishop, who had a strained look on his face.

'They don't smell, if that's what you're worried about.' Grent almost smiled as he glanced towards the road. He was led down the steps and was soon on the level where the cars parked. It had been raining and he could feel the wet seeping into his socks and onto his feet, but he didn't care. As they opened the front gate to let an ambulance in, he saw his chance and started to run.

'Stop him!' Bishop ordered. A half dozen or so officers and staff turned as if in slow motion and watched Grent running, their faces screwed up in the rain. Bishop knew Grent wouldn't get out, but he saw Ambrose give chase. 'Leave him, Ambrose, he's not going anywhere.'

'No, sir. He's not trying to—'

And then he saw what Ambrose had seen. Grent was running towards the ambulance that had just entered. Thirty miles an hour, through the rain, desperate to get to where it needed to be. Its flashing blue lights strobed across the scene, making Grent look like a figure from a silent movie, sixteen frames per second, arms flailing above his head. At the last moment Bishop caught sight of his eyes, large and pale as he threw himself in front of the vehicle. The driver didn't stand a chance and Grent's body bounced off the front of the bonnet with a sickening thud and got wrenched underneath. It was crushed by the wheels and rolled into a heap, smeared and mangled like graffiti on the pavement.

Ambrose took one look at the body and vomited by the side of the road.

An hour later, Bishop made his way to the Chief Constable's office. He was feeling resentful tonight. Resentful and angry. He knocked once. Twice.

'Come in!'

Franks looked up when he entered and gestured to the seat opposite his desk. Bishop sat and waited in the silence. Eventually the Chief Constable pointed at the whisky in front of him. Bishop nodded and wondered if this was going to be a zero-conversation meeting. Have a drink, stare at each other for a bit. Franks will shrug and I'll have to leave. Slightly less nervous but slightly more inebriated. He held his drink in one hand, swirling it quietly. Watching the ice bounce from side to side like tiny tugs.

Franks raised an eyebrow, nodded oh so gently and then spoke:

'We can consider the John Pickford case closed.'

'Yes, sir.'

Franks relaxed in his chair but Bishop wondered if it was over. 'Now – on to something entirely different,' the Chief said, and Bishop almost laughed and had to choke the urge.

'We're putting the killing of Natasha Ormand and the attack on Miss Lily-May Brown and Miss Wakefield as collateral damage between two rival drug gangs. Another statistic for the six o'clock news. Nobody has claimed responsibility as yet for the murder of Saulius Yosovov. He was a contract killer, apparently.'

'I heard that too, sir.'

'CCTV had been disabled at the tower block, and there appear to be no witnesses willing to testify, but there will be an independent investigation by the Met Violent Crime Task Force.'

'May I ask why, sir?'

He had sounded more bitter than he meant to.

'You may not.' The colour on Franks' face changed and there was a wash of deep red on his cheeks. 'That will be all, DI Bishop.'

Bishop nodded shakily. Franks offered his whisky as a salute. The glasses chinked together but Franks didn't make eye contact. Bishop nodded and downed his in one. He stood up, hid the wobble in his legs and managed to walk in a straight line to the door. He turned to Franks, but the moment he spoke he regretted it.

'I shouldn't have let Timothy Grent go, sir.'

'No, you shouldn't have.' A folder appeared from a drawer and was placed in the middle of the desk. A pen was picked up. The lid uncapped. 'There will be an enquiry. We will have to see how the sword falls.' He drained the glass and went to refill it. 'That will be all, DI Bishop.'

'Yes, sir. Thank you, sir.'

In the corridor he leaned his head and shoulders against the wall. He stayed like that for several minutes. Then eventually pulled himself away and headed outside.

Bishop felt the chill despite his jacket as he made his way towards his car.

A new shift was coming on. Young officers who could survive on two hours' sleep and live on pizza – all moving with exaggerated purpose. Bishop was so tired he was starting to feel old. Thompson was ten years his senior but over the past week he felt as though they could have been twins. He leaned against his car and lit a cigarette. Fiddled with his car keys until he discovered by accident that the car door was actually unlocked. He didn't remember leaving it like that. He looked around as if the shadows had eyes and when the phone rang he nearly dropped it. He checked the number. It was Holly.

'Hey,' he said.

'They said you had already left the station.'

'We're going to meet at the Robin Hood pub tonight in the forest,' Bishop said. 'Let our hair down a bit. The landlord is giving us a deal. Shall I come and pick you up?'

'No,' he heard her say. 'It's fine.' It was as if she were only half listening, her voice vague, as if she were elsewhere. 'I'll meet you there. And I'm going to need something a lot stronger than hot chocolate tonight,' she said.

'Me too,' he nodded, and disconnected the phone.

Seventy-two

'Where are you taking me, Sis?'

'Shssh,' Holly said playfully. 'Too many questions.' She reached out and took Lee's hand. A left, a right and into the conservatory. A large building with glass veranda and doors leading outside. It was a beautiful evening, a cloudless sky and the moon was bright and made patterns of white by their feet. 'When was the last time you came in here?'

'I don't recall.'

'See – the garden looks different from this angle.'

Lee went up to the window. 'It's still one minute and thirty-seven seconds.'

She reached into her jacket pocket, pulled out an iPod and pressed play. Music began. A waltz. Lee turned and stared at her.

'Seriously?'

'Yes.'

'I don't know, Holly. I'm tired.'

'Come on, Lee.' She held up her arms. Her movements slow, almost dreamlike. 'I need it more than you tonight.'

He stepped closer until they stood opposite. Her right hand went onto his back. His right hand on her left shoulder. Their other two hands clasped together at shoulder height.

'One foot in front of the other. Right?'

'Something like that. After you, sir.'

'Thank you, madam.'

They started to dance. She went with the music. Swayed. He couldn't lead so she did, but he was grateful for it until he scuffed against her feet.

'Shit, sorry,' he whispered.

'Don't apologise,' she whispered. 'Are you enjoying this?'

'Not really.'

'Let me guide you, Lee.'

She heard him sigh and sensed him close his eyes. He reached in and held her tighter. The waltz was long gone now. It was more of a hug with tiny movements around the feet. A gentle swaying from side to side and she could feel his whole body alive but tense. He almost pulled away at one point but she held him tighter and said in his ear:

'I've got you, okay? I'm never going to let you go.'

He stopped dancing and suddenly stepped back, staring her in the eyes.

'Do you promise?'

'I promise,' she said, but wasn't sure if she believed it herself.

He nodded. Seemed grateful, then she rested her head on his chest and they began to sway again with the music. Round and round. Finding the rhythm. Her toes stepping up and down, light touches on the shiny floor.

'Who brought me here, Holly? This life. This choice. Was it me?'

'I don't know.'

She felt his fingers gently brush against her hair, and wondered how much he missed human contact, being in here. How much he missed touch and interaction. There was always talking, there were always people around. All these people to share stories with, but to touch? The senses. One of those that was overlooked. We all needed it sometimes. Ever since we were babies. Being cuddled and held. Nurtured. And as we got older we oftentimes lost it. Put an arm around us. Let our head fall on their chest and let us cry. Some people never had that and that was the cruellest of things. We all craved it but most of us—

He pulled away abruptly as if he had been reading her thoughts. 'Enough now, Holly,' he said. His hands fell away from her face, slack and powerless.

'You want to stop?'

'Enough,' he mumbled. He lowered his head and started to cry.

Holly walked around the garden. She stopped and took her shoes off when she was halfway around. Wet grass between her toes and she counted the trees and bushes. One minute thirty-seven seconds one way. One minute thirty-seven seconds the other way just to change the view. She was thinking of Bishop when a voice came from behind.

'Holly, do you want to come in? We're going to turn the lights out.'

She nodded and aimed away from the darkness.

Lights out.

Seventy-three

'I will never understand the part of me that did these things to those boys. Perhaps I am a monster. I'm not a hundred per cent evil though. I'm not. Do you believe me, Holly?'

John Pickford patted his thin hair to one side of his head. There was a curious lack of expression on his face.

It was quiet, apart from the clock ticking on the far wall, underneath which stood a prison officer. The chair was comfortable – the only thing in the small grey room that was. There was a plastic table between them and for the briefest moment Holly thought she could have been with Lee again. But this was John Pickford, and this was Wandsworth prison where he would eat three hot meals a day and fold laundry twice a week, and would no doubt count the days until his lawyers were ready for his trial. He had already pleaded not guilty to all charges by reason of diminished responsibility. She didn't know who his psychologist would be, who would put him through Hare's Psychopathy Checklist, and part of her didn't care. She heard boots outside the doorway. Voices. Loud and violent. Doors slamming. Then sudden quiet.

'The press have been quite disrespectful to me,' he said. 'May I quote, please?'

She nodded.

'"I thought he would have more of a presence around him – I was almost disappointed but he was quite insignificant. You would walk past him in the street and never look twice ..." the *Daily Star*. Not exactly a quality rag.' He became very still and watched her with a hint of regret. 'I wondered if there was something special about you when you first came to my office. The way you stared. You didn't look at the room, you watched it. As if it were alive, as if it could somehow speak to you.'

'It did eventually.'

'Hmm.'

'I found Stephen. Was he the first?'

He laughed and gave a strange, twisted smile, avoiding Holly's eyes.

'You want to look behind the curtain, Holly?'

'Sibling rivalry that ended in blood.'

'You make it sound so simple. All murderers are unique. Wouldn't you agree?'

'Yes.'

'I would describe myself as an obsessive ponderer. I spent years fantasising about it. Picking over every detail like a shade of paint until I could create the perfect picture in my head. My cognitions were very graphic. I even knew what sound he would make when he was dying.'

'And did you find what you were looking for when it was done?'

'Fleeting.'

'But enough?' He didn't respond. 'And you killed Stephen in Wanstead Park?'

'Yes.'

'Why did you bring him home?'

It was hard to tell if he was surprised or simply annoyed by her question.

'I would go searching for him in the forest with mother,' he said. 'Every weekend we would walk through the trees and she would watch young boys playing, catch a glimpse of one of them with short blond hair and I could almost feel her heart cry out. One Saturday I led her to a point between two trees. Stephen's body was literally five feet away. If she had knelt down and rummaged for a while she would have found him. It was the most exhilarating experience I have ever had. I had to bring him back to the house. I can't quite . . .'

He seemed suddenly distracted, as if something else were going on, but then he started again:

'Sometimes we have no idea what we're looking at. There was a point when the memory made me feel old because I'd been carrying it for so long. And it was always there. The same way you walk into the house and the sofa is there, and the prints are on the wall, and the wallpaper, and the wooden banisters and the dark red curtains. It's always there. Memories are like that too. They're always there but some of them drag you down.' There was an edge to his voice now. 'I brought him back because I wanted to punish my mother even more.'

Holly gave a little shake of her head.

'Memories aren't just experiences, Holly. You walk into an old room and you get hit by its memories. I used to think I hated my mother's room, but the reality was I hated my mother.' He licked his lips and leaned forward. Their hands were almost touching. 'When Stephen disappeared, I thought she would turn to me. But she didn't. She turned ever further away.'

'When did you first start hating your brother?'

'Hate is a very strong word. After he was born I felt as though I didn't exist. It's the cruellest thing to be ignored. To have no voice. Never to catch someone's eye. I don't understand life. I can't work out if it's good or bad. Pain. Hurt. Love lost.'

'Love lost?'

'We all have loves that we have lost and I am no exception. No matter what you think of me.' He actually smiled as he then said: 'So I collected his body from the forest. I put him in his bed as if he were asleep. Undressed him. Cleaned him and made him wear a pair of white underpants. Put his head on the pillow. "Mum!" I said. "Stephen's come home! Mum!" She rushed into the bedroom, there were tears in her eyes as she saw the lump under the covers and then she pulled away the blanket.'

He took a moment. Then began again with the same cold indifferent tone.

'I thought she'd be so happy. In one way I feel as though I put her out of her misery.'

'The coroner said you strangled her.'

'The coroner, the coroner, the coroner. The coroner isn't here, Holly. It's only you and me.' He looked at her. His eyes blurred. 'I strangled them both with his school tie. Stephen liked school. He was very good in classes. He loved to write.'

'So did Noah Beasley. Tell me about church.'

He waved vaguely across the desk.

'Why?'

'You went to St Mary's church on Roding Lane.'

'Have you visited?'

'This morning, before I came here. It's very beautiful,' Holly said.

'I got to sing there after Stephen had gone. A special treat. Mother came to watch me on New Year's Eve. The stained glass on the window above the pulpit. He watched me when I sang.'

'Who watched you, John?'

He twisted his hands away.

'Gabriel.' And then, as if she didn't quite understand: 'He's been with me ever since.'

Holly felt suddenly dirty. Talking to this man. This killer of children. And she wondered if somehow they were watching her. Stephen, Noah, Matthew.

'Why did you choose these boys?'

'They looked like my brother. But it was more than that. They had Stephen's vulnerability. His peacefulness. An attribute I simply loathed. I wanted to take it away.'

'Your life as John Andrew Pickford is over. You killed your brother, your mother. Matthew Cotton, Noah Beasley and your neighbour, Denise Woolcott.'

John stifled a laugh: 'Oh, she of the thick ankles. I hope you cleaned up my rockery after you dug her up.'

'Was there anybody in between? Are there other boys in the forest that we might find?'

'No.'

'Elijah Eaton?'

'I don't know who that is.'

'He was thirteen when he went missing five years ago.'

'Not me. I had Stephen next to me every night for the past eighteen years. I didn't need anything more.'

399

'Until Eileen.'

He looked puzzled for a moment then nodded.

'Harper was a surrogate for your brother, wasn't he?' Holly said. 'A method of assuaging your guilt. You cared for him. Loved him. And then Eileen took him away.'

'I thought I could control my urges, the feelings that I had, by having someone else in his place. I wish I could say I'm sorry. But I'm not. It wasn't me that did it. It was something inside of me that I just responded to.'

They both waited with the silence between them until he finally said:

'How is my mother?' He shrugged slightly and carried on when she didn't respond: 'She even spoke to me when she had no tongue. Soft words. Beautifully soft, and I can still smell her. And you think I'm not insane?'

'Why did you want to see me, John?'

He held eye contact with her for a second longer before taking an envelope from his jacket. His arm reached out, caused a shadow to cross Holly's face as he left it on the table.

'Someone told me you might appreciate this.'

He got up from his seat and strode out of the room.

Holly stared at the open door as if she had been given a clue that she didn't quite understand. She picked up the envelope.

There was something small and heavy inside.

At her flat, the Harland Miller once again hung proud over the fireplace, the case files neatly packed away in a folder on one shelf.

As she removed the envelope from her jacket a twinge of uneasiness ran through her. She opened it, tilted it up, and John Pickford's St Jude necklace fell into her palm. She closed her eyes and took a moment. Then went swiftly into her murderabilia room. She didn't stay long, time enough to hang the necklace on the inside of the door handle. It rattled when she pulled it to.

And for the first time ever, she locked the door.

Seventy-four

Holly got to the Robin Hood pub in Epping Forest an hour later.

The evening was young, but the bar was already full of early drinkers and the task force had massed at the rear by the exit to the gardens. They erupted in a roar of support as she entered and Thompson bought her a pint of Guinness.

'There you go,' the big man said.

She took a sip. Then said:

'Where's Bishop?'

'Yeah,' Thompson wiped a meaty hand through his hair, 'where is the big guy?'

After twenty minutes Holly found herself alone at a table, watching the team, content to be away from the others, but somehow involved. Even though she couldn't reach out a hand and touch anyone she felt connected.

They had the heat lamps on outside and without them it would have been cold, but with them there was pleasant glow as she walked past and leaned against the wooden banister at the rear of the decking. Warmth and laughter behind.

Cold forest in front. It was so quiet she could hear the wind rustling through the trees. She was staring at the stars when she heard him. Bishop coming from the bar, beer in hand, looking around. Searching for someone. Her? Yeah, he saw her. Raised his glass. Took a sip but didn't take his eyes off her.

Number 4 in the magazine.

She felt him lean up against the railing next to her as he held up a cigarette. Offered her one. After Bishop lit it she paused on the exhale. Holding it in. Filling her lungs with smoke and her head with the fairies.

'Fuck. That's strong.'

They chinked glasses.

She smiled but wanted to move on. Got serious:

'Thank you, Bishop. For what you did for me.'

He nodded and smoked for a few beats. Careful not to look at her when he said:

'I'll always be here for you.'

She felt herself welling up. Broke the emotion with a smile and shook her head. *If I reach out and take your hand, she thought. Will you hold it and follow me wherever I go? Will you trust me and hold a secret and still love me for it?* She wanted to open her heart, open what was left, was about to—

'This case. We couldn't have done it without you. You never stop, do you?' he said. 'Why?'

'Because there is no finish line.'

She had started this job full of apprehension. The last case had almost killed her. She hadn't realised it until now but she was good at this. Murderers, rapists, show yourselves. I'm ready for you now. Bring it on . . .

Lipski's voice suddenly came from behind:

'You two guys coming in? Thompson is doing karaoke.

403

"YMCA", for Chrissakes! You gotta see it.' She went inside again and the two were left alone. Bishop peeled himself from the railing.

'You want to watch a fat old man sing a song?'

'Oh – are you going to have a go as well?'

'Fuck me. You are so rude.'

She howled with laughter until she had tears falling down her cheeks. He joined in. The sort of laughter where your chest actually hurts and your cheeks ache.

'William Bishop,' she was smiling.

Hold my hand. Walk with me.

'We can talk about other things,' she said after a while. 'Doesn't have to be all about death and killing and . . . '

'Life and everything else in between?'

'Something like that.'

So they did talk about other things and at the end of a few minutes they were laughing and smiling and Holly felt the tension evaporating from her body. The drink was helping and she finished her Guinness. He put an arm around her and held her for a minute and she could feel his body warmth. And in that moment Holly thought that if she died there and then, everything would make sense.

'You want another one?' he asked.

'Only one. Don't want to piss off Dr Breaker too much.'

'Who's Dr Breaker?'

'My specialist who has a crush on me.'

'Fuck Dr Breaker,' he smiled and she watched him head into the pub. Stayed a moment longer with her thoughts and then Thompson came out. The big guy was staggering and looked about to topple when he said:

'You gotta come in. The team wants a word.'

Dead trees under a metallic sky. Lingering frost and shadows deep.

Holly Wakefield turned her back on the forest.

Inside the pub the rest of the squad made way for her.

Bishop was standing to one side, smiling and offering a shrug. This was their doing. Not his. Thompson grinned:

'We all clubbed together and got you something.'

He pulled a small box with a ribbon on it from inside his jacket. Tossed it to her. She caught it but there were a few jeers as if she hadn't. She pulled off the ribbon and opened it up.

And then she started laughing.

'Bastards.'

It was a Mars Bar.

Acknowledgements

I would once again like to thank my superhero agent Luigi Bonomi – he can now fly and has X-ray vision – along with Alison Bonomi and Hannah Schofield at LBA. You guys rock and throw me armbands when I threaten to capsize. Thanks to Nicki Kennedy, Sam Edenborough, Jenny Robson, Katherine West and May Wall, my foreign rights agents at ILA – you work tirelessly for me and possess powers that most people cannot comprehend.

A huge thank you to my publisher, Emma Beswetherick at Little, Brown, who has once again done a superb job of editing and working tirelessly alongside me. She has also faced the reality of a decaf soya latte with honey and helped me get rid of the cat. And to Hannah Wann, Jo Wickham, Kate Hibbert and the larger team at Little, Brown. Cover design, sales and marketing, thank you once again for everything.

Have you read the first gripping thriller in the Holly Wakefield series?

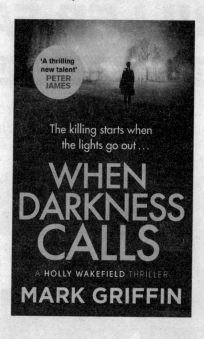

When DI Bishop approaches criminal psychologist Holly Wakefield to investigate a recent killing, Holly is horrified by the dismembered bodies and the way they have been theatrically positioned.

More shocking still is when the pathologist reveals this is not the first time she has seen these mutilations. It means a serial killer is out there, and they're going to kill again – soon.

Holly is used to chasing serial killers. But this killer has something in common with Holly that she's kept hidden for as long as she can remember. And for the first time since she was a child, Holly is forced to face the darkness of her past . . .

Available in paperback and ebook now.